'*Mission to Paris* is as intricate and enjoyable as anything Furst has written . . . Furst's high level of surface period detail is expertly deployed to make us feel as if we're stranded in the past without a guide. Nothing is needlessly explained; it just happens quickly and thrillingly' *Guardian*

'The writing in *Mission to Paris*, sentence after sentence, page after page, is dazzling. If you are a John le Carré fan, this is definitely a novel for you' James Patterson

'*Mission to Paris*, the twelfth novel in the series, contains some of Furst's best writing to date . . . Furst is a romantic moralist working in a version of the realist tradition . . . line-for-line he beats his rivals hands down' *Independent*

'Alan Furst's *Mission to Paris* is a brilliant thriller noir of Second World War espionage' *Daily Telegraph*

'Paris in 1938 is cleverly evoked in this tale of a Hollywood actor who is drawn into a web of international espionage and pitted agains Hitler's worst. The French capital is the real star, partying hard with a sense that the lights are about to go out'
Sunday Express

'This is a world filled with a rich cast of characters from an old central Europe – a half-continent we are only now getting to know again – already haunted by the spectre of impending doom. A great read' *The Times*

'Alan Furst's subject is the death of old Europe. His books are spy novels told in a style that is at once meticulously detailed – the complete menu, the vintage of the champagne, the colour of the tablecloths – and impressionistic . . . brilliantly captures the tense and frightening atmosphere during the last days of free Paris'
Literary Review

'Memorable and wonderfully readable. It also leaves you hungry for more' *The Spectator*

'Set around the Second World War, Alan Furst's novels are steadily making their way into the public's affections – and not before time . . . the characters and setting are beautifully realised'
Mail on Sunday

By Alan Furst

Night Soldiers
Dark Star
The Polish Officer
The World at Night
Red Gold
Kingdom of Shadows
Blood of Victory
Dark Voyage
The Foreign Correspondent
The Spies of Warsaw
Spies of the Balkans
Mission to Paris

MISSION TO PARIS

Alan Furst

PHOENIX

A PHOENIX PAPERBACK

First published in Great Britain in 2012
by Weidenfeld & Nicolson
This paperback edition published in 2013
by Phoenix,
an imprint of Orion Books Ltd,
Orion House, 5 Upper St Martin's Lane,
London WC2H 9EA

An Hachette UK company

A CIP catalogue record for this book
is available from the British Library.

Printed and bound in Great Britain by
Clays Ltd, St Ives plc

The Orion Publishing Group's policy is to use papers
that are natural, renewable and recyclable products and
made from wood grown in sustainable forests. The logging
and manufacturing processes are expected to conform to
the environmental regulations of the country of origin.

www.orionbooks.co.uk

In the 1930s, the Nazi government of Germany, bitterly resentful at having lost the 1914 war, determined to destroy its traditional enemy, France. Force of arms lay in the future, but a small bureau in the Reich Foreign Ministry undertook operations to weaken French morale and degrade France's will to defend herself. This strategy, using ancient and well-proven methods, was known as political warfare.

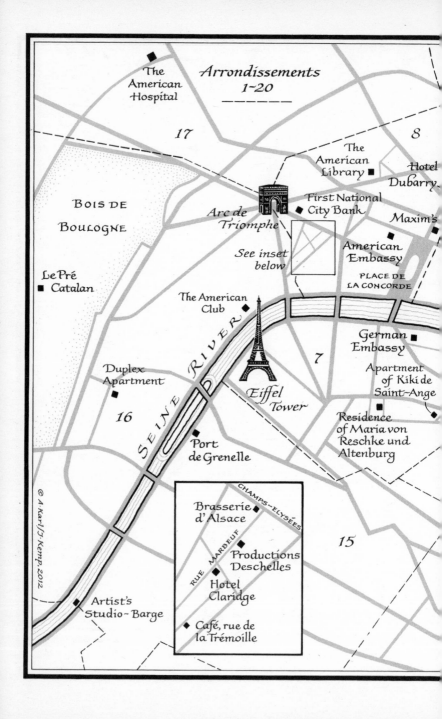

GERMAN
MONEY

IN PARIS, THE EVENINGS OF SEPTEMBER ARE SOMETIMES WARM, EX-cessively gentle, and, in the magic particular to that city, irresistibly seductive. The autumn of the year 1938 began in just such weather and on the terraces of the best cafés, in the famous restaurants, at the dinner parties one wished to attend, the conversation was, of necessity, lively and smart: fashion, cinema, love affairs, politics, and, yes, the possibility of war – that too had its moment. Almost anything, really, except money. Or, rather, *German* money. A curious silence, for hundreds of millions of francs – tens of millions of dollars – had been paid to some of the most distinguished citizens of France since Hitler's ascent to power in 1933. But maybe not so curious, because those who had taken the money were aware of a certain shadow in these transactions and, in that shadow, the people who require darkness for the kind of work they do.

The distinguished citizens, had they been willing to talk about it, would have admitted that the Germans, the political operatives who offered the bounty, were surprisingly adept. They knew how to soften a conscience, presented bribery as little more than a form of sophisticated commerce, of the sort that evolves in *salons* and offices and the private rooms of banks – a gentleman's treason. And the operatives could depend on one hard-edged principle: that those who style themselves as *men of the world* know there is an iron fist in every velvet glove, understand what might await them in the shadows and so, having decided to play the game, they will obey its rules.

Still, human nature being what it is, there will forever be *somebody,* won't there, who will not.

One such, on the fourteenth of September, was a rising political star called Prideaux. Had he been in Paris that evening, he would have been having drinks at Fouquet with a Spanish marquis, a diplomat, after which he could have chosen between two good dinner parties: one in the quarter clustered around the Palais Bourbon, the other in a lovely old mansion up in Passy. It was destiny, Prideaux believed, that he spend his evenings in such exalted places. And, he thought, if fucking destiny had a shred of mercy left in its cold heart he would just now be hailing a taxi. Fucking destiny, however, had other things in mind for the future and didn't care a bit what became of Prideaux.

Who felt, in his heart, terribly wronged. This shouldn't be happening to him, not to *him,* the famously clever Louis Prideaux, *chef de cabinet* – technically chief of staff but far more powerful than that – to an important senator in Paris. Well, it had happened. As *tout Paris* left for the August migration to the countryside, Prideaux had been forced to admit that his elegant world was doomed to collapse (expensive mistress, borrowed money, vengeful wife) and so he'd fled, desperate for a new life, finding himself on the night of the fourteenth in Varna, the Black Sea port of Bulgaria. *Bulgaria!* Prideaux fell back on his lumpy bed at a waterfront hotel, crushed by loss: the row of beautiful suits in his armoire, the apartment windows that looked out at the Seine, the slim, white hands of his aristocratic – by birth, not behaviour – mistress. All gone, all gone. For a moment he actually contemplated weeping but then his fingers, dangling over the side of the bed, touched the supple leather of his valise. For Prideaux, the life preserver in a stormy sea: a million francs. A soothing, restorative, million, francs.

This money, German money, had been meant for the senator, so that he might influence the recommendation of a defence committee, which had for some time been considering a large outlay for construction on the northern extension of the Maginot Line. Up into Belgium, the Ardennes forest, where the Germans had attacked in 1914. A decision of such magnitude, he would tell the committee, should not be made precipitously, it needed more time, it should be *studied,* pros and cons worked through by technicians who understood the whole complicated business. *Later,* the committee would decide. Was it not wise to delay a little? That's what the people of France demanded of them: not rash expenditure, wisdom.

All that August, Prideaux had temporized: what to do? The suitcase of money for the senator had reached Prideaux by way of a prominent hostess, a German baroness named von Reschke, who'd settled in Paris a few years earlier and, using wealth and connection, had become the ruling despot of one of the loftiest *salons* in the city. The baroness spent the summer at her château near Versailles and there, in the drawing room, had handed Prideaux an envelope. Inside, a claim ticket for the baggage office at the Gare de Lyon railway station. 'This is for you-know-who,' she'd said, ever the coquette, flirting with the handsome Prideaux. He'd collected the suitcase and hidden it under a couch, where it gave off a magnetic energy – he could *feel* its presence. Its potential.

The senator was in Cap Ferrat, wouldn't return until the third of September, and Prideaux sweated through hot August nights of temptation. Sometimes he thought he might resist, but the forces of catastrophe were waiting and they wouldn't wait long: his wife's ferocious lawyer, the shady individuals who'd loaned him money when the banks no longer would, and his cruel mistress, whose passion was kindled by expensive wines with expensive dinners and expensive jewellery to wear at the table. When unappeased she was cold, no bed. And while what happened in that bed was the best thing that had ever happened to Prideaux, it would soon be only a memory.

He had to escape before it all came crashing down on him. *Take the money*, Prideaux's devil whispered. The Germans have more where that came from. Go to, say, Istanbul, where a perfect new identity could be purchased. Then, on to exotic climes – Alexandria? Johannesburg? Quebec? A visit to a travel agency revealed that a Greek freighter, the *Olympios*, took on a few passengers at the Bulgarian port of Varna, easily reached by train from Paris. Stay? Or go? Prideaux couldn't decide but then, after an exceptionally uncomfortable telephone call from one of his creditors, he took the money and ran. Before anyone came looking for him.

But they were looking for him. In fact, they'd found him.

The senator had been approached on September fifth, in his office. No, the *package* hadn't arrived, was there a problem? His *chef de cabinet* was up at Deauville, he had telephoned and would return in a few days. The committee meeting? The senator consulted his calendar, that would be on the eleventh. Surely, by then . . .

In Berlin, at von Ribbentrop's Foreign Ministry, the people at the political warfare bureau found this news troubling, and spoke to the bribery people, who were very troubled indeed. So much so that, just to make sure, they got in touch with a dependable friend, a detective at the *Sûreté Nationale* – the French security service – and asked him to lend a hand. For the detective, an easy job. Prideaux wasn't in Deauville, according to his concierge, he was staying indoors. The concierge rubbed her thumb across the pads of her index and middle fingers and raised an eyebrow – *money*, it meant. And that gesture did it. At the Foreign Ministry they had a meeting and, by day's end, a discussion – *not* at the ministry! – with Herbert.

Slim, well-dressed, quiet, Herbert made no particular impression on anybody he met, probably he was some kind of businessman, though he never quite got around to saying what he did. Perhaps you'd meet him again, perhaps you wouldn't, it didn't particularly matter. He circulated comfortably at the mid-level of Berlin society, turning up here and there, invited or not – what could you do, you couldn't ask him to leave. Anyhow, nobody ever did, and he was always pleasant. There were, however, a few individuals in Berlin – those with uncommonly sharp instincts, those who somehow heard interesting things – who met Herbert only once. They didn't precisely avoid him, not overtly, they just weren't where he was or, if they were, they soon had to be elsewhere and, all courtesy, vanished.

What did they know? They didn't know much, in fact they'd better not. Because Herbert had a certain vocation, supposedly secret to all but those who made use of his services. Exceptional services: silent, and efficient. For example, surveillance on Prideaux was in place within hours of Herbert's meeting with his contact at the Foreign Ministry, and Prideaux was not entirely alone as he climbed aboard the first of the trains that would take him to Varna. Where Herbert, informed of Prideaux's booking on the *Olympios*, awaited him. Herbert and his second-in-command, one Lothar, had hired a plane and pilot and flown to an airfield near Varna a night earlier and, on the evening of the fourteenth, they called off their associates and sent them back to wherever they came from. The Greek freighter was not expected at the dock until the sixteenth and would likely be late, so Prideaux wasn't going anywhere.

He really wasn't.

Which meant Herbert and Lothar could relax. For a while, at least, as only one final task lay ahead of them and they had a spare hour or two. Why not have fun in the interim? They had a contact scheduled at a local nightclub and so went looking for it, working their way through a maze of dockside streets; dark, twisting lanes decorated with broken glass and scented with urine, where in time they came upon an iron door beneath a board that said UNCLE BORIS. Inside, Herbert handed the maître d' a fistful of leva notes and the one-eyed monster showed them to a table in the corner, said something amusing in Bulgarian, laughed, made as though to slap Herbert on the back, then didn't. The two Germans settled in to drink mastika and enjoy the show, keeping an eye on the door as they awaited the appearance of their 'brute', as they playfully referred to him. Their brute for *this* operation; Herbert rarely used them more than once.

Lothar was fiftyish, fat and jolly, with tufts of dark red hair and a red face. Like Herbert, he'd been a junior officer during the Great War, the 1914 war, but they never met in the trenches – with five million men under arms an unlikely possibility – but found each other later, in one of the many veterans' organizations that formed in Germany after the defeat of 1918. They fought a little more in the 1920s, after joining a militia, killing off the communists who were trying to take over the country. By the early 1930s Herbert had discovered his true vocation and enlisted Lothar as his second-in-command. A wise choice – Lothar was all business when it mattered but he was also good company. As the nightclub show unfolded, he nudged Herbert with an elbow and rumbled with baritone laughter.

In a space cleared of chairs and tables, a novelty act from somewhere in the Balkans: a two-man canvas horse that danced and capered, the front and rear halves in perfect harmony. Done well, this was by itself entertaining, but what made it memorable was a girl, in scanty, spangled costume, who played the accordion as she stood centre stage on a pair of very sexy legs. The men in the club found them enticing, bare and shapely, as did the canvas horse, which danced nearer and nearer to the girl, the head lunging and feinting as though to nuzzle her thighs, then turning to the audience: *Shall I?*

Oh yes! The shouts were in Bulgarian but there was no question of what they meant. 'Will it have her?' Herbert said.

'I should think so,' Lothar said. 'Otherwise people will throw things.'

The one-eyed monster brought fresh mastika, the shouts grew louder, the accordion played on. At last, the horse found its courage and, having galloped around the girl a few times, stood behind her on its hind legs with its hooves on her shoulders. The girl never missed a beat but then, when the horse covered her breasts with its hooves, and to the absolute delight of the audience, she blushed, her face turning pink, her eyes closing. As the horse began to move in a rhythmic manner familiar to all.

A little after ten o'clock, a white-haired man with a skull for a face entered the nightclub and peered around the room. When Herbert beckoned to him he approached the table and stood there a moment while the attentive one-eyed monster brought a chair and an extra glass. 'You would be Aleksey?' Herbert said. 'The Russian?'

'That's right.' German was the second language of eastern Europe and Aleksey seemed comfortable speaking it.

'General Aleksey?'

'So I'm called – there are many other Alekseys. How did you recognize me?'

'My associate in Belgrade sent me a photograph.'

'I don't remember him taking a photograph.'

Herbert's shrug was eloquent, they did what they wanted to do. 'In security work,' he said, 'it's important to take precautions.'

'Yes, of course it is,' Aleksey said, letting them know he wasn't intimidated.

'Your contract with us calls for payment in Swiss francs, once you've done your job, is that right?'

'Yes. Two thousand Swiss francs.'

'If I may ask,' Herbert said, 'of what army a general?'

'The Russian army, the Czar's army. Not the Bolsheviks.'

'So, after 1917, you emigrated to Belgrade.'

'"Emigrated" is barely the word. But, yes, I went to Belgrade, to the émigré community there. Fellow Slavs, the Serbians, all that.'

'Do you have with you . . . what you'll need?'

'Yes. Small but dependable.'

'With silencer?'

'As you ordered.'

'Good. My colleague and I are going out for a while, when we return it will be time for you to do your work. You've done it before, we're told.'

'I've done many things, as I don't care to sweep floors, and Belgrade has more than enough émigré taxi drivers.' He paused a moment, then said, 'So . . .'

From Herbert, a nod of approval. To the question he'd asked, an oblique answer was apparently the preferred answer. As General Aleksey poured himself some mastika, Herbert met Lothar's eyes and gestured towards the door. To Aleksey he said, 'We have an errand to run, when we return we'll tell you where to go. Meanwhile, the floor show should start up again any time now, you may find it amusing.'

'How long will you be gone?'

'Not too long,' Herbert said, rising to leave.

Prideaux had packed in a hurry, forgetting his pyjama bottoms, and now wore the top and his underdrawers. Alone in a foreign city, he was terribly bored, by ten in the evening had read, for the third time, his last French newspaper. He was also hungry – the desk clerk had brought him a plate of something that couldn't be eaten – so smoked the last of his Gitanes followed by the first of a packet he'd bought at the Varna railway station. Surely he couldn't go anywhere; a night-time tour of the Varna waterfront with a million francs in a valise was an invitation to disaster. Stretching out on the bed, he stared at the ceiling, tried not to recall his former life, and fantasized about his new one. *Rich and mysterious, he drew the attention of women . . .*

A reverie interrupted by two hesitant taps on the door. *Now what?* Somebody from the hotel; if he remained quiet, perhaps they would go away. They didn't. Thirty seconds later, more taps. He rose from the bed and considered putting on his trousers but thought, *who cares what servants see?* and stayed as he was. Standing at the door, he said, 'Who is it?'

'The desk clerk, sir.'

'What do you want?'

No answer. Out in the harbour, a ship sounded its horn. From the room above, the floorboards creaked as somebody moved about. Finally, whoever was in the hall again tapped on the door. Prideaux opened it. The man in the hallway was slim and well dressed and not a desk clerk. Gently but firmly, the man pushed the door open, then closed it behind him as he entered the room. 'Monsieur Prideaux?' he said. 'May we speak for a moment?' His French was correct, his accent barbaric. He looked around for a chair but there was no such thing to be found, not in this room, so he settled at the foot of the bed while Prideaux sat by the headboard.

Prideaux's heart was beating hard, and he hoped desperately that this was something other than what he suspected. 'You're not the desk clerk, sir.'

Herbert, his expression on the mournful side, shook his head slowly. 'No,' he said. 'I am not.'

'Then who are you?' But for the whine in his voice, this would have been indignant.

Herbert said, 'Think of me as a courier.'

'A what?'

'A courier. I've come here to recover something that belongs to us – it certainly doesn't belong to you.'

Prideaux looked puzzled. 'What are you talking about?'

Herbert, no more than slightly irritated, simply said, 'Please.'

'I don't know what you want, sir, I simply got fed up with life in Paris and came down here. How does that concern you, whoever you are?'

Herbert turned towards the window – this was growing tiresome. 'I hope there's no need for violence, Monsieur Prideaux, my associates are downstairs but please don't force me to bring them up here. Better that way, believe me. I am, as I said, a courier, and my instructions are to take the money you've stolen back to Berlin. After that, we don't care what you do or where you go, it doesn't concern us.'

Prideaux collapsed very slowly; the hauteur in his expression drained away, his shoulders slumped, and finally his head lowered so that he stared at the floor.

Herbert took no pleasure in this – a show of humiliation was, to him, unbearable weakness. And what might come next, he wondered. Tears? Hysterics? *Aggression?* Whatever it might be, he didn't want to see it. 'I'm sure,' he said, his voice reaching for sympathy, 'there was a reason. There's always a reason.'

Prideaux started to rise, but Herbert stood up quickly, raised a hand like a traffic policeman stopping a car, and a defeated Prideaux sat obediently back down on the bed. Herbert stayed on his feet, stared at Prideaux for a moment, then said, 'Monsieur Prideaux, I think it will be easier for both of us if you simply tell me where the money is. Really, much easier.'

It took a few seconds – Prideaux had to get control of himself – then he said, so quietly that Herbert could only just hear the words, 'Under the bed.'

Herbert slid the valise from beneath the bed, undid the buckles, and peered inside. 'Where are your personal things?' he said.

Prideaux gestured towards another valise, standing open at the foot of the bed.

'Did you put any of the money in there? Have you spent some of it? Or is it all, every franc of it, in here? Best now to be truthful.'

'It's all there,' Prideaux said.

Herbert closed the valise and pulled the straps tight. 'Well, we'll see. I'm going to take this money away and count it and, if you've been honest with me I'll be back, and I'll give you a few hundred francs – at least something for wherever you're going next. Shall I tell you why?'

Prideaux, staring at the floor, didn't answer.

'It's because people like you can be useful, in certain situations, and people like you never have enough money. So, when such people help us out, with whatever we might need, we are always generous. Very generous indeed.'

Herbert let this sink in. It took some time, but Prideaux eventually said, 'What if I'm . . . far away?'

Herbert smiled. Prideaux's eyes were cast down so he didn't see the smile, which was just as well. 'Monsieur Prideaux,' Herbert said, as though he were saying *poor Monsieur Prideaux,* 'there is no such thing as far away.' Then he stepped into the hall and drew the door shut behind him.

Herbert left Lothar to watch the hotel, likely unnecessary but why take chances. Prideaux, he thought, had taken the bait and would remain where he was. Herbert then returned to the nightclub, told General Aleksey where to find Prideaux and described him, in his pyjama top and underdrawers. Thirty minutes later, as the canvas horse capered and danced to the music of the accordion, Lothar and the Russian returned. Herbert counted out two thousand Swiss francs, General Aleksey put the money in his pocket, wished them a pleasant evening, and walked out the door.

10 September, 1938. In Berlin, the Ribbentropburo – the political warfare department named for Foreign Minister Joachim von Ribbentrop – had its offices in the Reich Foreign Ministry at 3, Wilhelmstrasse. Senior bureaucrats from the ministry liked to take a morning coffee in the dining room of the vast and luxurious Hotel Kaiserhof, on the nearby Wilhelmplatz. This was especially true of the Deputy Director of the Ribbentropburo, who could be found, at seven in the morning, at his customary table in the corner, his sombre blue suit vivid against the background of shining white tablecloths.

The Deputy Director, an SS major, had formerly been a junior professor of social sciences, particularly anthropology, at the University of Dresden. He was an exceptionally bright fellow, with sharp black eyes and sharp features – it was sometimes said of him, privately, that he had a face like an axe. This feature did him no harm, it made him look smart, and you had to be smart to succeed in the political warfare business; you had to understand your enemy's history, his culture, and, most of all, his psychology.

The Deputy Director's morning ritual made him accessible to junior staff, of the courageous and ambitious sort, who dared to approach him at his table. This was dangerous, because the Deputy Director did not suffer fools gladly, but it could be done and, if done successfully, might move the underling one rung up the very steep ladder of advancement within the bureau. On the morning of the tenth, a fresh-faced young man carrying a briefcase presented himself to the Deputy Director and was invited to sit down and have a cup of coffee.

After they'd spent a few minutes on the weather and the state of the world, the young man said, 'A most interesting document has found its way to my desk.'

'Oh?'

'Yes, sir. I thought it worth bringing to your attention.'

'And it is . . . ?'

The young man reached into his briefcase and brought out a press clipping. 'I have it here, with a translation – the document is in English.'

'I read English,' said the Deputy Director. He then snapped his fingers and extended a hand to receive the interesting document.

'It's taken from the Hollywood newspaper called *Variety*,' the young man said as the Deputy Director glanced at the clipping. 'And reports that the movie actor Fredric Stahl is coming to Paris to make a film.'

'He is influential? In America?'

'Not really, he's just an actor, but I believe we can make use of him once he gets to Paris. He will surely receive attention from the French newspapers and the radio.'

The Deputy Director finished reading the release and handed it back to the young man. 'What do you propose?'

'To put him on the list maintained by our French section.'

'Very well, you may add him to the list, and make sure that what's-his-name who runs the section does something about it.'

'You mean Herr Hoff, sir.'

'Yes, Hoff. Have him work up a background study, all the usual items.'

'I'll do that, sir, as soon as I return to the office.'

14 September. After midnight, the liner *Ile de France* rising and falling on the mid-Atlantic swell, a light sea breeze, the stars a million diamonds spread across a black sky. *And,* Stahl thought, *a woman in my arms.* Or at least by his side. They lay together on a deck chair, she in formal gown, he in tuxedo, the warmth of her body welcome on the chilly night, the soft weight of her breast, resting gently against him, a promise that wouldn't be kept but a sweet promise just the same. *Edith,* he thought. Or was it Edna? He wasn't sure so would avoid using her name, perhaps call her . . . what? Well, not *my dear,* anything was better than that, which he found stilted and pretentious though God knew he'd said it a few times. Said it because he'd *had* to, it was written so in the script and he was Fredric Stahl, yes, the Hollywood movie star, that Fredric Stahl, and he'd made a fortune using phrases like *my dear,* which melted the hearts of women from coast to coast when spoken in his faintly foreign accent.

Thus Warner Bros. 'Why not Fredric Stahl, hunh? With that European accent?' And just how hard he'd worked to get that accent right they'd never know. He certainly wasn't alone in this; the English Archie Leach had become Cary Grant by sounding like a sophisticated gent from the east coast, while the Hungarian Peter Lorre developed a voice – insinuating, oily, and menacing – that suggested vaguely Continental origin.

'Penny for your thoughts,' the woman said.

'Such a beautiful night,' he said.

She moved closer to him, the gin on her breath strong in his nostrils. 'Who would've thought you'd be so nice?' she said. 'I mean, in person.' In response, he put his arm around her shoulders and hugged her a little.

They'd met on the night the *Ile de France* sailed from New York, at the captain's table in the first-class dining room. A long-suffering, pretty wife she was, her husband three sheets to the wind when they appeared for dinner. Soon he announced, in the middle of someone else's story, that he owned a Cadillac dealership in Bryn Mawr, Pennsylvania. 'That's on the Main Line, in case you don't know.' By the third night his table companions knew very well indeed, because he kept repeating it, and at last his wife, Edith, maybe Edna, dealt with the situation by taking him back to their cabin. She then reappeared and when, after dessert, Stahl said he was going for a walk on deck, she caught up to him at the portholed doors to the dining room and said, 'Can I come along for the walk, Mr. Stahl?' They walked, smoked, leaned on the rail, sometimes she held her hair back to keep it from blowing around. Finally he found a deck chair – the sling in French Line colours, the footrest polished teak – and they snuggled down together to enjoy the night at sea.

'Tell me, umm, where are you going in Europe?' he said.

'It's Iris – I bet you forgot.'

'I won't again.'

'Paree,' she said. 'Brussels, Amsterdam, Geneva, Rome, Vienna. There's more, oh, ah, *Venice*. I'm still forgetting one.'

'Maybe Budapest.'

'Nooo, I don't think so.'

'Berlin?'

'That's it!'

After a moment, Stahl said, 'You'll see a lot.'

'Where are *you* going, Mr. Stahl?'

'Just to Paris, to make a movie. And please call me Fredric.'

'Oh, is that all? "Just to Paris"? "To make a movie"?' A ladylike snort followed. She was already writing the postcard. *You'll never guess who I . . .* 'Are you French, Fredric?'

'I was born in Vienna, wandered about the world for a time, lived and worked in Paris, then, in the summer of 1930, Hollywood. I'm an American now.' He paused, then said, 'Tell me, Iris, when you planned the trip, did you think about the politics, in Europe?'

'Oh who cares – they're always squabbling over something. You can't go to Spain, 'cause there's a war there, you know. Otherwise I expect the castles are all open, and the restaurants.'

He could hear approaching footsteps on the iron deck, then a ship's officer flicked a torch beam over them, touched the brim of his cap and said, '*Bonsoir, Madame, Monsieur.*'

'What's it called, your movie?'

'*Après la Guerre.* That would be *After the War,* in English. It takes place in 1918, at the end of the war.'

'Will it play in Bryn Mawr?'

'Maybe it will. I hope so.'

'Well, we can always go to Philadelphia to see it, if we have to.'

It was true that he'd 'wandered about the world'. The phrase suggested romance and adventure – something like that had appeared in a Warner Bros. publicity bio – but it didn't tell the whole story. In fact, he'd run away to sea at the age of sixteen. He was also not really 'Fredric Stahl', had been born Franz Stalka, forty years earlier in Vienna, to a Slovenian father and an Austrian mother of solidly bourgeois families resident in Austria-Hungary for generations. His father was beyond strict; the rigid, fearsome lord of the family, a tyrant with a face like an angry prune. Thus Stahl grew up in a world of rules and punishments – there was hardly a moment in his early life when he wasn't in trouble for doing something wrong. He had two older brothers, obedient little gentlemen and utterly servile – 'Yes, papa,' 'As you wish, papa' – who studied for hours and did well in private academies. He had also a younger sister, Klara, and if he was the bad boy of the family, she was the angel and Stahl adored her. A beautiful little angel, with her mother's good looks. Inherited, as well, by the boy who would become an actor and take a new name.

It was said of him by those who made a living in the business of faces and bodies that he was 'a very masculine actor'. Stahl wasn't sure precisely what they meant, but he knew they were rich and not for nothing. It referred, he suspected, to a certain inner confidence, expressed by, among other things, a low-pitched voice – *assurance,* not just a bass register – from an actor who always sounded 'quiet' no matter how loudly he spoke. He could play the sympathetic lawyer, the kind aristocrat, the saintly husband, the comforting doctor, or the good lover – the knight not the gigolo.

His hair was dark, combed back from a high, noble forehead which rose from deep-set eyes. Cold grey eyes – the grey was cold, the eyes were warm: receptive and expressive. Just enough grey in those eyes for black-and-white film, and even better – it turned out to his great relief – in technicolour. His posture was relaxed – *hands in pockets* for Stahl was not a weak gesture – and his physique appropriate for the parts he played. He'd been scrawny as a boy but two years as an Ordinary Seaman, scraping rust, painting decks, had put just enough muscle on him so he could be filmed wearing a bathing suit. He couldn't punch another man, he wasn't Clark Gable, and he couldn't fight a duel, he was not Errol Flynn. But neither was he Charles Boyer – he wasn't so *sophisticated*. Mostly he played a warm man in a cold world. And, if all his movies were taken together, Fredric Stahl was not somebody you knew, but somebody you would very much like to know.

In fact he was good at his profession – had two Oscar nominations, one for Supporting Actor, the other for the lead in *Summer Storm* – and very much in control of gesture and tone but, beyond skill, he had the single, inexplicable quality of the star actor or actress. When he was on screen, you couldn't take your eyes off him.

Stahl shifted slightly in the deck chair, the damp was beginning to reach him and he had to suppress a shiver. And, he sensed, the weather was turning – sometimes the ship's bow hit the oncoming wave with a loud smack. 'We might just have a storm,' he said. It was, he thought, time to get Iris back where she belonged, the cuddling had devloped a certain familiar edge.

'A storm?' she said. 'Oh, I hope not. I'm afraid I'll get seasick.'

'You'll be fine. Just remember: don't stay in your cabin, go someplace where you can keep your eyes on the horizon.'

'Is it that easy?'

'Yes. I spent two years at sea, that's how I know.'

'*You*? A sailor?'

He nodded. 'I ran away to sea when I was sixteen.'

'Your poor mom!'

'I wrote them a letter,' he said. 'I went to Hamburg, and for a month all I did was sweep out the union hall, but then a Dutch ship needed a deckhand and I signed on and saw the world – Shanghai, Batavia, Calcutta . . .' This had been the purest possible luck; Stahl had gone to sea in the spring of 1914, before the war, on what by chance was the ship of a country that remained neutral, thus he was spared service for the enemies of Austria-Hungary.

'Say, you've had some adventures, haven't you,' she said.

'I did. In 1916 we were shelled and set on fire, just off the coast of Spain. An Italian destroyer did that.'

'But, you said "neutral" . . .'

'We never knew why they did it. Exuberance, maybe, we didn't ask. But we managed to reach the port of Barcelona, where I got help from the Austrian legation. They could have sent me off to fight in the trenches, but instead they gave me a job, and that was my military service.'

'What did you do?'

'I opened the mail. Made sure it got to the right people.'

She started to ask a question, but then a gust of wind hit her and she said 'Brrr' and burrowed against Stahl, close enough now that her voice was soft. 'So,' she said, lingering on the word, 'when did you decide to become an actor?'

'A little later, when I was back in Vienna.' The *Ile de France* lifted and fell, hitting another wave. 'I think, Iris, it might be time for you to go back to your cabin, your husband's probably beginning to wonder where you are.'

'Oh, Jack sleeps like a log when he's drunk.'

Nonetheless, she wasn't coming to Stahl's cabin. She didn't really want to, Stahl felt, maybe she wanted to be asked. But, in any event, what he didn't need was a public row with some lush over a wife's shipboard infidelity. With certain actors, Warner Bros. wouldn't have cared, but not Fredric Stahl. He put a hand on her cheek and turned her face towards him. 'One kiss, Iris, and then back to our cabins.'

The kiss was dry, and tender, and went on for a time because they both enjoyed it.

The storm came full force after midnight, the liner pitching and rolling in heavy seas. Stahl woke up, grumbled at the weather, and went back to sleep. When he left his cabin in the morning, the exquisite art deco carpets had been covered with rolls of brown paper and, up on deck, the sky was heavy with dark cloud and every wave sent spray flying over the bow. Returning to his cabin after a long walk, he found the ship's daily news bulletin slipped beneath the door.

The French Line wishes you good morning. Temperature at 0600 hours 53°. The Paris weather 66° and partly cloudy.

The 1938 Salon d'Automne will open 5 October at the Grand Palais in Paris. The International Surrealist Exhibition remains open at the Galerie des Beaux-Arts, 60 artists, including Marcel Duchamp, and 300 works, including Salvador Dali's 'Rainy Taxi'.

Yesterday at the European Championships in Paris, the Finnish runner Taisto Mäki set a new record in the 10,000 metre race, 29 minutes, 52 seconds.

The British Prime Minister Chamberlain goes to Berchtesgaden today for consultations on the Sudeten issue with Reichs Chancellor Hitler.

In Hollywood, filming has begun on 'The Wizard of Oz' with Buddy Ebsen, allergic to his costume, replaced by Jack Haley.

Great Britain has ordered its fleet at Invergordon to alert status.

Pittsburgh halfback Whizzer White, injured in a loss to the Eagles, has said he will play against the NY Giants on Friday.

The first-class shuffleboard tournament has been postponed until 1400 hours tomorrow.

It was dusk when the *Ile de France* docked at Le Havre, and a brass band greeted the passengers at the foot of the first-class gangway. A band made up, according to the fancy writing on a giant bass drum, of municipal sanitation workers. Wearing blue uniforms and caps, working away at a spirited march, they could surely not *all* have been short and stocky with black moustaches, but that was Stahl's impression. As he stepped onto the pier, a shout rose above the cornets and trombones. '*Mr. Stahl! Fredric Stahl!*' Who was this? Or, rather, *where* was he? He was, Stahl now saw, attached to a hand waving frantically above the heads of people waiting to meet the passengers.

With difficulty, the man wormed his way through the crowd and stood in front of Stahl. He was not much over five feet tall, with a hook nose and a beaming smile, nattily dressed in a tan double-breasted suit. What remained of his hair was arranged in strands across his head and plastered down with oil. Reaching up, he grasped Stahl's hand, gave it an enthusiastic pump, and said, 'Welcome to France, I am Zolly!' When Stahl didn't react he added, '*Zolly Louis,* the Warner man in Paris!' His accent was from somewhere well east of the dock in Le Havre.

'Hello, Zolly, thanks for meeting me,' Stahl said.

Then the flashbulbs went off. The floating lights of the afterimages made it difficult for Stahl to see much of anything, but he didn't need to see. Instinctively, he turned his head slightly to the left, to show his right, his better, side, and his face broke into an amiable smile, accompanied by a raised hand seemingly caught in mid-wave. A voice called out, 'Over to here, Mis-ter Stahl.' Stahl turned towards the voice and, blind as a bat, smiled away.

'He speaks French, boys,' Zolly called out. Then, an aside to Stahl, 'I made sure the press got here.'

A man with a small notebook appeared from the after-image. 'Jardine, of *Le Matin*,' he said in French. 'How was your voyage?'

'I enjoyed every minute of it,' Stahl said. 'The *Ile de France* is a fine ship, one of the best. Luxurious, and *fast*.'

'Any storms?'

Stahl shook his head, dismissing the idea. 'A smooth voyage in every way. Maybe I ate a little more than I should have, but I couldn't resist.'

Now a different voice: 'Would you say something about your new movie?'

'It's called *Après la Guerre,* being made for Paramount France and produced by Monsieur Jules Deschelles.'

'You know Monsieur Deschelles?'

Zolly cleared his throat.

'By reputation,' Stahl said. 'He is well regarded in Hollywood.'

'This movie,' Jardine of *Le Matin* said, 'is it about the, ah, futility of war?'

'You might say that,' Stahl said, then, as he considered going on, Zolly said, 'That's enough, boys. He'll be available for interviews, but right now Mr. Stahl would like to get to Paris as soon as possible.'

As the photographers took a few more shots, working around to get the *Ile de France* as background, a beautiful girl appeared at Stahl's side, firmly taking his arm and smiling for the cameras. Stahl's expression didn't change but, out of the corner of his mouth, he said, 'Who the hell is this?'

'No idea,' Zolly said. As he led Stahl away from the crowd, the Warner man in Paris glanced back over his shoulder. Winked? At the young woman he'd promised . . . ? This was all in Stahl's imagination, but it was a highly experienced and accurate imagination.

Zolly Louis had a car and driver waiting on the pier. Since Stahl had already cleared customs and border control – the passports of first-class travellers were stamped in their staterooms – and his baggage would be delivered to his hotel, he was free to head south to

Paris. The car was stunning, a grand four-door sedan that glowed pearlescent silver, with the graceful curve and sweep of an aerodynamic masterpiece. Curiously, the steering wheel was set in the centre of the dashboard, so a passenger could sit on either side of the driver.

Who, Stahl thought, certainly looked like a relative of Zolly Louis – similar height, and a similar face, except for a thin moustache. 'Meet your new driver,' Zolly said. 'My nephew, Jimmy.' Handing Stahl a business card, Zolly said, 'Call him anytime.' Jimmy, sitting on a pile of seat cushions, nodded to Stahl – bowed might have been a better description – and said in English, 'So pleased to meet you, sir,' one word at a time.

Zolly opened the rear door for Stahl, climbed in behind him, and said, 'Now we go. To the Claridge, Jimmy, and make it snappy.'

The Hotel Claridge, on the rue François 1er, was not at all where Stahl wanted to stay but somebody in Paris had made the reservation and Stahl hadn't complained. The Claridge was where rich Englishmen took suites, close to the Champs-Elysées, a *quartier* of fancy cinemas, overpriced restaurants, and hordes of tourists. Stahl meant to find somewhere else as soon as he could.

As they left the pier, Zolly said, 'How about this car?'

'Very impressive,' Stahl said.

'The 1938 Panhard Dynamic,' Zolly said. 'It's all the rage in Paris.'

The lights of Le Havre soon faded away behind them, replaced by the rolling fields of the night-time countryside. When Stahl lowered his window and inhaled the scent of it – damp earth, newly cut hay, a hint of pig manure – he was taken with a sudden rising of the spirit. And the more he inhaled this fragrant air, the better he felt, as though some part of his being had lain dormant in California but had now come back to life. *Perhaps I have a French soul*, he thought, *and it knows it's home.* Home at that moment was a starless night, a steady wind, not a human to be seen. Except, now and again, a sleeping village; stone houses with closed shutters, the local café – a dimly lit window with figures gathered at a bar – then farm fields again, divided by ancient trees and tangled underbrush. Le Havre was only two hours from Paris but the land between was France, dark and silent and very old.

It was quiet in the car, even with the window down, only the hum of the engine and the brush of tyres on the road. Stahl, in a pensive mood, lit a cigarette – on the boat he'd changed over to Gauloises, replacing his Lucky Strikes – and thought about a conversation they'd had as they began their journey. It was no more than genial chitchat, making the time pass, which began in English but changed soon enough to French. Zolly Louis was rather a different individual when he spoke French. English for Zolly was the language of the promo man, the salesman, the drummer, whereas in French he was close to circumspect. The way Stahl put it to himself, Zolly Louis spoke the French of the émigré. Familiar to Stahl, who'd spent seven years in Paris as an émigré among émigrés, which was a long way from what Americans meant when they called themselves expatriates: expatriates could go home, émigrés couldn't.

That side of Zolly had made Stahl curious. 'Tell me,' he'd said, 'the name "Zolly" is short for . . . ?' He'd wondered if it might be, perhaps, Solomon. 'Short for Zoltan,' was the answer. 'What else?' Even in the darkened back seat, Stahl caught the flicker in Zolly's eyes. Stahl then asked where he was from. This question was answered with a shrug, spread hands, *who knows?* Finally Zolly said, 'In some parts of Europe, the Roumanians say you're not Roumanian, the Hungarians say you're not Hungarian, and the Serbs don't say anything. That's where I'm from.'

Stahl didn't pursue it and, after a silence, Zolly changed the subject and asked about the new movie – what about it had so appealed to him that he was willing to leave Hollywood? Stahl didn't care to tell the truth and said he liked the role, and the idea of working in Paris. Zolly nodded, and let it go. But Stahl had understood him perfectly: *Any day now, Europe's going up in flames. What are you doing here?*

Zolly, I wish I knew.

In July, Stahl's agent at the William Morris Agency, Baruch 'Buzzy' Mehlman, had told him he'd be meeting with Walter Perry, the studio's *éminence grise,* and Jack Warner himself, in Perry's office. When Stahl showed up, prompt to the minute and shaved to perfection, Perry said, 'Jack's upstairs in a meeting, he'll join us as soon as he can.' Which meant never, of course, but Stahl got the point: when Walter Perry spoke, he spoke for Jack Warner, and everybody at Warner's knew it. And what Jack had to say was: We're loaning you out to Paramount France, to make a movie at Joinville, Paramount's studios outside Paris. And in return the Paramount star Gary Cooper will be making a western for Warner. 'Naturally,' Walter Perry had said, 'you'll need some time to think it over. We'll send you a synopsis, take a look at it, talk it over with Buzzy, then let me know. But I should tell you, Fredric, you'll make Jack really happy if you say yes.'

The synopsis wasn't bad, the money, by the time Buzzy got done with Paramount, would be something more than his usual $100,000 a picture, and so Fredric Stahl decided to make Jack really happy. Which, Walter Perry told Buzzy, who told Stahl, it did. So, good, go to Paris. Still, in all this there was something that wasn't quite right. He couldn't have said why, it simply felt – *odd.* When he told friends about it, there was a certain moment of hesitation before they congratulated him, so he wasn't alone in wondering if there somehow wasn't more to this, perhaps studio politics, perhaps . . .

It was Zolly who broke into the reverie. 'Time for *pipi,*' he announced, Jimmy stopped the Panhard and the three of them stood side by side at the edge of the road and watered a field.

Paris.

The night manager of the Claridge took Stahl's passport – the police collected them late in the evening and returned them by morning –

then personally led Zolly and Stahl up to the reserved suite. Abundant flowers and chocolates had been provided, as well as a bottle of Badoit, since American visitors feared European tap water. When the manager and Zolly left, Stahl stretched out on a chaise longue and had just closed his eyes when his luggage arrived, accompanied by a hall porter and a maid who opened his wardrobe trunks and began to unpack and put away his clothing. Stahl retrieved a sweater and a pair of corduroy trousers, then went out to find Paris.

His Paris. Which was found by crossing the Seine on the Pont d'Alma and, eventually, entering the maze of narrow streets of the Sixth Arrondissement, the Faubourg Saint-Germain. And if the damp earth of the French countryside had lifted his spirit, being back in his old *quartier* was as though a door to heaven had been left open. Walking slowly, looking at everything, he couldn't get enough of the Parisian air: it smelled of a thousand years of rain dripping on stone, smelled of rough black tobacco and garlic and drains, of perfume, of potatoes frying in fat. It smelled as it had smelled when he was twenty-five.

A warm evening, people were out, the bistros crowded and noisy. On the wall of a newspaper kiosk, closed down for the night, the day's front-page headlines were still posted: CZECHOSLOVAKIA DECLARES STATE OF EMERGENCY. And, below that, GERMAN DIVISIONS PREPARE TO MARCH. Two women walking arm in arm passed by and when Stahl looked back over his shoulder he caught one of them doing the same thing and she laughed and turned away. In a café at the corner of the rue du Four and the rue Mabillon, an old woman with red hair was playing a violin. Stahl went into the café, stood at the bar, ordered a cognac, saw his reflection in the mirror, and smiled. 'A fine evening, no?' said the bartender.

'Yes it is,' Stahl said.

In the morning, Stahl woke up suddenly, jolted into consciousness by a chorus of bleating taxi horns down on the street. Like a flock of crows, he thought, once disturbed they became violently loud and indignant. Now he needed coffee, reached for the telephone and in a few minutes a tray was brought up with coffee and a basket of croissants. He broke the tip off one of them, which produced a shower of pastry flakes, ate the tip, then ate the croissant, then ate all the others, then ate the flakes. As he finished up, a bellboy arrived with an envelope on a silver tray. Inside the envelope was a handwritten note from Zolly Louis, who said he had to be away for a day or two, please stop by the office at 7, rue Scribe, near the American Express office, where Mme Boulanger would be waiting for him.

Warner Bros. France was, according to the directory in the lobby, on the third floor. Stahl pressed the button to call the elevator and was about to take the stairs when he heard whirring and grinding above him, peered up through the wire cage and saw the cables on the bottom of the car, then, very slowly, the tiny elevator itself. Up on the third floor, searching through the gloom of a long corridor, he found the name of the company on a pebbled glass door, which opened to an office furnished with well-used desks – cigarette burns on the edges – black telephones, and Warner movie posters: *42nd Street, Captain Blood, The Adventures of Robin Hood* – showing Errol Flynn in green hat with feather and Olivia de Havilland in a sort of wimple – and *The Life of Emile Zola*, released a year earlier. It was, by way of the story of the Dreyfus affair, Warner's, in fact Hollywood's, first anti-fascist movie. And in prominent position, between two grimy windows, a poster of the actor who'd made a great deal of money for Warner, Porky Pig.

Stahl stood at the open door; a man was gesturing as he argued on the phone, a girl typing at great speed, eyes on a pencilled draft. Then: 'Ah, *voilà!* He arrives!' A woman in a rather snug knit suit was rising from her swivel chair, evidently Mme Boulanger. Fiftyish and determined, with bright red lips and fingernails, she was one of those businesswomen who wore a hat in the office – a black pillbox with a bow on one side. Holding a cigarette in one hand, she brushed his cheeks with her lips. 'Elsa Boulanger,' she said.

'Good morning, Madame Boulanger.'

'Have a seat,' she commanded, turning her swivel chair to face him. 'I'm to do your publicity – the Warner star in Paris part. Paramount will work on the movie itself. Did you have a good voyage? Did your luggage arrive? Are you comfortable in your hotel? Have you seen *Le Matin*?' She handed him a newspaper folded open to two photographs. There he was, with the *Ile de France* in the background, as he smiled and waved. The second photograph showed the young woman holding his arm, the caption below read, *Fredric Stahl is welcomed to France by the film actress Colette Dulac.*

'Who is she?' Stahl said. 'She just . . . appeared.'

Mme Boulanger shrugged. 'Nobody,' she said. 'But she wants to change that, I'd say.' She paused, and stubbed her cigarette out in a café ashtray that said SUZE. Stahl turned the newspaper to see what was above the fold and found a review of *Le Quai des Brumes,* a Marcel Carné film starring Jean Gabin. 'I'd like to see this,' Stahl said. 'I knew Carné, at least to say hello to, when I worked here.'

Mme Boulanger leaned towards him and lowered her voice. '*Mon cher* Monsieur Stahl,' she said, the *my dear* not without affection, then hesitated as she took the paper away from him and ran her finger along the text below his photograph. 'What is this all about? This line, "Monsieur Stahl told *Le Matin* that his new film, *Après la Guerre,* will be about 'the futility of war'." Is there any special reason you said that?'

'I didn't say it. The *Le Matin* man put it in a question and I, well, I did no more than agree. I really didn't know what to say.'

'You will have to be more careful here, you know.'

'Careful?'

'Yes, these days, careful.'

Stahl tried to laugh it off. 'Isn't war always futile, Madame Boulanger?'

Mme Boulanger wasn't amused. '*Le Matin, mon cher,* is a very rightist newspaper.'

Stahl was puzzled and showed it. 'Rightist?' he said. 'The French right is against war? Has turned pacifist?'

'In its way. The press and politicians on the right try to persuade us that resistance to Hitler is futile. The German military is too large, too strong, their machines are new and efficient and deadly, and their passion for a fight unequalled. Poor France can never win against such a powerful and determined force. That's what we're being fed, over here.'

'What do they want France to do?'

'Negotiate, sign treaties, acknowledge Hitler's supremacy, let him do whatever he wants in Europe as long as he leaves us alone.'

Stahl shook his head. 'I had no idea.'

'You are Austrian by birth, no?'

'Viennese.'

'What do you think about what goes on over there?' She nodded her head in the general direction of France's eastern border with Germany, a little more than two hundred miles from where they sat.

'Sickening,' he said. Mme Boulanger's expression barely changed but Stahl could tell she was relieved. 'And dangerous,' he went on. 'I can't bear to watch Hitler in the newsreels.'

'*Le Matin* doesn't know where you stand, but they offer you an opportunity, as an actor, as an artist, to speak out against European war.'

'Perhaps I'll let them know,' he said. Then added, 'Where I stand.'

'Perhaps you'll find a way to keep *out* of politics, Monsieur Stahl. For actors it's much the best idea. Those of us who work for your success would prefer that *all* the people who go to the movies feel affection for you. Why annoy those who don't like your political views?'

Stahl nodded. 'You are a sensible person, Madame Boulanger.'

She smiled, reached out and rested two fingers lightly on his knee. 'You are a successful man, a movie star, let's keep it that way. How long are you in Paris?'

'Four months? Less? It's hard to know, I have to meet with the producer and the director, then I'll have a better idea.'

Mme Boulanger swivelled back to face her desk, picked up an appointment book, its pages thickened by notes in blue ink, and thumbed through it. 'I see people from the newspapers on a fairly regular basis, and I'll set up a few interviews. And by the way, is this *Après la Guerre* an outcry against war? Umm, the *futility* of war?'

Stahl shrugged. 'Three soldiers, foreign legionnaires, try to return home from Turkey after the 1918 armistice.'

'And you play . . . ?'

'Colonel Vadic, of obscure Balkan origin, the leader, and much-decorated hero. I may get to walk with a stick.'

Mme Boulanger's face lit up. 'I like that,' she said. 'A *human* story.'

Walking back to the hotel, Stahl sensed that the city's mood had changed. Sombre today, the Parisians, unsmiling, eyes down, something had reached them on the morning of 19 September. The headlines weren't so different than the day before, all to do with the possibility of a German march into Czechoslovakia. If that happened, France was obliged by treaty to go to war. Years earlier, in the last months of 1923, as Stahl was beginning a new life in Paris, war was a thing of the past – the last one so brutal and vicious that all the world knew there could never be another. At least all the world of the Faubourg Saint-Germain. In the Left Bank cafés that autumn, the word was barely mentioned, the talk was about paintings, books, music, scandals, reputations, and who was in whose bed. As Stahl's French grew better, as he picked up the argot, the slang, he fell in love with the world of the cafés.

He'd come a long way to get there. When he was twenty and working at the legation in Barcelona, the war ended, the Central Powers had lost, and the legation gave all its employees steamship tickets to the Austro-Hungarian port of Trieste. From there, Stahl had made his way to Vienna. Returned home, where to his mother he was a prodigal son, to his father a self-indulgent wastrel. He managed to live at the family apartment for a few weeks, then fled to stay on friends' couches, and finally found a room in a cellar, half of which was given over to the storage of potatoes. A stage-struck friend – from one of the most aristocratic and impoverished families in the city – had taken to hanging around the great Viennese theatres, the

'Burg' and the Volksoper, and Stahl joined him and found an occasional job as an extra. He couldn't sing, but enthusiastically mimed the words, and it was always good to have a handsome face in the crowd cheering the king. He carried his first spear in *Aida,* wore his first muttonchops – and had his first addictive sniff of the spirit gum that stuck them to his face – in *The Merry Widow.* In time, he won dramatic roles at some of the city's smaller playhouses, worked hard, was noticed in reviews, and began to build a career.

He loved acting.

He'd been born to act – at least he thought so but he wasn't the only one. It was the pure craft of it that excited him. When the circuits closed between actor and audience, when a line drew a laugh or, better, a gasp, when a pause lasted for precisely the right interval, when lines were picked up smartly from fellow players, when a silent reaction meant more than spoken words, he felt, and began to crave, that excitement. He loved also – that month anyhow – an actress named Berta and, in the spring of 1923, Berta decided to try her luck in Paris and Stahl went with her. There they lived passionately together for six weeks, almost, until she seduced a successful playwright and left for a better arrondissement. But Stahl wasn't going anywhere. When he'd arrived in Paris it was as though a switch had been thrown in his life: everything at home and in school that had been 'wrong' with him was now somehow right.

He worked hard to speak decent French, discovered the cafés where theatre people went, became one of them, and found roles he could play, even if he had to memorize his lines phonetically. By 1925 he'd been recruited for his first work in film – silent at the time, which forced the actors to communicate with face and body. Then, after Warner Bros.' *The Jazz Singer* in 1928, the dam broke – the first French talking picture, *Les Trois Masques,* appeared in 1929. Later that year, Stahl had the lead role in his first sound film: the wealthy owner of a factory (Stahl) secretly goes to union meetings, falls in love with a tough slumgirl factory worker, defends the dignity of the working class, loses his family and his factory, runs away with the girl, and is shot dead at a street march in the last scene. And then, who happened to be in Paris on the honeymoon of his third marriage but Milt Freed, an executive at Warner Bros.

Despite the fact that he and his new wife spoke only the most basic restaurant French, they took in a movie.

'Stalka! Franz Stalka!'

Stahl had just entered the hotel lobby. Shocked at hearing his real name, he stared at the man who'd called out to him: a chubby fellow with a shining bald head and a fringe of grey hair. Who was this, rising from a lobby chair, newspaper still in one hand, a huge grin on his face? Stahl had no idea, then he almost remembered, and then he did. Last seen, what was it, twenty years ago? By now the man was hurrying towards him.

'It's me, Stalka, Moppi, you can't have forgotten!' This in pure Viennese German.

'Hello, uh, Moppi.' This sudden incarnation was Karl Moppel, his boss at the Austro-Hungarian legation in Barcelona, lo these twenty years ago. A man he'd always called Herr Moppel, though he vaguely remembered other people at the legation using the nickname.

Moppi shook his head. 'Ach, I should have called you Fredric Stahl – of course I've followed your career. What are you doing in Paris?'

'I'm here to make a film.'

'Fantastic. I'm so proud of you, *we're* proud of you, all the old gang.'

'I'm glad, that's very kind of you to say.'

'Can we have coffee?' Moppi said, looking at his watch. 'I'm supposed to meet somebody but she hasn't shown up.'

'Let's just sit in the lobby, all right?'

'Of course. I can't believe I've run into you.' They took two chairs separated by a rubber tree. 'I've often wondered what became of you, over the years. Then, maybe five or six years ago, I saw your picture on a poster at a movie theatre and I thought, I know that fellow!

That's Franz Stalka, who worked for us in Barcelona. I was delighted, really, delighted. What a success you've become.'

'What brings *you* to Paris, Moppi?' Something inside Stahl curled up and quivered when he said that silly name.

'Me? Oh, I work in the embassy now. Still a diplomat, old Moppi. It was the Austrian embassy but it's German now, since the *Anschluss* in March.'

'Were you pleased, when that happened?'

Moppi looked serious. 'It was unsettling, I'll tell you that, and I didn't like it at all, not at all. But you know, Franz – may I call you Franz?'

'Please do.'

'The political situation was very bad, we were on the brink of civil war in Austria and, in a way, Hitler saved us. Anyhow, beyond flags and things like that it doesn't mean very much. Except calm and prosperity – how does one go about disliking that, I ask you?'

'It would be difficult,' Stahl said.

Moppi sat back and gazed affectionately at Stahl, then slowly shook his head. 'Just imagine, I know a Hollywood star.'

'I'm the same person,' Stahl said. 'Older.'

Moppi roared and wiped his eyes. 'Yes, isn't it so, I try not to think about it.'

Now Stahl looked at his watch.

'I'll bet you're busy, a fellow like you,' Moppi said.

Stahl offered a smile of regret that meant yes, he was busy.

'Say, I have an idea, before you rush off. Some of the old gang from the military intelligence are in Paris now, one's a diplomat, another has business here, why don't we get together for a grand Parisian lunch? Talk over old times.'

'From the what?'

'Why our section at the legation – what did you think we were about?'

'Moppi, I opened the *mail*.'

'Yes you did – the so-called "Señor Rojas" writes to the consul, the so-called "Señor Blanco" requests a visa to visit his poor mother,

"Señor Azul" has inherited a small house in Linz. That was what you called "the mail", Franz, some of it, the important letters. Just the day-to-day details of a military intelligence section, quite humdrum in fact. No shooting, eh?' He laughed.

Stahl sat there, his mind working at all this when a well-dressed woman came quickly towards them. 'Oh, Moppi, I'm so sorry,' she said. 'I could not find a taxi.'

'Look who's here, Hilda!' Moppi said, then, 'Moppi, *manners*. Frau Hilda Bruner, allow me to present Herr *Fredric Stahl*.' He beamed.

The woman blinked and stared. 'Well, well,' she said. 'You're the movie star.'

'Yes, that's me,' he said, just rueful enough. They shook hands, her hand was warm and she held tight for a moment longer than usual.

Moppi looked at his watch, which was thin and gold and expensive. 'Later than I thought,' he said. 'We'd better go off to the restaurant or we'll lose our reservation.' He put his hand out and Stahl shook it. 'You will have a lunch with us, maybe next week, won't you? At least say you'll think about it.'

'I certainly will . . . think about it, Moppi. Wonderful to see you. And a pleasure to meet you, Meine Frau.'

Moppi reached into the side pocket of his jacket, produced a business card and handed it to Stahl. Then he took Frau Bruner's arm and the two of them headed for the door. Moppi looked back at Stahl and smiled, then called out, 'See you soon!'

As Moppi and Frau Bruner left the hotel, Stahl retreated to his suite. He had no memory of any intelligence section at the Barcelona legation. He assumed that, as in any foreign outpost, the Austro-Hungarian diplomats, especially the army and naval officers, tried to learn what they could of Spanish political and military institutions, but Stahl could recollect no codes, no secret writing, no discussion of operations, nothing like that. He'd read the names of the addressees, opened the envelopes, sometimes looked at the first few lines to make sure they were going to the right person, then sorted them into the proper mailboxes, that was all. Maybe Señores Red, White, and Blue had sent letters, but that meant nothing to an eighteen-year-old clerk. When the mail was done, he'd filed papers, emptied wastebaskets, delivered envelopes in the city, run errands, did whatever they told him to do. Yet this man Moppi – good God! – wanted him to *believe* he'd been involved in clandestine work, because . . . Because why? Because it made him vulnerable? Vulnerable to what? Some byzantine form of blackmail? Well, they could forget that. He'd never loved Austria, had disliked the smug hypocrisies of its culture, and now he hated what it had become: a land of Nazi Jew-baiters and book-burners. So he wasn't going to have lunch or any other contact with Moppi and his pals. He would be polite, distant, and impossible to approach, and that was that.

The Claridge version of a desk, an escritoire with glassed-in bookcase above the hinged writing surface, was by a window and Stahl set Moppi's business card down on the polished wood and had a good look at it. The address was the German embassy on the rue de Lille. The card itself was impressive, printed on heavy stock, the letters sharp black against a crisp white background. *Like new,* he thought. And, when he picked up the card and held it at eye level, he caught a faint whiff of fresh ink.

24 September. Now, finally, he could go to work. He'd been invited to a one o'clock lunch with Jules Deschelles, the producer for *Après la Guerre*. Deschelles had his office at 28, rue Marbeuf – just up the street from the hotel – a turn-of-the-century building with a doorway flanked by a wholesale butcher and a men's haberdashery. Not fancy here, commercial and busy, which allowed Deschelles to pay a reasonable rent for an Eighth Arrondissement address. Crossing the first courtyard, Stahl found a second, then walked up to the fourth floor.

Spotting a door with PRODUCTIONS on it he reached for the doorknob, only then noticing that it said PRODUCTIONS CASSON. Wrong producer! He knew of Jean Casson, who made dark, tasty little films about Parisian gangsters with hearts of gold and wildly stunning girlfriends. PRODUCTIONS DESCHELLES was further down the hall, past a spice importer and a travel agency.

In the office there was a tough old bird of a secretary and Deschelles himself. He was about Stahl's age, an ascetic sort of man, tall, thin, and exceptionally pale, with a scholar's face – a scholar of some very esoteric subject – and glasses with fine silver frames. He seemed, to Stahl, finicky, holding his head back when he spoke, pursing his lips as he listened. Without ceremony, Deschelles handed him a copy of the script, *Fredric Stahl* carefully written in the upper corner of the cover. 'I thought about mailing a script to you in Hollywood,' Deschelles said. 'But it wasn't any good. Do you know of Etienne Roux?'

Stahl didn't.

'He wrote the novel *Trois Soldats,* three soldiers, and a first draft of the screenplay. This is a second version, by two Parisian screenwriters who've been produced a dozen times.' Deschelles stood up, retrieved a book from a pile on the windowsill, and handed it to Stahl. 'Look it over if you have a moment, but eventually I'd like to have it back.'

Stahl opened the book to the first page:

> At the end of the war, three soldiers found themselves far from home and penniless. Their enlistments were up, they had long been separated from their regiment, and they were, despite all the battles they'd fought, alive. This they had not foreseen, but soon set about making plans to find their way back to their native land.

'Roux attempted the universal,' Deschelles said. 'The time was modern but unspecific, there were no nationalities, and the countries they passed through were not named. Very poetic, you could say, but my screenwriters had no patience for *that.* They rewrote it so the war now ends in 1918, the soldiers are in the French Foreign Legion, and the movie opens with them in a Turkish prisoner-of-war camp. They try to get—'

'Yes, that was in the synopsis.'

Deschelles went on to discuss the director, Emile Simon, who Stahl had never heard of but, as Deschelles described his career, was a familiar type – one of those dependable, competent technicians that no film studio could live without. He'd made a number of films, one of which Stahl remembered – it had played in American theatres – but had not seen. 'He's Belgian, from Antwerp,' Deschelles said. 'Not in any way the eccentric genius, far from it. Emile is good-natured, easy to work with, and he's never made an actor look bad.' After a moment, Deschelles added, 'And he is *very* excited at the prospect of working with you, as all of us are. It will add a dimension to this film we never thought we'd have. A surprise, of course, but the best kind of surprise.'

'A surprise?' Stahl said. 'What they said in California was that Paramount started this project with the idea that I'd be in it. Not so?'

Deschelles hesitated, then proceeded carefully. 'Ah, it's my understanding that the idea came from Warner Bros. There was negotiation as to which Paramount actor could do a film for Warner, and that turned out to be Gary Cooper.' He paused, then said, 'We had originally cast Pierre Langlois as the lead, Monsieur Stahl, we'd signed a contract. And Pierre wasn't so pleased to lose the role and Paramount had to find him something else.'

'Really,' Stahl said, because Deschelles had gone silent and he had to say something. 'I wasn't aware of all this. You're sure?'

'I am. Well, maybe better to say as sure as anyone can be in this business. As you know, some films, by the time they reach the movie theatres, have led very complicated lives. Yet, even so, there on the screen is the most tender love story, or a great battle between a hero of the people and a wicked king.' After a moment, he said, 'You're not, um, *disappointed*, are you?'

Stahl smiled and said, 'Far from it.' In his imagination he could hear Buzzy Mehlman's voice: *Just do the movie, Fredric, let me worry about what goes on behind the scenes.*

Deschelles looked relieved – Stahl's delivery of the *far from it* line had been persuasive. 'You're aware,' he said, 'that a French production is often chosen, by the American award committees, as the best foreign film of the year – since 1931 that's been true. Perhaps Warners sees it from that angle; success in France, followed by success in America, and then in the international markets. Which will make you more valuable, in future productions.'

Stahl nodded in agreement, but this was courtesy. *Somebody* wasn't telling the truth and, if he understood what Deschelles had said, that somebody was Walter Perry. Buzz Mehlman had a very wry touch when it came to the mechanics, and the ethics, of the film business and Stahl could imagine him saying, 'What? A movie studio *lied*? Oh no!' Nonetheless, here he was, in Paris with a contract and a movie to be made: this was his *career,* but he had no idea how to protect himself. In fact, he'd been put in a position where he had to do as the studio wished. Once again, in Stahl's imagination, a dark grin from his agent. As the silence in the office grew, Deschelles finally said, 'Shall we go out and have something to eat?'

They left the office, walking towards the river on the sunny, windy afternoon, Deschelles chatting about the other people who would be working on the film, Stahl responding now and again, the script and the novel firmly beneath his arm. Eventually they arrived at a Lebanese restaurant and settled in at a table. 'I hope you like Lebanese cuisine,' Deschelles said.

Stahl said he did.

As he looked over the menu, Deschelles said, 'I always order the mezze, but the portions are generous so, if you don't mind, I'll get one order we can share.'

'I don't mind at all.' This wasn't true, Stahl very much liked the little appetizers served as mezze, but producers as a class, spending a lot of money every day, could be stingy in small matters. When Deschelles excused himself to go to the WC, Stahl opened the script and paged through it, stopping to look at some of his character's lines. COLONEL VADIC, as the script had it, is at a castle in Hungary, and explains how he, as a Slav, rose to command – normally reserved for

French officers. Wounded in battle, he was declared '*Français par le sang versé*' – French by spilled blood – which in the Foreign Legion qualified him to become an officer.

Deschelles returned, a delicious mezze arrived soon after – stuffed grape leaves, salty white cheese, falafel – Stahl's favourite, mashed chickpeas fried up in little pancakes – and hummus, Stahl's other favourite. As the main course was served, ground lamb and pine nuts baked in layers, Deschelles nodded his head towards a nearby table and spoke in a confidential voice, 'I think you've been spotted.'

As Stahl followed Deschelles's eyes, a man sitting alone at the table became interested in his newspaper. 'He knows who you are and he wants to stare,' Deschelles said, 'but that's very rude here. He's avoiding us now, because he's been caught at it.' Stahl had been stared at many times in public, but some sort of intuition suggested that this man wasn't a movie fan, he was something else.

For dessert, they shared three small squares of baklava.

Back at the Claridge, Stahl was headed for the elevator when the manager called out to him, 'Oh Monsieur Stahl.' Stahl went over to the desk. 'A letter for you, sir, delivered by hand. The messenger asked that it be given to you in person.'

Stahl thanked him and went up to his suite. Inside a manila envelope, a formal envelope held a folded note card: on the front, printed in some elaborate form of italic: *The Baroness Cornelia Maria von Reschke und Altenburg.* When he opened the card he found the message: French written in careful, spidery script: 'My dear Monsieur Stahl, I can only hope you will forgive an invitation on such short notice but I've just now learned that you are in Paris and I am a most devoted admirer of your films. I am having a cocktail party at six tomorrow evening and would be so very pleased if you would join us. Please telephone my secretary, Mlle Jeanette, at INV 46-63 if you would like further information.' The signature, *Maria von Reschke,* was a thing of beauty, as was the address, a street in the Seventh he had never heard of.

He read the note a second time – who was this? German nobility in Paris? Expatriate German nobility? Well, he thought, why not. Artists didn't own the rights to expatriate life. And he liked the idea of *le cocktail*, as the French called such a gathering; with a dinner you were good and stuck, but you could leave a cocktail party. He knew that sooner or later he would have to find a social existence in Paris and here was a good place to begin. But, for no reason he could define, he thought he'd better call Mme Boulanger at Warner France. A young woman answered, then Zolly Louis picked up an extension phone. 'How's it being?' Zolly said in English. 'Everything okay?'

Stahl assured him all was well. Had he ever heard of a certain Baroness von Reschke? 'Of course!' Zolly said. 'She's famous, she's got one of the three important *salons* in Paris. You're invited over there?' He was. 'You should go, Mister Stahl. You'll meet the crème de la crème, *chez* the baroness – bankers, fashionable women, *ambassadors*. And then, the other two will invite you to their *salons*. They *hate* each other, these hostesses!'

So that was decided, he would go. He hunted around in his closet to see where the maid had put the shoes he wanted to wear, found them, and set them out in the hall to be polished. As he closed the door he realized it was very quiet in the suite, and the evening stretched out ahead of him. He undressed, put on a bathrobe, and settled himself lengthwise on a sofa with his copy of *Après la Guerre*. But not for long. Just turning the cover and reading the stage directions for the first scene produced in him a sharp little pang of familiar anxiety that meant *work*.

But he didn't want to work – the fading light outside the window, the gathering dusk, had reached him. It was *l'heure bleue* – time to be meeting a lover, or looking for one. Well, he had nowhere to go. He put the script aside, went to the desk, found Hotel Claridge stationery, and began to write a letter to Betsy Belle in Hollywood.

Betsy Belle (born Myra Harzie in Ottumwa, Iowa) was his official fiancée; *fiancée* being Hollywood code for lover, for the woman who accompanied you to parties, and a convenient euphemism for studio publicists and gossip columnists. She'd been discovered by a talent scout at an Iowa high school pageant, where she'd played the role of a corn, and when she'd arrived in Hollywood she'd quickly become a successful starlet. Blessed with a cupid's-bow mouth that revealed two white teeth, a snub nose, and bright blonde hair that she wore like a teenager, Betsy had appeared in a number of movies, but had also grown older every year, until available parts were rare. Betsy also happened to be smart, and not at all the innocent she played on the screen. Of the cupid's-bow shape of her upper lip she would say, 'It makes me look like a fucking rabbit.'

He and Betsy didn't precisely live together, truer to say that she stayed with him at his house some of the time, then, wanting to be by herself, would retreat to her apartment. 'In this town,' she explained, 'getting people to like you is what takes up most of your time, so it's my luxury to hide from the world.' What Betsy Belle really liked was muggles, marijuana, and on nights when they were together she'd put on one of her Django Reinhardt records – 'I'se a Muggin'' her favourite – and smoke away, first becoming very entertaining, then highly aroused, eventually heading for Stahl's lap. This wasn't now and then, this was always, and at first Stahl had thought it was something about him. But, on reflection, he realized it was her nature, her own internal catnip – desire simply wouldn't leave her alone. The wolves of Hollywood wouldn't leave her alone either, so being Stahl's 'fiancée' was at least some protection. Certainly she didn't expect fidelity in Paris, and Stahl knew she'd find herself somebody else soon enough. Still, despite all the practical sentiments, he really liked her and she was, no matter what else went on, a true friend.

It was, by the third draft, a sweet letter. He loved Paris, he missed her. Not original but from the heart. And how many letters like this, he wondered, would be in that morning's mail?

25 September. When Stahl came out of the hotel, Zolly Louis's nephew Jimmy, in grey chauffeur's uniform and cap, leapt smartly from the driver's seat, opened the door of the silver Panhard, and said, 'Good

evening, sir.' Stahl gave him the Baroness von Reschke's address, and the car swung out into a slow line of traffic. For the occasion, Stahl had worn his best suit: double-breasted in thin, midnight-blue wool with natural shoulders, a handsome fit, perfectly cut by the custom tailor Isidor Klein in downtown Los Angeles. Mr Klein did not advertise, his telephone number was passed from successful producer to powerful agent to prominent actor, and his services required time, several fittings, and a lot of money. To the suit, Stahl had added a custom-made shirt, a shade or two off white, and a dove-grey and Renaissance-red tie from Sulka.

It didn't take long enough to drive to the baroness's house, so Stahl got a tour of the royal Seventh until 6.45, then Jimmy turned off the rue du Bac and into a street of private mansions built in the seventeenth and eighteenth centuries. 'You inherit these,' Jimmy said as Stahl stared out the window. 'Or they are *very* expensive.' He pulled into a porte cochere, a man in a suit opened the door and asked for Stahl's name. Parked beyond the entry were a few glossy black automobiles and two silver Panhard Dynamics, glowing softly in the light of the streetlamps.

The cocktail party was in the drawing room, where splendid old paintings in elaborate gold frames – lords and ladies and cherubs and a few bare breasts – hung on the boiserie; walnut panelling that covered the walls. It was a stiff, formal room, with draperies of forest-green velvet, maroon taffeta upholstery, spindly chairs from royal times – chanting in chorus *don't dare sit on me* – and a mirror-polished eighteenth-century parquet floor. Against one wall, a huge marble-topped hunting table with gilt legs, a place to toss your pheasants when you came in from the field, and flanking the sofas, end tables held silver *objets,* marble hounds, crystal lamps with butter-coloured silk shades, and heavy vases of white gladioli. If this room didn't intimidate you, Stahl thought, nothing would.

The party was in full swing – the sound of thirty conversations in a haze of cigarette smoke and perfume – and Stahl, standing at the ten-foot-high doors, had the impression that the guests went with the room: a few stunning women, some imposing, white-haired dowagers, a balding gent with a pipe – the pet intellectual? – a sculpted beard or two, even a couple of ceremonial sashes; an exotic species of royalty, perhaps the Margrave of Moldavia or something like that. And now, here came what must be the baroness, face lit with delight and a grand hostess smile. 'Monsieur Stahl! We're *honoured*. Oh thank you *so* much for coming.' She was, Stahl thought as he took her claw, a very formidable woman: perhaps fifty, with stylishly set straw hair and a white face, skin drawn tight as a drum with the bone in the centre of her forehead faintly evident, a blue vein at one temple, and uncomfortably penetrating greenish eyes. For the early-evening party, she wore a powder-pink cocktail dress.

'You're staying at the Claridge?' she said. 'I just love that hotel, so much quieter than the Ritz.'

A glass of champagne was put in his hand, a silver tray of caviar blini flew past. 'They certainly make you comfortable,' Stahl said. 'But I'll be there for, three months? Four?'

'Months in a hotel . . .' she said.

'I'm thinking about an apartment.'

At that she brightened. 'Then you must let me help you, dear, I *know* people.'

Stahl's gracious nod meant that he appreciated the offer.

'I have a friend who writes about film for the newspapers, according to him you're Viennese, is that correct?'

Over her shoulder, Stahl faced a vast painting, and found himself looking into the shining eyes of a King Charles spaniel on a courtesan's lap. 'Yes, I was born and raised in Vienna.'

'I was there a month ago, it's a very vibrant city nowadays, after some difficult years.'

'It's been a long time since I visited,' Stahl said.

'Do go, dear, when you have a chance, I think you'll be pleased.'

Very pleased, swastikas everywhere.

The baroness sensed what his silence meant. 'Well, Europe is changing, isn't it,' she said. 'For the better, I'd say – perhaps it's been destroyed for the last time. My most fervent hope, anyhow, and surely yours.'

'It is.'

The baroness's lips curved upwards at the corners and her eyes narrowed, the smile of a huntress. 'Then we must do what we can to make sure of that, don't you agree?'

'I don't think I can do very much,' Stahl said. 'I'm no politician.'

'But you never know, dear, do you, about these things. Sometimes an opportunity presents itself, and then . . .'

Stahl had gone as far as he wanted with this and said, 'And do you enjoy living in Paris?'

'Enjoy? I'm passionate for it, completely passionate.'

'I am as well.'

'Then how lucky we are! I bought this house five years ago, though I worried that as a German I might not be welcome here. Fortunately, that's not the case – Parisians, bless their souls, take you as you are, they care more about style, about character, than they do about nationality. So, I thought, perhaps we *can* live together, and there's hope for poor old Europe after all. And, you know, there are some very well-regarded people, very *accomplished* people, in Paris who've discovered Berlin, the new Berlin, at last recovered after the war, after the financial crisis. They go for a weekend and when they return they say, "To hell with 1914, we had the warmest welcome in that city." I must tell you the mood there is extraordinary; confident, forward-looking. Say what you will about Herr Hitler, perhaps not one's favourite politician – yes, yes, I know, he's the most awful little man, but the results! Prosperity, dignity restored, that you must see for yourself!'

The baroness took his arm and led him further into the room, which was so crowded that they brushed against shoulders and backs. 'What a crush,' the baroness said. Then, leaning closer to him, she said, '*Everyone* wants to meet you, you know, they're just pretending to ignore you. Good manners and all that. Now, who shall you meet?'

'I leave it to your ladyship.'

'Oh pfui, Monsieur Fredric Stahl, you must call me Maria.' They pressed further into the room, then the baroness said, 'Now here's a fine fellow.' The fine fellow, tall, lean, and slightly stooped, turned towards the baroness, who said, 'Hello there, Philippe, look who's here!'

The fine fellow wore an elegant grey suit, his thick grey hair perfectly in place, his smile irresistible. 'Could you be Fredric Stahl? The movie star?' As he said this, his eyes, his face, radiated an almost palpable warmth.

'Monsieur Fredric Stahl,' the baroness said, a rich pride in her voice, 'allow me to present Monsieur Philippe LaMotte.'

LaMotte's handshake was powerful. '*Enchanté,*' he said. 'I am your greatest fan.'

'Martine!' the baroness called out, spying a special friend. 'I leave you in good hands,' she said to Stahl. 'We'll talk again, may I depend on it?' There was a gentle, and momentary, tightening of her hand on his arm, then she was off.

'I can't quite believe I'm standing here with you,' LaMotte said. 'For me, you'll always be in that garden, rain pouring down on you, watching the woman you love embracing, what was he? Race-car driver, snake-in-the-grass . . .'

'In *Summer Storm.*'

'Yes, the raindrops falling into your drink. But I am especially fond of *A Fortunate Woman.* You're a doctor in Manhattan and this woman comes to your office and she . . .'

'Actually, the part was originally written for Barbara Stanwyck.' Stahl knew from experience that LaMotte was going to recount the story of the film, and offering a bit of Hollywood gossip could politely break the flow.

'Really? Barbara Stanwyck? That would have been wonderful. She's the best actress in Hollywood, at least for me.'

'Surely one of them,' Stahl said. *Time to deflect,* he thought, and said, 'What sorts of things do you do in Paris, Monsieur LaMotte?'

'Just another businessman,' LaMotte said apologetically. 'I'm the managing director of the Rousillon company, in Epernay.' He raised his glass so that the light caught the bubbles and said, 'Rousillon Brut Millésime – we're drinking our champagne.' And, his tone slightly amused, added, 'And if you haven't heard our slogan, it's "Champagne, the only drink you can hear."' He held the glass to his ear and listened theatrically.

Stahl imitated the gesture, but he'd had the glass long enough that the characteristic fizzing sound was no longer audible.

'A fresh glass, perhaps,' LaMotte said. He looked around, but the servant with a tray of glasses was on the other side of the room.

'He'll get here,' Stahl said. 'It's very good champagne.'

'Thank you, but to tell you the truth, I find my other work more absorbing.'

'And that is?'

'I'm one of the directors of the Comité Franco-Allemagne. Do you know what that is?'

'Forgive me, but I don't.'

'You'd know if you were living in Paris,' LaMotte said. 'It was started in 1930, by a German called Otto Abetz, a simple drawing teacher in the public schools of Karlsruhe whose father had been killed in the war. The basic idea was that German and French veterans of the war would work together to keep it from happening again. And it's been something of a success, because veterans, men who've actually done the fighting, are highly respected in both countries.'

'That sounds like a very worthwhile undertaking,' Stahl said. 'The baroness was talking about something similar.'

'Rapprochement,' LaMotte said. 'Do they have the word in English?'

'You don't often hear it, but it's used. To mean the re-establishment of harmony, of good relations. The baroness was describing her own experience, here in Paris.'

'She's a great supporter. She's terribly rich, you know, and very generous. This is the sort of organization that's only effective if it has money to spend. We were, from the beginning, often in the news, in the papers and on the radio, and even in *Time* magazine. We sponsor visits, back and forth, meetings in Paris and Berlin, we hold the occasional press conference, and we're always available to react as political events unfold – we're trying to deal with problems in Czech-oslovakia right now, but it's not easy.'

'What's your approach?'

'Anything but war. That's *always* our approach. And the public in Europe has been very sympathetic – in Paris, Berlin, London, every-where. We've worked hard for that. About four years ago, for instance, I suggested we build an organization for young people – they must learn early how terrible war is. The idea was, French youth and Ger-man youth would together create a bridge of understanding, to work together for rapprochement, for mutual respect and reconciliation. We have summer camps – free summer camps – and a magazine, *Notre Temps,* our times, that's widely read and reports on all our activities.'

'Nothing wrong with that,' Stahl said.

'You wouldn't think so, would you. But we have our enemies, par-ticularly from certain political factions who do nothing but press for French rearmament.' LaMotte shook his head, more than a little anger in his expression. 'And who will bankrupt the nation to do it. Spending millions of francs on warplanes and cannon while the needy go unfed. When the states of Europe try to intimidate their neigh-bours with new guns and ships, the next step is war, as we learned in 1914 to our great sorrow.'

'Then you are, perhaps, a pacifist?'

LaMotte shrugged. 'I'm just an honourable businessman who loves his country. But these people will have us at war if they get their way. *Bellicistes* we call them, warmongers. Back in 1936, when we had the so-called Popular Front, a communist front, they wanted to arm the Republicans fighting in Spain. Well, we put all the pressure we could on the government, and France remained neutral, but the government still sent four hundred aeroplanes to the Spaniards, se-cretly. There were investigations in the senate, and the numbers kept changing, but law meant nothing to them and the country saw that.'

Stahl wondered how to answer this, and said, 'Well, our newspa-pers . . .'

Just then a very appealing woman appeared at LaMotte's side. She wore a tight cloche hat with chestnut hair swept across her forehead, her eyes were heavily made up and looked enormous, and she wore a tied rope of pearls above a low neckline. Looking at Stahl she said, 'Oh Philippe, are you going to keep our guest all to yourself? I trust you're not talking *politics*.' She grinned wickedly at Stahl.

'Me?' LaMotte said. 'Politics? How could you think such a thing?' He laughed and said, 'Kiki de Saint-Ange, may I present Monsieur Fredric Stahl.'

She dropped a cool hand into Stahl's and said, '*Formidable*, to think someone like you would turn up *here*.'

LaMotte said, 'It was a wonderful surprise to meet you in person, Monsieur Stahl, and I hope to see you again sometime, if your schedule permits.'

'It's been a pleasure,' Stahl said.

'What a courteous fellow you are,' Kiki said. 'Philippe can be amusing, but you've landed among the most boring, stuffy old mummies in France. These are the aristos who got away in 1789!'

'Oh? Well, you're here.'

'I am standing in for my parents, Monsieur Stahl, so I have to be here, but not for long.'

'Won't you be missed?'

'Not me. And I'm going to a much livelier party than this.'

'That sounds exciting,' Stahl said.

'Why not see for yourself? Not a soul will know who you are, they don't *go* to American movies.'

This hit home, for it summoned his former life in the city, but he didn't think he could just disappear.

She moved closer to him, her voice lowered. 'So we shall conspire, you and I. When I can't stand it any more I'll let you know, then you can do as you like. Where I'm going it's a *very* different crowd.'

Stahl hesitated. 'The Baroness von Reschke would think . . .'

Kiki flicked her fingers from her lips, the kiss floated in the air. From the corner of his eye, Stahl spotted the baroness, cutting her way through the crowd like a determined shark. 'Here she comes now,' Kiki said. 'Cinderella's stepmother. Perhaps I'll see you later.'

She slipped away, to be replaced by the baroness. 'My dear Monsieur Stahl, there's someone here you absolutely must meet . . .'

It was eight-twenty when he escaped. Kiki de Saint-Ange, now wearing an embroidered evening jacket, was lighting a cigarette by the doors, made eye contact with Stahl, and left. Stahl followed her. Outside he found a classic autumn drizzle, and as he caught up to Kiki she said, 'Now, a taxi.'

'No need for that,' Stahl said and led Kiki to the Panhard. Jimmy Louis leapt from the car and opened the back door, Kiki got in, and Jimmy closed the door and led Stahl around to the other side. 'We're going up to Boulogne-Billancourt, the *quai* on this side of the river,' Kiki said. Jimmy took the rue de Grenelle, heading west, but not for long. Suddenly the Panhard jerked to a stop and Jimmy said, *'Merde,'* under his breath, as though to himself, then added one or two elaborations in deep argot that Stahl couldn't understand.

Stahl leaned forward. 'What's *wrong*? Is it the car?'

'No, sir, not the car.' Clearly much worse than that, whatever it was. They had stopped by the Mairie, the mayor's office of the Seventh Arrondissement, where a group of people stood in front of the doors, with more arriving.

'Excuse me for a moment, sir,' Jimmy said, left the car, and joined the crowd.

'Any idea what's happened?' a puzzled Stahl said to Kiki.

She knew. *'Affiches blanches,'* she said. 'We're in for it now.'

Stahl had no idea what she meant. White notices? At the Mairie, Jimmy was working his way towards the doors. 'They must have just posted them,' Kiki said. 'Nobody at the party said a thing.'

'"Them"? What are they?'

'Mobilization notices,' Kiki said. 'Telling the men of Paris, telling men all over the country, that they must join their reserve units. *Tomorrow*. We're at war, Monsieur Stahl.' She found a cigarette and lit it, then threw the gold lighter angrily into her handbag. 'So, that's that,' she said.

Jimmy came trotting back to the car. 'Categories two and three,' he said.

'Not general?' Kiki said.

'No, *mobilisation partiale* – it's in big letters.' He got behind the wheel, then sat there. 'I'm in category three, so I'll be on the train at dawn, Monsieur Stahl. I'm very sorry, but I have to go and fight. I'm sure Zolly will find someone for you.'

'Can you take us up to the party?' Kiki said. 'Later we'll find a taxi.'

'There won't be any taxis,' Jimmy said. 'The drivers will be home, packing and saying goodbye.'

'Then we'll use the Métro, or we'll walk,' Kiki said. 'And if they start bombing us, we'll run.'

'What sort of unit are you in, Jimmy?' Stahl said.

'Infantry,' Jimmy said, and put the car in gear.

War came to the '*very* different crowd' that night, its long shadow sometimes a presence in the room, but the crowd fought back; defiant and merry and to hell with everything. They had the radio on, tuned to Radio Paris, the official state network, which played light classical music interrupted by news bulletins: mobilized men must report to their units in the east, extra trains would be running from the Gare de l'Est on the Boulevard de Strasbourg. And the government wished to emphasize that war had not been declared. 'Yet!' cried the party guests every time they heard the announcement. Of the thirty or so people crammed into an artist's studio, four or five of the men had been mobilized. Somebody said, 'We who are about to die salute you,' and that set the wits among them to shouting every possible obscene variation on the phrase. It kept them busy, it kept them amused, it chased the doom away.

The party was on a barge, tied up to a wharf in a long line of working barges where the city of Paris bordered the industrial suburb of Boulogne-Billancourt. The host, a cheerful old gent in a paint-spattered shirt, had a huge tangled grey beard with a breadcrumb caught in the middle. He gave Kiki a powerful hug, put his arm around Stahl's shoulders, and led them both around the room. He'd built himself a studio on the barge; removed some of the deck planking and installed a set of angled windows above the curve of the bow. So, with little space for hanging paintings, he'd used easels to display his work. Not Picasso, but not bad, in Stahl's opinion. After the tour they found a place to sit, Stahl took off his jacket and tie and turned up the cuffs of his shirt, while Kiki slipped out of her embroidered jacket. 'It's from Schiaparelli,' she told a woman who asked. Mildly abstract nudes seemed to be the artist's favoured style. One of which, a few feet from where Stahl and Kiki sat – on a love seat obviously rescued from a fire – had a face Stahl recognized. There was Kiki de Saint-Ange, lying languorous and seductive on a sofa, a 'Naked Maja' that imitated the Goya painting. 'I see you keep looking at that,' she said, teasing him. 'It's not a bad likeness, though I seem to have been grey-green that afternoon.'

They called him 'Fredric', the men and women getting drunk together on strong, sour wine poured from ceramic jugs, smoking up the host's hashish, petting the barge cats, now and then each other. The barge's bedroom, partly obscured by a lank curtain, served those who simply had to shed their black sweaters and make love despite the coming storm, or because of it. Two or three of the guests told Stahl he looked familiar, had they met before? Stahl just smiled and said he didn't think so. What with the long hours at the baroness's party, he was tired of being *the* Fredric Stahl and had packed it in for the night.

Needing some air, he made his way up to the deck, then noticed a young man who'd apparently done the same thing. He was one of those heading east in the morning and when their eyes met Stahl thought he might be close to tears – perhaps he'd sought privacy for that reason. They stood there in silence, then the man spoke. 'You know, my life hasn't been too bad, lately,' he said, voice unsteady. 'But now those bastards are going to get me killed.' He shook his head and said, 'No luck. No luck at all.' Stahl didn't answer, there was no answer. He just stared at the silent lights across the river and felt the heavy current in the deck beneath his feet. He had half turned to rejoin the party when there was a white flash that lit the clouds in the eastern sky, followed by a sharp crack of thunder. Maybe. Stahl and the young man looked at each other. Finally Stahl said, 'I think that's thunder.' The young man nodded, *yes, probably thunder.* Then they went back to the party.

Stahl and Kiki left sometime around three in the morning – long after the last Métro at eleven-thirty – and set out to walk back to the Seventh, where Kiki had an apartment. There were no taxis, the streets were deserted. They were not far from the apartment when suddenly, out of nowhere, the city's air-raid sirens began to wail. They stopped dead, listened for the sound of aeroplane engines, and stared up into the rain. 'Should we do something?' Stahl said. 'Go indoors?'

'Where?' Kiki said.

The buildings were dark, the shops had their shutters rolled down. 'I guess we won't,' Stahl said. They trudged on, past piles of sand in the streets. Somebody at the party had told them about the sand, de-livered throughout the city by sanitation workers, meant to be taken up to the roof and stored there, in case the Germans dropped incendi-ary bombs. 'Then,' the guest said, 'when a bomb falls on your roof and starts to burn, you use the sand to put out the fire, and you must remember to bring a shovel. But in Paris nobody has a shovel, so maybe a spoon.'

At last, exhausted and soaked, they reached Kiki's door, where she kissed him quickly on the lips and went inside. Then it was a long walk back to the Claridge, and after four when he got there. The desk clerk took one look at him and said, 'I'll send someone up to get your suit, sir. We'll press it, it will be as good as new, sir, you'll see.' In the room, Stahl took everything off, put on a bathrobe, and waited for the porter. Standing at the window, he searched the sky, but no bombs fell on Paris that night.

When the telephone woke him at nine, Stahl struggled to sit up and reached for a cigarette. On the other end of the line, an excited Jules

Deschelles. 'All is not lost!' Deschelles said. 'Have you seen the papers? Daladier and Chamberlain are going to Munich to meet with Hitler, a last chance for peace.' Daladier was the Premier of France, Chamberlain the Prime Minister of Great Britain.

'I thought the war would begin today,' Stahl said.

'Oh no, not yet, there's still hope. We've lost Emile Simon, our director, he's been called back to Belgium. However, they might let him go, we'll see. Then some of the crew, grips and electricians, were sent to their units in Alsace – we'll see about them as well. So, there will be a delay, but don't book passage, the movie will somehow get made.'

'What will happen to the Czechs?'

For a moment, Deschelles was silent, then he said, 'Who knows? Perhaps they will fight, perhaps they won't. Are you concerned about that?'

'Well, I don't want to see them occupied.'

'No, of course not, nobody wants that,' Deschelles said. 'I just felt I should make sure you aren't worried about the film. And there's a lot we can get done while all this madness works itself out.'

'I can learn lines,' Stahl said.

'That's the spirit! And I'll have our costume designer get in touch with you, perhaps today or tomorrow.'

'Good. I'll wait for the call.'

Deschelles said goodbye and hung up. Stahl tried to go back to sleep.

29 September. The costume designer, a woman named Renate Steiner, had arranged to meet with Stahl at her workroom, in Building K at the Paramount studios in Joinville, a working-class suburb southeast of Paris. He'd then telephoned Zolly Louis, who told Stahl he was still looking for a driver. 'I'd be happy to do it myself,' Zolly said, 'but I don't drive so much, maybe you can find a taxi.' In fact there was a taxi, on the morning of the twenty-ninth, waiting near the front of the Claridge. The driver was an old man in a clean white shirt buttoned

at the throat, who had an artificial hand – a leather cup enclosing the wrist, a leather glove with thumb and fingers set in a half-curled position. 'A German did that to me,' the driver said as they drove off. 'I could get a better one, but it's expensive.' He explained that the taxi belonged to his son. 'Just now he's driving an army truck, up around Lille, much good it will do him or anybody else,' he said and spat out the window.

In time they reached Joinville and the driver, when Stahl handed him a hundred francs – twenty dollars – agreed to wait until Stahl was done with his appointment. The studios were vast – bought by Paramount in 1930, then used as a movie factory, making as many as fourteen versions of a new film in fourteen languages spoken by fourteen casts, thus making money fourteen times out of a single vehicle. This was possible because everybody everywhere liked to go to the movies, talking movies that talked in their own language. So the classic line of the American Saturday night: *Say, honey, whattaya say we take in the new show at the Bijou?* was repeated in its own linguistic version around the world. And still was, though by the time Stahl reached Joinville it had, with the development of new sound technology, become a dubbing studio: an actor moved his lips in French, the audience heard Spanish.

Stahl, in the course of a long search for Building K, stopped for a time to watch a moustachioed gaucho with a guitar singing *'te amo'* to a señorita on a balcony as the cameraman peered through his lens and the technicians squatted out of the frame. It was mostly, at Joinville, pretty much the same movie – love ignited, love thwarted, love triumphant. Just like, Stahl told himself with an inner smile, Hollywood.

Eventually, he found what he was looking for: a one-storey, rust-stained stucco Building K, situated between Building R and Building 22 – the French were staunchly committed anarchists when it suited them. Renate Steiner's workroom was spacious, long wooden tables held bolts of fabric, boxes of buttons in every colour and size, boxes of zips, cloth flowers, snips of material (*I'll want that later*), and spools of thread, attended by every imaginable species of mannequin – from wire mesh to stained cotton, some of them in costume: here a Zouave, there a king's ermine, and in between a pirate's striped shirt and a convict's striped outfit.

Steiner sat before a sewing machine, matt black from constant use, SINGER in gold letters across the side. As she looked up to see who her visitor was, she ceased working the pedals and the two-stroke music of the machine slowed, then stopped. 'Fredric Stahl,' she said, her voice pleased to see him. 'I'm Renate Steiner. Thank you for coming out here.' She stood and said, 'Let me find you a place to sit,' walked to the end of the table and whipped a caveman's bearskin off a chair. As she moved her own chair to face his, she said, 'Not too much trouble finding me?'

'Not so much – I'm used to studio lots.'

'Yes, of course. Still, people get horribly lost out here.' She settled herself in the chair and took off her silver-rimmed glasses.

She was in her early forties, he guessed – a few silver strands in dark hair stylishly cut to look chopped off and practical – and wore a blue work smock that buttoned up the front. Sitting close to her, he saw that she was very fair-skinned, with a sharp line to her jaw and a pointy nose that suggested mischief, the tip faintly reddened in the chill of the unheated room. Her eyes were a faded blue, her smile ironic, and subtly challenging. The face of an intellectual, he thought – she would be partial to symphonies and serious books. She was dressed for the chill, in a long, loose skirt, thick black wool stockings, and laced, low-heeled boots. She wore no make-up he could see but somehow didn't need it, looking scrubbed and sensible.

'So then,' she said. '*Après la Guerre*, an appealing title, isn't it, what with . . . everything going on right now. What do you think of the script?'

'I've read through it a couple of times, and I'm almost done with the book – normally I would have finished it but it kept putting me to sleep.'

'Yes, I felt the same way, but the script is better. Much better, would you say?'

From Stahl, a nod of enthusiasm. 'It has real possibilities, depending on who directs – Jules Deschelles was going to tell me who will replace Emile Simon but so far he hasn't. A lot will depend on how it's shot, on the music, and . . . but you know all that. You've been doing this for a while, no?'

'Ten years, give or take. I started in Germany, with UFA, but we, my husband and I, had to leave when Hitler took power in '33. We weren't the sort of people he wanted in Germany – my husband was a journalist, a little too far to the left. So, late at night, we ran like hell and took only whatever money we had in the house. I wondered if we weren't just scaring ourselves with this whole Nazi business but, a month after we left, some of our old friends disappeared, and you know what's gone on there since '33. After all, you're from Vienna, or so I've read, anyhow.'

'I left when I was sixteen, but that had to do with family, not politics. Later I went back for a few years, then lived in Paris before they brought me out to Hollywood.'

'Do you like it there?'

'I try to. I don't think anybody actually *likes* it, not the people I talk to. Mostly they feel some mixture of gratitude and anxiety, because it pays a lot but after a while you discover it's perilous – you can really say the wrong thing to the wrong person, and it's probably wise to understand that a career in movies is temporary. On the other hand, I like America. Well, I like *Americans,* I'm not sorry to be one of them, as much as I am.'

She shrugged. 'You're an émigré, like us. I don't suppose you'd prefer to speak German, we can.'

'Oh no, I have to speak French right now, think in French as much as possible.'

She was silent for a moment, then, for no particular reason, smiled at him. 'Well,' she said. 'I suppose we have to go to work, get you measured up to be Colonel Vadic. Where's he from, your colonel?'

'"A Slav" is all it says in the script. In the book he's from somewhere in the Balkans.'

'Deschelles saw something there, in the book, let's hope he was right,' she said, then stood and drew a rolled yellow tape measure out of the pocket of her smock. 'Could you stand in front of my mirror?'

Stahl stepped onto a wooden platform in front of the mirror. Renate Steiner took a long, appraising look at him and said, 'You're nice and tall, aren't you. Thank heaven, or your forebears. There are some very handsome, very short actors in this business, and the producer has to cast a very short woman as the love interest or the actor has to stand on a box.' She found a pad and pencil on the table and said, 'Could you hold your left arm out straight, palm facing me?'

Stahl did as he was told. Renate put her glasses back on, clamped the pencil between her teeth, then stretched the tape from the tip of his middle finger to his armpit. She studied the tape where it met his finger, steadied the end under his arm, and said, 'You're not ticklish, are you?'

'Not for a long time.'

'That makes this easier, now and then we've had comedy in here.' She let the tape go and wrote down the measurement and said, 'By the way, may I call you Fredric?'

'Yes, I prefer it.' After a beat he said, 'Renate.'

Measuring his other arm, she said, 'We've got plenty of Foreign Legion uniforms in stock, we'll just have to do some alterations.'

'Will I be wearing the kepi with the white neckcloth?' In his voice, *I hope not.*

'Not if *I* can help it,' she said firmly. 'That's been seen too often, in the *worst* movies – the audience will expect you to burst out in song. "Oh, my desert maiden . . . ", that sort of thing.' He smiled, she glanced up at him. 'No,' she said, 'you'll wear a classic officer's uniform, and since Vadic has been in a Turkish prison camp we'll have to fade it, soil it, give you a little rip in the shoulder.'

'That sounds just right,' he said. 'When I made silent films in Paris they stuck a kepi on me but it was too small . . .'

She said, 'Would you face the mirror, please?' and stepped up onto the platform, running the tape across his shoulders.

'. . . which made it so hot they had to wipe the sweat off my face.'

'That won't happen, not at *chez* Renate – I try to keep my actors comfortable.' She reached up and measured his head. 'Your hat will fit perfectly, colonel.' She next took his neck measurement, then drew the tape tight around his waist. 'Please don't do that,' she said. 'Just let everything settle in its natural position, you're not at the beach.' Stahl relaxed his stomach. 'We all have tummies, don't we?' she said. Then she knelt in front of him and, looking up at him, she said, 'We come now to the inseam.' This measurement was taken from the very top of the inner thigh. 'You can hold the sensitive end if you like.'

Stahl grinned despite himself. 'No, I don't mind, I'll just close my eyes.'

She laughed politely, then went ahead and took the measurement, exactly as his tailor, and past costume designers, had done it. 'There,' she said, 'you can open your eyes now.' Next she did the wrist, after that, the neck. Then she said, 'We're just about done,' and circled the tape around his hips.

'Bigger than you thought?' Stahl said, a laugh in his voice.

'Oh, normal, maybe a *little* bigger,' she said. 'But you aren't the only one.' She was, he knew, referring to herself. She rolled the tape back up and put it in the pocket of her smock. They returned to their chairs and Stahl, glad that the work was finished, lit a cigarette. Renate, looking at her notepad, said, 'Colonel Vadic will also wear an old suit – all three of them will. This is when they have to get rid of their uniforms, after they've been arrested as deserters . . .'

'And almost executed. Blindfolded, tied to the post . . .'

'They buy suits in Damascus, in the souk,' she said. 'You know, I think Paramount might let Deschelles shoot on location. He's trying, anyhow, wants to use Tangiers for Damascus, and do the desert scenes nearby.'

'We can only hope,' Stahl said. 'Because you know what studio desert sets are like, beach sand blown around by fans, and . . .'

Suddenly, a man and a woman on bicycles skidded to a halt in front of the open door. 'Renate!' the woman called out, her voice breathless and excited. Renate rose and walked over to the door, Stahl followed her. 'Have you heard?' the woman said. She spoke German with a sharp Berlin accent. 'Excuse me, sir,' she said to Stahl in French, 'but there is finally good news. Very good news.'

'Hello, Inga,' Renate said. 'Hello, Klaus.'

'They've made a deal with Hitler,' Inga said, now back in German. 'He takes the Sudetenland, but promises that's the end of it, and he signed a paper saying so. They had to put pressure on the Czechs, of course, who were going to fight. Now they've agreed not to resist.'

'This is good news, thank you for telling me,' Renate said. Her tone was courteous, and far from elated.

Inga again apologized for the interruption, then she and Klaus pedalled away on their bicycles. 'I suppose that's good news,' Stahl said. 'Surely for this movie, it is.'

Renate said, 'Yes, I suppose it is,' her tone tentative and thoughtful. 'Maybe not so good for the Czechs, though. And I have Jewish friends who settled in Karlsbad, in the Sudeten Mountains, when they fled Germany, and now they'll have to run again. But it *is* good news, for me and Inga and Klaus, because if France goes to war with Germany, all the German émigrés here will be interned. That's a rumour, but it's a rumour I believe.'

Stahl spent another fifteen minutes with Renate Steiner, then went off to find his taxi.

The driver had managed to get hold of a newspaper, a special edition with the headline WAR AVERTED, then, in smaller print, *Hitler Signs Agreement in Munich* with a photograph of Neville Chamberlain smiling as he waved a piece of paper. Heading away from Joinville, the driver was ambivalent – yes, his son would be demobilized, would return to his family and his taxi, and about this he felt a father's great relief. On the other hand, he didn't trust Hitler. 'This man is the neighbourhood bully,' he said, anger tightening his voice. 'Don't they see that, these diplomats? You appease a thug like Hitler, it just makes him greedy for *more,* because he *smells* fear.' Distracted by his emotions, he took a route through Paris on the left bank of the Seine, entering the city via the Thirteenth Arrondissement and continuing into the

Fifth on the *quai* by the river. To reach the Claridge, he should have taken the right bank, which Stahl noticed, without any particular concern.

But, as they reached the foot of the Boulevard Saint-Germain, traffic slowed down, and soon the taxi could move only a few feet before it had to stop. The driver swore, and with his good hand swung off the boulevard onto a side street. Here, however, the traffic barely crawled, and when he tried to return to Saint-Germain, a policeman stopped him and said, 'You'll have to go back the other way – they're marching on the boulevard.' The driver raised his hands, he surrendered. So Stahl thanked him, paid the fare, added a generous tip, then headed for the Métro station on the Place Maubert. By the time he got there he was mixed in with the marchers, students angered at the Munich agreement, with signs that said SHAME! and chants of 'Down with Daladier!' At last he reached the Métro, to find its grilled gate shut and a hand-lettered sign that said *On Strike*. Well, no surprise, the Métro-workers' union was a communist union and would strike if angered by government policy.

With an oath that was more sigh than curse, Stahl set out for the hotel. Not a bad day for a walk: grey clouds above the city, a chill in the air, the forces of autumn were gathering. As he made his way up the boulevard, he realized that a lot of the marchers were women – many of the male students had apparently been mobilized. He then began to notice small knots of men gathered on the pavement, glaring at the marchers, sometimes turning to each other and making comments that drew a snicker from their pals. The marching students ignored the sneering crowd. Until one of them joined the march, just long enough to bump the shoulder of a student, who turned and said something as the man laughed and retreated back to the pavement.

And then, about ten feet away from Stahl, a man wearing a grey hood with eyeholes cut in it came running out of an alley waving a metal rod. Some of the marchers stopped to see what was going on, somebody shouted a warning, a second hooded man followed the first and swung his metal rod, hitting a woman in the side of the head. As she sank to her knees, a drop of blood running from beneath her hair, the man swung the rod back, preparing to hit her again. Stahl ran at him, shouting 'Stop!' as he grabbed at the rod. The man swore, words muffled by the hood, and Stahl barely held on, until the man stopped pulling at the rod and pushed against him, so that he stumbled into the girl on her knees, who yelped as Stahl fell over her. When the man lifted the rod over his head, Stahl kicked at him, then got himself upright. In time for the rod to hit him in the face. With salty blood in his mouth, he rushed at the man and punched him in the centre of the hood, which knocked him back a step.

This was not the only fight on the boulevard – there were hooded men with rods attacking marchers on both sides of him, people on the ground, shouting and screaming everywhere. Stahl spat the blood out of his mouth and went after the man who'd hit him. And now tried to do it again. Stahl dodged away from the rod, which landed on his shoulder, grabbed the bottom of the hood and tore it off, revealing a fair-haired teenager with the sparse beginnings of a moustache. His eyes widened as Stahl threw the hood at him and punched him again, square in the mouth. Sputtering with rage, the teenager swung the rod back over his head, but a girl student wearing broken glasses got the fingernails of both hands into the side of his face and raked him from forehead to jaw. He didn't mind hitting women but he didn't like women hitting back so he hesitated, turned, and ran away. Somebody grabbed Stahl from behind, somebody very strong, lifting him off his feet as he tried to fight free. 'Calm down,' a voice said. 'Or else.' The arm around his chest was wearing a police uniform, so Stahl stopped struggling.

As more police arrived, Stahl's arms were pulled back, and handcuffs snapped on his wrists.

They had two holding cells at the Fifth Arrondissement prefecture, so the marchers and the attackers – 'the fascists', the students called them – were separated. In Stahl's cell, the walls bled moisture, and one of the graffiti carved into the stone was dated 1889. A woman in the cell lent Stahl her compact, its mirror revealing a livid purple bruise which ran down the right side of his face. The inside of his upper lip had been gashed by his teeth, his head ached terribly, his right hand was swollen – possibly a broken knuckle – but the worst pain was in his shoulder. Still, in a way he'd been lucky: if his nose was broken there was no evidence of it, and he had all his teeth.

He wound up sitting on the stone floor, back against the wall, next to a man about his own age, who explained that he was a Métro worker, a motorman, and had been on a picket line when the *'cagoulards'*, hooded ones, had attacked them. 'Very foolish,' the motorman said. 'We gave them a thrashing they'll remember.' Stahl offered him a cigarette, the motorman was grateful. 'How did you do?' he said to Stahl.

Stahl shrugged. 'I hit one of them, a couple of times.'

'Good for you. I don't imagine you do much fighting.'

'No,' Stahl said. He started to smile but it hurt. 'I had a couple of fights at sea, when I was a kid. The first one didn't last long – I drew my arm back, then I was looking at the sky and they threw a pail of water on me. The guy was built like an ox – a stoker.'

The motorman was amused. 'You don't want to fight a man who shovels coal all day.'

'My face was numb for hours,' Stahl said. 'The other one was with a mess steward, that went better. We punched each other for maybe a minute, then the crewmen separated us – we were both finished, gasping for breath. So I didn't win, but I didn't lose.'

'Oh, I'd say you won – they probably left you alone after that.'

'Then I guess I won.'

The motorman was released an hour later – his union had sent a lawyer. It was dawn before Zolly Louis showed up. 'The police couldn't find you,' Zolly said.

'How did you know to look for me?'

'A journalist called the office. Was it possible that Fredric Stahl was arrested for fighting? A witness was almost sure he'd seen a movie star taken away. You weren't at the hotel, so we called the police. Eventually, the *flics* figured out where you were.'

'What did you tell the journalist?'

'That you were on a train to Geneva.'

Zolly had paid somebody off, and a sergeant led them down a tunnel which eventually led to a street behind the prefecture. 'Just in case there's a reporter in front,' Zolly said. 'Or, God forbid, a photographer.'

30 September. Hervé Charais, a news commentator on Radio Paris, was lying in bed that afternoon, propped up on a pillow so he could better feast his eyes on his exquisite little Spanish mistress, one Consuela, as she stood naked before a dressing-table mirror and, in profile, bent over to peer at a non-existent blemish on her forehead. While Consuela was very much worth looking at, Hervé Charais was certainly not; soft and squat and pudgy, he walked splay-footed, so waddled like a duck. But Hervé Charais had a most cultured, mellifluous, and persuasive voice, and therein lay his considerable popularity. Across the darkened room, Consuela held back her thick hair and squinted at her reflection: a thirty-five-year-old face above, the body of a fifteen-year-old below. *Like a Greek statue,* he thought, a statue that could be warmed up to just the proper temperature – 'but only by you,' as she put it.

And to think it had all started with an accident! Some months earlier, she'd spilled a drink on him when he was out with friends at a nightclub. That led to an apology, and that led to a new drink, and that led, in time, to this very room. 'Come back to bed, my precious,' he said tenderly.

'Yes, in a moment, I have something on my forehead.'

And soon you'll have something somewhere else.

'Don't you have to write your commentary, for tonight?'

'It's mostly written, in my head anyhow.'

'Is it about Czechoslovakia?'

'What else?'

'So what will you say?'

'Oh, nothing special. The nation is relieved, surely, but maybe just for the time being.'

'Why don't you say something about the Sudeten Germans? They seem to have been forgotten in all this . . . whatever you call it.'

'You think so? What do you have in mind?'

'Just what happens to all these people who live in the wrong country, the poor Poles, the poor Hungarians, the poor, other people. But also the German minority living in Czechoslovakia, one hears the most frightening things, rapes and beatings by the Czech police, houses burned down . . .'

'You believe that? Mostly we think it's Nazi propaganda.'

'Some of it surely is . . . exaggerated. But my mama always used to say, where there's smoke there's fire.'

'Well, maybe, I don't know.'

Consuela turned to look at him. 'If you did at least *mention* them you'd be the only one on the radio. Everybody has forgotten how this crisis started.'

'Mmm,' he said. *It started in Berlin.*

Consuela appeared to have found the blemish, for she bent further towards the mirror. 'Just a tiny mention,' she said. 'It would show fairness, it would show that you care. Your listeners will like that, it's the best part of you.'

'I'll think about it,' Charais said.

'Ah, now you make me happy.'

'Done yet?'

'I suspect it's *you* who aren't done yet, are you?' She walked towards the bed, her breasts jiggling prettily with every step. 'How you look at me!' Closer and closer she came. 'So what goes on under that blanket, eh? You want to show me?'

By cable, 30 September, from Rudolf Vollmer, director of the National Press Guild of Germany, to J. L. Ferrand, a senior executive of the Havas Agency, the French wire service:

My dear Monsieur Ferrand,

Allow us to express our great pleasure that you have accepted our invitation to deliver a lecture to The National Press Guild on 17 October. This cable is to confirm the arrangements for your visit.

You will travel by Lufthansa Flight 26 from Paris on the afternoon of 15 October, to be met by a car that will take you to the Hotel Adlon, where you will occupy the Bismarck Suite on the top floor. Your lecture will be at 8.00 p.m. in the Adlon ballroom. We anticipate a large audience, and translation will be provided. On the 18 October, at 1.30 p.m., you are invited to dine with Foreign Minister von Ribbentrop in the Minister's private dining room. After lunch you will meet with Reichs Chancellor Hitler. You will return to Paris on 19 October, on Flight 27 from Berlin.

The honorarium for your lecture will be as specified: 100,000 reichsmarks, or, if you prefer, 50,000 American dollars. We look forward to meeting you, and to an interesting and much anticipated lecture on the role of the press in maintaining peace and stability in today's Europe.

With our most sincere and respectful good wishes,

Rudolf Vollmer
Director
The National Press Guild of Germany

2 October. Telephone call from Philippe LaMotte, managing director of Champagne Rousillon of Epernay, to Albert Roche, publisher of the newspaper *Le Temps*.

'Albert, good morning, how are you?'

'A busy day – a busy time! But, for the moment, all goes well.'

'Did you get to Deauville at all? During the, ah, crisis?'

'We did. We had tennis friends and we played all weekend. You and Jeanette should come up and take us on again, really Philippe, you stay in Paris too much, it isn't healthy.'

'We should, and soon, before it starts raining.'

'So, my friend, are you selling champagne?'

'Oh yes, thanks to *Le Temps*. Going to the full-page advertisements has made a real difference, and we're considering taking space in five issues a week instead of four. You know we compete with Taittinger and Moët et Chandon, and we're determined to outsell both of them by the end of the year.'

'Well, they're good advertisements, and we're all in love with the girl you're using – how did you *find* her?'

'By looking long and hard – we saw photographs of every model in Paris. Tell me, Albert, were you satisfied with Monday's editorial?'

'You mean "A Time to Reflect"? I thought it well written.'

'Oh it was, well written, but we found it timid. You know my personal view on this – that France and Germany can never go to war again. Why not come out and say it? Especially now, that the peace has been preserved. And you must give Germany some credit for that. At the last minute, Hitler chose diplomacy over arms, perhaps that ought to be said – *somewhere*, why not in *Le Temps*?'

'No special reason, it makes sense.'

'You're not personally against the idea, are you?'

'Not at all. I can have a word with Bonheur.'

'A reasonable editor – I've always thought so.'

'He is. I suspect that the, um, *perspective* you describe simply didn't occur to him.'

'Perhaps it should have.'

'And so I'll tell him – we still have time for Wednesday's edition, and Bonheur works quickly when he wishes.'

'That would make us all very happy, Albert. We really believe in *Le Temps*, it's the perfect place for our advertisements.'

'Well, that makes *me* happy. I can send over the early edition, if you like.'

'That would be wonderful, Albert. Now, tell Jeanette to expect a call from my wife, and prepare to be savaged on the court!'

'We'll give you a game, I can promise you that.'

'Looking forward to Wednesday, and we'll talk later this week.'

'Until then, Philippe. Goodbye.'

'Goodbye, Albert.'

When you are in Paris, you have to make love to somebody.

Stahl was not immune to this, nobody was. And now that life would go on, now that he would not be blown up by a bomb, now that he would make a film, he couldn't bear to be every night alone. The sandpiles had vanished, the gas masks – insufferable to the entire population over the age of ten – had been returned to the closet, the taxis were back. And as the autumn skies closed in over the city, as the lights in the shops went on at dusk, he grew lonelier and lonelier. He consulted a telephone directory and left a message with a maid for Kiki de Saint-Ange. She called back that evening, her voice warm and surprised. A drink at Le Petit Bar? She loved Le Petit Bar, she loved the Ritz, could he pick her up Friday at six? On that night, the simple act of walking out the hotel door excited him.

Kiki on Friday night: a black silk cap, snug and shimmering on her chestnut-coloured hair, a very different cocktail dress than the one she'd worn at the party, hem above the knee, neckline daring, in black wool crepe soft and thin enough to show her body when she moved. With silver-grey pearls and earrings, and precise but assertive – child-of-the-night – make-up on her eyes. At the tiny bar, they settled on chairs before a low table, they ordered champagne cocktails, they chatted, he explained the fading bruise on his face, she looked horrified, then sympathetic, then laid a hand on his forearm, *poor thing, brave man, such dreadful times these are, what will become of us?* Would she care to have another cocktail? *Oh yes, why not?* Even at the Ritz, a pretty couple. He heard his voice, low and rich – a tale of seafaring, a tale of Hollywood, the adventurer, the wanderer. Her turn: the country house of her parents by the Loire, picking wild strawberries, lost in the forest with her best friend Lisette, a sudden downpour. A husband in Paris, an Italian nobleman, how sad when these things went wrong. 'Another cocktail? I don't know . . . oh what the hell . . . I don't know what's got into me but tonight I don't care.' She met his eyes.

There was a line of taxis outside the Ritz but they walked, out of the Place Vendôme where jewellers waited, up into the cluster of streets near the Opéra. It wasn't that cold but it was cold enough – she shivered and leaned against him, he put his arm around her and could feel warm skin beneath the thin fabric of her raincoat. Down a side street, a blue neon sign, HOTEL DUBARRY; only two windows wide, anonymous, cheap but not dangerous. He never said a word, neither did she; they slowed down, stopped, then turned together and went up the single step to the door. The proprietor was casual, as though expecting a couple like them to appear around this time of the evening. 'A room for tonight?' he said. On the third floor, she cranked the window open and a breeze ruffled the sheer curtains. She was, when her clothes were off, smaller than he'd imagined – narrow shoulders, bare feet flat on the brown carpet, a hesitant smile – and, when he embraced her, even smaller. It was more pleasure than passion, as they played, courting urgency, which duly showed up, stronger than he'd thought it would be and welcome, very welcome.

AGENT
OF
INFLUENCE

12 OCTOBER, 1938. THE LEAVES WERE TURNING ON THE PLANE TREES that lined the boulevards, women brought out their scarves, and Jules Deschelles held a luncheon in a little bistro, Mère this or Chez that, near the Luxembourg gardens. Twelve settings, gleaming white and silver, were laid out on the big table on the second floor, where some of the cast and technicians who were to make *Après la Guerre* would dine together. For Stahl, the event brought a measure of relief, but also some anxiety.

Relief came in the introduction of the female romantic lead, Justine Piro, a veteran actress of the Parisian stage and film world, not quite a star of the first rank but a good name on a marquee, who would play the Hungarian adventuress, down on her luck and stranded in Damascus. When they were introduced, Stahl took her hand and brush-kissed her on both cheeks, then they took a good, long look at each other. *Can we succeed together?* Justine Piro – accented on the last syllable in the French pronunciation – was dark, hair and eyes, dressed simply, and not a beauty in midday restaurant light. But Stahl suspected that on screen she would be stunning, a mysterious transformation wrought, in certain individuals, by photography – 'the camera loves her' a common saying in the movie business. Nobody could really explain how this worked, but work it did. Stahl also met the soundman, the set-lighting man, and the crucially important character-lighting man, whose job was to emphasize and refine facial expression and physical presence. He could make you a better actor by moving a light one inch. Stahl thought Renate Steiner might attend, but Deschelles explained that she was out at the Joinville studios, working on another movie. The musical composer who would score the film had not yet been hired.

Anxiety came with the arrival of the second lead, the one-named character actor known as Pasquin. Single-named male actors, like Fernandel and Raimu, typically had the adjective 'beloved' permanently stuck to them in print, and so it was with the beloved Pasquin. He was, however, in his professional reputation, not much loved at all. 'Feared' said it better. Pasquin was enormous, enormously fat, with three chins and a cherub's round cheeks, above which tiny, jet-black eyes glittered with malice. Pasquin had a ferocious temper, and he drank: a volatile combination.

Pasquin was, like Fernandel and Raimu, a southerner, and early in his career had played in movies set in Provence and Marseille. In one of them, *Alphonse Gets Married,* the production's director, famously hard to please, called for take after take of a certain shot – action at Alphonse's elaborate wedding feast – and by the nineteenth take, the character played by Pasquin revealed a new and unexpected dimension. The placid and philosophical village baker now scowled and hissed his line, 'What if she doesn't want to?' This was meant to be spoken in a whining voice by a helpless and befuddled man. But not now. The way Pasquin delivered the line it now meant that 'if she didn't want to', he would tear her head off and throw it through the window. 'Cut!' said the director. At take twenty-five, a half-crocked

Pasquin lost his famous temper and took it out on the feast. As he swore and shrieked, hams and chickens flew through the air, the bride was showered with olives, the director struck in the face by a hurled artichoke, and soupe au pistou spattered the ceiling and the camera.

In *Après la Guerre,* Pasquin would play the earthy sergeant to Stahl's melancholy warrior Colonel Vadic, and Stahl liked the casting well enough, though how the sergeant retained his girth in a Turkish prison camp might require some ingenuity by the screenplay writers. When Pasquin arrived at the bistro – late, his breath reeking of wine – he squeezed Stahl's hand in a vicelike grip and muttered, 'So now Hollywood comes to France.' Stahl just smiled – *I hope you don't expect me to answer that.* Pasquin was trouble, but he was exceptionally popular. *With a strong director . . .* Stahl told himself hopefully, then turned away to talk to the set-lighting man.

And there would in fact be *a strong director.* As the cheese plate went around the table, Deschelles announced, like the cat that got the cream, that he had signed Jean Avila to direct the film. Stahl's outward response was properly impressed and appreciative but he immediately understood this was either a brilliant choice or a catastrophe. Everybody knew the name Jean Avila: twenty-five years old, with two masterpieces to his credit, the first suppressed by the French government, the second recut, and ruined, by film distributors. He came from a violently political family, his father, a famous Spanish anarchist, strangled in a French prison in 1917. Avila himself followed his father's politics, but his genius was, for anyone who'd contrived to see either of the films, beyond question. In Stahl's view, Deschelles had shown himself, and surely Paramount, to have serious ambitions for this movie.

Stahl left the restaurant – after yet one more delicious lunch barely tasted, a professional commonplace – with Justine Piro, and they walked for a time in the early-autumn afternoon and talked amiably. She said she liked his work, and he sensed she might actually mean it. He enquired about her life, she told him she was married to a physician and had two girls, eight and eleven. They got on well together – at least in the daily world, what might happen on a movie

set God only knew – and in time she took the Métro back to the Sixteenth Arrondissement. As Stahl crossed the Seine, he was happier
and more excited with every step. Maybe *Après la Guerre* had a
chance to be a good film, maybe even very good. So the message waiting for him at the Claridge didn't bother him all that much. Not at
first, anyhow.

Stahl read the message in the lobby. *12.25. Mme Brun at the American embassy telephoned, please call her back at Concorde 92 47.* His
reaction developed slowly, so he was still a film star as he got on the
elevator, but by the time he reached his rooms he was an émigré, and
called immediately. 'Ah yes, Monsieur Stahl,' Mme Brun said.
There was a pause, as though she had to consult a list to see what
they might want with this Monsieur Stahl. Apparently, she found
it. Could he be so kind as to visit the embassy, when convenient? Mr
J. J. Wilkinson, the Second Secretary, wished to speak with him. Stahl
said that he could. And would it, she wondered, a note of *oh dear* in
her voice, *possibly* be convenient tomorrow morning, at 11.15? It
would. Mr Wilkinson's office was in the chancery building, by the
Hotel Crillon – he knew where that was? Yes, he did. Mme Brun's version of *thank you and goodbye,* now that she had what she wanted,
was effusive, and genteel.

Stahl, moments earlier, had been his most optimistic and confident self, but the prospect of the meeting made fast work of that.
What could they want? Was there some sort of *problem*? Sternly, he
told himself to cut it out. This was most likely no more than a courtesy call. But it didn't feel like a courtesy call, it was as though he'd
been *summoned.* No, no, he was Fredric Stahl, a well-known and respected performer, and need have no fear of any government. But another instinct, an older, deeper instinct, told him just how wrong he
was about that.

In a quiet grey suit and the plainest tie he owned, he took a taxi to
the Avenue Gabriel, just off the Place de la Concorde, and arrived well
before the time of the meeting. He was expected – an official escorted

him to the top floor of the chancery, where he waited in a chair outside J. J. Wilkinson's office. A minute before noon, the door opened and the Second Secretary waved him inside.

It was a large, comfortable office with a window on the courtyard, a bookcase with numbered volumes on one wall, an official portrait – an oil painting – of President Roosevelt on the wall above the leather desk chair, the desk bearing stacks of paper, reports, memoranda, correspondence. J. J. Wilkinson, in shirtsleeves and loosened tie, his jacket over the back of the chair, was all smiles and affability. He was about fifty, Stahl guessed, with the thickening body of a former athlete and a heavy, boyish face. He might be cast as a guest at one of Jay Gatsby's parties, scotch in hand, flirting with a debutante. Was he, perhaps, an Ivy League alumnus, making his way easily through a familiar world? Maybe. In the corner, a squash racquet leaned against the wall. Wilkinson indicated the chair across from his desk and said, 'Thanks for dropping by, Mr Stahl, sorry about the short notice but this wretched business with the Czechs has kept us from our normal routine.' He glanced at a page of handwritten notes and said, 'Anyhow, as a resident alien of the US you're supposed to check in with us when you arrive in Paris. Not everybody does that, of course, and we don't really mind, but this visit will take care of it.'

'Thank you,' Stahl said.

'So, yes, ah, you've been a resident alien for eight years. Any thought of taking US citizenship?'

'I intend to. I've been meaning to go to the class, fill out the forms . . . but I've been in one movie, then right away another . . .'

'You surely have, and very successfully. I've seen you, of course, but I never remember movie names.' His tone was apologetic. 'Only that I enjoyed them. And with American movies you see in Paris, it's always someone else's voice, speaking French, which, frankly, bothers the hell out of me. The last time I saw John Wayne, and he said, "*Maintenant regardez,* Slim", it tickled me so bad my wife poked me in the ribs.' He grinned at the memory. 'Anyway, what do you think of Paris, these days?'

'Not the same as it was, back in the twenties, but not so different. It's still the city you fall in love with, despite the politics.'

'Pretty grim, all this hostility, no?'

'It is. The French didn't used to be so, um, *concentrated* on it. Before, it was more like a game, but now it's a war.'

Wilkinson nodded, *I'm glad you agree with me.* 'I'll tell you something, by trade I'm a lawyer in a Wall Street firm, but I worked for the Roosevelt campaigns in '32 and '36 and, believe me, there was plenty of rough stuff going on. But, compared to France, in the last few years, it was child's play. And now, with war coming . . .' He paused, then said, 'I saw an announcement of your arrival in the *Paris Herald* and I admit I wondered, I mean, what the hell made you come here now?'

'Jack Warner,' Stahl said.

Wilkinson laughed, a bass rumble, and his eyes lit up. 'I should've figured that out,' he said. 'But there's a story about Jack Warner which might explain it. A few years ago, the Warner Bros. representative in Berlin, a man named Joe Kaufmann, was beaten to death by Nazi Brown Shirts – they didn't like it that he was a Jew – and Warner closed the Berlin office. Then he started to make anti-fascist movies, and he got letters threatening to burn his house down. The other moguls, Goldwyn and Harry Cohn and the rest, don't want to get involved, but Jack Warner decided to fight, bless his heart.'

'Well, the decision to have one of his actors do a movie in Paris came from the top, from Jack Warner, personally.'

'Glad you came? Showing the flag?'

'I'm not sorry. Actors are told, "always avoid politics, it's bad for the box office", but I found out right away you can't.'

'How so, found out?'

'Two weeks ago I was caught in a street march and got hit in the face with a steel rod. That's the worst, but it started earlier. I was invited to a cocktail party – a *salon* – and they carried on like crazy, peace with Germany, peace with Germany, all we want is peace.'

From Wilkinson, a knowing smile. 'Which hostess? There are four or five – they're infamous.'

'The Baroness von Reschke. What a terror! And there was someone else, a man called, what's his name, he makes champagne, DeMotte? No, LaMotte. Philippe I think.'

'Ah yes, the Comité Franco-Allemagne, a Nazi propaganda outfit.'

Stahl stared at Wilkinson. 'You mean . . . *literally*? Nazi as in managed from Berlin?'

Slowly, Wilkinson nodded up and down. 'Yes indeedy. You're shocked?'

'I guess I am. Isn't that, um, espionage?'

'Properly called "political warfare". One form of espionage.'

'The French government must know what's going on, can't they do something about it?'

'They know everything, but they don't do anything.'

'Why not?'

Wilkinson raised his eyebrows, surprised that Stahl didn't know the answer. 'Political repercussions?' he said, as though reminding Stahl about the nature of the world. 'Politicians in power have to run for re-election, so what are they handing their opponents? They'll be accused of being against peace, against negotiations; they'll be called warmongers. And they'll lose the election, which means leaving Paris, and going back to some town in the Auvergne. But that's only one part of it, the other part is worse. The French know they were finished in 1917, and they were, until American troops showed up. So they're scared to death they'll push Hitler too far, scared to death of war – they lost a million and a half men the last time, and more than twice that wounded. And they know they'll lose again if the Wehrmacht crosses the border.'

'But, the Maginot Line . . .'

Wilkinson sighed, burdened by knowing more than was good for him. 'The Maginot Line is a political tactic of the French right. Supposedly it protects the nation, which believes in it as though it were magic, which means the French won't fully mobilize, won't spend enough money on armament, and won't invade Germany. It virtually pleads for Hitler's mercy, and it won't work. It's meant to *delay*, as the

French wait for the British to show up, and then they both wait for America. Meanwhile Hitler builds offensive weapons, tanks and warplanes.' He moved a marble pen stand to the centre of his desk, picked up a stapler and circled it above the marble stand, then pressed the top and a staple popped out and clicked against the stand. 'I could make an airplane noise, but you get the idea. That used to be the Maginot Line.'

'So what can they do?'

Wilkinson shrugged.

Stahl was silent for a moment, trying to sort out what Wilkinson had told him. If his statements about the baroness and LaMotte were true, then some very rich and powerful people in Paris were working for the enemy. Finally he said, 'What do they want with *me,* these people?'

'You're an important person, Mr Stahl, well known, respected, from a powerful part of the world. People will listen to what you say, they may even change their minds. I recall you once played a doctor, is that right?'

'Dr Lawton, in *A Fortunate Woman.*'

'That's it. Kindly Dr Lawton – strong, wise, and compassionate. Who wouldn't believe Dr Lawton? All this together, your status, and your character on screen, add up to what we call an "agent of influence".'

Stahl saw this was true, and became acutely uncomfortable. 'Should I make some kind of, what, public statement?'

'What would you say? "I believe in democracy"? "I believe in America"? That would be fine with the Germans, America doesn't want to fight a war any more than the French do. We have our own Maginot Line, it's called the Atlantic Ocean.'

'Then the hell with these people, I don't have to go to their *salons.*'

'You certainly don't. But that doesn't mean they won't put pressure on you.'

'Why would they?'

'The people in Berlin, in von Ribbentrop's Foreign Ministry, are persistent when they want something. And their people in Paris take orders, so . . .'

Now Stahl started to get mad. Why was this happening? Why him? He wanted nothing to do with the whole rotten business.

Wilkinson read him perfectly. 'Don't blame *me* for this,' he said. 'I'm on your side.'

'What should I do?'

'Stay away from them, see what happens.'

There was, suspended in the space between them, an *or* that lingered silently at the end of Wilkinson's sentence. *Or, if not, you could,* something like that. Stahl knew it was there, felt the bare ghost of what it might demand from him, and thought *Oh no you don't.* A Hollywood phrase he'd heard from Buzzy Mehlman suddenly came to him: *What is this meeting about?* Now Stahl thought he knew. 'You're not asking me to spy on these people, are you?'

'No.'

'Then what *are* you asking?'

Wilkinson leaned forward, clasped a pair of big, meaty hands together and rested them on his desk. 'That you be careful, that you don't let them use you if you can keep them from doing it. There's no point in your finding out what's going on and who is involved, the French know that already and so do we. Anyhow, you're not a spy, that takes nerves of steel, and soon enough becomes a full-time job. And I'm no spymaster. America has military attachés who do that and we don't have an overseas spy service.'

Stahl nodded that he understood, though he didn't believe Wilkinson was being fully honest.

'On the other hand,' Wilkinson said, then let the phrase hang there for a time. 'On the other hand, the people in the White House need to know as much as they can about what's going on over here, and that's one of the jobs an embassy, any embassy anywhere, has to do. So, if, in your time over here you, ah, *stumble* on something, something important, it wouldn't be a bad idea if you let me know about it. That isn't the official duty of an American in a foreign country but we're all in this together, and if you feel like an American it's not the worst thing to act like one.' Wilkinson took a moment to let that sink in, then said, 'Okay, the hell with all that stuff, tell me about the movie you're making.'

In the days that followed, Stahl found himself thinking about the meeting at the embassy more than he wanted to. He felt foolish to have been naive about the political realities in France, after all he was European, off in California for eight years but still, shouldn't he have known? Perhaps not. For one thing, this level of corruption was new, at least new to him. When he'd lived in Paris, the talk in the cafés took corruption as a regrettable but natural human undertaking – a means to weasel one's way to wealth and power, merely one of the darker traditions of Old Europe. There followed, in the cafés, a shrug. But that corruption was never thought to be at the tips of foreign tentacles. It was, back then, *French,* like good wine and good lovemaking.

Meanwhile, in the US, it wasn't much discussed. Americans were tired of the antics of slippery European politicians – a plague on all their houses! Europe was, as the woman on the *Ile de France* had put it when they shared a deck chair, a place where the bickering and squabbling never ended: sometimes they even shot each other, but they would shoot no more American boys. Thinking about the deckchair conversation, Stahl recalled a scene in a 1936 MGM film called *Libeled Lady,* with Jean Harlow, and Spencer Tracy as a newspaper editor. At one point, Tracy is in a newsroom and a reporter asks him, 'What'll we use for a headline?' Tracy says, 'I don't care. Anything. "War Threatens Europe."' The reporter asks, 'Which country?' and Tracy responds, 'Flip a nickel!'

In Stahl's Hollywood world, only the émigrés – the studio violinist from Germany, the make-up woman from Roumania, the scene painter from Hungary – followed European politics and the miseries of European Jews and communists and intellectuals. But the talk at a Warner commissary table, much of it heatedly leftist, quieted down when a 'real American' came by. Americans didn't want to worry about foreign troubles, they had plenty of their own.

Thus it fell to somebody like Wilkinson to worry, because 'the people in the White House' needed information. That was slightly odd, once Stahl had a chance to think about it. Wouldn't it be the Department of State – what Stahl thought of as the Foreign Ministry – that needed to know what was going on? Well, he was a foreigner, an émigré, and there were a lot of things he didn't understand. Still, he was grateful that Wilkinson had told him what was going on, it meant he could protect himself. So when a note from the Baroness von Reschke reached him at the Claridge – 'my friends were absolutely delighted to meet you, and I hope you will join us . . .' – Stahl tore it up. The note went on to say that the exquisite Josephine Baker would be giving a private performance. Likely in her skirt made of bananas, Stahl thought, but she won't be wearing it for me. He found great satisfaction in letting the note go unanswered – *take that, you Nazi witch, I'm being rude!* Maybe not a blow for democracy, but at least something.

And then, when he was handed a telephone message from Herr Moppel, he tore that up as well. Dear old Moppi was the very last person he wished to see. But Moppi didn't give up so easily, and called again the following day. This time Stahl was in his suite and answered the phone. 'Franz! Hello! It's me, Moppi!' Stahl was brusque and cold. He was at work on a film, he really had no time for social engagements. Goodbye. Bang went the phone, *fuck you*. This felt even better than ignoring the baroness, and Stahl sensed he'd avoided trouble, real trouble.

20 October. The director of *Après la Guerre*, Jean Avila, had finally made his way to Paris and telephoned the principal actors, asking them to come out to Joinville for a preliminary read-through of the script. They gathered at ten in the morning, on a set that was available until 2.00 p.m., a set for a romantic farce, *Cinéma de Boulevard*, in fin de siècle Paris. The actors settled on fringed velvet sofas and chatted until Jean Avila came hurrying through the door. 'Here at last,' he said. 'They held me up for three days at the border.' Avila seemed well

beyond his twenty-five years. He had long, black, wiry hair, a lean body, and a face marked by the character lines of an older man, which gave him the sort of brooding good looks that women fell for. Starting with Stahl – 'pleased to have you here,' he said, 'very pleased' – he introduced himself to each member of the cast.

At first, the reading went well. 'Let's begin on page thirty-six,' Avila said. 'The top of the page, where Colonel Vadic and the others are trying to get food from the Turkish farm woman.' That line, 'There she is, looking out the window,' belonged to Gilles Brecker, who had a faint Alsatian accent and, with blond hair and steel-framed glasses, looked like a cinematic German. He would play the war-loving lieutenant, eager to fight again after getting out of the prison camp.

'Justine, would you read the farm woman?' Avila said.

Justine Piro, wearing slacks and a sweater, her hair swept up in a kerchief, said, 'Go away, or I'll set the dogs on you.'

'We hear the dogs barking.' Avila said, reading the stage direction.

The fat, burly Pasquin lit a cigarette and planted a thick forefinger on the page. 'What's wrong with her?'

'It's the uniforms,' Stahl said.

'Dear madam,' Pasquin crooned. 'A little something to eat?' He mimed bringing food to his mouth and twice smacked his lips. Avila looked up and smiled.

'Let's just kick down the door and take whatever she has,' Brecker said, the impatience in his voice nudging anger.

'Hasn't there been enough of that?' Stahl said, sounding tired of the world. 'And what if she resists? What then? Will you beat her?'

'We must eat,' Brecker said. 'We need our strength.'

'We will eat, lieutenant, we will find something, somewhere. Maybe at the next farm,' Stahl said.

Pasquin cupped a hand to his ear. 'What's that? Did I hear a *chicken*?'

Avila read the stage direction: 'An old man wearing a tweed cap and an ancient suit jacket and holding a shotgun is seen stage left. We see his face, then he gestures them away with the shotgun.'

From Stahl: 'As I said, the next farm.'

From Avila: 'The three legionnaires trudging along a dirt path, the wind is blowing, the sun beats . . .' Avila stopped dead.

The door had flown open, every one of them stared. In the door-way stood Moppi, bright red in the face, breathing hard as though he'd been running, wearing a green loden jacket and an alpine hat with a feather. 'Franz!' he called out. 'Oh no, I'm so sorry, I've inter-rupted your work. But I couldn't reach you on the phone, so I thought I'd come out to the studio . . .'

'Herr Moppel,' Stahl said, his voice quiet but ice-cold. 'Would you kindly get out of here? Can't you see we're working?'

A woman appeared at the doorway, also breathing hard, appar-ently Moppi had outdistanced her in a race to the studio building. 'Pardon, pardon,' she said. 'This man insisted, at the reception. I *told* him he couldn't come here but he wouldn't listen. Shall I get the guard?'

'No, you needn't, I know when I'm not wanted,' Moppi said, sounding sullen and hurt. 'Goodbye, Franz, all I wanted to do was make a time for lunch.'

'Go away,' Stahl said. 'Don't ever come back.'

Moppi left, the woman glared at him, then again apologized and closed the door behind her. All the others turned and looked at Stahl. 'Who's Franz?' Pasquin said, honestly confused.

'My name before I was an actor,' Stahl said. 'I was born in Aus-tria.'

This was met with silence. Then Avila said, his voice incredulous, 'That man is a *friend* of yours?'

Stahl thought quickly and said, 'A friend of my family, long ago. He knew me as a child, now he's discovered I'm a *movie actor.*'

The silence continued. Then it was Justine Piro who saved the day. 'My God,' she said, 'I was afraid he was going to yodel.'

Laughter broke the tension. Avila said, 'Where were we?' But then looked up from his script and said to Stahl, 'How on earth did he know where you were?' It was the question of a man who'd grown up in a family that spent its life dodging the secret police of many countries.

Stahl shook his head. 'I don't know. Did he call Deschelles's office?'

'He didn't *follow* you, did he?'

'Oh Jean,' Piro said. 'Don't say such things. Please.'

'He might have,' Stahl said. 'I think he's maybe a little . . .' He circled a finger at his temple.

'No, he's just a German,' Pasquin said. 'They always find a way.'

Avila lit a cigarette, so did Stahl. 'Well, to hell with him,' Avila said. He looked down at his script and said, 'The three legionnaires trudging along a dirt path . . .'

Stahl was back at the Claridge by three. He took off his jacket and sat down hard on the edge of the bed. A few minutes later, he called the desk and asked for a glass of Pepto-Bismol to be brought up to his suite. This would settle his stomach and calm his nerves and Stahl needed all of that. When the Pepto-Bismol arrived – on a silver tray, with a linen napkin – Stahl drank the chalky stuff and waited for it to take effect. Then, still shaken, he went to the window and, for the first time in his life, peered down at the street below and tried to see if someone was watching him.

There was a letter for him the following morning, a letter from America, the name on the return address was Betsy Belle. He sat on a couch in the lobby and opened the envelope, reluctantly, because he had a strong premonition about what was in there, and this turned out to be the case. In the careful script of an Iowa schoolgirl, Betsy was telling him goodbye. She knew he would understand, she was sorry, they'd had such good times together and she had, always would have, loving feelings for him. But she'd met a man, older than her, but kind and considerate, who worked in the accounting office at MGM. He had proposed marriage, after they'd seen each other a few times, and she had accepted. 'My life was just going on, going noplace in particular, and I had to do something. Maybe I'll get a part in a movie sometime, but maybe I never will. That's cruel, but it might happen. I always leveled with you Fredric and truth is I feel like I've been saved. I took my things from the house, so what's done is done.' She signed the letter 'Love, Betsy.'

He'd suspected something like this was coming but still it hurt him. They'd been closer than he'd realized, but a future together hadn't been part of the bargain and women didn't work like that forever, so now she'd been 'saved'. He hoped that was true, he didn't want bad things to happen to her. Deeply, he didn't.

23 October. 'Hello, Kiki, it's Fredric Stahl. Would you like to go to a movie?'

'Oh yes, I *would* like to. When?'

'How about tonight?'

'Tonight?'

'If you can, or maybe Friday if you can't.'

'Well, I'd like to do *something*.'

'Tonight is possible?'

'What time?'

'I'll come and get you at eight – it's an eight-thirty show.'

The line buzzed. 'Eight will be fine.'

'I'll be there then.'

Maybe he was taking a chance, he thought – Kiki had some connection to the baroness and her crowd – but not much of a chance, and he was terribly lonely. According to Kiki, it was her parents who'd been invited to the von Reschke cocktail party, she had stood in for them, and she'd had no good words for the baroness's friends, preferring the company of the Bohemian crowd on the artist's barge. So he hoped. And then, after all, if she were part of some sinister plot against him, what could she do? Anyhow, he didn't think she was manipulating him, he just didn't.

It had rained, and it would rain again, on that chilly October evening. And as Fredric Stahl made his way through the Seventh Arrondissement, the city once again captured his heart: bittersweet autumn air, fallen leaves plastered to the cobblestones, lamplit rooms seen from the street – a night that sent his spirit aloft in a kind of melancholy elation. When he turned a corner, he discovered a woman wearing a raincoat over lounging pyjamas, waiting in a doorway while her spaniel visited the base of a streetlamp. Passing by, Stahl wished her a good evening. 'It is that, monsieur,' she said, with a conspirator's smile. 'And a good evening to you.'

Stahl had chosen a movie theatre near Kiki's apartment so they could walk. It wasn't that he wanted to see a particular movie, he wanted to go to the movies, and walking there was part of it. The theatre was showing *Algiers,* a Hollywood remake of *Pépé le Moko,* with the French Charles Boyer and Stahl's fellow Austrian Hedy Lamarr. As they left Kiki's building he told her what was playing. 'You haven't seen it, have you?'

'Oh no,' she said. 'But I wanted to.' As the first few drops of rain fell and the wind rattled the leaves left on the trees, she took his arm.

In the darkened theatre, an usherette with a torch led them down the aisle to, at Kiki's direction, an empty row. Almost immediately, a Pathé newsreel began. Stern music accompanied the narrator's voice for a marrying-and-murdering insurance salesman who'd been arrested in Toulon. Excited strings as bicyclists raced through a village street in the mountains. A few bars of triumphant brass – a perfume heiress in goggles and leather headgear rode on the wing of a monoplane. Then the drums and trumpets of war as Franco's Moorish soldiers charged across a dry riverbed. Finally a Wagnerian march, the volume much louder now. 'In Berlin, Adolf Hitler takes the salute . . . ,' said the narrator as German soldiers, tall and fiercely serious, goose-stepped past a reviewing stand draped with swastikas. 'Fucking *Boche*,' said a voice in the theatre. 'Shhh!' said another. Then it was time for Charles Boyer.

As the famous jewel thief Pépé le Moko, and a fugitive from French justice, Charles Boyer is trapped in the Casbah, the 'native quarter' of Algiers. 'A melting pot for all the sins of the earth,' said the voice-over. As the credits ran, Kiki took Stahl's hand and held it on top of the raincoat folded on her lap. Stahl moved closer so that their shoulders were touching. When Hedy Lamarr came on the screen, Kiki, her mouth by Stahl's ear, whispered, 'Do you think she is very beautiful?' Her breath smelled of licorice, with just a bare hint of wine.

'Everyone says she is,' Stahl said.

'Does she always wear so much make-up?'

'We all do.'

A tough police inspector arrives from Paris. He's come to arrest the wily jewel thief. Kiki moved Stahl's hand from the folded raincoat to the top of her wool skirt and the soft thigh beneath it. He was stirred by this and wanted to respond, but Kiki had hold of his left hand and his right was too far away. It occurred to him that he might say something, then it occurred to him that there was nothing to say, and a turn of the head to look at her wasn't the right thing either. So he watched the movie.

Where the French inspector leads a search through the narrow streets of the Casbah. As they approach one of Pépé's many hideouts, three beggars in three adjacent doorways rap their staves on the street doors, warning Pépé and his gang. It was getting very warm where Kiki's hand held his. She changed positions and gave him a delicate squeeze, which he returned. Now Inspector Slimane, an Algerian detective in a tarboosh, and Pépé's amiable opponent, is telling the jewel thief that the date of his future arrest is written on the wall of his office. Stahl was absorbed in the clever dialogue so it surprised him when Kiki, with a decorous parting of her legs, moved his hand beneath her skirt, where it rested partly on the hem of her silk panties, on her garter belt, and on the smooth skin of her inner thigh. Now

Stahl had to turn and look at her. But Kiki's profile showed nothing, her eyes were fixed on the screen, she was watching *Algiers*, whatever might be going on elsewhere had nothing to do with her.

Meanwhile, Hedy Lamarr dines with her awful husband and his awful friends in a little restaurant. The shafts of light from the projector shifted as the images changed, the sound track crackled beneath the voices of the actors, and Kiki moved Stahl's hand to the very centre of her damp panties, and then beneath. Making sure he stayed where he was, she changed hands, her left hand set on top of his, while her right hand crept under his raincoat, nudged his legs apart, and, slowly and with one or two hesitations as she struggled with the buttons, undid his fly. From Stahl, a kind of pleasurable sigh, very brief and completely spontaneous. Surprise. Nice surprise. And then, raising her panties with the back of her hand, she began to move his fingers.

Again he looked at her. At first her face was without expression but then, slowly, her eyelids lowered and her lips parted as her fingers rode on top of his. Her other hand tightened where she held him, her chin lifted and her mouth opened, a little, a little more, and then completely as she exhaled and a soft, breathy *ah* escaped her.

Now the hand that had gripped him hard relaxed, as Kiki rested the back of her head against the theatre seat. That grip, he realized, had not been meant for his pleasure – she'd simply held on to something that excited her while she watched whatever movie played behind her closed eyes. The jewel thief Pépé le Moko is led into a police trap – tempted by his passion for Hedy Lamarr, and for Paris, which he longs to see once more. The ship that will sail for France pulls away from the pier, Pépé runs from the police and is shot. As he lies dying in Slimane's arms, the detective says, 'We thought you were going to escape.' Then, Pépé's last words: 'I have.' Kiki took a handkerchief from the pocket of her raincoat and wiped her eyes.

26 October. Jules Deschelles telephoned and told Stahl that it would be three weeks before Joinville had space available for them. He'd

tried to argue but Paramount wouldn't budge. So Stahl and the others would learn their lines, continue the read-throughs, then start to rehearse. Deschelles regretted the delay, but maybe all for the best as Jean Avila and his cameraman would be going off to Syria and the Lebanon to scout locations. In fact, Deschelles might join them. Of course, if those countries didn't work out, they could always go to Morocco.

An hour later, as Stahl was about to leave for Joinville, a call from Mme Boulanger at the Warner publicity office. After a few opening pleasantries she said, 'I have an interview for you. It's tomorrow – whenever you can be available.'

'Who's doing the interview?'

'I doubt you know him. His name is Loubec, he writes sports and entertainment features for *Le Matin*.'

Again, Le Matin. 'I wonder if that's a good idea,' Stahl said, treading carefully. 'What with all the politics.'

'You'll manage,' Mme Boulanger said firmly. 'It's my job to get press coverage, Monsieur Stahl – you aren't going to turn me down, are you?'

'What's he like, this Loubec?'

From Mme Boulanger, a theatrical sigh that meant, *Oh no, he's being a prima donna.* 'I've run into him before, he's rather workmanlike, gets the information, writes it down. Just another journalist, dear. I'll hold your hand if you like.'

Stahl hesitated, then said, 'I guess I should do it. Where do we meet?'

'In your hotel, he's bringing a photographer.'

'All right. I'll likely be back from Joinville around five and I'll see him at – six?'

'I'll let him know. If you don't hear from me it'll be at six. How's everything else going? How's *Avant la Guerre*?'

'It's *Après la Guerre,* and the omens aren't so bad.'

'Superstitious, love? Don't dare to say it's good? Oh you actors! You're probably excited.'

'Too soon, too soon for that. Thanks for getting me the interview, Madame Boulanger.'

'You're welcome, but the truth is, he came to me.'

27 October. Loubec was prompt. They called up from the desk and Stahl said he would be right down – the idea of being interviewed 'in his suite at the Claridge' somehow felt wrong to him. He wore slacks and a dark-blue sweater – after twenty minutes of trial and error with his wardrobe – and had ordered up a good stiff whisky and soda. He was tense about this interview, apprehensive, and the drink helped.

They met at the desk and Stahl led the way to a table in the nearly deserted hotel bar. The photographer, bearded, bored, and rumpled, sat at the neighbouring table and fiddled with his camera. 'Would you care to have something?' Stahl said, looking from one to the other.

'No, thank you,' said Loubec. The photographer shrugged – if Loubec wouldn't, he couldn't. Loubec, in his mid-thirties, was pale and fair-haired, with a smooth, expressionless face and glasses with clear plastic frames. He flipped up the cover of his notepad and riffled through the pages until he found what he wanted. 'Thank you for agreeing to the interview, Monsieur Stahl. Do you mind if René takes a picture or two while we're talking?'

Stahl did mind. Unposed photographs, the subject caught un-aware by the camera, could make you look like a madman or the vil-lage idiot. 'One or two, but no more,' he said. 'And I'd prefer to do it when we're done talking.'

René couldn't have cared less. 'As you like,' he said.

'So,' Loubec said, 'can we start by going over the titles and dates of your movies? And the award nominations? I have them listed, but I just want to make sure I didn't miss something.'

This was done quickly enough – Loubec basically had it right, though Stahl wasn't certain about some of the dates. 'I won't try to use it all,' Loubec said, 'just the highlights. Now, looking at your date of birth, it seems you were likely the right age for military service during the war, but that isn't covered in your Warner bio. Did you serve in the army? Perhaps you were exempt?' Loubec's pencil hovered over the empty space on his notepad page.

'I was at sea, on a neutral ship, when the war began. The ship was damaged by gunfire but we made it to Barcelona.'

'And that was . . . ?'

'In 1916.'

'With two years of war remaining.'

'When I went to the Austrian legation, they gave me a job. As what's called an "office boy."'

'What were they like? The other Austrians, I mean.'

Where is this headed? 'What were they like?' Stahl said. 'They were like people who worked in an office.'

'So, "ordinary", you'd say.'

'Yes. Why do you ask?'

'Well, you're of German origin and . . .'

'I was born in Vienna, but I left when I was sixteen – I believe the bio says that.'

'Sorry, I should've said Austrian. I'm afraid that many people here in France think it's the same thing. My point is, you weren't in the trenches shooting at French soldiers. And your experience of Austrians during the war wasn't, militaristic, or anything like that.'

Stahl shook his head, clearly ready to move to another subject.

'Have you been, since you arrived in France, the subject of any anti-German, I should say anti-Austrian, hostility?'

'No, of course not.'

'There is some considerable anti-German sentiment here in France, Monsieur Stahl.'

Stahl shrugged. 'Not on movie sets, the subject doesn't come up.'

Loubec turned the page back to his questions. 'You've arrived in France during a period of considerable turmoil, some people say that war is coming, did your American friends think you were brave, or maybe foolish, to come to France?'

'No. They might have wondered, but nobody said anything.'

'Do they believe that war is inevitable? Or do they hope that diplomacy can resolve political differences?'

Stahl let his irritation show – Loubec had manoeuvred him into a political discussion he'd meant to avoid. As he leaned forward, a flashbulb popped as René took a photograph. Stahl rubbed his eyes and stared at him. 'Pardon,' René said. 'It's dark in here.'

'Should I read back the question?' Loubec said.

'No, naturally they hope there won't be a war. They don't want to see people killed, cities burned down. Do you?'

Loubec's face was so immobile, so opaque, that for a moment Stahl wondered if there was something wrong with him. 'I don't,' Loubec said. 'But, sad to say, there are politicians who are dedicated to preparation for war, massive rearmament, anti-German propaganda, because they have dismissed the idea that France and Germany can come to any rapprochement. But, perhaps, you agree with them.'

'I don't,' Stahl said. 'But I don't spend time worrying about it, I spend my time preparing to make a moving picture.' Stahl hadn't raised his voice, but the emphasis was there. 'It's called *Après la Guerre,* produced by Jules Deschelles for Paramount Pictures.' Stahl smiled, meaning he wasn't angry, but . . .

'Of course we'll talk about the movie, but my readers are interested in your views, Monsieur Stahl, what sort of fellow you are – one's life is more than one's profession, no?'

Stahl smiled again. 'Maybe less than you think, Monsieur Loubec.'

'Very well, then tell me this, are you concerned about the possibility that, if war breaks out, you might not be able to finish your film?'

Stahl lit a cigarette, then looked at his watch. 'I believe it will be finished,' he said. *And that's that.*

'Maybe it would be better if countries never again went to war. As an artist, do you believe that?'

'That it would be better?'

'Yes.'

'Who doesn't believe that?'

Loubec shrugged. 'Now, can you say something about *Après la Guerre?*'

As Loubec's pencil worked away – *obediently,* it seemed to Stahl – he repeated his memorized summary, hitting the points that made the movie sound dramatic and exciting. Loubec asked a tame question or two, then they left the hotel and René took a number of photographs. But Stahl never saw them.

Le Matin reached the news-stands at 5.30 in the morning, Stahl had one back in his suite by 5.45. The front-page headline said that the insurance salesman from Toulon, who'd married four women, then poisoned them and taken their money, had been sentenced to death at the conclusion of his trial. In the grainy photograph, a fat little man with a moustache was being taken down the courthouse steps by two policemen. Above the right-hand column, a smaller headline: VON RIBBENTROP CALLS FOR GERMAN CONTROL OF DANZIG. The German foreign minister was photographed shaking hands with Josef Beck, his Polish counterpart. Of the two, von Ribbentrop had the larger smile.

Stahl hunted through the paper and, towards the back, across from the racetrack results, a mid-column photograph caught his attention: a man with an intense and mildly disturbed expression on his face, a serious man, leaned forward, his mouth parted as he began to speak. A good photograph, really, nothing to do with being a movie star, simply a concerned, notably handsome individual. At the top of the column was a publicity still: Stahl holding a doctor's bag as he stood in a doorway, with the caption *Fredric Stahl as Dr Lawton in 'A Fortunate Woman'.* This photo was beneath the story's headline:

AMERICAN ACTOR FAVOURS DIPLOMACY

In smaller print, a subhead:

Hollywood Star Fredric Stahl
Speaks Out for Rapprochement

Stahl's first try at a reaction was *mild irritation because it doesn't matter,* but slowly, inevitably, anger began to build inside him. It wasn't that he'd never been manipulated – not in his business it wasn't – but there was a certain arrogance, almost bravado, in the way it had been done. And, worse, he had watched it happening to him but could do nothing about it. And this was what took a whetstone to the edge of his anger.

The story was nothing but sweetness and light. Surely it made Philippe LaMotte and the Baroness von Reschke happy as they ate their morning croissants. As far as Stahl was concerned, the story went: anti-German feeling in France was muted, except in the case of certain politicians who were anxious to rearm, who were preparing to take the nation into war. '"Do they want to see people killed, cities burned down?" a puzzled Stahl asked this reporter.' And, a few sentences later, 'Who doesn't believe that it would be better if countries never again went to war?' The man who said this was clearly, as the first paragraph pointed out, a highly respected and accomplished American. So, went the innuendo, that's what important Americans are thinking.

Stahl had always admired good work and he admired it now. Loubec was a sneaky little bastard but he was good at his job. Did the story matter? In the greater scheme of things, maybe not all that much, just another drip from the leaky faucet. But, Stahl supposed, the people who'd done this knew that it was a slow but effective way to create a flood.

Mme Boulanger waited until a decent eighty-thirty before she called. 'Well,' she said, 'what did you think?'

'You know,' he said, 'I realized what was going on but I couldn't stop it. Will it matter?'

'To your career? No, not much, not at all. I have to translate the story for Warner publicity in Hollywood, but I doubt they'll do more than take a quick glance to make sure you haven't said anything dreadful.' She paused a moment, then said, 'Also, a copy goes to somebody named Walter Perry, I expect he's important but I don't know who he is.'

'An *éminence grise,* Jack Warner's personal stand-in.'

'Well, so they care about you, you're a valuable asset.'

'Were you disturbed by it, Madame Boulanger?'

'Oh, maybe a little. Those aren't my political views – it's the *Le Matin* line. Did you mean what you said?'

'Not the way it came out.'

'Ahh, journalists,' she said. 'But, aside from the fact that you stuck your nose into French politics, it's not that damaging. For one thing, an American reader would think you simply care about peace and don't hate Germans. They have no idea what goes on here. None. And, speaking of that, I think you'd do well to meet a friend of mine. His name is André Sokoloff, of Russian extraction but completely French, completely Parisian says it better.'

'Who is he?'

'The senior correspondent for *Paris-Soir,* which is sort of the *New York Times* of France. Have lunch with him, he'll tell you some things you ought to know.'

'Things I ought to know?'

'They're after you, Monsieur Stahl. I surely didn't mean to help them but I did, so this is my way of helping you protect yourself.'

'There's more to come, you mean.'

'That I can promise you. As the English detectives say in the mystery novels, "the game is on".'

Stahl ordered coffee and croissants, had his breakfast at the window, and watched the brown leaves go swirling down the rue François 1er. He felt better, Mme Boulanger had made him feel better, that was her job. When a client was the subject of bad press, she helped them get through it. He couldn't say exactly how she managed to do that, but the tone of her voice had a lot to do with it – an unstated but clear message: *this is not the end of the world.*

Done with breakfast, he caught a whiff of his underarms – he'd had a difficult morning – and realized he'd better shower before he went out to Joinville. So he was naked when the phone rang. Stahl was no psychic, he couldn't foresee future events – sometimes a very fortunate thing – but he knew who this was and he was right.

'Franz, good morning. I hope I'm not disturbing you, is it too early?'

He didn't slam the phone down – he wanted to, but he didn't. He knew, since his meeting with Wilkinson, that he was talking to the enemy. So then, what did the enemy have to say? Something Wilkinson could use? Maybe it didn't matter but, in case it did, he wasn't going to sacrifice it for the simple pleasure of slamming down a phone. 'Hello, Moppi,' he said, some resignation in his voice.

'I was wondering if you'd seen today's *Le Matin*.' Moppi was not at all his usual blustering self, he was, for him, quiet, subdued, delicately sympathetic.

'Yes, I saw it.'

'I must admit I was surprised . . . at what you said.'

'You were?'

'Yes, it really didn't sound like you. Nothing wrong with the – *sentiments,* of course not, you just don't seem like somebody who would talk about politics in a foreign newspaper. But maybe I'm wrong.'

'You're not wrong. The quotes weren't inaccurate but they were presented in a way that made me into something I'm not.'

'Ach!' said Moppi in Austrian despair. 'These journalists have no decency.'

'Well, next time I'll know better.'

'Maybe you should be glad it wasn't worse, if you understand me.'

'Worse? How?'

'Oh, for example, you were briefly in jail. Imagine what a French newspaper could make of that!'

How did . . . 'I was caught in a street march. I was never charged with anything.'

'Of course not! You're *important,* a *star*. But still, they could have suggested *anything,* some terrible accusation. And then, even the fact that you were discreetly set free, without publicity, could be used against you. Big movie star, look how the powerful are treated differently from you and me. *L'Humanité,* the communist party newspaper, would give it prominent space.'

'But they haven't, have they?'

'Thank heaven. In truth, the story in *Le Matin* wasn't so bad, by now the market women are wrapping fish in it.'

'Moppi, I have to go out in a little while . . .'

'Forgive me, Franz, I blabber too much, my wife . . . I am calling to ask of you a favour, not that you owe me anything, you don't, but my position in the embassy concerns culture, and I could be in difficulties if you won't have a little lunch with us.'

'When?'

'Tomorrow, at Maxim's. Are you allowing me to hope, Franz?'

'I'll look at my schedule later today and call you back. Maybe even tomorrow morning – is that too late?'

'Why no. No! Not at all!' The old exuberant Moppi had returned from wherever he'd been hiding. 'Believe me, you won't regret it.'

Oh no?

Stahl showered and shaved and dressed – casually, corduroys and a loose grey shirt – for work. He wasn't sure what he wanted to do about the lunch invitation and went back and forth; from *confront these people* to *get as far away as you can,* then gave up – he would decide later. But, if he *was* going to lunch the following day, he had to telephone Jean Avila. This wasn't so easy; Stahl could only hope he hadn't seen the story. A vain hope. 'I didn't realize,' Avila said, 'that you were so interested in French politics.'

'I'm not.' After a moment he said, 'You *read* that paper?'

'You know I don't, but a friend felt obligated to tell me about it.' Some tartness in his voice suggested what he felt about such 'friends'.

'They twisted everything I said. I thought I was doing *publicity.*'

'You were, in a way, but their publicity, not yours. You have to be careful, Fredric, everything in this accursed country is so symbolic, a few words may mean more than you suspect – it's like speaking in *code.*'

'I spent this morning learning all about that,' Stahl said ruefully, 'and I won't be talking to *them* again. Jean, I may have to go to a lunch tomorrow, can you work around me?'

'Come to the set at ten, as usual, then stay until twelve-thirty. All right?'

'Thank you, Jean, and thank you for being understanding about that trash in the newspaper.'

'See you later, my friend, and don't stop to talk to any journalists on the way.'

29 October. Jimmy Louis drove Stahl to Maxim's in the glowing silver Panhard. Moppi and his pals wanted a movie star, very well, they would have one. Stahl had decided to accept the invitation. He'd certainly heard Moppi's threats, about the newspapers, and he'd heard him say they knew more about him – his night in jail – than he'd thought they did. *We're watching you.* So he would go to lunch, and if he heard something interesting he'd let Wilkinson know about it. He would listen to them, and then he would find a way to let them know that it ended there, that he wouldn't be intimidated. They might accept that, or they might not, and, if they didn't, they would attack him in the press and he would have to fight back. A public brawl. Warner Bros. wouldn't like it, Deschelles wouldn't like it, so the longer he could put that off the better for him. Not unwise, he thought, to sacrifice two hours in defence of his career. But he'd go no further, he was done with them, and they were about to find that out.

He had Jimmy drive around until 1.20, then they pulled up in front of the restaurant. Inside, spectacular opulence – Maxim's had been established in the Belle Epoque, before the turn of the century, when life in Paris was, for a time, sweet and golden, if you had the money for sweet and golden. With the arrival of Art Nouveau in the 1920s, the restaurant was redecorated, and there it stopped. Stahl paused at the maître d's station, but he was immediately led into the dining room, where he saw mostly businessmen and a sprinkling of tourists. And here came Moppi, red in the face and wiping his bald head with one of the restaurant's enormous linen napkins. Moppi pumped his hand and tried to take Stahl, his greatly desired prize, by the elbow, but Stahl slipped away.

At a table in the centre of the room, five faces were eagerly turned towards him as he approached. Stahl was introduced – all German names – and he realized they had managed to round up one of his 'friends from the legation', an older man when Stahl knew him in Barcelona, now very old and very nervous. Stahl instinctively doubted this man lived in Paris, suspecting that he had been imported for the occasion. Even during the pre-lunch menu chitchat, all the men at the table deferred to the leader, one Emhof, whose speech was German, not Austrian. He was a good-sized gent – they were all good-sized except for the imported guest. Emhof was pop-eyed, which gave him a fervent stare no matter where he looked. He had a bass rumble for a voice, a vast belly, and a Nazi party pin – a swastika with a diamond at its centre – in his lapel. He was sitting to Stahl's left, and smelled of smelly cigars. Taking the wine list in hand, he produced a pair of heavy, black-framed glasses, put them on, then tilted them upwards for sharper vision in the restaurant light. The wine waiter stood patiently by Emhof's chair – *this will be worth the wait* – and Emhof finally said, 'We'll have the Château Margaux.'

'The 1932, monsieur?'

'The 1899, and you might as well bring two bottles. No, three.'

'Very good, monsieur.'

Emhof turned towards Stahl and leaned back, taking off his glasses. 'We're pleased you could join us, Herr Stalka – or would you prefer to be called by your Hollywood name?'

'As you wish, Herr Emhof. I was born Stalka, it's still that way in my passport.'

'And it's . . . ?'

'Slovenian.' *As you well know.*

'Slovenian! So beautiful there, such majestic mountains. You ski, I would suppose.'

'Not so much, sometimes on vacation I tried it, but my family was more Viennese than Slovenian, my mother and father's people had been there for a long time.'

'And your family lives there still?'

'They do.'

'But you are far away, in California. Do you manage to see them?'

'Not for a long time, I'm afraid.'

Moppi cleared his throat and said, 'Perhaps you might . . .' But Emhof stared at him and he shut up.

'And Hollywood? You're happy there? I understand that the movie business is almost entirely a Jewish business, am I right? Is that entirely comfortable? Or are you perhaps yourself of Jewish origin?'

'I was raised as a Catholic, but I am not a religious person. And I'm very comfortable with whatever Jews work in Hollywood, it really doesn't matter.'

'We had them in the German film industry, though many of them have moved on. Yet the business seems to thrive so we don't much notice the – absence.'

The man on Emhof's left, young and ambitious-looking, said, 'Do you follow today's German films, Herr Stalka?'

'I don't.'

'Pity. It's a very vibrant industry. UFA, our principal production house, makes hundreds of films and the best of them are quite good, just like Hollywood, I imagine.'

'I'm sure they are,' Stahl said.

The waiter arrived. Emhof – and all but Stahl echoed his choice – ordered a Maxim's classic: Tournedos Rossini, tender beef filet topped with foie gras and a sliver of truffle, and, another classic, the Pommes Anna, thinly sliced potatoes layered with butter and pressed into a block. Stahl ordered the Filet of Sole Albert, named for the famous Maxim maître d'hôtel.

As the waiter left, Emhof said, 'Tell me, Herr Stalka, does Hollywood make films about mountaineering?'

'I don't think so,' Stahl said. 'At least I don't know of any.'

'Extraordinary. We have been producing them in Germany since the mid-twenties. Have you not seen Arnold Fanck's *Der heilige Berg*?

"The Holy Mountain"? Where our own Leni Riefenstahl is the lead actress?'

Stahl shook his head. He knew only of Riefenstahl's propaganda films, about the Nuremberg rally of the Nazi party, and the '36 Olympics – young people with beautifully defined muscles.

'It's very popular in Germany,' Moppi said, 'the mountain film.'

'It's a national *passion*,' the man to Emhof's left said. 'We all must climb, must make our way up the incline of life to the sunlit peak of success. A journey, a journey requiring great fortitude, great inner strength.'

'No doubt.' Out before Stahl could stop it, this was lightly flavoured with derision – the Viennese taste for irony was returning as he spoke German.

Emhof raised his eyebrows. Moppi rushed in. 'So much do we enjoy the mountain movie, Franz, that a film festival is scheduled to take place in Berlin. Forty mountain films will be shown! That will be exciting, no?'

Stahl could only imagine. As for mountains in the movies, what came to mind was his musician friends' amusement at a certain film cliché: when a mountaintop was shown, the shot was always scored with a long, triumphant note from a horn. Finally he said, 'Always good to have a film festival.'

'Yes, we think so too,' Emhof said.

The wine appeared, and with some ceremony the bottles were placed on angled silver wine-rests. 'Shall I open all of them, monsieur?'

'Naturally,' Emhof said.

When all six glasses were poured, Emhof said '*Sieg Heil*', and raised his glass as the other four Germans repeated the toast. Stahl looked away, and two or three heads turned towards them at nearby tables.

Yes, Stahl thought, Château Margaux was transcendent – if only he'd been with a lover or with friends, he would have enjoyed it.

The lunch arrived soon thereafter; an appetizer plate of caviar with blini and chopped egg. And then the tournedos. As the plates were set down, all the Germans said, 'Ahh.' Had this been a table of Parisians, some light conversation would have been maintained – to talk while dining demanded a certain level of skill. Not the Germans, they fell on the tournedos with avid concentration, while the old man from Stahl's Barcelona days ate in such a way, eyes never leaving his plate, that it occurred to Stahl it might have been some time since he'd had a good meal. Meanwhile, Stahl ate some of his sole.

As the plates were taken away, Emhof dabbed at his mouth with a napkin and said, 'The French can cook, that much we must say for them.'

The others nodded and agreed.

'And they must be encouraged to continue, no matter what,' said the man next to Emhof.

No matter what? This remark, with just a hint of knowing under-tone, was, Stahl sensed, meant to go over his head and resonate with the man's colleagues.

Emhof intervened, making sure the man to his left did not elaborate. 'It isn't only cooking, there are many things that the French – ' He was winding up to expand on this theme but he stopped dead and his face lit with anticipation as a waiter appeared, rolling a cart that held a large pan, cordials, and a plate of crêpes – here were the makings of Crêpes Suzette!

'Oh-ho,' said Moppi, grinning and rubbing his hands.

'I wonder,' Emhof said, turning to face Stahl, 'if you would be willing to listen to an idea that's just now occurred to me.'

'I will always listen,' Stahl said.

'Our festival of mountain movies begins in November, in Berlin, and we are going to offer a number of prizes, in various categories; technical achievement, performance, umm, spiritual value – just like the Oscars.' He paused, Stahl waited. 'So, of course, if there are prizes, there must be judges. Is there any chance you would consider coming over – even for a day, I know you're a busy man – to be one of them? Think of the film-makers, how excited they would be just to *meet* a man of your stature. And there is quite a substantial honorarium to be paid, twenty thousand reichsmarks – ten thousand dollars in American money. Only a day's work, Herr Stalka, Herr Fredric Stahl, and Lufthansa will fly you over and back. What do you think?'

'I think I won't be coming to your festival, Herr Emhof. And I won't be coming to any more lunches, and I won't be answering Herr Moppi's telephone calls, or letters, or telegrams. And if Herr Moppi shows up again at a movie set where I'm working, I'll have him arrested. Have I made myself clear?'

'Speaking of movies,' said the man to Emhof's left, addressing all at the table, 'I saw once again, last week, the magnificent Marlene Dietrich in *The Blue Angel*.'

'What an actress,' Emhof said.

'Oh she was wonderful, wasn't she,' Moppi said. 'What was she called? I can never remember.'

'Lola Lola,' said Emhof. 'Memorable, one of our greatest films.'

'Right! Lola Lola!' Moppi said.

Stahl rose, placed his napkin by his plate, said, 'Good day, gentlemen,' and walked towards the door. Behind him, the old man said, 'Good day, sir.' At a table near the maître d' station sat a very respectable couple, drinking wine and waiting for their next course. The man, dressed to perfection in a dark suit, crisp white shirt, and sober tie, his mouth set in prim disapproval, turned his head towards Stahl and, just for an instant, met his eyes, then looked away. Stahl continued towards the door. The last thing he heard from the table of Germans was a cry of delight as the liqueurs in the crêpe pan were set ablaze.

The cast out at Joinville worked hard the following day. Stahl and the others had not yet 'dropped their scripts', but they could rehearse by glancing over their lines and setting their scripts aside, which freed them to move around and add physical action to the dialogue.

In the film, the three legionnaires have found a morning's work, cleaning an olive-oil mill in a small Turkish town. When they are paid – much less than promised – they replace their tattered uniforms with old clothing from the local souk. They are then seen on a platform at the railway station, waiting for a local train which will eventually take them to the last stop in Turkey where, since they have no papers, they plan a clandestine crossing at night, into Syria. They expect that Syria, a French colonial possession since the end of the Great War, will be a place where they can acquire passports and money.

They ride for a few stops, and begin to believe their plan will work, but then they are discovered by a conductor and, without tickets, they are thrown off the train in some tiny village. In the same carriage, the character played by Justine Piro is also unable to produce a ticket and she is pushed out the door of the railway carriage. Her character, called Ilona, says she is an impoverished Hungarian countess, and needs only to reach Hungary, where she has money and family. In return for the legionnaires' protection, she will help them when they get to Budapest.

Having identified Stahl's Colonel Vadic as the leader of the trio, she seeks to enlist his sympathy. 'How on earth did you wind up in Turkey?' Vadic asks her.

'My fiancé was a diplomat, sent to Istanbul when the war began, and he brought me there.'

'What happened?' the lieutenant asks.

'What often happens,' she says.

'He abandoned you?' Pasquin's sergeant says. '*You?*'

Avila broke in. 'The sergeant doesn't really believe anything she says, Pasquin, but he is amused by her lie, so he should smile with that line.'

The sergeant, it later turns out, is correct – Ilona is not Hungarian, not a countess, and there never was a fiancé. Pasquin and Justine Piro worked at the two-line sequence for a time, trying it in a slightly altered form on each repetition, as Avila commented and suggested different variations.

By 3.00 p.m., when the costumed upper-class rakes and ingenues arrived for their boulevard comedy, the cast of *Après la Guerre* had been at it for five hours. As they prepared to leave, Avila took Stahl aside and asked if he would mind going over to Building K, where Renate Steiner, the costume designer, needed him for a fitting. Stahl was worn out, it had been a long rehearsal and, after the lunch at Maxim's the day before, he'd had trouble sleeping. But of course he had to go off to Building K.

At Building K, a different Renate Steiner. Dark-haired and fair-skinned, with a sharp jawline and a pointy nose, she wore the same blue work-smock over a long dress, thick stockings, and laced boots. But her smile, ironic and subtly challenging, was not to be seen, and her faded blue eyes, that had caught his interest, were swollen and faintly red. Was something wrong? He didn't know her well enough to ask. Better just to assume her life, like his, like everybody else's, had its ups and downs.

'Thank you for coming over,' she said. 'I'm sure you're tired – when you work with Avila you don't take time off, because he never does.'

'I'm used to hard work,' he said. 'All going well?'

She shrugged. 'Well enough, I guess. Let's get you into uniform, Fredric.' She nodded towards a curtain in one corner, her changing room, and handed him the uniform. 'While you change clothes, I'll get your boots,' she said.

He reappeared as Colonel Vadic, his Foreign Legion uniform bleached out and artfully torn at the sleeve. She looked him over with a critical eye, then shook her head. *Lord, why me?* As she snatched a lump of tailor's chalk from her work table she said, 'I'm training a new seamstress, so there *will* be mistakes.' With a strong hand she grabbed the shoulder of his tunic, moved it back and forth, then flat-tened it out and drew a line for a new seam. 'And I have three more of these,' she said, irritation in her voice. 'A duplicate of this one, be-cause God-only-knows what happens on movie sets, one even more distressed, for your travels in the desert, and the last one, terribly ratty, that you try to sell at the used-clothing stall in the souk. The merchant has a funny line about it, if I remember correctly.'

It took some time – there was something wrong with each uni-form – and the late-afternoon light outside the windows began to fade towards an early dusk. Holding a few pins between her lips, she knelt and changed the length of his trousers, then stood, stared at him for a long minute, and said, 'Let's get rid of that button on your breast pocket.' She found a razor blade with a covered edge and sliced off a button. 'I'll fix the flap so it doesn't lie flat but I don't need to do that now. Have a look.'

He turned and faced the full-length mirror. 'It looks just right,' he said. In the mirror, he could see her over his shoulder. From a desk by the far wall, a telephone rang – the French signal, two short rings. Then again, and a third time, but Renate didn't move. She pressed her lips together and closed her eyes. The phone continued to ring. It was as though the two of them were frozen in place. At last the ringing stopped and she sank down in a chair and held her hands over her face. Stahl turned around. From beneath her hands, in a voice fighting through tears, she said, 'I'll have to pull . . .' She stopped, then went on, 'I'll have to pull the threads out, where the button was.' Stahl waited patiently, a sympathetic man in a tattered uniform.

She dropped her hands and said, 'Oh you must forgive me.'

His voice was low and gentle as he said, 'There's nothing to forgive.'

The kindness undid her. She took a handkerchief from the pocket of her smock and wept silently, hiding her face behind the white square. When the telephone rang again, one sob escaped her. Stahl couldn't bear it. He walked over to her and rested a light hand on her shoulder. Then was startled as she suddenly rose from the chair, threw her arms around him, and pressed her face against his chest. He held her carefully, desperate to say *something*, but what came to him, some version of *please don't cry*, was worse than silence. At last the phone stopped ringing, she let him go and went and stood by her work table, turned away from him. 'I don't know what to say.'

'You needn't say a word.'

'It's just that . . . I have trouble at home. Bad trouble. Trouble I can't fix.'

'That's very hard for a woman.'

She nodded, then blew her nose, took a deep breath, and exhaled. 'He calls me and says frightening things, he wants to . . .'

'To what?'

'I can't say it out loud. He is going to . . . he doesn't want to live any more.'

'Your husband?'

'We're not married but yes, he is my husband.'

'Renate,' Stahl said softly, 'I can go outside, you know, have a cigarette . . .'

From Renate, the suggestion of a nod, then, quietly, 'I know.' She paused, then said, 'I really can't bear it any longer. I just can't.'

'Would it help you to talk about it?'

A brief shrug, then once again, trying to calm herself, she took a breath and let it out. 'An old story, I expect you know the whole thing. He was an important journalist in Berlin, but he is nothing here. He can't write in French, not well enough he can't. So he does a few pieces, diatribes, for the émigré magazines and gets a few francs, but it's me who makes the money.'

Stahl was silent. He went behind the curtain, retrieved his pack of Gauloises, took one himself and offered her the pack. She drew one out, he lit both cigarettes. 'Thank you,' she said.

'You're right. I *have* seen this before, but if he can somehow hang on, life will improve.' And, yes, it sometimes did, but often it did not, and émigré suicides were all too common.

'I tell him that. He says he has lost his manhood.'

Her face was taut with anguish, Stahl tried to say something, anything. 'Oh, men can be like that, it's . . .'

'Fredric, I think I am done for the day.'

'I understand, let me change and I'll be gone in a minute.'

'Please don't be angry with me. He will call again, and it's easier if I'm alone when I talk to him. It can go on . . . for a long time.'

Stahl changed quickly, struggling to unlace the heavy boots. The phone rang as he reached the door. He waved goodbye to Renate, who nodded gratefully and lifted the receiver.

2 November. In northern Europe, the fog of autumn had settled over the cities. When Stahl looked out of his window at dawn, the street lay under a white mist that shifted with the wind and there were halos on the streetlamps, automobiles were no more than dim headlights moving slowly past the hotel, while pedestrians appeared for a moment, then faded into shapes and vanished.

Later on, at the desk in the lobby of the Claridge, there was a letter from the Baroness von Reschke on her elegant notepaper. Yet another cocktail party was planned, her friends were hoping he could make a little time for them, and she was eager to see him again. 'I had hoped we could be closer, my dear, could take tea together some afternoon, just the two of us, but I will settle for your enchanting presence at my party.' She meant? Oh Christ, she'd made it very clear what she meant. Tête-à-tête, so to speak, literally head-to-head but people went on from there, didn't they. South. That was where *she* wanted them to go. In front of a camera he would have reacted darkly, in the lobby he just made a face.

Also: a telegram from Buzzy Mehlman, his agent, who had seen a translation of the *Le Matin* article. Stahl was astonished at the speed of the response, and counted the intervening days on his fingers. Had Mme Boulanger sent the story by cable? *Spare no expense*. This made Stahl uncomfortable – could it really be all that important? And the text of Buzzy's message didn't make him feel any easier:

Great article in Le Matin stop Good coverage of film and
Stahl successes stop Political opinion puzzling we think that
unnecessary stop No reaction from Warner Bros but one story
like this plenty stop Hope you're healthy and loving Paree you
can always telephone if you like stop

Signed: Buzz

Mme Boulanger, true to her word, had scheduled a lunch for him that afternoon with André Sokoloff, the lead journalist at the newspaper *Paris-Soir.* Jean Avila would be spending the day with his production designer and art director in another building at Joinville, where sets were being built for the movie, so Stahl had the day off. The lunch was at 1.00 p.m. at a brasserie just off the Place Bastille. Stahl, tired of being driven around, took the Métro.

Mme Boulanger had made sure the brasserie people *knew who he was,* thus the *propriétaire* himself, one Papa Heininger – all straight-backed dignity and old-fashioned courtesy – greeted Stahl and showed him to 'our most requested table'. Table 14, according to a heavy silver stand, which may have been their most requested table, but it had a hole in the vast mirror above the banquette. Otherwise, Stahl thought, the brasserie was the perfection of its type: hurrying waiters with old-fashioned whiskers, abundant gold leaf and red plush, and the very air itself, a heady blend of perfume, tobacco smoke, and grilled sausage. At least one room in heaven, Stahl thought, would smell like this.

André Sokoloff arrived a moment later, moving at the fast pace of the man who is perpetually late; a cigarette between his lips, a buckled leather briefcase beneath his arm. He was, Stahl thought, the essential Parisian, the essential Parisian *journalist.* After they'd shaken hands, Sokoloff sat opposite Stahl and said, 'You know this place? The famous Brasserie Heininger?'

'Famous for what?' Stahl said, suspecting that a joke lay ahead.

'It's a restaurant with a *story,*' Sokoloff said. 'See that hole in the mirror? A year ago, in June I think, they had a Bulgarian headwaiter here, called Omaraeff, much too involved in émigré politics, who got himself shot in the ladies' WC. He was hiding in a stall and pulled his pants down, which, since it was the *ladies'* WC, was a mistake. "A fatal mistake", as we say. Meanwhile, another member of the gang kept the dinner crowd entertained by running a tommy gun around the dining room – remember I said *Bulgarian* émigré politics, which tend to be dramatic. Well, there went all the mirrors, except for the one behind you, which had only a single bullet hole and was left as Omaraeff's memorial. Now that wouldn't matter, in this city, if the *choucroute* wasn't top-notch, but it is. You like *choucroute garnie,* sauerkraut and sausage?'

' "Like" really isn't the word. It's well beyond that.'

'Good. It always includes a sublime frankfurter and a pork chop. And to drink, I expect Warner Bros. would buy us champagne, but beer is what you want with *choucroute*.'

'*Dark* beer,' Stahl said. 'And plenty of it.'

'I can see we'll get along just fine,' Sokoloff said, and half turned to look for a waiter, who rushed over to the table. Sokoloff was about Stahl's age, good-looking in a craggy way, with a face careworn beyond his years, tousled brown hair, the dark complexion of the Latin French, and a certain set of the mouth: eager to laugh if it got the chance. As the waiter trotted off, Sokoloff said, 'When the beer comes, we should drink to the estimable Mme Boulanger, she's one of the good souls in this rats' nest – I mean Parisian journalism.'

'With pleasure,' Stahl said. 'She's been a friend. And I begin to think I need to have as many of those as I possibly can.'

'That's *always* true,' Sokoloff said. 'Now we could follow one of our unwritten laws – no talk about politics or work during a meal. But, if you don't mind, I'll break one more rule today and we'll do it anyhow. So then, tell me what's going on.'

'These people – only *Le Matin* so far but I get the feeling there's more coming – are, how to say, *after* me.'

Sokoloff grinned. 'After *you*? Only in your honour am I not sitting facing the door.'

'Is it that bad?'

'Not yet, but give it time.'

'Well, I'll let you know if a Bulgarian émigré comes through the door with a tommy gun.'

'Do that, and we'll continue our conversation under the table – which might be the best place to talk about the savage *Le Matin*. But I should start by telling you about *Paris-Soir,* where I work. We are the most respected – or hated, depends who you talk to – news organization in Paris, we also publish magazines, *Marie Claire* and *Paris Match,* and we own the station known as Radio 37. Saint-Exupéry has written for us, so has Cocteau, and Blaise Cendrars. But the most important thing about *Paris-Soir* is that we don't take bribes – not in any form. We have a wealthy publisher who is as much of an idealist as any publisher can be. We also occupy the democratic centre; with the communist *L'Humanité* far to our left, and *Le Matin* and others well to our right. When Henry Luce said in *Time* magazine that French newspapers sold their editorial policies to the highest bidder, he was sued for libel by *Le Matin, Le Journal,* and *Le Temps* – three newspapers of the right who sold their editorial policies to the highest bidder.'

With a tray balanced on the splayed fingers of one hand, the waiter arrived. Resting the tray on a service rack, he set a platter on the table and said, nearly sang, *'Choucroute garnie!'* then added a crock of hot mustard and two glasses of dark Alsatian beer.

Stahl raised his glass and said, *'Salut,* Mme Boulanger.'

Sokoloff imitated Stahl's gesture and said, 'Mme Boulanger.' Then he drank and said, 'Mm. Anyhow, the newspapers here are divided like the country, where cordial animosity has become something much more dangerous. This smouldered away for years, then came the Popular Front of 1936 – socialists, democrats, and communists – with Léon Blum, who is Jewish, as prime minister. The parties of the right were enraged; a fascist gang dragged Blum from his car, beat him badly, almost killed him. And if anyone wondered why, they wrote on the walls MIEUX HITLER QUE BLUM, better Hitler than Blum. Yes, mean-spirited, yes, caustic, but, in the end, far worse. In fact, they meant it.'

'Meant it? Meant what? That Adolf Hitler should govern France? I'm sorry but I find that hard to believe.'

'So do I. Or, rather, so *did* I. What the right has in mind is that Hitler would *dominate* France – with treaties by preference but with tanks if necessary. Democracy – which to the right is another way of saying "socialism", if not outright Bolshevism – to be destroyed, and replaced by a Bonapartist authoritarian government which will finish with the labour unions and the intellectuals once and for all.'

Stahl had assembled a forkful of sauerkraut, speared a bite of frankfurter, spread some mustard on it, and raised the fork halfway to his mouth. There it stayed. He raised his head and met Sokoloff's eyes. 'That is . . .' He hesitated, then said, 'That's treason.'

'Not yet.'

'I don't understand,' Stahl said. 'Am I just being naive?'

'You're a well-meaning European who's been away from Europe for eight years, during which time political life has changed. What hasn't changed is the power of money – it was the big banks, the insurance companies, and the heavy industries that brought down the Popular Front. They are secretive about what they do, they crave anonymity. But there is also the magnate, the *gros légume* – the big vegetable – the warrior of the right. We have more than our share of those, it seems.'

'And they are?'

'For example Pierre Taittinger, of the house of champagne, who formed his very own fascist gang, the *Jeunesses Patriotes,* the young patriots, and introduced the symbolic blue beret as part of his, and their, uniform. For example François Coty, who famously said, "perfume is a woman's love affair with herself", and hid crates of weapons in his château at Louveciennes, on the outskirts of Paris, for *his* fascist gang, *Solidarité Française*. For example Jean Hennessy of the cognac firm, and the Michelin brothers, the tyre people, thought to be responsible for a terrorist bombing on the rue de Presbourg. These are people who work to bring down the government by force, and replace it with one more to their liking. Some of them have their own newspapers, some support, and arm, their own private militias, but all of them have one thing in common.'

'Which is?'

'They are French.'

'But I'm told there is also German money, a lot of it, buying influence in the French government, and used to support propaganda, political warfare, that is meant to destroy the French will to fight.'

'What you say is true, and *now* you have treason.'

Stahl returned to his lunch and his beer, but Sokoloff's last comment didn't go away. In the brasserie, the lunchtime symphony rose in volume – the clatter of silverware and china, spirited chatter, laughter, exclamations of *'Mais oui!'* and *'C'est terrible!'* Did they know? If they knew, did they care? The French looked away from evil, it drained the pleasure from life. *Perhaps,* they thought, *it will just go away.* In his very soul, Stahl wanted them to be right.

Sokoloff, sensing Stahl's change of mood, looked guilty. 'Oh well,' he said, 'let's have another beer. Yes?'

Stahl said, 'What the hell, why not.' Then, after a moment, 'What is it with the Germans? They didn't used to be like this.'

Sokoloff shrugged. 'They lost a war and it made them furious, now they want to destroy us. Hitler has, at times, a certain twinkle in his eye, you know? *What a sly fox am I* – something like that. He means he conquered two nations, Austria and Czechoslovakia, without firing a shot, and France is next. He said in *Mein Kampf* that France should be isolated, then destroyed. Have you looked at a map lately? We're surrounded by fascist dictatorships: Italy, Portugal, soon enough Spain, and Germany itself. Switzerland, Belgium, the Netherlands; all neutral. Others, like Hungary, bullied into alliance with the Nazis. We no longer *have* friends, the world is becoming, for us, a very cold place.'

'Well, *I'm* your friend,' Stahl said, *as though that meant anything.*

'I know you are, and you're an American, which makes you a very welcome friend.'

'So then, what can I do? What should I do? Nothing?'

Sokoloff thought it over, then, with a rather wistful smile, said, 'I don't think I have an answer. I will tell you, as a friend, to be careful. They, and I mean the French and the Germans, will attack their enemies – especially in the press. All they've done so far is *use* you, bad enough, but it can be much worse.' He paused, then said, 'Have you ever heard of a man named Roger Salengro?'

'No.'

'He was Blum's Minister of the Interior – that means he directed all the security forces, all counter-espionage. Salengro wasn't going to stand for their nonsense, so they attacked him. A particularly nasty little magazine, called *Gringoire,* wrote that Salengro, who fought bravely in the last war until he was captured, allowed himself to be taken prisoner on purpose, to save his life, an act of cowardice. This was a lie, but *Gringoire* kept repeating it until, one day, when Salengro went to the ministry, the soldiers guarding the entrance refused to salute him. They had come to believe the lie. Salengro's heart was broken, and he went home and killed himself.'

'That's vile,' Stahl said.

'It is. But better for you to know about it.'

Stahl nodded, the story reaching him as he stared out at the crowded room. 'I don't know,' he said. 'Maybe I should just go back to America.'

'Give up? Ruin your career? You won't do that.'

'No, probably I won't. I can't.'

'You're not the type. The people in Hollywood cast you as they do for a reason, Monsieur Stahl, they build on what is already there.'

'Perhaps, some day, I will do an interview with you, Monsieur Sokoloff.'

'Maybe some day, but not yet. As we used to say in the trenches, keep your head down.'

Stahl placed his knife and fork on the plate, then lit a cigarette.

Trying to ease the gloom he'd felt after talking to Sokoloff, he decided to walk for a while, taking the narrow, sunless streets of the Marais, the ancient Jewish quarter, in the general direction of the hotel. For a long time, nothing had changed here; tenement walls leaned over crooked lanes, the markets had kosher chickens hung on steel hooks, men wearing yarmulkes spoke Yiddish together – but stopped speaking until he'd passed by – and the women, heads covered with shawls or scarves, did not meet his eyes. It was, he thought, as though he were in some shtetl in Poland.

Still, by the time he left the district he was at least hopeful. He felt he could deal with his problems and do in Paris what he'd come here to do. Which wasn't politics. He had faced down Moppi and his dreadful friends, and, in André Sokoloff, he had a new ally, without doubt a good man in a fight. Slowly, he regained himself – this wasn't the first trouble in his life and it surely wouldn't be the last, but he'd dealt with it before and he would now. A taxi cruised slowly by his side, inviting him to ride, Stahl raised a hand, the taxi stopped. And, on the way to the Claridge, just looking out at the streets made him feel better.

Reaching his rooms on the top floor of the hotel, Stahl tried to use his key but the door, already unlocked, swung open, slowly, as he pushed against it.

Inside, a man was sitting on the sofa, apparently waiting for him. Actually, not quite sitting, *lounging* said it better – he had one leg hooked over the arm of the sofa, his body resting against the cushions at an angle. A magazine that Stahl had left on the night table lay open on his lap. Was he a hotel thief? He wasn't acting like one. He was tall, wearing a brown jacket and grey slacks, his collar unbuttoned, his tie pulled down. He had scant, colourless hair combed back from a high forehead, pale eyes, pale skin. To Stahl, he looked like a Scandinavian, perhaps a Swede, maybe a businessman. On the floor in front of the sofa was a small bag of pebbled black leather, like a doctor's bag.

Stahl took a few steps towards the telephone on the desk, then put his hand on the receiver, ready to call downstairs, but the man just watched him as though he were an object of some, but not much, interest. 'What are you doing here?' Stahl said. 'This isn't your room.'

In German, the man said, 'I stopped by to talk to you, Herr Stahl.'

Again, Stahl looked at the black bag. 'Are you a doctor?' he said, truly puzzled.

'No, I'm not a doctor,' the man said.

'I'm going to call the desk and have you thrown out. Or arrested.'

'Yes?' said the man, as though Stahl had commented about the weather.

Stahl picked up the phone, but the man didn't move. 'It won't take too long,' he said. 'Just a brief conversation is all I require, then I won't trouble you any further.'

Stahl put the receiver back but kept his hand on it.

'How was your lunch with Herr Sokoloff?' the man said.

'That's none of your business.'

'No? Maybe it is. He's surely not a proper friend for you.'

Stahl almost laughed. 'What?'

'I think you are a little confused, Herr Stahl, about who your friends are. You are really being rather . . . difficult.'

'Am I,' Stahl said. 'You're German?'

The man nodded slowly, no expression on his face. 'Proud to be,' he said. 'Especially the way things are going now.'

Stahl waited. The man unhooked his leg from the arm of the sofa and sat forward, elbows on knees, fingers clasped. 'What we've learned in Germany is that life goes very well when everybody does their job, and does what they're told to do. Harmony, as we call it, is a powerful force in a nation.'

'I'm sure it is. But, so what?'

'Well, we've told you what we want you to do, to come to Berlin, to appear at our film festival, but you seem disinclined to obey, and this is troubling.'

Stahl stared at the man with an expression of combined disbelief and distaste.

The man smiled to himself and gently shook his head. 'Ah, defiance,' he said, his voice soft and nostalgic – he remembered defiance, from some bygone age long ago. 'Quite a bit of *that,* at the beginning, before we came to power, but we're patient, hardworking people and in time we cured it. It turns, we've found, with persistence on our part, to disbelief, and, in time, to compliance. Oh, people think the most violent thoughts, you can't imagine, but that stays inside. On the outside, however, in the daily world, the individual does what he's told, and then there's harmony. Much of Europe is finding this harmony not so bad as they feared, and soon all of us will work together.'

'No doubt,' Stahl said, sarcasm cutting a fine edge on the words. 'You've broken into my room like a criminal, you've said what you came to say, now get out.'

'You're angry. Well, I understand that, but you'll have some time to think this through, not a lot of time, but some, and I expect you'll come to see where your interests lie. It's *easier,* Herr Stahl, to try and get along with us, to do what we tell you to do – is it really so much? Ask yourself. A brief trip to Berlin, fine food, good company, people saying flattering things – would that be so bad?'

'Stop it,' Stahl said.

The man stretched, then looked at his watch, like someone who is tired but has things to do before he can relax. 'Please don't be rude to me, Herr Stahl, that isn't good for either of us.' He stood, stood rather abruptly, like a schoolboy's feint, and Stahl, despite himself, reacted – didn't move a muscle but the flinch had been there and he knew it. The man grinned, amused by his tactic, picked up his black bag, walked casually to the door, and said, 'Good afternoon, Herr Stahl. One way or another, we'll be in touch with you.'

Was the 'you' subtly inflected? Very subtly inflected? Or, Stahl wondered, had he just heard it that way. The man nodded to him and left the room. Stahl heard him walking away down the corridor and shut the door but the lock didn't click shut. He tried again, and the same thing happened. The lock no longer worked, and now he would have to get it fixed.

3 November. At 3.30 on the afternoon of the third, the senior staff of the Ribbentropburo – the political warfare bureau of the Reich Foreign Ministry, named for Foreign Minister von Ribbentrop – held its weekly meeting. In a general way, their mission was similar to that of Goebbels's Propaganda Ministry, but Goebbels's people supervised all internal culture – the painters and the writers and the composers, the films and the newspapers – while the bureau operated mostly abroad, and was far more clandestine and aggressive in its methods. 'We don't send out press releases,' they liked to say, 'we send out operatives, and then *other* people send out press releases.'

This was an important meeting, decisions had to be made, and some of the men around the table had their jackets hung on the backs of their chairs and their sleeves rolled up. Herr Emhof, of the bulging eyes, attended the meeting but was not of sufficient stature to merit a place at the table, so sat on one of the chairs ranged around the walls and did not speak unless spoken to.

The agenda for this meeting was a typed list of thirty-eight names, which represented thirty-eight problems that had to be resolved. There were hundreds of names in the bureau's files, and most had agreed, some gladly, some not so gladly, to do what the bureau had determined they should do; thus there was no point in wasting time on them. The thirty-eight names, however – people of various backgrounds, all pertinent to the bureau's operations in France – had to be dealt with because they represented potential failures. The Reich Foreign Ministry did not accept failures, so you couldn't really afford, if you worked there, to have too many of them on your record, or you would find yourself working somewhere else. Perhaps at the coal administration, or the department of gasoline rationing, or, at the very worst, you might have to take your wife and family and pets and go off to work in Essen, or Dortmund, or Ulm – exiled.

The meeting was led by the Deputy Director of the bureau, an SS major who had formerly been a junior professor of social sciences, particularly anthropology, at the University of Dresden. He appeared, as always, in civilian clothes, a dark-blue suit, and he was exceptionally bright. A little young for his senior position, a smart, sharp-witted fellow on the way up in the Nazi administration.

The warm air in the room was thick with cigarette smoke, a grey November drizzle outside, and the men at the cluttered table – stacks of dossiers, notepads, ashtrays – made slow but steady progress as they worked their way down the alphabetized list; it was almost five by the time they reached the names beginning with the letter S. They disposed of the first three quickly, then came to the priest Père Sébastien, Father Sébastien, who preached fervently against Nazi atheism at an important church in the city of Lyons. Over the past few months, the bureau had made sure he was besieged by letters from the pious in various parts of France, negative – though gravely respectful – commentary had appeared in the Lyonnais newspapers, and the Vatican had been contacted by German diplomats in Rome.

Why, they asked, was Père Sébastien so obsessed with the religious institutions of a foreign nation? Was he not using the pulpit to advance his own, rather leftist, political agenda? Should he not, the Lord's Shepherd, be paying more attention to the tending of his own local flock?

'The Vatican doesn't exactly disagree,' said the man who saw to operations in the Rhône Valley, 'but the administration is slow as a snail, very tentative, and very cautious.'

'Are our Italian friends willing to help?' said the Deputy Director.

'To date they are useless. They say they will intervene, but then they do nothing.'

'Can we prod him?'

'No, no, let's not. He has a true sense of mission, that will only inspire him.'

The Deputy Director thought for a moment. 'Yes, I suppose you're right. Priests!'

Here and there at the table, an appreciative laugh.

'Perhaps I can do something,' said the Deputy Director. 'I will have a word with our Vatican diplomats, they might just have to *insist* – it's the lepers on Martinique who require such a passionate fellow.'

The man in charge of Lyons made a note – though a secretary seated on one of the chairs kept a record of the meeting in shorthand – and work on the list continued. The journalist Sablier had died in a motoring accident – 'Ours?' 'No, the hand of fate, a mountain road' – and the owner of a small chain of radio stations, Schimmel, a Jew, had put his business up for sale and was going to emigrate to Canada.

'The emigration papers are truly filed?'

'Yes, we checked.'

'That brings us to' – he ran his finger down the list – 'Monsieur Sicot.' Sicot was the publisher and editor of a small socialist newspaper in the city of Bordeaux.

'He rants and raves,' said the man in charge of Sicot. '"The Maginot Line will not save us!" On and on he goes, calls for fleets of fighter planes. He was highly decorated in the Great War and is a fanatic patriot.'

'Who won't listen to reason.'

'Not Sicot. Not ever.'

'Then he'll have to have business problems. Perhaps the advertisers, perhaps the unions, perhaps the bank that holds his notes. Can this be done?'

'I'll go to work immediately, it will take some research.'

'Use the SD' – the intelligence service of the SS – 'and see what you can do. I'll expect a report at our meeting the first week of December. Now then' – he paused, again consulted the list – 'to Fredric Stahl, the movie actor.'

'No good news, I'm afraid,' said the man in charge of Stahl. Called Hoff, he was a plain, middle-aged man who'd served twenty years in the Foreign Ministry with very little distinction – but no serious missteps – then made his way to a position in the bureau through seniority, longtime alliances, and a rather late but practical membership in the Nazi party. 'He moved a little,' Hoff said, 'attended a luncheon, but there he stopped.'

'He's an *actor,* no? What's the problem? Nervous about his career? Studio control?'

'Some of that, but we suspect he's concerned about his, um, we can call it integrity – being faithful to his political beliefs.'

'His what?'

'Integrity.'

The Deputy Director was a very smooth man, but he had a temper, and it was getting towards the time when he wanted a drink and dinner. 'And so?' he said, voice rising. 'And so we kiss him goodbye?'

'We may have to.'

'Somebody give me the goddamn file.'

Hoff shuffled through the dossiers in front of him, where was it? Not this, not this . . .

'*Now,* Hoff. *Now!*'

'Yes, sir. Here it is.'

The Deputy Director opened the dossier by slamming the cover against the table, then, using his index finger, searched through the typed reports of contacts and surveillance. 'We want him to visit the Reich, for a *day,* for a single *day,* to judge some little movie festival, is that correct?'

'Yes, sir.'

'Well, I'll tell you what, Herr Hoff.' By now the Deputy Director was almost shouting. 'He *will* visit the Reich. And we *will* take his photograph for the newspapers, with fucking *Goebbels* we'll take his photograph, and he will pick some idiot as a winner and we will take another photograph as they both hold a fucking *bouquet*! Do I make myself clear?'

'Yes, sir. Very clear.'

The Deputy Director read further, slapping each page down as he turned it over. 'So, he was visited in his hotel room. What a blow! Is anything else planned?'

'Not for the moment. I thought it best to seek your counsel.' Hoff had moved his hands off the table and hidden them in his lap because they were shaking.

'Seek my counsel? Oh, very flattering, Hoff, you're seeking my counsel. Well, here's my *counsel:* you think up something to make this man behave, and you send me a memorandum before you do it. Is that understood, Herr *Hoff*?'

'Yes, sir.'

'And, if you cannot persuade him to put aside this saintly *integrity* – Christ! What a word! – and do what we want, you can have some-body get in touch with, ah, Heinrich, and instead of visiting the Reich he can visit the devil. Oh, excuse me, I forgot he's a saint, so he can visit the angels.'

From down the table, a small, hesitant voice: 'It's not Heinrich, sir, the man who does these things for us is called Herbert.'

3 November. At 7.15, Stahl decided to stop worrying and go out for dinner. Too often that day he'd caught himself brooding about the man who'd entered his room, and all the rest of it, which he suspected

was exactly what they wanted him to do. Therefore, he wouldn't. He could have gone down to the hotel restaurant, but the food there was rich and elaborate, living up to its price, and really much fancier than he liked. So he put on a pair of corduroys and a comfortable jacket, with a wool scarf and a pair of leather gloves to keep him warm, walked over to the Champs-Elysées, then down to a big Alsatian brasserie that served the commercial residents of the quarter – butchers from the wholesale meat markets on the rue Marbeuf, office workers, and shop clerks. It was a big, rough, loud sort of place, where you could eat cheaply by ordering the plat du jour, or in grander fashion, oysters, lobster, champagne, if you were in the mood and had the money. For Stahl, always steak au poivre, a tough, delicious steak, barely cooked, and more frites – crisp, golden, and brown at the edges – than you thought you could eat, though you were usually wrong about that.

He was just seated at a table when Kiki de Saint-Ange walked through the door, peered about, discovered Stahl, and came hurrying towards him. She was very good to look at that evening, a black afternoon dress beneath her raincoat – a vivid memory from their night at the movies – and a violet and grey scarf arranged in the complicated style Parisian women were taught at birth, arty gold earrings, and her little knitted cap. Stahl was delighted to see her, a friend welcome when one thinks one will be dining alone, but for the question *what's she doing here?* The more contact he had with his German enemies, the more sensitive he became to coincidence.

'I *hoped* it was you,' she said, slightly breathless. 'I saw you on the boulevard, from a distance, and I thought, 'Is that Fredric?' My eyesight is terrible – it wouldn't have been the first time I chased down a stranger. May I join you? Maybe you're expecting somebody.'

'Please,' said Stahl, standing up and waiting until she was seated. 'I'm not expecting anybody. What brings you to the neighbourhood?'

'Ai! *Horreur!* I had to see my attorney, he has his office up the Champs-Elysées, and I'd finally got done with him and was walking down the hill, upset, close to tears, and hello, there you were! At least I suspected it was you and, honestly, I really hoped it was.'

'What's going on?'

'Darling, may I have a cognac? A double?'

'Ah, Fredric, *manners*! Yes, of course, forgive me.' Stahl signalled to the waiter, who made eye contact, meaning *yes, I see you, be patient*.

'What's going on,' said Kiki, 'is that a year ago, my lovely old aunt, whom I adored, got sick and died. I used to go and stay with her when things were too awful at home, she had the sweetest little house, down in the Sologne, do you know it? It's where the Parisian aristocrats hunt wild boar, and anything else they can shoot at. There are hunting lodges down there but she just had a country cottage, in a kind of hidden valley, looking out at the river Sauldre. In her will, she left the house for my sister and me to share, which was not a problem at all, but then there was every sort of legal complication that comes with inheritance. Fredric, if you hate somebody and want to ruin their life, die and leave them a house in France. Anyhow, I just spent two hours with the lawyer and, when I said close to tears, I meant tears of frustration. I got so angry I finally said, "Let's give the damn thing to a charity," to which the lawyer replied, "Impossible, mademoiselle, it cannot be done until you have taken legal possession of the property."'

The waiter rushed over, Stahl ordered two double cognacs while in his mind a cartoon version of a steak au poivre grew wings and flew away. He sensed the evening would end with the two of them in bed together, and disliked making love on a full stomach – *the stag grows thin during the rutting season* and all that. And he'd always preferred sex to food. 'You have my sympathy,' he said. 'I've spent hours in lawyers' offices, my nose shoved in the worst side of humanity.' He shook his head at the memory. 'Still, I expect it will all work itself out, in time.'

From Kiki, a glum smile. 'You really are an American, my dear. Hopeful, optimistic. Some things here, believe me, *never* work out – lawsuits, property disputes, absurd legal entanglements – these things can go on for *generations*. I just want it over with.' She looked rueful for a moment, then said, 'You would have liked that house, we could have had a very nice weekend there.'

'I'm sure I would have, though I'd likely leave the boars alone.' A moment of silence, the waiter appeared with the cognacs, a napkin riding atop each glass. Stahl took a sip, pure fire all the way down, and said, 'So what have you been doing?' And then – strange what the mind did when you weren't watching it – 'Have you seen the baroness lately?'

Kiki seemed surprised. 'You know, I actually have seen her, that German witch, I was at her house for an afternoon card party.'

'You were?'

'Yes, trapped, you might say. She'd invited my crowd, girls who grew up together in the Seventh Arrondissement, went to the same school, la-la-la. I couldn't say no.' Stahl took out his Gauloises, offered one to Kiki, and lit both. 'That's just the way it is here. So we gossiped and laughed and tried to play bridge; I'm not very good at it, dreadful really. Anyhow, tell me about yourself.'

What about himself could he tell her? Surely not the truth, for, Gallic to the core, she had no desire to hear about personal problems and, beyond that, in the fogbound land of intrigue, he thought he'd rather not test her loyalties. 'Oh, life goes on,' he said, not without charm. 'I'm spending time out in Joinville, rehearsing. It's work, but it's the work I do and I like doing it. Most days.'

Kiki nodded. 'I hope I didn't interrupt your dinner, you *were* planning to eat, weren't you?'

'Actually I wasn't. I got tired of being in my room, thought I'd come down here and have a drink. Hotels are a kind of curse of the movie business, even very nice hotels.'

'It is a very nice hotel, isn't it, the Claridge. Or so people say.'

'You've never been there?'

'No, my dear, I haven't.' As she said this, her eyes met his.

'It's very, oh, *luxurious* would be one way to describe it. And quiet, when the traffic dies down at night.'

'And discreet, I'd imagine. Perfect discretion for all that money, which I imagine appeals to the guests.'

'Yes, one feels one can do . . . almost anything, really.'

'Anything at all, unknown to the prying eyes of the city,' she said, as though quoting from a certain kind of novel. She picked a shred of tobacco off her tongue with her red fingernails, then said, 'And do you find that – stimulating?'

'You know I *do*, Kiki,' he said, playing at sincerity, 'now that you mention it. Once the door closes . . .'

'One can only *imagine*,' she said. 'Like the little hotel we found, the night we had a drink at the Ritz.'

He smiled, acknowledging that he'd enjoyed it in the same way she had. 'Yes, lovers on the run, fleeing to an anonymous room.'

'But that's not the Claridge.'

'No, the fantasy there is quite different,' he said.

She'd slipped her shoe off, and a soft foot now rested on top of his. 'Oh yes? Well, I wouldn't know,' she said.

'Because you haven't been there.'

'No, I haven't.' The foot made its way up his leg, then returned.

The waiter appeared at the table, two menus in hand.

'We're just having drinks,' Stahl said. *'L'addition, s'il vous plaît.'*

At the Claridge, she would, to her 'surprise', be seduced; a proper, a time-honou red, hotel fantasy. *In all innocence, she accompanied him to his room, but, once there* . . . And she did, somehow, contrive to suggest the demure maiden. 'It's so terribly *warm* in here,' she said.

'It's the warm dress you have on,' he said. 'That's why.'

'But if I were to take it off . . .' Quite worried, Kiki.

'Oh you needn't be concerned,' he said. 'Not with *me*.'

'Well . . . ,' she said, uncertain, then took her dress off and draped it neatly over the back of a chair. 'There. That's better.'

And then, even half-stripped, in high heels and lacy bra and panties, she played the ingenue – explored the suite, room to room, discovering the flowers in a crystal vase, stroking the sleek wood of the escritoire, thrilled to be among such elegant things. Stahl followed her eagerly – she was a pretty woman, prettily made, champagne-cup breasts, derriere the classic inverted ace of hearts, swaying as she roamed about.

Eventually she wandered back to the bedroom, took off her shoes, and stood with feet together, head bowed, arms by her sides, at his mercy. Cautiously, he embraced her, but she was rigid, anxious, moved not an inch. By happenstance the mirror on the bedroom door was directly behind her, so he took the waistband of her panties between delicate fingers and turned down the back, the result especially provocative in the mirror. 'Oh,' she said, 'what are you doing to me?' He knelt before his victim and lowered her panties to her ankles, took them off, moved her legs apart, then, with his thumbs, more parting, and he touched her with his tongue. 'Oh no,' she said, *not that*. She kept her role in play, though it grew difficult, and in time he took her hand and led her to the bed *and there ravished her*. They both, Kiki and the virgin Kiki, did very much like being ravished, *her girlish passion at last released*. But by then she acted no longer, and let the guests in the rooms on either side of the suite know about it.

4 November. Fredric Stahl felt light and good that morning, a night of lovemaking an effective antidote to a sea of troubles. He'd come slowly awake at five, discovered a warm Kiki next to him, warmed her a little more, then fell back asleep. His interior go-to-work clock woke him promptly at 8.30, then, following coffee and croissants, he got a taxi, dropped Kiki off at her apartment, and continued out to Joinville. An exquisite autumn day, the sky its darkest blue, the North Sea clouds sharp-edged and white against it, the world would go on, life would get better.

Justine Piro was there when he arrived, as was Pasquin, who was his usual grumpy self but even he felt the sweetness of the day and said so. Jean Avila appeared a few minutes later, accompanied by his cameraman, and Renate Steiner, looking worried and harassed, stopped by, nodded to Stahl, and managed half a smile. She carried a thoroughly grimy straw boater with a crushed top and a torn brim, meant for Piro's desert scenes. Piro tried the hat on, became Ilona, the fake Hungarian countess, and delivered the line, 'I cannot go on like this for one minute more, gentlemen, I cannot, and I *will* not.' She was wonderfully arrogant and imperious, but the battered hat made her hauteur look silly and everyone laughed. Then they waited for Gilles Brecker, the Alsatian with blond hair and steel-framed glasses, the movie's lieutenant. At last, just when Avila had begun to look at his watch, Brecker came through the door.

Rather awkwardly, he came through the door, because his left arm was in a cast, carried by a sling. Nobody said a word, although Avila opened his mouth, then self-control won out and he remained silent. And they waited – politely, 'Good morning, Gilles' and such – until he took a breath and said, 'Please don't worry, it's only six weeks.'

Six weeks. 'You've broken your arm,' Avila said evenly. He'd tried for a simple statement of fact, but the accusation in his voice, though faint, was audible.

'My wrist,' Brecker said.

'Were you in an accident?' said Piro, a truly good soul, her expression kind and caring. She still wore the hat.

'Does it hurt?' Stahl said. He felt sorry for Brecker, but there was something about the sudden bad luck that nagged at him.

'I can work,' Brecker said defensively. 'It just takes getting used to.'

'All right,' Pasquin said, out of patience. 'What happened?'

'Well, I was out last night, I'd had a quarrel with my friend and I was very hurt, very angry, so I went up to La Fourche.' La Fourche, the fork, where the Avenue de Clichy joined the Avenue de Saint-Ouen, was infamous, a cluster of bars and bawdy nightclubs, a sexual bazaar where any and all tastes were easily accommodated. 'It was after midnight in this little place on the rue Saint-Jean and everyone was drinking, *really* drinking, and some sort of fight started between two men who were standing at the bar. It was dark, people were shouting, pushing and shoving, and someone swung a chair. I don't have any idea who he was trying to hit, but who he did hit was me. I hardly felt it, I thought I might have a bruise, and I got out of there, found a taxi, and headed home. But by the time I got there my arm was turning terrible colours so my friend took me down to the hospital on the Ile de la Cité, the doctor said it was broken, put the cast on, and gave me some pills.' Brecker stood there for a moment, clearly miserable, and said, 'I'm sorry, everybody, but it just *happened,* it was an accident.'

Was it?

The question hit Stahl hard and frightened him – *physical* fear, in the stomach. Was this an attack on *him*? Had the Germans sent a message? *We will destroy your movie.* He didn't know, maybe it was an accident, maybe he was seeing phantoms. But the suspicion was there and, he knew, it wasn't going to go away.

Now I have to do something.

In his mind he spoke the phrase, a pledge to himself.

On the set of the boulevard farce, the recovery began. Avila was already talking about shooting around Brecker once production started, somebody wondered if the lieutenant might have had his wrist broken at the prison camp, or perhaps it could be explained as an injury received in battle before the legionnaires were captured. Somebody else thought that idea might work if a dirty cloth were used to hide the white cast. But Stahl didn't really follow the discussion and didn't take part in it. He would finish the day's rehearsal, return to the hotel, and make a telephone call. In his mind, as the others went back and forth, he saw an image of the phone on his desk.

He called the American embassy and asked for Mme Brun, who quickly came on the line. Did he wish to speak to Mr Wilkinson? Thank you Mme Brun, but what he really needed was to meet personally with Mr Wilkinson. And it was urgent. 'I see,' Mme Brun said. 'Can you stop by at six this evening? I'm sure he'll have time for you.'

Stahl was there early, at 5.40, prepared to wait in the chair outside the office, but Wilkinson saw him immediately. Affable and welcoming, he said, 'Hey, Mr Stahl, come on in. We're fixing all sorts of problems today.'

Wilkinson's office itself, as Stahl sat across from the diplomat, was comforting. Somehow the most commonplace things – the oil painting of Roosevelt on the wall, the squash racquet in the corner, the bulky presence of Wilkinson himself – inspired in Stahl a sense of American strength which, at that moment, felt very reassuring. Stahl lit a cigarette, Wilkinson, jacket off, tie pulled down, lit a cigar and made notes as they talked.

Stahl held nothing back, sensing it was crucial to tell Wilkinson the truth, in detail. Wilkinson was a good listener, didn't interrupt, didn't react, but the best thing about the way he listened to Stahl's narrative was that he managed to give Stahl the impression that he'd heard all this before, it wasn't new, it wasn't as bad as Stahl feared. And there was more than a possibility that something could be done about it.

When Stahl wound down – Brecker's wrist, the fight in the bar – Wilkinson waited for a moment, then said, 'What do you want to do, Mr Stahl?'

'I wish I had more ideas,' Stahl said. 'But the one that stays with me is to go to the police, maybe the Sûreté, the Deuxième Bureau.' The counter-espionage service of the French military, which Stahl knew well from French novels of intrigue – Inspector Maigret, other heroes from other books, were often involved with the Sûreté. 'Until I talked to André Sokoloff, and earlier to you, I didn't appreciate the *scale* of this thing. I expect the secret services might be interested in what's going on.'

'Very reasonable, the very thing I would do if I weren't sitting behind this desk.' Wilkinson puffed at his cigar, making sure it didn't go out. 'But if you think it through, it may not be such a good idea. For example, the police, say a detective from the Eighth Arrondissement where your hotel is located. Somebody broke into your room, did he steal anything? Other than your peace of mind? That should come under some law but it doesn't.' Wilkinson smiled ruefully, Stahl nodded, rueful as well. 'And of course you informed the manager at your hotel.'

'I didn't.'

'Oh?' Wilkinson played the detective rather well, one eyebrow raised.

'I knew what would happen: a lot of flapping of hands and apologies and "*terrible!*" this and "*c'est insupportable!*" that and on and on, then nothing is done. In fact, what could they do?'

'And did you report the incident to the police?'

'Not that either.'

'So the next line is: 'Monsieur, I don't see how I can help you.' And to break into somebody's room is actually against the law. Will you tell the police you were forced to go to an irritating lunch at Maxim's?'

Stahl didn't bother to answer.

'Misrepresented by a newspaper interview? What law did that break? The law of newspaper honesty?' Wilkinson started to laugh, then said, 'I'm not being cruel, Mr Stahl, but you have to realize these people are no fools, they're not going to leave themselves vulnerable to the police.'

'And the Sûreté? This is, after all, part of a conspiracy against the state.'

Wilkinson's mood changed. He leaned back in his desk chair and clasped his hands behind his head, revealing damp circles on the underarms of his shirt. 'Do you keep secrets, Mr Stahl? Is that something that matters to you? Because what I am going to tell you is confidential – it's not a state secret or anything like that, but I'd rather people didn't know we talked about it.'

'I don't tell secrets,' Stahl said. 'I don't really know why I don't, it's just part of my character. Gossip is in the bloodstream of Hollywood, but I don't take part in it, in fact I really don't like it.'

Wilkinson pursed his lips, then nodded to himself, choosing to believe what Stahl had said. 'I think I may have told you earlier that the French know all about German conspiracies, but they do nothing. Here's an example, and it involves your friend Sokoloff, who is somebody who can be believed. Two years ago, in 1936, a German spy came to the offices of *Paris-Soir,* in fact to Sokoloff, and brought with him a stolen dossier. He was done with working for the German services and this was an act of – revenge? Idealism? Who knows. Now I never saw the dossier but I know, generally, what was in there. Names, dates, transactions, everything one would need for a determined counter-attack against Nazi political warfare. If that dossier had been made public, some very big heads would have rolled in this country. It would have *changed* things, shown Germany's real intention towards her neighbour. Conquest.'

'And? I can't imagine Sokoloff did nothing.'

'No, he did what he should have done, though not what every journalist would do – the spy chose prudently when he went to Sokoloff. The dossier, and a record of what the spy said, were passed to French military intelligence. And *then* nothing happened. This decision to do nothing may have a lot to do with the present state of French politics – some people can be accused, but others, higher up, can't be. They're too powerful. But that's a theory, my theory, and there could be all sorts of other explanations.'

'And the spy? What happened to him?'

'Vanished. As spies do. There was some talk that he went to London.'

'So, you're saying I shouldn't approach the Sûreté.'

'No, Mr Stahl, that may be something you should do, but not now. And, if you do, you should know that they might not respond. Better for you, at the moment, to think about the future, what comes next.'

'I wish I knew,' Stahl said. 'I'm going to have a drink after I leave here, but, beyond that . . .'

'You're going to work, you're going to make a movie. Now, speaking of the movie, I have to say that the possibility of an intentional attack on this man, Becker?' – he glanced at his notes – 'Brecker, in order to put pressure on you, is extremely unlikely. For someone to use a chair to break somebody's wrist in the midst of a brawl in a dark room, to be able to do this on purpose, is nearly impossible. If the chair had hit Brecker in the shoulder you would never even have heard about it. Not that they wouldn't try to damage the movie, they would, they would do just about anything you can imagine and some things you can't.'

Now Stahl felt better, realizing that Wilkinson probably had it right. 'I mentioned the festival of mountain cinema. If I don't go, what would they do?'

'You can find that out by not going.' Wilkinson paused, then said, 'There's no question of your going, is there?'

Stahl spoke slowly, saying, 'There wasn't, at first, the very idea of helping them was . . . sickening.'

'If you went it would certainly become known, here and in Hollywood. It might well damage your career, isn't that so?'

'The director, Avila, wouldn't like it, maybe the producer as well, he's hard to read. On the other hand, if I said that Warner Bros. asked me to go, they might not hold it against me.'

'Well, yes, but what about Hollywood?'

Stahl didn't answer immediately. Finally he said, 'They might not notice, it would happen far away, in Europe, and, if they did notice, they very well might not care. The studio executives may dislike the behaviour of the Nazi government but they still do business in Germany, all they can, it's a big part of the foreign market. The German exhibitors will only show certain films – they'll take nothing with politics, they like musicals, they like dancing peasants, buxom maidens, singing pirates – but those sell plenty. Germans love to go to the movies, it's encouraged, Hitler and Goebbels and Goering are big movie fans. Hitler has a passion for being seen in public with actresses, for being photographed with them, while Goebbels takes them to bed, and Goering's wife Emmy *was* an actress. All of which adds up to this: if I appear at a festival in Berlin it could be seen as publicity, nothing more.'

'But you hate the idea of going, don't you?'

'I hate the idea of doing what these people want me to do. And then, what will they want next?'

'That's worth considering – it wouldn't end there.' They sat in silence for a moment, then Wilkinson said, 'Are you tempted to go, Mr Stahl? Even if the attack on Brecker was an accident, you saw what might happen.'

From Stahl, a reluctant yes – a nod and a grim face. He would be backing away from a fight and he didn't like it.

'I believe,' Wilkinson said thoughtfully, 'that it might not matter if you went. A sacrifice, for your pride, but a sacrifice made for tactical reasons; for the movie, even for your country.'

Again, Stahl nodded. 'Do you know, Mr Wilkinson, the worst part of this whole thing?'

Wilkinson waited to hear it.

'Being attacked, and not fighting back. Just sitting here and letting them come at me.'

'That I understand,' Wilkinson said. 'But I hope you realize you're not the only one. I mean, *I* would never think badly of you for not fighting, I'm a *diplomat,* I make myself agreeable to some of the most vile people on earth, I smile at them, I make them laugh if I can, I sit next to them at state banquets where I listen to them boast and brag about their triumphs, and then I suggest another glass of wine and then another. To them, I'm the most genial fellow in the world. And they are murderers, vicious, filth.'

'Yes, but in time . . . In time you act against them, if you can.'

'Maybe. I do what I do on behalf of our government and, if the policy is to defeat them, then I will work hard at it, with pleasure.'

Stahl glanced at the window, which looked out over a darkened courtyard. Down below he could hear the sound of footsteps, maybe high heels, crossing the cobbled surface, and then a woman laughed.

'You mentioned something,' Stahl said, 'the last time we spoke, about information, about my telling you if I found out something interesting, maybe important.'

'What are you saying, Mr Stahl?'

'Perhaps I would discover something, if I went to Germany.'

'Oh I doubt that. What would you do? Meet a Wehrmacht general and try to get information? "Say, General Schmidt, how's that new tank performing?" Believe me, you'd just get into trouble.'

'Well, it was a thought.'

'Put it out of your mind, that's dangerous stuff, not for you.'

'Really? Why not for me?'

'Spying is a brutal business, and, if you get *caught* . . .'

'What if there's a war and France is lost? What if I might have done something, anything, even a small thing, and didn't? What would I think of myself? I put that as a question but the truth is I know the answer. These people, these Nazis, are scum, Mr Wilkinson, but from the perspective of being here, in Europe, in Paris, it looks to me like they're winning.'

'They are. Right now, today, they are. And that's from somebody who knows a lot more than you do.'

'But you say there's nothing I can do.'

'Oh, I didn't quite say *that*.'

ESPIONAGE

IN GERMANY, IN AUGUST OF 1938, A JEWISH ÉMIGRÉ COUPLE CALLED Grynszpan was informed by the authorities that their residence permits had been cancelled and they would have to reapply for permission to remain in the country. They knew they needn't bother; the Nazi government wanted to get rid of them, two among seventeen thousand Jews of Polish origin, all of whom would have to return to Poland. In March of that year, however, Poland had annulled the citizenship of almost all resident alien Jews in Germany and Austria. So the Grynszpans couldn't stay where they were, but had nowhere else to go. On 26 October, the Gestapo resolved this paradox by arresting twelve thousand Jews, taking whatever they owned, putting them in boxcars, then herding them across the border to the Polish town of Zbaszyn, where the Poles refused to admit them.

Stranded in a field outside Zbaszyn, the Jews were without shelter and had very little to eat. So the Grynszpans, desperate for help of any kind, sent a postcard to their son, Herschel, who had fled Germany in 1936, at the age of fifteen, and was living illegally in Paris. On 31 October, Herschel Grynszpan received the postcard but there was nothing to be done, not by him, not by anyone he knew. Unable to help the people he loved, he was caught up in that particularly volatile mix of sorrow and anger and, by 7 November, he could bear it no longer. With the last of his money, he bought a revolver and ammunition, took the Métro to the Solférino station, walked to the German embassy on the rue de Lille and told the reception clerk he wished to speak with an official. The clerk told him he would be seen by a junior diplomat called Ernst vom Rath and sent him upstairs. When Grynszpan entered the office, he raised the revolver and shot vom Rath five times. Grynszpan, a farewell postcard to his parents in his pocket, made no attempt to run away, and was arrested by the French police. Vom Rath was taken to the hospital, where he died on 9 November.

The Nazi leadership was enraged – the more so for being shocked. How could such a thing happen? A *Jew,* a member of a weak and degenerate race, had had the audacity to attack a *German*? Imagine! Jews didn't fight back, they were expected to be meek, and to suffer in silence. So Herschel Grynszpan's action was seen as a racial insult, an *intolerable* insult, for which the Jews must be punished. How? Minister of Propaganda Josef Goebbels met with Chancellor Hitler, and they determined that the German people would avenge the insult with attacks on the Jewish population – in Berlin, and throughout Germany. Thus, on the night of 9 November, at 11.55 p.m., an order was issued by the Gestapo:

BERLIN No. 234404   9 NOVEMBER, 1938

To all Gestapo Stations and Gestapo District Stations

To Officer or Deputy

This teleprinter message is to be submitted without delay:

1. At very short notice, *Aktionen* against Jews, especially against their synagogues, will take place throughout the whole of Germany. They are not to be hindered. In conjunction with the police, however, it is to be ensured that looting and other particular excesses can be prevented.

2. If important archival material is in synagogues, this is to be taken into safekeeping by an immediate measure.

3. Preparations are to be made for the arrest of about 20,000–30,000 Jews in the Reich. Wealthy Jews in particular are to be selected.

4. Should, in the forthcoming *Aktionen,* Jews be found to be in possession of weapons, the most severe measures are to be taken. SS reserves as well as the General SS can be mobilized in the total *Aktionen*. The direction of the *Aktionen* by the Gestapo is in any case to be assured by appropriate measures.

Gestapo II Müller

This teleprinter message is secret.

9 November. The Lufthansa flight to Berlin would leave Le Bourget Airport at 10.20 a.m. A photographer from the Paris office of the DNB – Deutsches Nachrichtenburo, the German press agency – was at the airport, waiting to photograph Stahl as he climbed the stairway that was wheeled up to the door of the aeroplane. *Starting early,* Stahl thought. *Very thorough, very Teutonic.* But it would be a good photo – the handsome movie star in fedora and trench coat, the caption to read, *American movie star Fredric Stahl leaves for Berlin.* 'Over here, Herr Stahl,' the photographer called out. 'Could you give us a wave?' Then, 'Thank you. Another?' Well, Stahl told himself, you'd better be

as good an actor as they say. Otherwise, the photo would reveal a very anxious man, going off to meet a bad fate.

In the plane, Herr Emhof was waiting for him, black-framed glasses tilted over his bulging eyes as he read his morning newspaper. 'Ah, here you are, right on time,' Emhof said as Stahl settled himself in a seat across the aisle.

'Good morning, Herr Emhof,' Stahl said. 'A good day for flying.' True enough. Despite a low sky heavy with Parisian cloud, it was, everywhere but in Stahl's mind, calm weather. Stahl wasn't surprised to find Emhof waiting for him, making sure his package would be delivered to Berlin, bringing his treasure home. Once Stahl had made the change-of-mind telephone call to Moppi – who'd been so excited Stahl could hear him breathing – he knew the machine would be put in motion.

For Stahl, some serious thought had gone into that call, a matter of tone. What he'd finally come up with was not precisely apologetic, something closer to *I don't really know why I made such a fuss about this*. 'I spoke with the publicity people in Paris,' Stahl told Moppi. 'And they thought it was a good idea. So, off to Berlin!' Frivolous. Devil-may-care. It doesn't matter. In fact, the newly cooperative Stahl had elected to stay a second night in his suite at the Hotel Adlon, so he could be honoured at the banquet opening the festival, then would announce the winners at a second banquet the following night.

What he'd told Moppi was, like any good lie, partly true. He *had* spoken to Mme Boulanger about the journey – he didn't want her surprised, if she found out, didn't want her to think he had secrets. And though he couldn't tell her what he was really doing, he could lie persuasively, and *confided* to Mme Boulanger that 'someone at Warner Bros.' had suggested he go ahead and attend the festival. But he'd prefer, if possible, that nothing appear in the Paris press. She'd thought for a moment, then said, 'I don't see that they'd care, when you think about it, it has nothing to do with France.' As long as no press release was issued in Paris, she suspected the event would slide past without public notice.

He'd told Jean Avila the same thing. Avila had grimaced, his loathing of Nazi Germany was no secret, but he understood Stahl's position and simply said, 'As long as you're back on time, to hell with it.' And then, he just couldn't resist, 'If they put you in a camp, be sure and send me a postcard. "Dachau at Sunset" maybe, if they have that one.'

Very funny. No, not so funny.

Emhof broke into his reverie. 'Are you feeling well, this morning?'

'I am,' Stahl said. 'And looking forward to the festival.'

With one finger, Stahl touched the inside pocket of his jacket, making sure, yet once again, that what he carried in there was still with him. He didn't need to touch the pockets of his trousers, those were so full he could feel them against his body. 'It's quite safe, that way,' Wilkinson had told him in the stacks of the American Library. 'They wouldn't dare to search you. Not *you*.' Wilkinson had spread his hands and smiled – *that's why you're valuable*. Still, there was some considerable bulk to the money, two hundred thousand Swiss francs in thousand-franc notes – a little less than fifty thousand dollars. And then there was the crucial ten-reichsmark note, in his shirt pocket. Stahl had wanted to go back over the whole thing, making sure he had it all right, but heavy footsteps were ascending the stairs and Wilkinson had laid his index finger across his lips and with his other hand had gripped Stahl's shoulder. *Goodbye. Good luck.* Strong, J. J. Wilkinson, perhaps he'd played football, somewhere in the Ivy League. Then the diplomat walked away down the narrow aisle, leaving the Dewey Decimal 330.94s, European Economies, for Languages in the 400s.

Grey mist whipped past the aeroplane window, stubbled fields and dark evergreens below when it cleared. Emhof, saying, 'Perhaps you'd like something to read,' handed Stahl the day's newspapers, German newspapers. *Well good,* Stahl thought, a diversion. But of course it wasn't. On top of the stack, *Völkischer Beobachter* – the nationalist observer – the Nazi party newspaper owned by Adolf Hitler. Or perhaps *Das Reich,* owned by Propaganda Minister Goebbels? Stahl settled on the *Deutsche Allgemeine Zeitung,* supposedly the choice of German intellectuals.

Stahl had read his share of Los Angeles tabloids; dreadful crimes and humorous gossip – humorous as long as it wasn't about you – and he'd grown up with an Austrian press that could be venomous and often was, but what he had before him was something new. Hitler here and Hitler there, Hitler and his cronies everywhere. What a newspaper! It grovelled and fawned, down on its knees in the hope that its lord and master would present a certain part of himself for a kiss. After ten minutes – news of sports: how mighty the German shot-putters, how swift her sprinters, how noble her soccer players – Stahl set the newspapers on his lap and looked out of the window, then closed his eyes and pretended to doze, avoiding a potential conversation with Emhof. But solitude, alas, led Stahl to brood about what lay ahead of him. So it was a long plane ride. A long, long plane ride.

On landing at Berlin's Tempelhof Airport, the traveller was met by a force not unlike a storm; a powerful and dangerous storm – on its tide you could be swept away into a dark sea and never be seen again. The most sacred phrase of the Nazi creed was *Blood and Soil.* Well, here was the soil, the German earth, and before you could set foot upon such precious stuff you had to face its guardians, its border post. Where the uniforms of the SS were a shade of black that seemed to glow in the light of the overcast afternoon. Their polished boots glistened, their faces like white stone. The Alsatian shepherds on chain leads – no effete leather for us! – were as watchful as their masters, and the black and red swastika flags were hung as stiffened banners, which the wind was forbidden to disturb. Stahl approached the customs officers but he never reached them – Emhof cut in front of him, produced an identity card, then took Stahl's passport and had it stamped. Wilkinson was right: Stahl was too important to search, and ignored the stares of the officers as he walked past, his pockets stuffed with money.

The car waiting outside the terminal was a black Grosser Mercedes, its chauffeur standing at attention by the rear door. When Stahl and Emhof were settled in the back seat, Emhof barked out their destination and the chauffeur responded as though he'd been given a military order. And if Tempelhof Airport had been a kind of overture, the city of Berlin, when they reached its centre, was the Wagnerian climax. Uniforms everywhere, brown-shirted storm troopers with puttees bloused out above their boots, Wehrmacht officers in field grey, the navy in blue, the Luftwaffe in blue-grey, women in fur coats, men in homburgs and overcoats, and all of them, to a greater or lesser degree, marched. This country was already at war, though enemy forces had yet to appear, and Stahl could sense an almost palpable violence that hung above the city like a mist. And although he was not actually frightened, the street show had brought him to a state of high alert.

Emhof glanced over at him and said, 'Not much like Paris, is it?'

'No, not at all.'

'As you can see, we are a very determined people.'

Berlin was, Stahl thought, a movie set, meticulously designed for effect. People who saw this place – visitors, or an audience watching a newsreel – might wonder what sort of fool would dare to attack such a country. A quote about Goering that Stahl had read somewhere suddenly came to him: 'He loves war as a child loves Christmas.'

His suite at the Adlon, the Bismarck Suite – and there he was, in a gold frame on the wall, heroically painted with heavy white moustache and Pickelhaube spiked helmet – had all the luxuries and all the conveniences; for example a telephone in every room. These, Wilkinson had warned him, had microphones that were always alive, sending conversation in the room back to some technician wearing headphones as he sat in front of a console with dials and a wire recording machine. Best, if you had to speak privately, to disconnect the phone from its receptacle in the wall. Stahl's suitcase had been taken from the plane and driven quickly to the Adlon and it had already been unpacked – and no doubt searched. His evening clothes, for that

night's banquet, then the party in his honour on the following evening, were hung carefully in the closet, his brush and comb and tooth-
brush laid out by the shining porcelain sink. He undressed, stretched
out on the bed in his underwear and worked to calm himself down. *So
far, so good,* he thought. It surprised him – how much he wanted to do
this work, and do it successfully. Getting out of the Mercedes at the
entry to the Adlon, as the chauffeur held the door, he saw a few civil-
ians passing by and one of them, a rather elegant woman of some age,
her chin held high in a near desperate attempt at preserved dignity,
wore a yellow star on the breast of her woollen coat.

Stahl dressed for the banquet, then transferred the money and ten-
reichsmark note to his evening clothes. As Wilkinson had put it, in the
still, musty air of the library stacks, 'If you leave this money in your
room, you won't be coming back to Paris.' On the day before he
boarded the plane, the resident seamstress at the Claridge had sewn a
large inner pocket into the lining of his tuxedo jacket, much roomier
than the one on the left side. He was now more than glad he'd had this
done, for there was only a small back pocket on the trousers. Even so,
he had to stash a few thousand Swiss francs in the back of his cummerbund. *So I will not be dancing the polka tonight.* Precisely on
time, he made his way down to the Adlon's grand ballroom.

Splendid it surely was. Vast chandeliers glittered above, the white
tablecloths were dazzling, endless ranks of silverware marched away
from the side of every golden service plate, the satin draperies were
blood-red, and the centrepiece on the elevated centre table held an
exceptional display of marzipan tanks and fighter planes.

Very carefully, to avoid a shower of Swiss francs, Stahl withdrew
his typewritten speech – written in Paris with Mme Boulanger's help
– from his inner pocket. Herr von Somebody, the official host, spoke
first, welcoming the bejewelled ladies and beaming gentlemen to the
Reich National Festival of Mountain Cinema, 'and tonight's banquet
in honour of Herr Fredric Stahl, who is to select the festival's winners.' There followed a flowery tribute to the Führer, 'who has made

all this possible.' Stahl was then introduced, and gave a short speech, thanking everybody in sight, citing the importance of cinema to all the world's cultures, and looking forward to choosing the best mountain film of 1938, 'though I expect, given the general level of excellence, that will be an extremely difficult task.' When he was done, the guests – there must have been at least a hundred – rose to their feet and applauded.

The banquet began with a thin, and absolutely delicious, potato soup. It had been a long time – back in his days in Vienna – since Stahl had tasted good German food, and he made himself hold back on the soup, sensing there were perhaps even better things to come. Wild boar from Karinhall, the Goering estate, said the giant, both-hands-required menu. Leaving the soup, Stahl turned to the lady on his left, Princess von Somebody, with diamonds dripping down towards the cleft of a snowy bosom.

With the arrival of the wild boar, Stahl turned to chat with the director of the festival, who sat across from him, the German film producer Otto Raab. Stahl had never met him, but as Raab talked about himself Stahl realized that he knew this man, knew him from experience. Likely he'd started his artistic career in the provincial theatre, a local genius who had, driven by ambition, gone off to the great city – Berlin in this case – there to discover he was no genius at all, at best a worker bee, so that his passion to succeed soured and turned to bitter resentment. How did it happen that these people, many of them Jews, communists, sexual deviates, were set above him? They were snobs, arrogant and sure of their talent, this so-called elite, but they were no better than he was. They succeeded because they knew the right people, they hobnobbed, they worked their insidious magic and rose to the top, where they looked down their noses at the struggling Otto Raabs of the world.

But with the Nazi ascent to power in 1933, the Otto Raabs of Germany perfectly understood what it meant for them. Now it was *their* turn. They joined the Nazi party, and success inevitably followed. Now look! A respected producer of films, wholesome films, *German* films, a powerful man snubbed no longer. Raab had weak, watery eyes, and in the way they fixed on Stahl as Raab recounted various triumphs, there was the purest hatred. Stahl was careful with him, gently encouraging, keeping condescension at bay. After he'd had all he could stand of Raab, he turned to the woman on his right, the highly acclaimed film actress Olga Orlova.

Stahl knew something of Orlova, who had a complicated history. She was said to be a descendant of the Russian novelist Lermontov, had trained in the great Moscow Art Theatre with Stanislavsky, had fled with the White armies from the 1917 Bolshevik revolution, landed on her feet in Germany, become a film star, and a great favourite of that madly passionate film buff Adolf Hitler. Who made sure that photographs of the two of them together appeared in newspapers and magazines.

Orlova was, like many actresses, not so much beautiful as striking, memorable, with plain, strong features, upswept dark hair parted to one side, and animated eyes. She may have been over forty but looked younger – smooth skin, a well-tended body in a lime-coloured evening gown that revealed the bare shoulders of an athlete. She wore a necklace and earrings of small emeralds and, as she talked, Stahl noticed she had slim, delicate hands. Her voice was low, and sensual in a way that Stahl couldn't precisely define – she spoke intimately, but she was no coquette.

She admired him, she said, she knew his films. How on earth had they managed to lure him to this incredibly boring event?

'I'm living in Paris now, making a film for Paramount, and my studio thought it would be a good idea.'

'Ah yes,' Orlova said. 'There's more to this business than the screen kiss.'

'That's true.'

'It's certainly true for me. I started out in the theatre, acted my little heart out, Chekhov, Pushkin, Shakespeare in Russian. But the Bolsheviks put an end to that, so now I am in movies.'

'And a celebrity.'

'That I am. I work at it, and important people here seem to like what I do.'

'Surely one *very* important person,' Stahl said.

Orlova's smile was ever so slightly grim. 'One is chosen, some-times, it's not up to you. But it's not bad to be adored, and he is infi-nitely polite.'

'To you.'

'Yes, to me.' She shrugged. 'We have no intimate life, though the world is encouraged to think otherwise.'

'And you don't mind?'

'Mind gossip? No, do you?'

'Now and then, but it comes with the profession.'

'And makes private life difficult. Still . . .' For a moment, her eyes caught his in a certain way. 'I find *you*, for example, quite interesting.'

'I'm flattered,' Stahl said. 'But for people like us, privacy is almost impossible.'

'Almost,' she said. 'But not quite.' She paused for a moment, then said, 'Where are they keeping you?'

'Here.' He pointed upwards. 'In the Bismarck Suite.'

'Well, well, the Bismarck Suite. Then you're just down the hall from me.'

'Really?'

'Yes, I've taken the Führer's suite for tonight. I don't believe he's ever been there, but the hotel keeps it exclusively for him.'

'Where is it?'

'Just down the hall. The number one hundred is on the door.'

'I hadn't noticed.'

'No reason to, but now you know. I'll leave the door ajar.'

From behind them, a waiter cleared his throat. Startled, Stahl and Orlova turned to face him. He was a wiry little man with oiled, slicked-back hair and a smug, almost triumphant smile on his face. 'Excuse me, meine Frau, mein Herr, may I take your plates, please?' The words were commonplace but the tone was just insinuating enough to let them know their conversation had been overheard.

'By all means,' Orlova said. Her voice was dismissive, and faintly irritated.

The waiter took their plates, moving from Orlova's right to Stahl's. 'It is a pleasure to serve such glamorous people,' he said. The insinuation in his voice was now plainly evident. 'My name is Rudi, by the way.'

'Thank you, Rudi,' Stahl said, turning back to face Orlova.

The waiter bowed politely and said, 'Some people are known to reward good service.'

'We'll remember that,' Stahl said. 'Now go away.'

After another bow, the waiter, a slight redness to his cheeks, went off towards the kitchen.

'Rude little bastard, isn't he. How much of that do you think he overheard?' Stahl said. He had a bad feeling in his chest.

'It doesn't matter,' Orlova said. 'I do what I want. My private life is my own affair, and certain people know that very well.'

'Then I'll see you later.'

'After I go upstairs, give me a half-hour.'

Stahl looked to his left, meaning to resume conversation with Princess von Somebody, but Orlova put a hand on his arm. 'By the way, a silly thing but I want to leave a little something for the maid. Do you happen to have a ten-reichsmark note?'

'I do,' Stahl said. 'I'll bring it with me.'

When Stahl saw the waiters clearing space in the middle of the ballroom, and a small orchestra began to set up, he realized it was time to go. He took Princess von Somebody's hand, bent towards it, touched her skin with his lips and said good evening. The princess made a disappointed little mouth and said, 'Will you not stay for the dancing?'

'Forgive me, your grace, but I'm very tired, and I must rise early and watch the movies.'

'I see,' she said. 'Then good night, Herr Stahl, it was a pleasure to meet you.'

Stahl realized she'd expected to spend the night with him, so wished her the most gracious good-evening he could manage. Next he looked for Orlova, who was nowhere to be seen, and then, needing a breath of fresh air, he walked through the lobby to the door of the hotel, stepped outside, and took a cigarette and a lighter from his side pocket. He was about to light his cigarette when he smelled smoke. Not woodsmoke from a fireplace, the other kind, where something is burning that shouldn't be burning. He looked over at the doorman, a giant in a coat with epaulettes, who stood nearby, rubbing his hands to keep them warm – it was a chilly night, with a cutting little wind from the north. 'Is something on fire?' Stahl said.

'No, sir,' the doorman said.

Stahl looked up the front of the hotel but saw nothing. The smell was getting stronger. For a few moments he waited, listening for sirens, but the night was quiet. Curiously quiet, there was no traffic on what was usually, even late at night, a busy street. 'You're sure?' Stahl said to the doorman.

'Yes, sir. I am quite sure. But when you have finished your cigarette, it would be better to remain in the hotel for the evening.'

Why? But Stahl said his thank you and lit his cigarette.

12.30 a.m. Stahl walked down the hallway, couldn't find the Hitler suite, then went back the other way and found a door at the end which faced the corridor, a gold plate inscribed 100 screwed to the polished oak surface. And yes, it was slightly ajar. He knocked lightly, then entered. He was in a foyer, through an open door he could see a bedroom, and a pair of legs with bare feet. Olga Orlova was stretched out on the bed, her gown hiked up above her knees. She rose to a sitting position and smiled at him. 'My lover at last,' she said, eyes amused.

'I'm here, my darling.'

'Yes, I heard your carriage arrive. Do you have my reichsmark note?'

Stahl handed it to her. She opened a small address book on the night table and spoke the bill's serial number aloud, consulting her book to make sure the numbers matched. 'Really,' she said, 'I don't see why we have to do this. I've surely seen you enough to know who you are.' She handed the note back to him and said, 'For next time.'

Stahl began to fish the Swiss francs out of his tuxedo pockets, then unbuckled his cummerbund, retrieved the rest, and set the stacks on the satin coverlet. 'A lot of paper,' he said.

'How much?'

'Two hundred thousand francs.'

'That's the right number, I'll count it later. The telephones are turned off by the way, so we don't have to play the love scene.'

'They listen to *Hitler's* phones?'

She shrugged. 'Who knows what they do. I'm sure they're watching your room, so you'd better stay for an hour while we make passionate love.'

Stahl found a chair in the corner and sat down.

Orlova gathered up the money and put it in a large handbag with a shoulder strap. 'My spy bag,' she said. She poked around inside, then drew out a sheaf of very thin paper with tiny, spidery writing from top to bottom and edge to edge and walked it over to Stahl. 'Here's what your friends are expecting. There's quite a lot of it this time, Orlova has been *terribly* social these last few weeks.'

'Thank you,' Stahl said.

'If I knew how to do it properly, I would spit,' she said. 'But they didn't teach girls to do that, not in Czarist Russia. Maybe they do now, in their USSR.'

'Why spit?'

'If you read what I brought you, and I don't think you're supposed to, you'd know why. These monsters are bad enough in public, but you ought to get a taste of them in *private*. You'd spit too.' She lay back down on the bed and put her hands over her eyes. 'I am tired, Herr Stahl, Fredric. For years.' She was quiet for a time, Stahl thought she might be going to sleep, but she sat up suddenly and said, 'Christ! The goddamn hotel's on fire!'

'No, I made sure it isn't, but something is.'

Orlova's eyes were wide. 'I know that smell, I know that smell from 1917, that's a burning *building*.'

'Yes, I think it is.'

After a moment she lay back on the bed again.

'I wonder,' Stahl said, 'will there be talk, about our being together up here? If they're watching my room they know I'm not in there.'

Orlova turned on her side to face him. 'Talk? Not from the hotel people. For one thing, you could be anywhere in the hotel – the staircase in the Adlon is famous for night-time visits, you don't have to use the elevator. And even if they suspected something, when it comes to Adolf and his circle they keep their traps well shut. As for the morons who are running the festival, all they know is that I arranged to sit next to you. So what? Maybe I want to go to Hollywood.'

'Do you?'

'I don't know. I've thought about it.'

'They like foreign stars out there – you could be the next Marlene Dietrich. Anyhow, in time you may decide to try it.'

Orlova rolled onto her back and rubbed her eyes. 'Not much time left, Fredric, based on what's in your pocket.'

'Do they speak openly, in front of you?'

'No, but they like to talk to each other in what they think is a sort of code; winks, and pokes in the ribs, and too bad we can't let you in on the big secrets.' She was silent for a moment, then said, 'Now I'm going to take a nap, you should wait for an hour before you leave.'

3.40 a.m. Stahl had found it hard to go to sleep, had read a third of his Simenon novel, decided to have a brandy sent up to his suite but thought better of it, not wanting to call attention to himself. Finally, sometime after four in the morning, he drifted off.

Then, something brought him sharply awake.

What could have happened? A noise? A nightmare? A noise, for now he heard it again: shattering glass. Something of considerable size, plate glass, like a shop window. And there it was again, somewhere down in the street. He rolled off the bed, went to the window, and moved the drapery just enough so that he could see out. He thought he heard shouting, more than one voice, then, across the street from the hotel, a shadow went past, running at full speed. He caught only a glimpse but, with eyes fixed on the street, he saw a group of men, five or six of them, more trotting than running. They disappeared in the same direction the shadow had taken. Hunting him? He stood at the window for some time but saw nothing else, only a glow in the eastern sky. And the smell of burning was now very strong; acrid, unpleasant.

The young woman wore her shining blonde hair rolled in plaits above her ears – she was a peasant after all and, in the movies, that was the way pretty peasant girls wore their hair. As they also could be counted on to wear a dirndl – a tightly fitted bodice and full skirt, this costume in baby blue and white, so pure was she, toiling her way up the side of an alp. She climbed with the aid of a stick and with her other hand held a small brass urn to her breast. Poor Hans was in there – his ashes anyhow – cremated after being shot by a Jewish gangster in the evil city where he never *ever* should have gone, in the mistaken belief that he had lost her love. The violins worked away and, as she at last reached the crest, the sun just now rising above the neighbouring mountain, here came, as Stahl had anticipated, a long blast on an alpine horn. Triumph! True, there were tears in the girl's eyes, but there was also a fierce determination, hope for tomorrow: in the new Germany, this sort of tragedy must never happen again!

The film ended. Stahl was sitting in the middle row of a positively baroque movie theatre in downtown Berlin, a theatre with plaster angels and sconces and loges and plush seats, where he'd been taken to judge the best of the mountain movies. Not really his decision, of course. Emhof, seated next to him, said, 'I think I needn't tell you that you have just seen the festival's finest work.' Stahl thought he detected, in Emhof's eyes, a certain moisture. Had he been moved to tears?

'So,' Stahl said, 'the winner is *Das Berg von Hedwig*?' Hedwig's mountain.

'If you agree,' Emhof said.

'Well, I do agree. An excellent production, good acting, fine music, and produced and directed by Otto Raab.'

'Yes, of course Herr Goebbels's deputy will make the announcement, as Raab is the director of the festival.'

'That shouldn't matter, when such quality . . .' Stahl left it at that.

Emhof nodded. Stahl hoped he could now escape for the rest of the day.

He'd seen the newspapers that morning, which had reported that some German citizens, angered at the murder of the diplomat vom Rath, shot dead by a Jew in Paris, had attacked Jewish synagogues, setting them on fire, and breaking the windows of Jewish shops. This action, the papers said, was regrettable, but certainly understandable. The police and the Gestapo, concerned about further Jewish violence, worried about conspiracies, had arrested between twenty and thirty thousand prominent Jews. Local Berliners, the reports went on, had taken to calling the event *Kristallnacht,* after the crystalline appearance of shattered glass on the streets of German towns and cities.

Standing up to leave the movie theatre, Stahl counted the hours he had to endure before leaving this place. The Grosser Mercedes was waiting in front of the theatre and as Stahl was driven through the city he could see – and could hear – the streetsweepers shovelling up the broken glass. By the time he reached the Adlon it was mid-afternoon and all he wanted to do was escape: have a couple of brandies and fall asleep. He ordered the brandies and collapsed into a chair. Then the telephone rang.

He answered by saying, 'Yes?'

'This is the front desk. There's someone here to see you, Herr Stahl, could you be so kind as to come downstairs?'

Somehow it didn't sound like a front-desk voice. 'Who is it?'

'Oh, please forgive the *inconvenience,* but the gentleman does not give his name.'

Stahl hesitated, then said, 'Very well, I'll be down in a minute.'

He put on his jacket and straightened his tie. As he went out the door, he could see the back of a man waiting for the elevator, who turned around when Stahl's door clicked shut. It was the waiter from the banquet, wearing street clothes, his mouth twisted into a triumphant smirk. 'Remember me?' he said. 'Bet you thought you'd never see *me* again.'

Stahl wondered how he'd managed to make a telephone call from 'the front desk', then appear at the elevator – he must have, Stahl thought, used an empty room on the same floor. 'Yes, I remember you, your name is Rudi. Is there something you want?'

'Can't you guess? I asked for a small gratuity last night but you dismissed me, didn't you. Like a dog. "Go away," you said. But maybe you'll change your mind, Herr Stahl, maybe you'll decide I ought to have something after all.'

The waiter had moved towards Stahl, was now close enough so that Stahl could smell beer on his breath. Taking a step back, Stahl said, 'Would you like it now?'

Rudi seemed mollified. 'Well, I would like it, better late than never, as they say. But now you've insulted me, so it won't be a small gratuity, more like ten thousand reichsmarks.'

Ambitious blackmail, Stahl thought, $5,000. 'How much?' he said.

'You heard me, Herr Stahl.'

'Where would I get that kind of money?' Stahl was almost amused.

'You're a rich and famous man, you have plenty of money. But if you can't get at it, you'll have to ask your Russian, your bitch-in-heat Orlova. She'll surely help you. Want to know why? Because she wouldn't want me talking about what went on last night.'

'I don't think she cares,' Stahl said.

'Doesn't she? All right, then I'll just have a chat with my brother-in-law, who happens to work for the Gestapo. Maybe you two were plotting against the Führer, who knows? But they'll find something, these gentlemen, because they can *always* find something.'

Now Stahl was alarmed. 'I see, yes, you're right, you should have what you want. But it has to be tonight, I'm leaving in the morning.'

Rudi moved closer and said through clenched teeth, 'You *think* you're leaving but that's up to *me*. So you have until six this evening, which is when I have to go to work. Or maybe you want to stay in Germany for a while, it's up to you, maybe you'd like . . .'

'Where would I meet you?' Stahl said.

'I have a key for room eight-oh-two, down the corridor. Knock twice, then once.' He turned on his heel and headed for the stairway, then spun around, his face contorted by the memory of a thousand insults. 'You'd better be there, *mein Herr.*' The last two words he snarled, enraged by the polite form, enraged that he'd ever used it.

Stahl returned to his suite. Moments later, the room waiter delivered his brandies. He drank the first one immediately and told himself to calm down. He had only a thousand reichsmarks with him – five hundred dollars – and there was no way he could get any money in Berlin. Well, one way. In case of emergency, Wilkinson had asked him to memorize a telephone number which could put him in contact with Orlova. Now Stahl composed himself, took the pad on the desk and wrote down the number, praying that he had it right. 'It is dangerous,' Wilkinson had said, 'to call this number, don't use it unless you absolutely have to.'

Stahl asked the hotel operator for a line, then dialled the number, which rang twice, three times, four, five. He looked at what he'd written on the pad – was it 4, 2? Or 2, 4? He was about to hang up when a breathless woman's voice said, 'Hello?'

It wasn't Orlova's voice. 'I'm sorry to disturb you . . .'

'Wait a minute, I was just walking the dog. *Mitzi, sit!* Now, you were saying?'

'Is Olga Orlova there?'

'No, she's not here. *Mitzi!* Goddamnit!'

'It's quite urgent,' Stahl said.

'She's my neighbour, across the hall. Do you want me to knock on her door?'

'Yes, please.'

'Who's calling?'

'Tell her Fredric.'

'Oh, I see. Like that, is it. Very well, give me a minute.'

Stahl waited, drank off the second brandy and stared at the phone. Then he looked at his watch, the second hand sweeping around the dial. Finally, the receiver was picked up and Orlova said, 'Who is this?' She sounded irritated but Stahl could hear that she was also frightened. In the background, a small dog was barking.

'This is Fredric Stahl, Madame Orlova. I wonder if I might ask you for a favour?' Stahl's eyes were fixed on the baseboard, where the telephone wire was connected to a small box.

'Oh, of course. Are you calling from, ah, the hotel?'

'Yes, I am. I was wondering if you might be able to come over here.'

'I suppose I could, is something wrong?'

'I must speak to the audience tonight, at the banquet where I will announce the winners of the festival. And I'm having a woeful time of it, writing the speech. I don't really know the film industry here, and I don't want to sound ignorant.'

'I'm not much good as a writer, Herr Stahl.'

'Even so, some advice would be helpful. Is it possible you could come soon? Maybe even right away?'

Orlova sighed, *the things I'm asked to do*. 'I'll be there as soon as I can. Maybe some day you'll return the favour.'

'You need only ask, Madame Orlova.'

They hung up. Stahl settled down to wait. It was nearing four o'clock. Once she arrived, and Stahl told her what was going on, she would have to find the money and be back by six.

Orlova was almost frantic when she reached the room. When he opened the door of the Bismarck Suite she didn't say hello, she said, 'What's happened?' Stahl told her the story, her reaction a mixture of disbelief, fear, and anger. '*That* little man? Rudi? Rudi the waiter?' *He dared?* Then she got hold of herself and said, 'I'd better leave now, you said ten thousand reichsmarks?'

She was back at 5.40. By that point, Stahl, unable to sit down, was pacing back and forth and smoking one cigarette after another. He'd left the door open and she came rushing in. 'Christ, I couldn't find a taxi.' She sat on the edge of the couch. 'Anyhow, I have it.'

'From your bank?'

She looked up abruptly: *are you crazy?* 'From an umbrella shop,' she said. 'There's money in this city that will never see a bank; Jewish money, criminal money, *Nazi* money. All those bribes and thefts and . . .'

Stahl looked at his watch, then up at Orlova. For the meeting she'd changed outfits: under her open raincoat a revealing sweater and a tight skirt, made all the more provocative by the accessories of a prominent woman of the city – red silk scarf, tight black gloves, gold earrings, Chanel No. 5, and dark sunglasses. She was now the movie star of a waiter's fantasies. At 6.00 p.m. precisely they left the room. Stahl could hear her breathing, and could sense in her a powerful tension, which seemed to grow as they walked along the silent, carpeted corridor. In a whisper, Stahl said, 'Can you calm down a little?'

She didn't answer. It was as though she was so intensely fixed on the meeting that she hadn't heard him. Instead, she pursed her lips and expelled a short breath, then did it again.

In an attempt to distract her he said, 'Do you know this room? Eight-oh-two?'

She started to answer then worked her mouth, as though it was so dry she couldn't speak. 'A small room, I'd guess. For a servant or a bodyguard.'

As they stood in front of the room, Stahl saw that her hands, holding her bag, were trembling. He patted her shoulder. 'Just give me the money,' he said. 'Let me do it, he doesn't need to see you.'

She shook her head, jerking it back and forth, brushing off his suggestion as though it were absurd and irritating.

Stahl knocked twice, then once.

From inside: 'It's not locked.'

Stahl opened the door. It was a small room, meagrely furnished. Rudi was sitting in a chair by the wall at the foot of the bed and was cleaning his nails with a clasp knife. He looked up at them and set the open knife on his lap. 'Hello, Rudi,' Orlova said. She was now quite amiable and relaxed.

'You have the money?'

'It's right here.' She took an envelope out of her raincoat pocket, walked over to Rudi and handed it to him, then waited while he counted the twenty reichsmark notes. 'All is good?' she said with a smile.

Rudi nodded, and started to get up. Orlova put a hand on his shoulder, which startled him. 'I'll just take another moment,' she said. 'Will you accept my apology?'

This was unexpected. 'Maybe,' he said, sulky and uncertain.

'And that also goes for me,' Stahl said. Rudi stared at him, not quite comfortable with his victory. 'It was a long evening,' Stahl explained, 'and I was tired and I . . .'

At this point in the apology, Stahl was interrupted by a low sound, *thuck,* saw the automatic pistol and silencer in Orlova's gloved hand and realized she'd shot Rudi in the temple. His head fell back against the chair, his eyes and mouth wide open, as though he were surprised to find himself dead. A bead of blood grew next to his ear, ran slowly down his cheek, then stopped.

Orlova started to twist the long tube of the silencer, unscrewing it from the pistol. 'This was never going to end,' she said. 'So I ended it. Get his clothes off, everything but his underwear, and put that little knife in his pocket.'

Stahl was frozen, staring at Rudi.

'Please,' Orlova said.

He nodded and went to work untying Rudi's shoes. Orlova took them and lined them up beneath the chair. Stahl handed her the socks, trousers – after trouble with Rudi's belt buckle – jacket, tie, and shirt. When he was done, he saw that Orlova had folded everything into a neat pile. 'This will go on the chair,' she said. 'You put him on the bed, I'll write the note.' She had brought with her a pencil and a sheet of cheap paper. Stahl took Rudi under the arms and pulled backwards, which tipped the chair over. 'Shh!' Orlova said. 'Christ, be *quiet.*'

He dragged Rudi up onto the bed, raised his head and slipped the pillow beneath it. Orlova set the pile of clothes on the chair and put the note on the night table. Stahl read the note, written in unruly script: *I can stand it no longer.* 'Will that do?' Orlova said.

Stahl nodded. 'Of course the police might wonder if it's really suicide.'

'They won't pursue it. This is a certain kind of hotel, if a waiter killed himself, or if someone else killed him, doesn't matter. Not these days it doesn't. And there's a good chance the hotel will get rid of the body themselves – who wants to talk to the police?'

Orlova stood at the door and looked critically at the scene in the room. Then she placed the automatic in Rudi's hand, made a dent in the other pillow, as though a head had rested there, took a little bottle of perfume out of her bag and put a drop or two on the sheet below the dented pillow. 'What do you think?' she said.

'It looks like his lover bid him goodbye, then he shot himself.'

She took one last look around, then remembered to leave the pencil by the note. She looked at Stahl and said, 'It had to be done. In time, he would have denounced us, just as he said he would.'

Stahl nodded.

'I'll be going,' Orlova said. 'Enjoy the banquet.'

He got through it. As the grinning faces came to greet him, as medals caught the light of the chandeliers, as Goebbels's deputy spoke at great length and flattered him and flashbulbs popped, as he read out the names of the winning films. Otto Raab was deeply moved when Stahl, after a dramatic pause, announced that *Das Berg von Hedwig* had won the grand prize, a gold Oscar-sized statuette of a mountain with a movie camera on top. Stahl delivered his speech – a tepid joke about the lion at the Berlin zoo drew a great roar of laughter. He ended with praise for the Reich National Festival of Mountain Cinema; it was only the beginning, many more festivals would follow, as German film-makers climbed to the summit of their craft. When he was done, Goebbels's deputy presented him with a two-foot-high crystal sculpture of an eagle, a Nazi eagle, head and beak in profile, stiff wings outstretched, its claws holding a swastika in a wreath. The hideous thing was incredibly heavy, Stahl almost dropped it, but held on.

The morning flight from Tempelhof landed at Le Bourget at 2.30 p.m. There was a little bar in one corner of the terminal building where uniformed customs officers and airport workers in *bleu de travail* smocks took time off during the day. They stood at the zinc bar, drank red wine or coffee, smoked – there was always one with the stub of a Gauloise stuck to his lips – and talked in low voices. As the exhausted Stahl entered the terminal – carrying the paper-wrapped eagle, Orlova's notes in his jacket pocket – he was met by the smell of coffee and cigarettes and the sound of quiet conversation and thanked God that he was back in France.

Production for *Après la Guerre* began that afternoon, 11 November, with scenes that could be shot on sets built in the studios at Joinville, and a few exteriors using local settings. Location shooting was now to take place in and around Beirut, where it would be 'summer' – sunshine and blue sky – in December, so Deschelles and Avila were pleased with the weather, the cold rain and gloom of November, appropriate for scenes in the Balkans as the story wound to its finale. Some trouble with the screenwriters here, the script specified a death scene for Stahl's Colonel Vadic but Deschelles argued that they couldn't kill off *Fredric Stahl,* so it would have to be rewritten. He *almost* dies but, nursed back to health by the loving false countess, he survives. Avila argued the other way, Deschelles allowed him to lose gracefully, and in return agreed to ask Paramount for money to shoot the Hungarian castle scenes in a Hungarian castle.

The first time that cameras rolled in a film was traditionally a superstitious moment for the cast and crew, an omen of what was to come. Avila was smart, and chose a scene that he felt would go well – Pasquin's comic night of love with a heavy-set Turkish woman, the wife of a local policeman. The script called for a dog that had to

scratch at a bedroom door – the husband was on the other side, un-
aware that his wife had returned home, unaware that she was in bed
with Pasquin's sergeant. For this scene Avila had chosen a French
bulldog, a good character to play against the roly-poly Pasquin.

But the dog wouldn't scratch at the door, it simply stood there like
a rock while its trainer, on the other side of the door, called out first
commands, then baby-talk endearments, and finally tried to tempt it
with hazelnut ice cream, its favorite treat. Time went by, a certain
anxiety began to spread through the people on the set, a half-naked
Pasquin sat up in bed and shouted, 'Scratch the fucking door, goddamn it!' but the bulldog merely turned its head towards the source of
the noise and broke wind. *That* relieved the tension – the 'Turkish
wife' laughed so hard that tears rolled down her chubby face and her
make-up had to be reapplied.

At last, one of the prop men came to the rescue, with a trick he'd
seen in other productions. From his prop room he produced a stuffed
toy, a tabby cat. When he showed it to the dog, the animal went crazy,
it *hated* cats, and the prop man only just managed to snatch the toy
away before it was savaged. Avila was now poised to call out 'Action',
the cameraman was ready, the trainer took the tabby cat outside the
room and closed the door, and the dog stood there. Immediately, a
conference was held – do without the scratching at the door? From
Avila, an emphatic *no*. So the prop man tried one last thing: he pushed
the cat's tail beneath the door and when the trainer released the bulldog it galloped towards the tail and, when the prop man on the other
side whisked it away, the dog scratched at the door as though he was
trying to tear it to pieces. The cameras rolled, the policeman's wife
said, 'Oh my God, he smells my husband,' Avila said 'Cut!' and the
cast and crew applauded.

They were on the set until 5.30, Avila had met his day's quota – two
minutes of film – and Stahl, though he ached to go back to the Claridge and get into a hot shower, had one final chore ahead of him. Renate Steiner was expecting his appearance at her workroom in

Building K. Colonel Vadic had to wear, at several points in the film, a thin cotton long-sleeved undershirt with buttons at the top – a khaki-coloured garment meant to look like Foreign Legion issue. This could not be bought in Paris, so a seamstress ran one up, a duplicate to follow once Stahl had a fitting.

It was a long walk to Building K in the cold fading twilight but Steiner's workroom was warm, heated by a small charcoal stove in one corner. And Renate was glad to see him – a sweet smile, kisses on both cheeks. 'You seem to be doing better,' Stahl said. 'The last time I was here . . .' She'd been in tears with husband trouble.

'I'm sorry,' she said. 'One's personal life . . . But everything's different now.'

'You've made up? Your husband found a job?'

'My husband found a girlfriend,' she said. 'And off they went. I was miserable for a week, then I discovered how relieved I was to have him gone – thank heaven for sexy little Monique! Oh, that sounds terribly cold, doesn't it.'

'Not to me.'

She shrugged. 'If we hadn't had to run away from Germany everything might have been all right but . . . that's just what happened.'

'You do seem different,' Stahl said.

'Freedom,' she said. 'It's good for me. Now, Fredric, would you be so kind as to take off your shirt? You can go behind the curtain if you like.'

Stahl took off his sweater, then unbuttoned his shirt and hung it over the back of a chair. He was just muscular enough, no bare-to-the-waist pirate but not at all soft, that he didn't mind being seen in his skin. Steiner held the khaki undershirt up by its shoulders and showed it to Stahl. 'What do you think?'

'I like it.'

'It's your women fans who must like it, so it should show the outline of your shoulders and chest, then loosen a bit as it falls to the waist.'

'What do I wear down below?'

'Uniform trousers, then civilian trousers. These were voluminous

in the script and tied with a string but that's just writers, Avila wants
to show your bottom half. Now it's Gilles Brecker who gets the big
trousers. How is his wrist, by the way?'

'We're shooting around him for another two weeks, then he'll be
fine.'

Stahl slid the undershirt over his head; Renate had perched on a
high stool and lit a cigarette, shaking the match out as she looked
critically at the fit of the shirt. 'Can you turn sideways?'

He did.

'Now the back.'

He turned his back to her.

'Not bad,' she said. 'For a first try.'

She put her cigarette out in an ashtray and, pins in mouth, set
about refitting the undershirt. She was very close to him, he could
smell some sort of woodsy perfume, and when she reached up beneath the shirt her hand was warm against his skin. 'If I stick you just
yell,' she said, her words slurred by the pins in her mouth.

'I will,' Stahl said.

She kept on fussing with the shirt, stepping back for a look, then
repositioning the pins to move a seam. Stahl hitched up his trousers
because, to his surprise, not an unpleasant surprise, he'd become excited and he didn't want her to see it. 'What are you doing?' she said.

'Pulling up my pants.'

'Well, don't. Just stand still.' Then she said *'Merde!'* and withdrew her hand, a drop of blood on the ball of her index finger. This
she put in her mouth for a moment, took it out and pressed her thumb
against it. Looking for something to cover the pinprick, she walked
over to her work table. Stahl couldn't take his eyes off the back view.
She wore, as usual, a smock over a long skirt, which should have hidden the motion beneath but didn't quite. He hadn't noticed this the
last time he'd seen her – was she wearing a different skirt? Had she
changed for his eyes? That idea he liked very well but he knew it was
wishful thinking. Probably.

At the table she found a strip of adhesive tape, tore off a piece
with her teeth and stuck it on her finger. That done, she mumbled,

'Goddamn thimble,' and went rummaging through mounds of fabric, retrieved only a scissors and a magazine photo, then gave up. She turned, walked back and stood in front of him. 'You can take it off now,' she said. 'I'm sorry this took so long.'

'I don't care.'

'I expect you want to go home and have a drink.'

'I do.' Then, after a moment, 'Is there anything here?'

'There is, but . . .'

'But what?'

'I have Strega.'

'Strega!' *Of all things.* 'The witch,' he said, translating the Italian word. It was a liqueur made of mountain herbs, secret herbs – a strange taste, sweet at first, then something more.

She walked over to a cabinet, took out a bottle of Strega and two cloudy glasses, poured some thick, dark-gold liqueur in each, returned and handed him a glass. *'Salut,'* she said.

'To us,' he said and immediately regretted it. He was acting like a teenager.

'Yes,' she said. 'To us. You like it?'

'It's been a while since I've had it.'

'Myself I like it.'

'I like it too.'

'Good. Want some more?'

'Please.'

'Aren't you getting cold?'

'Not at all. I don't mind being undressed.'

'Hm. Well . . .' She took the undershirt back to her table and said, 'You've been very patient.'

He put his shirt back on, buttoning it as he walked over and stood next to her, their shoulders almost touching. For a moment, neither of them moved, then Stahl said, 'I guess I should go.'

'I will need another fitting once it's been resewn.'

'When is that?'

'Oh, tomorrow. Can you stop by when the filming's over?'

'I'll see you then.'

Stahl found a taxi on the street that bordered the studio and, set-tled in the back seat, felt the excitement of a man who'd found trea-sure. He'd been drawn to her the first time they met but she was married, off-limits. He had wondered what it would be like with her, then let it go. But when she'd told him she was free, when she'd flirted with him . . . She had, hadn't she? He hoped so because now he really wanted her, he wanted to fuck her – it was the same heat he'd felt as a schoolboy. What was it that reached him? What? She was no pinup girl, more the opposite: the minister's prim daughter, the well-curved spinster beneath the spinster skirt. In fact, Renate Steiner wasn't any-thing like that, she was a sophisticated, intellectual woman. That was her inner self, no secrets there, but her *outer* self, her face with its pointy nose and pale forehead, her concealed shape, *was* that of the fantasy spinster. And Stahl, after weeks of Parisian glamour, after the erotic tricks of Kiki de Saint-Ange, discovered that, at least for the mo-ment, he was again *sixteen*, and hot for one of the plainer girls in the school. Would she do it with him? In the back seat of the taxi it was already *tomorrow night* and his imagination undressed her: she would touch not one button, one popper, one waistband of her clothing.

There was a crowd of people in the street as they drove up the Champs-Elysées and the driver had to slow down and work his way through them. A few held signs, NEVER AGAIN and SAVE THE PEACE, and Stahl realized it was 11 November, Armistice Day, celebrating the end of 'the war to end all wars'. There'd no doubt been a military parade, an official parade, earlier in the day; this was just a crowd of people – workers, students, middle-class Parisians – who'd made a few signs. The driver asked Stahl what he thought about the march and Stahl said, 'Who doesn't want peace?' The driver turned halfway round and said, 'Amen to that, monsieur.' But to Stahl it was a dream, a hope. He'd seen Germany, and he knew there would be war.

The night of his return to Paris he'd met J. J. Wilkinson, as planned, in the waiting room of the American Hospital in Neuilly and, in the hallway by the WC, handed him Orlova's notes. They were together only a moment, but Wilkinson had said, 'You'll be invited to a party on the night of the eleventh, please be there if you can manage it and we'll have a chance to talk.' Stahl's time with Renate Steiner had, until this moment, undone his memory but now he realized he would have to go. The party was being given by an American woman, her name sometimes in the society columns, a longtime expatriate married to a French aristocrat. Oh well, he would at least have his hot shower at the Claridge. His heart sank a little, at the idea of going to a party, but the people marching in the street cured that. Going to a dinner party was the least he could do.

Wilkinson wasn't at the party. A dozen well-dressed people and a vast centerpiece of white gladioli, but no diplomat. A disappointed Stahl did the best he could, chatting right and left, telling a few movie stories, getting a laugh or two, resisting the urge to look at his watch. After dessert, as he headed dutifully off to the library for brandy and cigars, the hostess appeared by his side and said, 'There's a staircase behind that door at the end of the hall. Your friend is waiting upstairs.' She smiled at him and her eyes twinkled – nothing quite like a little intrigue.

The apartment was a duplex – there were a few of these in the Sixteenth Arrondissement – and J. J. Wilkinson, drink in hand, tie pulled down, was waiting for him in what had once been a small bedroom for a child – a model aeroplane, a Spad fighter, hung on a cord from the ceiling light fixture, and boys' books, *Poppy Ott and the Stuttering Parrot,* filled the bookcase. Wilkinson was sitting on a narrow cot covered with a camp blanket and rose to give Stahl his powerful handshake. 'First of all, thank you,' he said.

Stahl sat on the other end of the cot and told the story of his time in Berlin. Wilkinson made notes, interrupting only to make sure he had the names right. Stahl tried to be thorough, and hesitated only when it came time to tell Wilkinson about Rudi – was it wise to confess he'd helped to commit a murder? But to keep it secret wasn't a possibility – he had to trust Wilkinson. 'Now,' he said, 'this next part is difficult, but it happened, and you ought to know about it.'

Wilkinson nodded, took a sip of his drink, and said, 'Might as well.' *What could be so bad?* But when Stahl described what had gone on in room 802, Wilkinson sat bolt upright, his eyes widened and he said, 'Good God.'

Stahl shrugged. 'She had to do it, she said something about "this will never end", and she was right.'

'Yes, but . . .'

'I know,' Stahl said. 'I saw it, but I couldn't believe it was happening.'

Wilkinson reached over to the windowsill, took a half-smoked cigar from a clamshell and, after several tries, got it lit. 'I'm shocked,' he said, 'but maybe not *that* shocked, now that I think about it. People talk about tough women, "a tigress" and all that, but Orlova is the real thing.'

'You've met her?'

Wilkinson shook his head. 'She sent a friend to see someone else at the embassy. Everything after that was in letters carried by hand. But, to do what she does, under the nose of the Gestapo . . .'

'Anyhow,' Stahl said, 'I trust her report was worth it.'

'Not up to me, Fredric. But I suspect it'll be useful.'

Useful? 'I mean, fifty thousand dollars – I assume the government wouldn't spend money like that unless it was very important.'

Now Wilkinson stopped. He took a puff on his cigar, blew the smoke out, and stared at Stahl, trying to make up his mind. 'Very well, I think you've earned the right to hear a little more about this. I don't know what I'm supposed to tell you, or what stays secret – the truth is I don't know what the hell I'm doing, I have to make it up, to improvise, as I go along. Just promise me you'll keep your mouth shut – I don't mean to be rude, but no point in mincing words.'

'You have my promise,' Stahl said. 'I am *not* going to talk about it.'

Wilkinson nodded, but he was clearly uncomfortable. 'First of all, this is not government money. The USA doesn't spend money like that, maybe it should, but it doesn't. The money is, umm, donated? I guess that's the word. The Department of State and the military spend a little money for information but nothing like this. With Orlova, we don't even know where it *goes* – it's not some kind of sale, she demanded the money and we found a way to get it into Germany. Maybe she keeps it, maybe she pays agents of her own, maybe she gives it to the Reds.'

'The Reds? She's a Russian spy?'

'Who knows. Circumstantial evidence says she could be. She's got family, prominent family, still in Russia, I can't believe the Bolsheviks just let her pal around with Hitler and his crowd.'

'She works for you, she works for them . . .'

'And God knows who else.'

'But she doesn't get caught.'

'No she doesn't, and you just saw why.'

'I guess I did,' Stahl said. 'But still, the information is important.'

'Very important. We don't have a political spy service, but, um, people have to know what's going on.'

'People?'

Wilkinson pointed up at the ceiling with his index finger. 'People who live in a big, white, house, those people. Oh what the hell, *that* person.'

'The President.'

'Yeah, him.'

Stahl was sufficiently impressed that he had no idea what to say. At last, he managed a quiet 'Oh.'

From Wilkinson, a thin smile. 'America is isolationist, he isn't. America doesn't want to fight, he does. But he can't, politically can *not,* and what truly hurt was the appeasement at Munich – all over the US the sentiment was, "if the Europeans don't want to fight Germany, why should we?"'

'They don't know what goes on there,' Stahl said, more passion in his voice than he intended. 'If they did . . .'

'And if my grandmother had wheels she'd be a cart,' Wilkinson said. 'It's not that Americans don't know what goes on, endless articles have been written in the liberal press, in small magazines, but that has no effect on the population – people in small towns, "just plain folks", as they say. So FDR and the people around him are looking for an opening, some damning intelligence that lets the American people know *they're* threatened, not just some Frenchy with a moustache. The army and navy attachés do their jobs, they count aeroplanes and cannons and ships, but the president needs to know what the Nazis are up to, and he's enlisted his friends, rich and powerful friends, to learn what goes on. They have money, and plenty of nerve, and there's at least a chance they'll find something.' The cigar had gone out, Wilkinson looked at it in disgust and squashed it into the clamshell.

'I didn't set out to be in the Foreign Service, Fredric. As I told you earlier, I'm a Wall Street lawyer. But they got me appointed Second Secretary and here I am. Why me? Well, my mother's people came from Holland, a long time ago, we're one of those old Dutch families up the Hudson River and we're distantly related to the Roosevelts. This work is, as I said, improvisation, so we use whoever's around, if we can trust them.'

'Even movie actors,' Stahl said.

'Movie *stars*, Fredric.'

'At one point, I don't think I mentioned it, Orlova gave me back the ten-reichsmark note and said something like, "for next time". Is there a next time?'

'I don't know, maybe. Would you do it again if I asked you?'

'Whatever you want,' Stahl said. 'You know where to find me.'

12 November. Heading off for work, Stahl was beckoned by the clerk at the front desk, who handed him a letter from America. The return address said *The William Morris Agency,* with an address in Beverly

Hills that Stahl knew well. His agent, Buzzy Mehlman, had scrawled a note on agency stationery: 'Attaboy, keep up the good work! Buzz.' The note was accompanied by a clipping from the *Variety* gossip column where the phrase *we hear* headed every item.

> WE HEAR that Fredric Stahl's new film for Paramount France, *Après la Guerre,* has started production in Paris and that leading man Stahl is working hard at publicity for the European market.

Stahl was relieved. Apparently he needn't have worried what impression his trip to Berlin made back home. A deft hand, in the press release: he hadn't been in Germany, he'd been in *Europe*. Someone, somewhere, had protected him.

Out at Joinville, the day crept by at tortoise speed. Stahl couldn't stop thinking about what would follow the day's shooting – a visit to Renate Steiner's workroom in Building K. Script in hand, he went through the scene he'd play once the cameras rolled but, no matter how hard he tried to concentrate, his mind summoned images of what he hoped for that evening.

In the studio, a hayloft set had been built and here the legionnaires would spend the night – supposedly in Roumania, just across the border from Hungary. In this scene, Justine Piro's false countess Ilona and Stahl's Colonel Vadic first discover they are falling in love. Pasquin's and Gilles Brecker's characters have gone off to search for food, Ilona and the colonel are alone. Outside the hayloft window, the lighting designer had created twilight, the soundmen would provide distant rumbles of thunder, and the music, added later, would complete the illusion.

Ilona, in a black cotton dress, her hair worn loose and artfully disordered, is lying on her side in the hay, her head propped on her hand, the colonel sits with his arms clasped around his knees. The first shot took a long time to set up – Avila wanted Ilona's face lit a certain way and the spot had to be adjusted again and again until he was satisfied. Then, when he had what he wanted, there was a problem with the camera. Meanwhile, dust from the hay made Stahl and Piro sneeze, and Stahl's back started to hurt every time he got himself into position.

At last, the camera was ready and Piro delivered Ilona's line: 'You know, I was a little afraid of you, at first.'

In the distance, the thunder rumbled.

'Afraid? Of me?'

'Cut!' Avila shouted. The spot lighting Ilona's face was flickering on and off. 'Louis, we need another bulb.'

'It's not the bulb, chief.'

'Where's the electrician?'

'He's wiring the other set.'

'Would someone go and find him, please. *Quickly.*'

And so on, for hours. Every time they got something to work, something else didn't. Or a line was fluffed, or the thunder was too loud.

By three-twenty, Avila had had enough. 'The gods are against us today,' he said. 'We'll start here in the morning; nine-thirty sharp, everybody.'

Finally, Stahl thought. He felt drained, but some Strega and conversation in Building K would fix that, he just needed time to recover. Then, as he was headed to his dressing room to change out of his uniform, one of the studio office workers handed him a telephone message. *Wolf Lustig's office in Berlin telephoned, can you please call them back as soon as possible.* There followed a telephone number.

Stahl's first reaction was irritation – what the hell did *he* want? Stahl had never met Wolf Lustig but he knew who he was: one of the most prominent producers at the UFA studios in Babelsberg – Germany's Hollywood – and UFA was the biggest, and now almost the only, film company in Germany. Taking off his uniform tunic, Stahl wondered if he had to call back, then put off deciding until the morning. What would Wolf Lustig want with him? By the time Stahl had brushed his hair, he thought he knew. This was not film business, this was Emhof business, Moppi business. Somewhere in his mind, Stahl had decided that once he was done with the festival, those people would be done with him. *How naive,* he thought. Now the decision to call back would have to be taken in a different light. No, he thought, now he would have to call back, because that was 'Wilkinson business'.

Outside, the late-afternoon sun had broken through, shafts piercing the rain clouds, and the wet tiles on the roof of Building K shimmered in the light. The door to Renate Steiner's workroom was open, Stahl looked in from the threshold and called out, 'Hello? Renate?'

The response was a small shriek. Renate was standing on the platform in front of the mirror, in profile to Stahl, wearing a peasant blouse, panties, garter belt, black stockings, and no shoes. She hurried for the shelter of the curtain, leaving Stahl with an image of very white, full thighs and well-shaped legs. 'I'm sorry,' he said, 'I . . .'

From behind the curtain: 'Why are you so early?'

'Avila let us go.'

'Close your eyes.'

He heard her walking quickly, then opened his eyes to see her wrapped in the blue smock. 'Shall I try the entry again?'

She laughed. 'Bad boy, you surprised me.'

'I am sorry, I didn't mean to . . .'

'Oh it doesn't matter. Your undershirt's on a hanger by the platform. Why don't you try it on while I get decent.'

Stahl took off his blazer and shirt and pulled the undershirt over his head. In the mirror, the undershirt fit perfectly, falling just so across his shoulders. Meanwhile, Renate was again dressed as usual. As she approached him, he saw a faint rose colour on her cheeks. The glimpse he'd had of her had aroused him, the blush did nothing to change that. Renate stared at Stahl's image in the mirror, put her silver-rimmed glasses on, then took them off. 'What do you think?' she said.

'It's perfect.'

She took the bottom of the shirt and shook it, then let it fall back in place. 'Can you take a little walk for me?'

Stahl squared his shoulders in Colonel Vadic's military posture, walked to the wall, turned, stood for a moment, then walked back to the platform. 'Looks good to me,' Renate said. 'I won't keep you – I'm sure it's been a long day.'

'Well, you're not keeping me, but I imagine you have work to do.'

'First I'm going to have a cup of tea, would you like one?'

'You can make tea?'

'I have a hot plate. I can live for *days* in here if I have to.'

'A cup of tea would be very welcome.'

In the back of the workroom, she put a pot of water on a hot plate. 'I didn't mean to . . . shock you. I just bought that blouse and I wanted to try it on.'

'What's the verdict?'

'It's awful, I have to take it back. I don't know what came over me in the store.' They waited as the hot plate element began to glow orange. 'How was your time in Germany?' she said.

'Worse than I expected. How did you hear about that?'

'Somebody on the set mentioned that you'd gone – is it a secret?'

'No. Warner Bros. wanted me to go, they saw it as a boost for the German market.'

'Still, I was surprised . . . that you let them use you, use your reputation. And that you'd have anything to do with the Nazis.'

'I held my nose, and did what I had to do.'

'What's it like there, now?'

'Surreal. All these monsters strutting around as though they owned the world. And then, the night I was there they burned down the synagogues.'

The water boiled, Renate took a spoonful of tea from a canister, then added water to a small, chipped teapot. 'Now it must steep,' she said.

'You don't think badly of me, do you? For going there?'

'It doesn't matter what I think,' she said.

'To me it does,' Stahl said. She glanced at him, her faded-blue eyes found his, a momentary uncertainty in her expression, then she looked away. 'I was wondering,' Stahl said, the words deliberate, 'if later on . . . Would you like to go somewhere? Get something to eat?'

'Mm. I'd like to, but I don't think I can. I have to go home, then I'm going to see friends. You remember Inga and Klaus? My émigré friends?'

Stahl was blank, then did remember – they'd arrived on bicycles the night when it seemed Germany would go to war with Czechoslovakia. 'I do,' he said.

'An émigré evening,' she said. 'I don't really look forward to it. Now let me pour you some tea. Do you take sugar? I don't have milk.'

They talked for a while, mostly about the movie, until Stahl felt it was time for him to go. He thanked Renate for refitting his costume, and for the tea. She walked him to the door, said goodbye and turned her face upwards, expecting the Parisian kiss on each cheek. Then Stahl, for a moment, touched her lips with his. As he drew back, he saw the same look in her eyes, now not so much wary as hurt. That Stahl, being who he was, would want her, an easy conquest to satisfy a casual desire.

'Perhaps another time,' he said. 'We'll have an evening out.'

'Oh stop it,' she said, with one of her particularly ironic smiles. 'But it was nice to be asked.'

He hoped she might stand there and watch him walk away but he heard the door click shut on his second step.

It took more than an hour for the hotel operator to connect him with Wolf Lustig's office. There was a storm somewhere between Paris and Berlin, the line crackled with static and the woman in Lustig's office had to raise her voice, almost shouting in order to be heard. But shouting very courteously. Herr Lustig, she said, wished urgently to meet with him regarding an important UFA production. And soon Herr Lustig would be in Paris. However, his time there was extremely limited and busy. Would it be possible for Monsieur Stahl to meet Herr Lustig at a social function? They could talk there. And what social function was that? A cocktail party, given by the Rousillon champagne people, at the restaurant Pré Catelan in the Bois de Boulogne. Did he know it? He did. The party would be on the seventeenth, at five o'clock. Would his schedule permit him to attend? He thought it would. Oh, Herr Lustig will be so pleased.

In the hotel suite, Stahl turned on the radio, and found swing-band music recorded in New York – Artie Shaw playing 'Frenesi' and 'Begin the Beguine'. For a rejected lover, maybe the best thing on a lonely night: people wanted each other, then life got in the way but, if the songs told the truth, desire would not be denied. Not forever, any-how. Stahl brooded as the music played; Renate Steiner had misun-derstood him, he would have to try again, and they *would* be together. In Stahl's imagination it happened *this* way, no, *that* way, no . . . Even-tually he drifted off to sleep, and woke at four to find himself wearing a bathrobe and lying on the coverlet as rain fell on the city.

17 November. The Pré Catelan was a small white château. Located on a winding road in the vast Bois de Boulogne park at the western edge of the Sixteenth Arrondissement, it had been built in the 1700s, becoming a restaurant in 1906, and soon enough *the* place for elegant and luxurious celebrations. Stahl changed clothes at the studio and, with Jimmy Louis driving the silver Panhard, he managed to get there by six. The dining room had a high, domed ceiling, the walls featured marble columns and triple sconces, the windows looked past a grand terrace to the park's bare trees. Above the dining-room entry, a banner ran from wall to wall: ROUSILLON BRUT MILLESIME. Appar-ently, the party celebrated the new brand of champagne being mar-keted by Rousillon Frères. At the door, a lovely young woman welcomed him and handed him a glass of champagne. Now what? He was at the edge of a huge, chattering mob of people, loud and getting louder, quite merry an hour into the event. Somewhere in there was Wolf Lustig.

Then the Baroness von Reschke emerged, miraculously, from the crowd, her predator's lupine smile shining brighter with every step. 'Oh Monsieur Stahl, my dear Fredric, you're *here,* it's so good to see you!' She was as he remembered her, in a cocktail dress of puffy em-erald silk, blue vein at her temple, stylishly set straw hair. She took

Stahl's hand in both claws and said, 'I'm giving a dinner on the week-end, all sorts of interesting people, may I hope you'll join us?' Stahl said he would be leaving town. Behind the baroness, awaiting his turn with Stahl, was Philippe LaMotte, who Stahl had met at the baroness's cocktail party in September. LaMotte, he recalled, was an executive at Rousillon and a leader of the Comité Franco-Allemagne, the friendship society pledged to bring harmony to relations between France and Germany. The baroness fled, promising to be back in a moment, and LaMotte, in his exquisite suit, shook Stahl's hand. 'I wanted to welcome you personally,' he said. 'My favourite American actor. How is the world treating you, my friend?'

As well as could be hoped for, he was much occupied with work.

'Ah, but you managed to visit Berlin, everyone speaks of the impression you made there. A triumph, it's said.'

Stahl was not going to discuss Berlin, and asked LaMotte about the champagne business.

'Our brand is ordered everywhere, it is a great success.'

Stahl sipped the champagne, which was too fruity for his taste, and raised his eyebrows to show how good it was.

LaMotte glowed. 'Yes, yes, only the Epernay soil does this to the grape, hard, chalky soil, *bad* soil, the vines struggle to grow yet *this* is what they produce!'

'One can see why it's popular,' Stahl said.

'Still, we must advertise. Have you given any thought to what I mentioned the last time we met? To appear in our advertisements? You need only to hold a glass of champagne and look successful; the text might say something about having a glass of Rousillon champagne before you play a love scene.'

Alas, Stahl did not at the moment have the time, and . . .

Over LaMotte's shoulder, the baroness again materialized, this time with – Stahl recognized him from his photographs – the eminent German producer Wolf Lustig. Now Stahl, most especially after his recent experience of the Third Reich, had a determined loathing for the baroness and her fascist friends, but his reaction to Lustig was instant and visceral revulsion. His photographs did not do him justice. He smiled enthusiastically as they were introduced, the smile spread across thick, liver-coloured lips, and held his head in an unusual way, canted over towards his shoulder, which made him look like a licentious uncle bent on the seduction of an adorable niece – *seamy* didn't describe him. 'I'm honoured to meet you, Monsieur Stahl,' he said. 'You stand far above your colleagues in America.'

'You are too kind.'

Lustig seemed amused. *Of course I'm being too kind, do you not understand the art of flattery?*

'I expect the UFA is doing quite well at the moment,' Stahl said, trying to expedite the conversation to the point where he could run away.

'We are, sir. We Germans are a movie-loving people – what better after a hard day's work at the factory?'

'True everywhere,' Stahl said.

'I'm so pleased you could be here,' Lustig said. 'I've been wanting to discuss a project, yes, a certain project. A film, naturally. With quite a grand budget – we spend money when we see a good thing.'

And what good thing was this?

'It's a story from today's papers, may I tell you what I have in mind?'

Stahl nodded. His physical aversion to Lustig was growing stronger, it was like sitting next to the wrong person on the Métro and being unable to get away.

'It's called *Harvest of Destiny*, a romantic tragedy. The time is now, the place is the border between Poland and Germany, the eastern side of the Polish Corridor. The hero is a handsome young fellow called Franz, simple, honest, who works on the family farm – we see him gathering hay, feeding the cow, at home in the evening, reading by lamplight. One day, a wagon stops at the farm, the draught horse has pulled up lame. So far, so good?'

'I think I follow it,' Stahl said.

'It's a Polish farmer who's driving the wagon, which is full of potatoes or whatever it is, and he is that day accompanied by his daughter, Wanda. Need I say his beautiful daughter? I think not.' Lustig's eyes twinkled and he placed a warm hand on Stahl's arm. 'So now we have Franz and Wanda falling in love. He walks across the fields at night to see his girl but he's caught by Polish border guards, who give him a hard time. The plot moves along, Franz and Wanda come hand in hand out of the forest and we know what's happened. And next we learn that he has proposed marriage and she has accepted him.

'But all is not well. When Franz seeks permission from his father, he is warned: "Things have not always gone well between our two nations," the father says. "This is sorrowful but it is a fact and we would do nothing but worry about the two of you." Of course, we need a strong, sympathetic actor for the father . . .' Lustig let the sentence hang, waiting for Stahl to react.

'And that would be me?' said Stahl, a hardened veteran of producers' pitches.

'It's the *perfect* part for you,' Lustig said. 'Anyhow, the star-crossed lovers decide to run away together. We thought about having her pregnant, but the idea of a German fathering a child with a Polish woman is not acceptable. So they elope, and here they have adventures – swim a fast river, escape the brutish Poles who guard the border, whatever we can think up. In time they reach their destination, a city, which is, of course . . .' He waited for Stahl to take the bait, then said, 'Danzig.'

At this point, Lustig winked. Danzig was a disputed city – in Polish territory but with a majority German population, and the name had lately been in the news. So it was a significant wink. It meant that Lustig presumed Stahl was on his side, was complicit, was sympathetic to the Nazi version of *the Polish problem*. Hitler's phrase.

Lustig, having made his point, said, 'Franz and Wanda try to make a life in Danzig – he gets a job as a stevedore, but the Poles who work on the docks don't like Germans, and he is attacked by a Polish gang and beaten up. He fights back – fiercely, he fights – but when they cannot subdue him with their fists, they stab him, and he dies. It is left for the father, for you, to spell out the film's moral: that the European powers have stirred up conflict, and here is the tragedy that results when they won't make things right.' He paused and searched Stahl's face, then said, 'So? What do you think?'

'*Harvest of Destiny* you said. And what is the destiny?'

Lustig was surprised by the question. 'The destiny is war between Germany and Poland, unless Europe prevails on the Poles to see the light and agree to the Reich's demands.'

To this, Stahl did not respond. He was at the party to see what Lustig wanted with him, not to start a fight, not to throw bad champagne in his face, though the thought did cross his mind. 'Of course I appreciate your thinking of me for the role, Herr Lustig, but my contract with Warner Bros. would never allow me to take on a project for UFA.'

'Are you sure?'

'I am.'

'Well, not all the foreign actors remain in Hollywood. Emil Jannings, who you'll remember from *The Blue Angel,* has come back to Germany and is quite thoroughly happy and successful. And Maurice Chevalier, after some success in America, is now working in his native France. Have you ever considered something like this? A return to the homeland?'

'I haven't, Herr Lustig.'

'Perhaps you ought to think about it. Whatever you earn at Warner Bros. would be exceeded at UFA, you would be acting in your native language, and the choice of roles would be yours.'

'Again, thank you, but I will likely remain in Hollywood.'

Lustig shrugged. 'It's up to you, naturally. Perhaps events in the future will make the possibility . . . more appealing.' He waited, Stahl just stood there. 'Very well, I'm off to the buffet table. I will be in Paris for another day, meetings and more meetings, then I'll be going to Poland to scout locations for *Harvest.* That looks to be an interesting visit, have you ever been in Poland?'

'I haven't, Herr Lustig.'

'Come along, if you like, everything first class,' he said. 'Though what that means to the Poles I can't be sure.' He laughed at that, a snicker, and said, 'Who knows, a look at what goes on over there might change your mind.' Then he said goodbye, his soft hand found Stahl's and held it, and he was away.

Stahl breathed a sigh of relief and turned towards the door, only to find Kiki de Saint-Ange standing at his side. 'Remember me?' she said.

'Kiki, hello! What are you doing here?'

'Waiting for you. No, not really, I was invited, and it was such a boring afternoon . . .'

'Well, it's good to see you.'

That was true. Kiki looked her best – a black Chanel suit, chiffon blouse, a knotted rope of pearls, and tight black gloves. Her chestnut hair was cut short, with a swathe brushed across her forehead. She held a cigarette by her ear, her other hand cupping her elbow, and her eyes met his as she flirted with him. 'I think you're avoiding me, you know, you are *very* silent lately.'

'Not on purpose,' he said. 'It's just . . .'

'Or maybe you think I've exhausted my, my, umm, *repertoire*. Well, don't. I am the most *adventurous* girl.'

'You are, and I know it.'

'So where are you going after this?'

Stahl was severely tempted. Kiki held nothing back – unlike others he could name who held everything back. And he found himself wondering just what sort of wickedness she had in mind. Oh, what the hell, why not. As she took a puff on her cigarette and blew smoke from her nostrils, her eyes stayed fixed on his. With, now, pure enquiry.

'I have to meet my producer,' he said, and immediately regretted it. Why had he done this? He thought he knew – there was someone else he really wanted – but he'd surprised himself. *Not like me,* he thought.

'I see,' she said, an edge of anger in her voice. 'Your producer. Well, don't leave it too long, good things don't last forever.' She reached up and stroked his cheek with two gloved fingers.

'I will telephone you, Kiki,' he said. He kissed her lightly, left and right, inhaling the perfume in her hair.

———

19 November. The *Paris Herald* was brought to Stahl's room every morning with his coffee and croissants. He had, like many Americans living in Paris, become addicted to it. The lead stories were, as usual since Stahl's arrival, about political manoeuvres in European capitals. There was news of social goings-on, of sports – mostly football now – and the stock market. On the inside of the back page, a brief article caught Stahl's attention. A certain Professor James Franklin, on sabbatical from the University of Illinois, and his wife, Dorothea, had left Paris on a trip to Berlin and there vanished. It had been three weeks since they were last seen. German police were investigating.

Stahl read the article twice, then again. Was this an instance of random violence? Had they encountered criminals? It was known in Paris that some Americans had been confronted in German cities by Brown Shirts and, refusing to return the Nazi salute, had been badly beaten up. Some had died. These events were rarely reported, but they were known to occur. Or was there a reason for their disappearance – had they been caught doing something clandestine? Stahl was to see J. J. Wilkinson late that afternoon and he considered raising the subject, then decided he shouldn't. It would amount, implicitly, to an accusation: did you have something to do with this?

Stahl had his breakfast, then left the *Herald* on the tray for the room waiter to take away. Dressed for work at Joinville, on his way to the door, he read the article once again.

5.20 p.m. The Paris branch of the National City Bank, on the Champs-Elysées, had closed at five but Stahl, following directions, rang a bell by the door and was admitted, then escorted through the immense bronze doors to the vault and led to a private room reserved for safe-deposit box holders. Here Wilkinson awaited him.

After a very productive day on the movie set, Stahl was in a good mood – successful work almost always had this effect on him – and his narrative of the meeting with Wolf Lustig was lightened, here and there, by a touch of comedy. Traditionally, stories about god-awful movie producers were good for a laugh. But Wilkinson didn't find it so funny. He made Stahl go back over details – 'Are you sure he said that?' and so on, as though the report he would write was an especially important one. 'You've done well,' Wilkinson said, when Stahl wound down.

'Did I? I just stood there and let him talk. Do you suppose he really thought I was going to be in his wretched film?'

'He had a try at it, he was likely *told* to try it. And then he went further, proposing that you go to live in Germany.'

Stahl shook his head. 'How could anybody . . .'

'Think you might? The Nazis believe they're going to rule the world, and "believe" isn't the right word – they *know* it. So maybe, with a little persuasion, with a little pressure, they might get you to join them. After all, you went to Berlin, you did what they wanted. And it would have been a real triumph if it had worked. Imagine the German newspapers.'

'Well, he didn't stop there. As I told you, he invited me to go scouting for locations in Poland.'

'Yes, I'll be spying on Poland, why not come along.'

Stahl looked incredulous.

'Scouting locations?' Wilkinson said. 'That would perhaps include railways? Bridges? Ports? With a camera no doubt. What would you call it?'

'*That* never occurred to me. I'm afraid I'm not so smart about this . . . kind of thing.'

'Movie producers are catnip to spy services – they turn up everywhere, they spend a lot of money, they can reach important people, it's one of those useful professions.' Wilkinson put his notepad back in his briefcase. 'Anyhow, you've helped us. Roosevelt is about to go to Congress with a proposal for millions of dollars to be spent on rearmament. Five hundred million dollars, to be precise, which ain't chicken feed. And the only thing that will persuade Congress to spend this kind of money is some strong indication that there *will* be war in Europe. Hitler has been screaming about Poland lately, and suddenly it's in the French press. I don't know if you saw it, probably you didn't, but that fascist bastard Marcel Déat just published an opinion piece called '*Mourir pour Danzig?*' To die for Danzig? Who would want to die in some quarrel over a faraway city? So French public opinion is once again being, as they say, "harmonized".

'Now newspaper stories won't convince the honourable senator from Ohio, but what may convince him is being invited to lunch at the White House and told, not for publication, of course, that the Germans are making propaganda films about Poland. They're going down the same road they took in Czechoslovakia, but the Poles only just got their country back, twenty years ago, and they'll fight to keep it. And when they fight, Britain and France will have to declare war – they wriggled out of their treaties with the Czechs at Munich but they can't do that again.'

'I assume there's more than *Harvest of Destiny*.'

'There is. All sorts of things that add up, Orlova's notes included, and intelligence from here and there. The German administration in Danzig just threw all the Jews out of the city, for instance, and Danzig isn't *in* Germany, it's in Poland, supposedly administered by the League of Nations, so it will be a long lunch at the White House.'

'Mr Wilkinson, you aren't suggesting I go to Poland, are you?'

'No. That's potentially a trap.'

'A trap?'

'Maybe, could be, you never know. Talk about headlines! "Poles arrest American actor spying for Germany." I doubt you'd be going back to Hollywood after that. And you really might wind up working for UFA.'

'Good God.'

'Yes, kindly old Dr Lawton joins up with the Nazis.' The idea was horrifying but the way Wilkinson had put it amused them both. 'Better stay here in Paris,' Wilkinson said. 'And, even here, watch out for yourself. These people may seem absurd, like Wolf Lustig and Moppi and his pals, but absurdity can shield the truth, which is that these people are dangerous.'

———

Adolf Hitler was a man who needed an audience. When he spoke in public, the shrieking crowd drove him to his most passionate moments. In private, he required a circle of admirers, sitting rapt and silent as he delivered his monologues. Of course the people around him had to be the right people: senior military officers, old comrades from the early Nazi days, a few blonde women, maybe an actress or two, a sprinkling of diplomats. One such was a cousin of Propaganda Minister Goebbels, a young man called Manfred Mueller. Freddi, Hitler called him, and he was something of a court favourite. He wore owlish round glasses in tortoiseshell frames, stood – and sat – straight as a stick, laughed at Hitler's snide remarks, and carefully deferred to Hitler's powerful friends but not in a way that got on their nerves. He was just a very nice young man, easy to have around.

Sometimes the whole gang went off to one of Hitler's country retreats, the Berghof, say, in the mountain town of Berchtesgaden in the Austrian Alps. There wasn't room for everybody at the Berghof – Hitler liked his numerous bodyguards close by – so his guests would stay at the Berchtesgadener Hof, the local hotel. Since these were social events, couples were welcome, and Freddi Mueller was often accompanied by his wife, Gertrud, called Trudi.

Trudi Mueller was also easy to have around, always following the expected protocol: women were there to listen to what the men said and to appreciate their brilliance, laugh at their wit, look serious when important subjects were being discussed. In her thirties, she was pretty in a careful way, with smooth brown hair and fine skin. She dressed conservatively and, like her husband, had excellent posture. A perfect couple, the Muellers: attentive, unassuming, and perfectly correct in everything they did, in everything they thought.

Well, almost everything. Because Trudi Mueller had fallen in love with Olga Orlova. Did Trudi admit this, even to herself? Possibly she didn't, and buried certain desires so deeply that she could ignore their existence. But, whatever her dreams or reveries, and some of her dreams were unsettling, Trudi openly worshipped the Russian actress; thought her terribly glamorous, loved her beautiful clothes, loved the way she spoke – that Slavic undertone in her German, loved the way she held herself, loved the way her well-exercised body looked in a bathing suit. She saw Orlova, who was in her forties, as the successful older woman; sophisticated, confident, comfortable with her life. Trudi wouldn't have dared to think she could ever be *like* her, it was more than enough to be near her.

Now Trudi may not have known what she felt but Orlova surely did. She'd been in this position before, she knew the signs, and didn't mind – being desired was a daily commonplace for a film star and it was inevitable that sometimes women did the desiring. So Orlova knew. Trudi often touched her, her eyes had a certain light in them when the two of them talked, and she was responsive to Orlova's moods and fell in with them. Was something funny? They laughed together. Was something sad? They mourned together. Would it ever go beyond that? Here Orlova was uncertain. Trudi was from a certain social class, strict, conventional, and rigidly proper, where such feelings between women were not discussed, and, supposedly, never acted upon. Even in the 1920s, when open and fervent sexuality flourished in German cities, the Trudi Muellers of the world sniffed and pretended not to notice. As for Orlova, a life in the theatre and then in film had room for pretty much anything, as long as it was discreet, as long as, the saying went, it didn't frighten the cat.

Meanwhile, Orlova the professional spy sensed opportunity in Trudi's affections. She couldn't have said precisely what that was but felt its presence – something useful, a secret to be stolen, so she kept at it, and she and Trudi were often in each other's company. On days when the men up at the Berghof had private matters to discuss and the women didn't appear until dinnertime, the two of them would go walking in the mountains, take tea together in the hotel parlour – crackling fire on the hearth, bear and chamois trophy heads on the walls – and now and then visit in one of their rooms if the weather was bad.

And there came an afternoon in November when the weather was very bad indeed. It didn't start that way, was chilly and calm all morning. Freddi was in a meeting up at the Berghof. Orlova, having the sort of day when boredom becomes intolerable, knocked at the door of Trudi's room and suggested they take one of the trails up the mountain. She was already dressed for it: a ski parka, wool trousers – plus fours, buttoned over heavy socks below the knee – and a knit stocking cap, snug on her head, that hung down to her shoulder and ended in a fluffy pompom. The red cap made her look like a child, an elfin child, and Trudi said it was adorable.

Trudi was eager to go for a walk but she had to change into outdoor clothes. Orlova made as if to leave, so Trudi could dress in private, but Trudi insisted she stay, it wouldn't take too long. Orlova sat in a chair, Trudi took off her dress and hung it up, tossed her slip on the bed, and walked around in her underwear, gathering up a cold-weather outfit and chattering away. Something of a display, really, a show, and Orlova wondered idly if she knew what she was doing. Perhaps she did – turning to Orlova and saying, 'You don't mind, do you, if I go about like this?'

'Of course not.'

'After all, we're both girls.'

Trudi put on a heavy sweater and slacks, then lace-up boots. All the while she talked; they had the painters in their apartment in Berlin and the inconvenience, and the smell of fresh paint, was frankly testing her patience. Should they stay at a hotel? That seemed to her extravagant, didn't Olga think so? No? No doubt Olga was used to luxurious hotels but Trudi was so much more comfortable at home. On and on she went, talking to Orlova through the open bathroom door as she fixed her make-up. Watching her apply fresh lipstick, Orlova thought, *Must look good in case we meet a bear.*

At that moment, Orlova's eye happened to fall on a briefcase, leaning on the leg of a chair set before a small desk. Freddi's briefcase. Forgotten? Left on purpose? She wondered what might be in there, then Trudi came out of the bathroom and said, reaching for her coat, 'Ready at last!'

Outside, the clouds above the mountain had lowered while Trudi changed her clothes, and a white mist had blanked out the summit, which meant alpine weather on the way, but they were dressed for it. They walked through the town, past the little shops and the statue of

Goethe, then started up one of the trails. About twenty minutes later a few flakes of snow came drifting down – big, soft flakes that spun through the still air. Trudi wiped her face with her mitten, Orlova's cap turned from red to white. A wind stirred, then grew stronger and sighed through the forest, while the branches of the pine trees bowed with the weight of the new snow.

The trail had a gentle slope as it climbed the face of the mountain, the streets and houses below looked remote and serene, like a village in a painting, and Trudi grew confidential. Did Olga, she wondered, ever feel lonely? In truth, Orlova said, she didn't – she seemed always to have people around her. Trudi said that even in a crowd she sometimes felt very much alone. For a time, the grade steepened, which made conversation difficult as they worked their way upwards, but then it levelled out and Trudi said that she and Freddi had always wanted children – but did Orlova think every couple *had* to have them? Orlova didn't think so; people ought to be free to do as they liked. Trudi agreed – wistfully, it seemed to Orlova. Maybe in the future they'd have them, Trudi said, lately Freddi worked so hard, cared so very much about his job, that he was always tired. Every night, he was tired. 'He falls asleep when his head hits the pillow. It leaves me feeling, oh, "lonely" is the word, I guess.'

Just about here it occurred to Orlova that a comment about Trudi's sleepwear might be in order, but then she was distracted by the weather. A Muscovite by birth, she knew a thing or two about snow, which had started to come down thick and fast. They really couldn't see the town any longer and when she turned and looked back down the trail, their footprints had disappeared. In fact, the word 'blizzard' wouldn't have been all that wrong.

'Trudi, dear,' she said. 'I think we shouldn't go much further.'

'That's what I think,' Trudi said, apparently eager to return to the hotel, and they started back down the mountain, the going sufficiently difficult that now and then Trudi had to hold on to Orlova's arm. They were never really in trouble, but by the time they reached the hotel they were both red in the face and breathing hard. When Orlova dropped Trudi off at her room and said she was going upstairs to change, Trudi said, 'You will come back, won't you? And keep me company?'

'I'll see you in a few minutes,' Orlova said. 'Why don't you have them send up a bottle of brandy? It'll warm us up.'

In her room, Orlova hung up her wet clothes and put on slacks and a sweater, then stood for a time before her open suitcase, contemplating a small Leica camera. It wasn't a miniature camera, a spy's camera – discovery of such a thing would have been a catastrophe – but, equipped with a certain lens, it worked almost as well. It had done so in the past. Take it down to Trudi's room? Where Freddi's briefcase rested against a chair? How? In a handbag. Would there be an opportunity to use it? Orlova thought this through, and found no suitable strategy, but then, with a nod to the gods of chance, she dropped it in her bag.

Downstairs, Trudi was wearing a quilted pink bathrobe that hung down to her ankles. The bottle of brandy and two glasses had arrived, along with a message from the hotel telephone operator: the roads down the mountain from the Berghof were impassable, Herr Mueller would not be able to return until the morning. Trudi didn't seem all that disappointed, quite the reverse. 'So it's just you and me, tonight,' she said.

They sat together and talked for a while, then Trudi said, 'I've caught a chill, feel my hands.'

'Like ice,' Orlova said, rubbing them for a moment.

'I think I'd better take a bath,' Trudi said.

'You should, it will warm you up.'

Trudi slipped off her robe and walked into the bathroom, leaving the door open behind her. When the water was turned on, Orlova calculated that the sound would cover any noise she might make and headed for the briefcase. She unsnapped the latch and spread the sides open, to be greeted by a bulky sheaf of papers. A memorandum, something about *Plan* ALBRECHT. Another, this one to do with secretarial holidays. A draft for a report, script written in pen, the sentences hard to read. Then, from the bathroom, 'Olga, dear?'

'Yes?'

'Could you bring me my drink?'

'Be right there.'

Orlova managed to shuffle through a few more pages, then found Trudi's glass, poured in some more brandy, and took it into the bathroom. Through the steam, she could see Trudi's white body in the green water. 'Here it is.'

'Thank you. You can sit on the edge of the tub, if you like.'

'The steam is getting me wet, I'll wait for you in the room.' As she turned to go, the significance of one of the papers came to her: a list of names with numbers, reichsmarks, next to them. Which could have been anything, but now Orlova realized that she'd seen a crossed *L,* the *Ł,* which was pronounced W.

In Polish.

Orlova snatched the Leica from her purse, found the list, and laid it flat on the desk. She riffled through to the end, some thirty pages. She had only eighteen exposures left on the film in her camera, but she'd get what she could.

Now the splash of water in the bathroom stopped. Orlova glanced at the open door, her heart pounding, but there was only drifting steam. She returned to the document and snapped the first photograph. 'Olga?'

'Yes?'

'Do you think Freddi is a good husband?'

Calling out, 'Of course he is,' Orlova used the sound of her voice to conceal a turn to the next page.

'Oh, in a way he is, he's . . .' *Click.* Next page. '. . . kind and considerate.'

'There's much to be said for kindness.' *Click.* Next page.

'But shouldn't there be more?' *Click.* Next page.

'Do you mean physical things?' *Click.* Next page. 'Intimate things?'

'That *is* what . . .' *Click.* Next page. '. . . I mean, Olga.'

'It is important in love affairs.' *Click.* 'But a marriage isn't . . .' Next page. *Click.* '. . . a love affair.' Next page.

'Do you think . . .' *Click.* Next page. '. . . I should have a love affair?' *Click.* Next page.

The dialogue continued, with an occasional slosh from the bathroom as Trudi changed positions. Was there somebody Trudi liked? Well, yes, there was, could Orlova guess who that might be? Orlova said she wouldn't even try to guess. And what if Freddi found out? What *then*? There was no way he ever would. Orlova doubted that. Trudi persisted – the person she had in mind would *never* tell, of that she was sure. Then, as Orlova rushed to turn a page, it rattled, and Trudi called out, 'Are you reading the newspaper?'

Desperately, Orlova looked around the room. *Was there a newspaper?* Yes! There it was, on a chair. 'I'm just thumbing through it,' she answered. Then, from the bathroom, the sound of Trudi getting out of the tub, and, as she dried herself, Orlova took the final exposure, jammed the document back in the briefcase, closed it, and put the camera in her bag. 'I don't think anybody would ever know,' Trudi said.

Orlova hurried over to the chair, grabbed the newspaper and was standing there holding it when Trudi ran naked from the bathroom, jumped into the bed, pulled the covers up to her chin, and said, 'That felt so good, my bath.'

'Well, when you're chilled . . .'

'Olga, dear?'

'Yes?'

'Why don't you get in here with me and keep me warm?'

Orlova laughed and threw the newspaper back on the chair. 'I'm going to take my brandy upstairs and rest for a while.'

'Are you sure, Olga?' Trudi's voice had lowered, *I'm serious*. The question was overt and direct.

Orlova walked over to the bed and smoothed Trudi's hair back. 'Yes, Trudi, I am sure,' she said, her tone affectionate and understanding. Then she said, 'I'll be back later, and we'll have dinner together,' and left the room.

Climbing the stairs to the floor above, Orlova hoped that Trudi wouldn't hate her – she might, that was one possible reaction. But the alternative was too dangerous. In different circumstances, Orlova thought, she might have done it – a dalliance on a snowy afternoon in the mountains, a couple of hours of discovery and excitement, nobody the wiser. With Trudi, however, she feared all that heat stored up inside would explode in real passion, real love, not just a crush on an admired older woman. What then? Longing looks from Trudi Mueller in the midst of the Hitler menagerie? These people were shrewd, they had the sharpened instincts of survivors, and they might very well figure out what was going on. *No, impossible,* Orlova thought as she opened the door to her room. She would be particularly sweet to Trudi at dinner; she loved her like a friend, she loved her like an older sister.

Meanwhile, a roll of film.

3 December. As the first snow of the season whitened the grounds of the Joinville studios, the production of *Après la Guerre* was smoother and faster by the day. The anarchist Jean Avila turned out to be a not entirely benevolent despot and, with cast and crew doing precisely what they were told, the daily minutes of film went from two, to three, to, on some days, five. The romantic scenes between Colonel Vadic and Ilona absolutely *smouldered,* and were more than once applauded on the set. There was, to professionals like Stahl and Justine Piro, no higher praise than that.

Even *the message* – as, after a gun battle in a Balkan village, the dying Gilles Brecker tells Colonel Vadic that an honourable death is the most important part of life – was emotional and moving. This was in no small part Avila's victory, pressing the screenwriters, as he put it to them in a café, 'to calm this fucking thing down a little – trust your actors.' Because the lieutenant has fought bravely, because he's given his life to save theirs, the colonel pretends to agree with him. But in Stahl's reading of his lines, in the expression on his face as the camera moves to close-up, it is clear that Colonel Vadic has come to understand that death is death and, honourable though it may be, sorrowful beyond all else. At the end of the second day of shooting, when the sequence was completed, Avila took Stahl aside and said, 'Thank you, Fredric.' That wasn't the last of the filming, not quite, but soon they would be leaving Joinville, to shoot exterior scenes in and around Beirut. Except that Beirut had now become some remote place in Morocco. 'Where,' Avila told the cast, repeating what Deschelles had said, 'they are known to have sand. Plenty of sand. It's called the Sahara.' Once that was done, they would return to Paris, then go to the Hungarian castle – Paramount had agreed to pay! – for a few more scenes on location.

By the third of December, Orlova's letter had reached Paris by courier and Wilkinson knew about the film of the Polish list. And the price of the Polish list, copied out from the eighteen exposures, another two hundred thousand Swiss francs. Roosevelt's millionaire friends had been generous enough so that Wilkinson could pay, he told Stahl in the billiard room of the American Club, but the exchange was difficult. He had planned on using a ballet troupe based in Boston, headed from Paris to Berlin on a cultural friendship tour, but the willing dancer had been injured in a taxi crash on the Boulevard Saint-Germain.

For Fredric Stahl there was no reason, and even less desire, to go to Germany. In fact, he told Wilkinson, he would be going to Morocco, to a place called Erg Chebbi in the Ziz Valley. Wilkinson raised his eyebrows, Stahl said, 'Dunes.' The desert scenery was spectacular and had been used by other film companies. But Stahl said he would take on the job if Orlova could arrange for somebody – he doubted she'd be able to come herself – to meet him there. Wilkinson took out his notepad, rested it on the billiard table, and said, 'Can you spell it?'

Over the next few days, Stahl realized that the prospect of leaving Paris for a time was more than a little welcome. The city of moods had fallen into a kind of trough; Parisians were feeling the pressure and they didn't like it. *Il faut en finir,* they said, there must be an end to this. They were fed up with alarms – Hitler said this, Roosevelt said that – hopes high one day, dashed the next, optimism followed by gloom. So, enough! After the Munich appeasement, Hitler seemed to think he'd won; France was finished, the war was over. This scared the French, it scared the sophisticated Parisians, and Stahl could feel it.

And, almost despite himself, he became a collector of signs and omens. The Germans had installed a second news agency in Paris, the Prima Presse, that issued a flow of press releases quoted in French newspapers – more tanks, more planes, millions of men marching with guns and giving the Nazi salute. A garment manufacturer in Paris advertised its new *pyjamas d'alerte,* so women would have something attractive to wear in bomb shelters. And America made it clearer every day that help was *not* at hand. *Time* magazine's newsreel series, *The March of Time,* brought out *Inside Nazi Germany – 1938,* which featured happy, hardworking Germans toiling in field and factory. Stahl watched it with disgust. And read an article by a young woman, a rising intellectual star, in which she described the French political climate as 'a mixture of braggadocio and cowardice, hopelessness and panic'. A perfect description, Stahl thought. And on 6 December, France and Germany signed a friendship treaty, stating that 'pacific and neighbourly relations between France and Germany constitute one of the essential elements of the consolidation of the situation in Europe and of the preservation of the general peace.'

8 December. Deschelles had chartered two aeroplanes to fly cast, crew, and equipment to Morocco, with stops for refuelling at Marseille, and then Tangiers – for the three-hundred-mile flight to a military airfield at Er Rashida. From there, cars and trucks would take them to Erg Chebbi, where they would stay at a hotel called the Kasbah Oudami; the producer had secured all thirty rooms for ten days. They left Le Bourget Airport at dawn. More than a few of the cast and crew had never flown in an aeroplane and, when the flight turned bumpy and the plane hit air pockets, had to be calmed by the administration of strong spirits, which were not denied to the other passengers. The well-oiled Pasquin, it turned out, knew a selection of

incredibly filthy songs, which most of them had never heard before. But they weren't hard to learn.

An hour into the flight, Stahl changed seats with an electrician so he could sit next to Renate Steiner, first asking her if she minded. He managed to keep the conversation light and easy, he wanted her to understand that, everything else aside, he truly *liked* her, which he did. Once she relaxed she was good company, smart, funny, and Stahl realized he could make her laugh, in its way a powerful form of intimacy. A key to the heart? At the Kasbah Oudami she would, she said, be sharing a room with the actress who played Pasquin's conquest in a Turkish village. *Just in case he had any ideas.* Which he did. And when she dozed off, somewhere over the Mediterranean, his shoulder was available, but she leaned her head against the window, and Stahl, who'd equipped himself for the journey with a few S. S. Van Dine mysteries, opened one of them, trying to follow the clues as Philo Vance solved *The Casino Murder Case*.

It was after midnight by the time they reached the hotel. 'I'm going to take a walk,' Stahl said. 'Would you like to come along?'

'I'm worn out,' she said. 'But maybe tomorrow I might.'

Something in her voice caught Stahl's attention, the lowering, slight as it was, of a barrier. 'Promise?' Stahl said, unwilling to let her go.

She nodded and said, 'Yes, tomorrow,' accompanied by one of her ironic smiles. *I know what you want.* Now she was toying with him, he thought, but he didn't mind because it could lead him exactly where he wanted to go.

In good spirits he entered the hotel and started up the tiled stairway to his room which, as leading man, he did not have to share. But the good spirits quickly evaporated. The Kasbah Oudami, occupying a rebuilt section of an abandoned Berber fortress, was suffused with cold, blue light. The walls had been, a long time ago, painted blue, the paint now puckered and peeling, and the air was chilled and clammy. This was, Stahl thought, a good place to be murdered. Should he actually go for a walk? With all those Swiss francs in his pockets? Still, honour demanded that he at least go back outside, which he did, and discovered Avila standing in front of the hotel.

Avila's face lit up when he saw Stahl. 'Want to have a look at the desert?' he said.

'I was thinking about it,' Stahl said, uncertainty in his voice.

'We'll be fine,' Avila said, and off they went.

It wasn't much better outdoors – this was Africa, not Europe, and they both, walking through the twisty streets of Erg Chebbi, felt a certain, nameless apprehension. A slice of moon lit the town, which had no streetlamps, and the silence of the place was heavy enough to preclude conversation. A few minutes later they stood at the edge of the desert, where a steady wind blew across the high dunes and the silence was even deeper. 'Is it ominous, or is it just me?' Stahl said.

'It's something,' Avila said. 'Supposedly, we're still in France.' Morocco was a French colonial possession.

Stahl laughed.

'Deschelles made some sort of deal with the colonial authority,' Avila said. 'We had to use French territory, so it was between Morocco and the Lebanon, Beirut, and Morocco won.'

'Can you get this . . . the feeling of this place, on film?'

'Slow pan, no music, mostly silence. Sun rising over the dunes.'

'You sound like you can't wait,' Stahl said.

'You're right, I can't.'

It was too cold to stay for very long. As they walked back to the hotel, a caravan came in off the desert, a line of loaded camels clopping up the cobbled street, bells jingling, each rider wearing a burnoose, the end of the cloth wrapped around the face, leaving only the eyes exposed.

The following morning brought grey cloud, so they had to wait out in the desert until eleven or so, when the sun burned through and the cameras rolled. Stahl, Gilles Brecker, and Pasquin were back in their tattered legionnaire uniforms, slogging through the sandy wastes of eastern Turkey in the brutal heat. The wind kept drying their 'sweat', so the make-up man came running before every shot. Pursued by two policemen in a battered command car – previously seen in a British war-against-the-natives film and rented at a high price – they lie flat, just below the crest of a dune, when they hear the chugging engine. Brecker reaches inside his tunic and brings out the pistol he's stolen. 'Don't do that, lieutenant,' Stahl says. The lieutenant says that he won't be taken alive. Pasquin grabs the pistol and says, 'Get yourself killed if you like, but not *me*.' One of the policemen climbs out of the car, walks almost to the top of the dune, stands there for a moment, then decides he doesn't want to go any further.

At five in the afternoon, Stahl re-counted the money, put it in a manila envelope, and headed for the Erg Chebbi railway station. A small crowd, amid mounds of baggage, waited on the platform, gazing hopefully up the long, straight track that ran to the horizon, and ultimately to Algeria. The train was late, the crowd fretted and paced, then went silent as two French gendarmes strolled to the end of the platform and leaned casually against a baggage cart. Twenty minutes later, the chuff of a steam engine in the distance was followed by grey smoke, and the crowd prepared to board.

The last carriage on the train was almost deserted, the aisle between yellow wicker seats littered with newspapers and cigarette butts. Stahl passed a Moroccan man in a suit and fez, and two women in lavishly embroidered robes, then, at the end of the carriage, found what he was looking for: a European reading a copy of *Paris Match*. The photograph on the cover showed French soldiers peeling potatoes into a huge iron pot, somewhere, as the cover advertised, SUR LA LIGNE MAGINOT.

The man looked up as Stahl approached. He was of indeterminate middle age, fair-haired and fattish. German? French? British? He wore the white suit of the colonial European, and seemed prosperous and self-confident. Stahl slid into the seat across the aisle and gave the first part of the protocol, in German as specified: 'Excuse me, sir, does this train go to Cairo?'

The man looked him over carefully and said, 'No, it goes to Alexandria.'

Stahl had tucked the envelope in his trouser waist, far enough around so that it was hidden by his jacket, and now drew it out and handed it to the man across the aisle. 'I'm sure you wish to count it,' he said.

The man reached inside his jacket, produced an envelope, and handed it to Stahl. 'Have a look,' he said. His German sounded native to Stahl. Inside the envelope, typed on very thin paper, several pages of Polish names and numbers. The list had been copied on a German keyboard, and the Polish accents applied with a pencil. As Stahl examined the list, the locomotive vented a plume of steam with a loud hiss. Startled, he began to rise in order to get off the train before it left the station.

'Don't worry,' the man said. 'You have a few minutes yet.' Holding the money below the back of the seat in front of him, he thumbed through the last of the Swiss franc notes, then put the money back in the envelope. 'All is correct,' he said. Then he turned and looked out of the window, searching the platform. 'Did you see any other Europeans?' he said. 'Waiting for the train?'

'Two French gendarmes,' Stahl said.

'Anybody else?'

'No. Just passengers. Moroccan passengers, I would say. Is there a problem?'

'I don't think so. One becomes overly sensitive, doing this . . . kind of thing.' He meant to accompany his words with a casual smile but it didn't really come off. In fact he was frightened. 'Oh well,' he said. 'I didn't mean to alarm you.'

Stahl nodded to the man, rose, went back down the aisle, and left the train. As he walked through the village twilight, he heard the train whistle as it departed.

When Stahl reached the Kasbah Oudami, he asked the desk clerk for the number of Renate Steiner's room, then knocked on her door. She answered, wearing slacks and two sweaters, and seemed surprised to see him. 'I wondered if you might like to go for a walk before dinner.'

'Oh,' she said. 'Now I don't think I can go out.'

Stahl was disappointed and showed it. 'Well, if you can't, you can't.'

'It's Annette, the woman I'm sharing the room with. She's terribly ill, I don't think I should leave her alone.'

'I'm sorry, what's wrong?'

'She ate a sheep-liver kebab, from a street vendor, I may have to get her a doctor.'

'Then another time,' Stahl said brusquely, turning to leave.

She put two fingers on his forearm. 'I did want to go,' she said. 'For a walk, with you.' For a moment they looked at each other, then she said, 'I can't help what happened.'

'I know,' Stahl said. They both stood there. Stahl didn't leave, Renate didn't close the door. Finally he said, 'Shall we try again, some time?' He meant, he thought he meant, *go for a walk,* but it wasn't only that, there was more.

'Yes.'

'Maybe tomorrow, when we come back to the hotel.'

'I think we could, I don't see why not.' They stood there.

'I'll come down here, and we'll go,' he said.

She nodded and said, 'Tomorrow.'

'I'll see you then,' he said.

'I'm looking forward to it.'

'I hope Annette feels better.'

'I will tell her that.'

'So . . . good night.'

'Yes, good night.'

10 December. At seven-thirty the following morning, the hotel desk clerk knocked at Jean Avila's door. When Avila, who'd been up working since dawn, answered, the desk clerk said, 'Forgive me, monsieur,

for disturbing you, but a policeman has asked to see you. He's waiting downstairs.'

The policeman turned out to be a gendarme officer, a captain, very official-looking in khaki uniform, leather strap from shoulder to pistol belt, and red and blue kepi with glossy black visor. He was a handsome man, dignified, freshly shaved. He introduced himself to Avila, his educated accent from somewhere in the south of France, and said, his voice polite and firm in equal measure, that he regretted the inconvenience but he had to ask Avila to accompany him up to the gendarmerie headquarters in Er Rashida. 'And I must ask you to select another member of your crew to go along with us.'

'Why is that, captain?' Avila didn't like police and wasn't afraid of them.

'A question of identification; we require the statements of two individuals. I will wait for you here, monsieur.'

Avila went up to Stahl's room and told him what was going on, then they went downstairs together. 'Any idea what they want from us?' Stahl said.

'We're supposed to identify somebody, that's all I know.'

In the military command car, the captain drove and, once they were on the road to Er Rashida, he said, 'We have had a homicide. A male European, with no papers, found by the railway track a few miles from Erg Chebbi. Unfortunately, he may be somebody you can identify, somebody from your film company.'

Stahl was sitting behind the captain, and suddenly very glad to be there, though he made sure his reaction wasn't visible. But he knew who this was. *Why? What happened?* He recalled everything he could about the courier, then settled on the man's fear that he was being watched, perhaps followed, he'd noticed *something,* something threatening, and he'd been right. 'Any theories about what happened?' Stahl said, raising his voice above the car's engine.

'Theories?' the captain said. 'Robbery perhaps, our first task must be to find out who he is. Was.'

An hour later they were at the gendarmerie station at Er Rashida, the administrative centre for the Ziz Valley region. A sergeant at the desk took their passports and laboriously copied out their names and passport numbers. Then the captain led them down to a room in the cellar which served as a temporary morgue. On a long wooden table was a body beneath a sheet. When the captain drew the sheet down to the corpse's bare chest, Stahl saw that what he'd feared was true. It was the courier, fair-haired and fattish, though it took a moment to recognize the face altered by death. A red and black bruise circled his throat.

'Do either of you recognize this man?' the captain said.

Avila and Stahl said, in turn, that they didn't.

'Very well. You're sure?'

'We are,' Avila said. 'He's not part of the film company, I've never seen him before. How did he die?'

'Garrotte.'

A
GOOD
SOLDIER

17 December. 1.30 in the morning. Seen from the window of a taxi headed for the Claridge, winter Paris. On a bridge across the Seine, the streetlamps along the balustrade were no more than ghostly blurs of light in the river fog. Deserted streets after that, wet from an evening rain, one café still lit, with one patron, a woman in a fur hat with a glass of wine before her. Winter Paris, Christmas coming, the Galeries Lafayette would have its toy train running in the window, the station roof glittering with granular snow. Stahl thanked heaven for getting him back here alive.

He was in danger, so his intuition told him, yet not so much now. After what he'd seen in the cellar of the gendarmerie he'd *felt* it, nearby, waiting for him. Late that afternoon he had, as promised, seen Renate Steiner. And told her, because she would surely hear about it, what had happened at Er Rashida. Then all they did was walk around the village, both of them edgy and distracted, too much aware of what was going on around them. He dropped her off at the Kasbah Oudami, then went over to the telegraph office, where he did what he could to warn Wilkinson that Orlova might be in trouble.

Birthday greetings stop gift en route
stop our friend may be unwell stop send
card soonest stop Fredric

In his reaction to the murder Stahl had not been alone, Avila had also been alarmed – could it have been some spasm of anti-colonial politics? – and, for the next few days, he drove the company hard, wanting to finish the location shooting and get the hell out of there. So both Stahl and Renate had to spend long hours on the production – Stahl even lent a hand building rails for tracking shots out in the Sahara. The extra effort worked. The cast and crew left two days ahead of schedule, reaching Paris in the early hours of the seventeenth. On the aeroplane home, feeling that he'd somehow *escaped,* a relieved and talkative Stahl sat with Renate and went on about secret places – hidden parks, empty museums – that he liked to visit.

The taxi pulled up in front of the Claridge and, minutes later, Stahl, with a grateful sigh, slid into his sweetly welcoming bed. Exhausted, he slept deeply until 6.00 when his mental alarm clock jarred him awake: he had to see Wilkinson. By 8.30 he was at the neighbourhood Bureau de Poste, making an anonymous phone call to an emergency number Wilkinson had given him. An hour later, Stahl was once again in the stacks at the American Library, apparently searching the 330.94s, European Economies.

Minutes later, Stahl heard hurried footsteps on the staircase, then a smiling Wilkinson appeared. An outwardly relaxed and insouciant Wilkinson, wanting to reassure his rattled agent, but Stahl suspected he'd been shaken by the telegram. Wilkinson picked a book off the shelf, looked at the title, and said, 'Have you read this one? *Belgian Banking Practice in the Eighteenth Century?* Kept me up all night, I couldn't put it down.' He returned the book to the shelf and said, 'You seem to be okay.'

'I guess I am.'

'So, what went wrong?'

'I made contact with the courier, he gave me the list and I paid him. Then, the next day, I found out he'd been strangled and thrown off the train, money and papers taken.'

'Jesus!'

'Just so.'

'Could it have been a robbery? Happenstance, you know, coincidence.'

'Could've. Is that what you think?'

'No, it's not. God *damn* it, what a mess.'

'Did you warn Orlova?'

Wilkinson nodded, an unhappy nod but affirmative. Then he took a breath, blew it out, and said, 'Anyhow, you did the right thing, letting me know that something had gone wrong. It did take me a minute to figure it out – my first thought was "it's not my birthday", then I understood. And by "gift en route" you meant . . .'

Stahl drew the envelope from his pocket and handed it to Wilkinson, who took the list out and for a time, turning pages, looked it over. 'Hm, yes, good,' he said. 'They'll like this in D.C., some kind of German operation in Poland.' He turned a page and said, 'I suspect the Polish congressmen from Chicago might find out about it, and their votes matter.'

'Any idea what it means?'

'These people could be Nazi spies . . . some of the names are German, and there are ethnic Germans in Poland who secretly admire Herr Hitler. Or it could be a list of targets – some propaganda operation being run by the Ribbentropburo. Or it could be anything.'

'Do you think they've arrested Orlova?'

'It's possible, yes, maybe.'

'And if they knew about the courier, do they know about me?'

Wilkinson shrugged and spread his hands. Stahl waited. Wilkinson said, 'They didn't know about you when you made the exchange. If they had, you wouldn't be here. What happened suggests they were after the courier, but didn't get him until you'd left the train. Meanwhile, if the worst happened, they've arrested Orlova and, given their methods, they'll know about you soon enough.'

'And then?'

'I don't . . .' Wilkinson stopped, then said, 'Please understand, this has never happened to me.'

'Or to me,' Stahl said.

'Well, I guess you'll have to face the possibility that they'll come after you.'

'How?'

'Again, I can't say. But better I don't tell you not to worry, because you might believe me.' Wilkinson thought for a moment, then said, 'Is it possible for you to go back to California?'

'Not now. I have to finish the movie.'

'What if you didn't?'

Stahl drew his finger across his throat. 'It is the one thing you cannot do, you wouldn't work again, not in Hollywood you wouldn't.'

'But you'd be alive.'

'True, but I'll tell you a funny thing, I won't let them do that to me. Maybe I can't stop them from murdering me, but they won't destroy me.'

This earned, from Wilkinson, a faint but appreciative smile. 'You're a pretty good soldier, Fredric, you'll never get a medal, but you are.'

'What about you?' Stahl said. 'Would they come after you?'

'It's occurred to me,' Wilkinson said. 'But it's something I can't worry about.' Then he shook his head and said, 'Damn it all to hell, I wish this hadn't happened.'

Avila had given the company the day off after the early-morning return to Paris. Thoroughly habituated to the rhythm of daily work, Stahl didn't quite know what to do with himself. So he walked, a long walk, back to the Claridge from the American Library. Beneath an overcast sky, he wandered down side streets, paused at appealing shop windows, looked at the women as they passed him by, and had, in the way of people walking alone in a city, some conversation with himself. Yes, they might come after him, he thought, but brooding about it was pointless; what would happen would happen, though if he had the opportunity to fight back, then he'd fight them. Hard. Until then he decided to avoid, if he could, obsession with that part of his life. *Think good thoughts,* his mother had always told him. Well, that's what he would try to do.

On the aeroplane, he had asked Renate for her telephone number and written it down on a scrap of paper, promising to call when they were back in Paris. This scrap of paper had migrated: from his pocket to his desk, then to the top of his bureau, and back to his pocket. When he returned to his room at 2.20 he could wait no longer, and called her. No answer. But at 2.45 she was home. They talked briefly, then he asked her to have dinner – was there something special she liked to eat? Lyonnais cooking? Normandy veal? The line hissed for a time, finally he said, 'Renate?' and she said, 'Why don't you come over here? I can make something for us.' Her voice was strained, as though she feared his answer wouldn't be the one she wanted.

'Yes, of course, I'd like that,' he said.

'It's not very fancy over here,' she said. 'Surely not what you're used to.' Then she gave him her address and they decided on a time, 7.00 p.m.

Stahl had brought his favourite sweater to Paris, very soft wool, in horizontal grey and black bands, which hung loose from his shoulders. This he wore, along with chocolate-coloured corduroy trousers, some cedar-smelling cologne – not too much! – then put on his belted raincoat and found his umbrella.

It was a few minutes after 6.00.

Not very fancy was to say the least. The rue Varlin was in a poor *quartier* near the Canal Saint-Martin and the railyards in the Tenth

Arrondissement. Ancient workers' tenements darkened the narrow street and the taxi slowed as it bumped over broken cobblestones. Said the driver, 'Are you sure this is where you want to go?' A concierge, an old woman in a kerchief who walked with two canes, let him in and said, 'Steiner? On the top floor, monsieur.' Heading for the staircase, Stahl passed the tenants' mailboxes. No French names here – Poles, Italians, Germans – this was a building for émigrés. The wooden stairs had hollows worn in the centre, a family fight was in progress on the third floor, a hunting cat crept past him and he was happy enough not to see its quarry.

Renate was, as always, all in black, sweater and heavy skirt, with, tonight, nylon stockings and low heels. He liked her mouth, the natural colour of her lips, but this she had ruined with red lipstick and, when he brushed her cheeks left and right, he encountered scented face powder. She was very tense, taking off her glasses and putting them back on. While he had not foreseen her mood, he *was* carrying a bottle of good Bordeaux, which would do as an antidote. The evening wobbled a little with a search for a strayed corkscrew – 'I don't have wine very often,' she said.

It was a tiny apartment, the parlour furnished with little more than a battered old sofa, green velvet, that looked like a veteran of the flea markets. Smoothed across the back was a piece of Asian-looking fabric, either hiding or decorating. There were lots of books, in home-built bookcases painted red, and in stacks on the floor. A radio, hoarse with faint static, was playing a symphony. When the corkscrew was found, Stahl poured Bordeaux into mismatched water glasses. '*Salut,*' he said, wary of more affectionate forms.

They sat on the sofa, talked about *Après la Guerre*, talked about the weather. When the first glass of wine had been drunk and the second was on the way, she said, 'How do you like my little palace?' gesturing grandly around the room.

'It's a lot nicer than the places I lived in when I was here in the twenties,' he said. 'At least you have heat.'

'The building isn't heated,' she said. This was common in Paris; in winter people without offices to go to spent the day in heated cafés, reading books or newspapers, making a coffee last all afternoon. 'I have that thing,' she said, indicating a kerosene stove in the corner with a pipe that went into the wall, rags stuffed around the opening. 'My departed husband, not much of a mechanical man, believe me, installed it, but it hasn't killed me yet.'

'Perhaps this evening,' Stahl said. 'They'll find us together, dead as mackerels. Very romantic.'

She grinned, the wine was at work. He picked up the bottle and waggled it over her glass, his eyebrows raised. She drank off what remained, said, 'Please,' and he refilled her glass. 'This really is very good,' she said, and looked at him with her head to one side: *and so?*

Now? No, later. What's the hurry? He took out a cigarette and offered her the pack. Delicately, she drew one out and he lit it for her with his lighter. A board on bricks in front of the sofa held a vase of weeds, and a Suze ashtray purloined from a café. With one bony finger she moved it towards them. She had, he saw, at least not put polish on her pared-back fingernails.

'Tell me when you're hungry,' she said. 'I have good ham and butter and a baguette and a salad from the charcuterie.'

'For the moment, I'll stay with this,' he said, holding up his glass.

'Are you comfortable?'

'I am, yes.'

'Why don't you put your feet up?'

She stood, he raised his legs and stretched out full length. But he'd taken up too much of the sofa. She perched on the edge, then, with a jerk of her head, used a rough expression that meant *move it* and pressed a soft, heavy hip against his knee, making space for herself. He could have made more room by shifting his legs but didn't, just stayed as he was, where he could feel the warmth of her body beneath the skirt. 'Happy like that?' she said.

He smiled at her. 'What do you think?'

She took off her glasses and rested them on the arm of the sofa. 'It's starting to rain,' she said.

He could hear the thin patter on the roof above them. He took the wine glass in his left hand and put his right hand on her knee. She looked at it, then back up at him, and, after a moment, covered his hand with hers. He thought about sliding his hand upwards, bringing her skirt with it, then didn't. For a time they sat like that, the low-volume music and the sound of the rain made the room very still.

Now.

'I wonder if I could . . .'

'Merde!' she said. 'I forgot I bought candles. It's too bright in here, isn't it?'

With a small sigh he said, 'Much too bright.'

She rose and hurried around the sofa, returning with two short white candles set on saucers. She struck a wooden match on the box, lit the candles, then twisted around and turned off a lamp. Turning back to him she said, 'You were saying, monsieur?' Delivered with one of her best ironic smiles.

'Well, there was a preface to this, but now I'll just ask you.'

'And what were you going to ask?'

'Why don't you take off your clothes?'

'Oh,' she said. 'All right.' Then, 'Here? Or go into the other room and come back . . . without them?'

'Here. So I can watch you.'

She stood up, rolled her sweater over her head and tossed it on the floor. Then unbuttoned her skirt, let it drop, and stepped out of it. Next the shoes came off, which left her in white bra and panties, garter belt and stockings. 'Is this what you wanted to see?'

'Some of it. There's more.'

But in truth there was a lot. She was bigger than he'd imagined her, heavy breasts, hips, tummy, and thighs. Emphasized by a narrow waist.

'More?'

'Yes, everything.'

She bent over, reached behind her back, undid her bra and slid it down her arms, then cradled her breasts with her hands. He was already excited, but this gesture provoked him even more. 'So,' she said. 'Now you've seen me.' Her eyes fastened on his, she raised one of her thumbs and circled it around her nipple, which came erect as he watched.

Suddenly he sat upright, meaning to go and snatch the rest of her clothes off her, but she took two steps towards him, put a hand on his chest and made him lie back. 'Stay there,' she said. 'I like you as a sultan.'

'A *sultan*?'

'Something like that – a ruler who expects to be served.'

'A sultan. Do you have a towel I can wear on my head?'

She hadn't moved back and now, standing over him, inches away, she unhooked her garter belt, took it off, and removed her stockings. 'Anything else you want?'

Growing wildly impatient, he reached for the waistband of her panties but she took his hands and put them on his chest and said, 'Now, now.'

'Renate, take your pants down.'

She did, he gazed up at the vee between her legs.

Again he moved his hand towards her but she bent over, put her mouth on his and, as his tongue slid across her lips, climbed on top of him. But he still had his clothes on, so worked his hands beneath her. She gave him a little room, he pulled at the sweater until it bunched under his chin, managed to undo one button on his shirt, then yanked hard and the rest were torn off. Now, back curved, she let the tips of her breasts rub against his bare chest. He lay still for a time, face lit with pleasure, then put his arms around her and held her bottom in his hands and, when he tightened his grip, it drew from her a sharp intake of breath – startled and excited at once.

He let her go and tried to rid himself of his trousers, but she sat upright and worked her way backwards until she straddled his knees. 'Soon enough,' she said, 'but there's something I want to see.' In no hurry, she unbuttoned his fly, freed him from his shorts, and, taking it between thumb and two fingers, gave it a few slow strokes, clearly pleased with the view, then lowered her head, met his eyes, and opened her mouth.

———

Eventually they got his clothes off and went at it; one way, another way – she knelt on the sofa and rested her forehead against the back – and did everything they liked to do. She was not the vocal type, though when the moment came it was accompanied by a series of moaning sighs that every time recharged him, inspired him to start over until, when he once again wanted her, she said, almost laughing, 'I'm sorry but I don't think there's another one in there.' Then she led him to her bedroom, barely large enough to hold a narrow cot, with a yellowed shade pulled down over the window. There they talked quietly; he told her he loved her curved body, she said she loved the way he touched her, what his hands did to her. Thus they at least used the word, and there was more to say, but with ceaseless fucking and drumming rain and a wintry night in Paris they let it go at that and fell dead asleep.

It was the most adorable little tearoom, with chintz café curtains and pink linen tablecloths, on a tree-lined street across from the Tiergarten park, and Olga Orlova often went there when she was in Berlin and not out at the Babelsberg studio making films. That afternoon, the tenth of December, she didn't have anything in particular to do, so invited Trudi Mueller for tea at four o'clock. Trudi was an easy companion, who saved up tidbits from her daily life and could be depended on for table conversation. Since their encounter at an alpine hotel, when Trudi had revealed her romantic feelings for Orlova, the Russian actress had made sure they saw each other often and stayed friends. It was important, to the clandestine side of Orlova's life, that there be no bad feelings between them.

Trudi prattled away, a waitress served a pot of tea and a plate of cream-filled pastries, Orlova smiled or frowned on cue, but her mind was far away. One of her couriers, a Swiss attorney called Wendel, was en route to some godforsaken village in the Moroccan desert, and would eventually return to Berlin with payment for the list of Polish names she'd photographed while Trudi was in the bathtub. This list she'd copied – eighteen typed pages! – and sold to the Americans and the British. As for the photographs themselves, they'd gone immediately to her superiors in Moscow, who believed that she was fairly compensated for her work. *Very* quietly, she disagreed, and sold her stolen secrets to those who would pay dearly to get their hands on them. Orlova had starved in Russia during the civil war that followed the revolution, but now she made sure that would never happen again. She did wonder, sometimes, how long that kind of thing could go on, but put the thought out of her head. In fact, she would have an answer soon enough.

Orlova took a bite of a pastry and, to avoid a cream moustache, was dabbing at her mouth with a pink napkin, when she saw the jolly proprietor making his way across the room. But when he reached Orlova's table, he wasn't so jolly. 'Excuse me, Frau Orlova,' he said, 'but there is a call for you on our telephone.' His voice was professionally courteous but his manner was stiff and uncertain – this sort of thing was unusual and he didn't care for it, even with a customer who was very much a local celebrity.

To Trudi, Orlova said, 'Well, I suppose I must answer the telephone,' and laid her napkin on the table. Orlova the actress seemed mildly surprised and bemused by this intrusion, but Orlova the spy was terrified. The tearoom telephone was a contact point designated for extreme emergencies only, it had never been used before. She followed the proprietor back to the cashier's counter, picked up the receiver and said, 'Good afternoon, this is Frau Orlova.'

The chatter in the tearoom was loud and she pressed the receiver to her ear. On the other end of the line: a man's voice speaking German with a Slavic accent, a man's voice almost breathless with tension. 'Get out,' he said. 'Right away. Now. This minute. There are Gestapo officers in your apartment.' Then there was a click as the man disconnected. Orlova saw that the proprietor was hovering nearby so, for his benefit, she spoke to the dead line. 'Oh yes?' she said. Then waited as though someone were speaking. After a few seconds she said, 'Ahh, I see, I'm sorry to hear that.' Then she said goodbye and replaced the receiver. To the proprietor, who was still standing there, she apologized for the inconvenience. 'All is well?' he said.

'I'm afraid there's something I must attend to,' she said, asked for the bill and paid it, her heart hammering inside her.

Back at the table, she said, 'Trudi dear, please forgive me but I must leave immediately.'

Trudi's eyes, usually tender and caring, were suddenly wide with alarm. 'You've gone pale,' she said. 'What's happened?'

Orlova took her fur coat from the back of the chair and put it on. 'I've had bad news, I'm afraid I must go to the railway station.'

'Then let me drive you, I have the car today, Freddi is in Potsdam.'

Orlova started to say no, then realized it would be faster than looking for a taxi and said yes.

Dusk came early to Berlin in December, yet many drivers were stubborn about turning on their headlights and it was hard to see them. At Orlova's direction, Trudi, knuckles white as she gripped the wheel, worked her way towards the Lehrter Bahnhof, Berlin's international railway terminal. Watching the traffic as it came at them, Orlova fought for control of her mind, fought to suppress the sharp little flashes of panic so she could concentrate. She doubted she would survive a search of her apartment – the Leica camera, the Walther automatic – and she realized that her time in Berlin was over. Now she had to run, to some other country and, wherever in the world she went, she knew they would take her if they found her.

'Are you worrying, Olga dear?'

'What?'

'Are you worrying, I said. You're being very quiet.'

'Yes, I am worried.'

'Don't, please don't. Everything will turn out for the best, I promise.'

Trudi had taken at least two wrong turns, each time provoking loud blasts from the horns of irritated drivers, which made her visibly flinch. Her car was a small Opel and, given the rules of the road in Berlin, drivers of fancier models bullied the cheaper car. But, at last, they reached the Lehrter Bahnhof. Naturally there were crowds of SS men at the entries, and to Orlova's eyes they looked particularly grim and determined. They were, she thought, *waiting* for her. The Opel jerked to a stop as Trudi stamped on the brakes and said, 'Sorry.' Then, 'Well, here we are. Where are you going? Can you tell me?'

'Zurich.'

'Is there someone in Zurich . . .' Trudi didn't quite know how to finish this question but Orlova understood what she meant: a lover, perhaps a secret lover. For Trudi, a rival.

Possible answers tumbled across Orlova's mind; *my beloved aunt, who has only days to live, my oldest friend, who has only days to live*, but none of them sounded credible. Heavy traffic moved about the station, busy this time of night with travellers coming and going. Finally, Orlova said, 'Trudi, I think I had better tell you something. The fact is, I'm in trouble.'

'I knew it! I *felt* it!'

'Trouble with the Gestapo.'

'My God! What have you done?'

'Nothing. But I have enemies, vicious enemies who are jealous of my connections with important people, and they've spread terrible rumours about me. I didn't think that anyone would believe such things, but I was wrong.'

'You're running away, Olga, aren't you.'

'Yes, I am.'

'They'll catch you if you try to get on a train, that's where they look for people, it's in the newspapers all the time.'

'I know,' Orlova said. She had with her two passports, one her own, the other a false passport, a Swiss passport, with a different name. She always carried a lot of money, that was a basic rule of clandestine life. What she had to do was become that other woman, and get out of Germany. 'Trudi,' she said, 'can you find a small hotel somewhere?'

'I don't see why not,' Trudi said, pressed the clutch to the floor and forced the shift into first gear.

Driving away from the station, she took side streets, until they came upon a small building with a sign over the door, HOTEL LUXURIA. Trudi parked the car and the two women entered the hotel. Yes, they had a room available. When asked about luggage, Orlova explained that they'd missed their train and left their luggage in the baggage room. And, by the way, was there a pharmacy nearby? There was, a block away on the Bernauer Strasse.

It was a tired little room, a commercial traveller's room: twin beds with thin, floral coverlets, a single chair, a rusty sink, WC down the hall. Orlova described what she needed and, once Trudi headed off to the pharmacy, she lay down on one of the beds and stared up at the lightbulb in the ceiling. If she did manage to get away, what would she do with her life? She had money in Switzerland, enough to last for a few years if she lived frugally. As a fugitive, her movie star days were over. But then, her spying days were also over. What would it be like to live in obscurity, quiet as a mouse, always waiting for a knock on the door? A German knock, or a Russian knock. *My God,* she thought, *they will all come looking for me.*

Twenty minutes later, Trudi returned, with scissors and a bottle of hydrogen peroxide. Orlova said, 'Trudi, you are going to cut my hair. Short, very short, above the ears, like a boy.'

'I don't really know how, I'm afraid I'll make a mess of it.'

'No matter, just snip away, and when you're done you're going to make me a blonde.'

Trudi took a deep breath; she couldn't say no to her friend, she just had to be careful and take her time. 'Very well,' she said. 'I'll do as you ask. But if I'm going to use the peroxide, you'd better take off your dress, and your slip.' After a last look at her old self in the cloudy mirror above the sink, and as Trudi, scissors in hand, watched her, Orlova undressed.

The following morning, the newly blonde and boyish Orlova stood at the door, anxious to leave. But when she put her hand on the knob, Trudi stopped her. 'Wait, please wait,' she said. 'Just a few seconds. I lay awake for a long time last night, thinking about myself, and about my life, and I made a decision. Olga, I don't want to lose you, I want to run away with you if you'll let me. I know it will be difficult, and I will have to write to Freddi and tell him what I've done, but I don't want to go back to him. I want to follow my heart, I want to stay with you.'

Orlova was moved by this and showed it. And with all the kindness she could muster she said, 'You know I can't let you do that. Sharing the life of a fugitive will not make you happy. Please don't cry. I will never forget what you said, Trudi, I will always remember you, but I must go on alone.'

For a moment, Trudi fought back tears. Finally she said, 'All right, Olga, I understand, so I have only one last request. I would like a kiss, a kiss goodbye, a real kiss.'

They held each other, the kiss was warm and slow and touched with sadness. Then they left the hotel. At Orlova's direction, Trudi drove out of Berlin to nearby Wannsee. From there, Orlova spent a long day taking local trains until she reached the city of Frankfurt where, at the main terminal, she bought a ticket and, an hour later, was on her way to Prague.

18 December. Early in the morning, Stahl left Renate's apartment and returned to the Claridge. In the bathroom mirror, he found shadows beneath his eyes – that dissolute Colonel Vadic – so used a washcloth and cold water as a compress. Perhaps this helped, but not much. By nine o'clock he was out at Joinville, where they had to do retakes of scenes that hadn't, for a variety of reasons, turned out right. A mysterious hand on the back of a chair, a hat magically gone in mid-conversation, a line badly delivered, Pasquin's sergeant saying, 'Jean, let me try that again.' Before they started shooting, the make-up man worked on Stahl and removed the evidence of a night rather too well spent.

When Renate Steiner arrived on the set, carrying a different tunic for the lieutenant, she seemed all business, but she glanced at Stahl and a certain look passed between them. It was the look of those who see each other for the first time after making love, for the first time, the night before, and it made his heart soar. Then a technician approached with a question and Stahl had to turn away, but he would not forget that moment. Renate held up the 'blood'-spattered tunic by the shoulders and said to Avila, 'This will be much better, Jean. Now he's really been *shot*.'

At the end of the day, Stahl walked over to Renate's workroom but she wasn't there so he returned to the hotel and telephoned her. He would pick her up at 7.30, they would have dinner at Balzar, an active, noisy bistro in the Sixth. 'We can have the mâche-betterave,' he said, a salad of beets and sweet little clumps of mâche lettuce with a mustard-flavoured dressing. 'Then perhaps a steak-frites or a ragout of veal. Everything there is good.'

When he arrived at the rue Varlin tenement, the concierge welcomed him back with a sly but affectionate smile: she knew, she approved. On the top floor, Renate was still getting dressed so Stahl sat on the sofa, recalling favoured details of what had gone on there the night before. When the telephone rang, Renate said 'Now what?' and answered with a brusque 'Hello?' She listened for a moment, then turned to Stahl, clearly puzzled, and said, 'It's for you. How would . . .' She didn't finish the question, simply handed him the receiver.

'Yes?' he said.

'Is it Herr Stahl on the line?'

'Yes, who is this?'

'My name doesn't matter, Herr Stahl, not at the moment, anyhow. I'll tell you when we meet.' His German was refined and educated, his voice smooth.

'Why would we meet?'

'I believe you might be able to help us. We're trying to resolve a . . . trying to resolve certain questions that involve your friend Olga Orlova – the actress. Have you seen her lately?'

'No. What questions are you talking about?'

'Mmm, better that we discuss these things in person. Are you planning a visit to Germany any time soon?'

'I'm not.'

'No matter, we can meet in Paris. Always a pleasure to be there.'

'Herr whatever-your-name-is, I don't think I can help you. My regrets, but I must go now.'

'Of course. I understand,' the man said, his voice sympathetic. 'Perhaps my colleagues in Paris will be in touch with you.'

Stahl handed the receiver back to Renate and she hung up. Shaken, he reached for the cigarette pack in his pocket.

Renate stood there for a moment, silent and uncertain, then said, 'Were you expecting a telephone call here?' She was being careful, trying to make the question sound offhand; she didn't mind, she was just curious. Then she added, 'From someone who speaks German?'

'No, it was as much of a surprise to me as it was to you.'

'Then how did he know where you were?'

'I don't know.'

'This is very strange,' she said. 'Has it happened before?'

She won't let it go. So, how much to tell her? With a sigh in his voice he said, 'I am, unfortunately, of some interest to certain German officials. The worst kind of German officials.'

'Oh. Well now I understand. German officials of the worst kind who are evidently following you around the city. Will they be joining us for dinner?'

'Renate, please, if you can find a way to ignore this . . .'

She cut him off. 'I'm an émigré, Fredric, a political refugee. I don't *like* strange phone calls.' She was going to continue but something suddenly occurred to her – from her expression, something she'd almost forgotten. 'Does this have anything to do with that vile little Austrian who appeared on the set? The man in the alpine costume?'

Stahl nodded, and tapped the ash from his cigarette into the Suze ashtray. 'The same crowd. They've been bothering me ever since I came to Paris.'

She thought it over. 'Is that why you went to Berlin? To appease these people?'

Now he had to lie. He couldn't reveal what he'd done in Berlin. 'No, the Warner publicity people liked the idea, so I agreed to go.'

'You couldn't refuse?'

'Let's say I didn't, maybe I should have.'

She took off her glasses, her faded blue eyes searching his face, her witchy nose scenting a lie. Finally she said, 'I *want* to believe you . . .'

She didn't finish the sentence but he knew what came next. He looked at his watch. 'Maybe we should . . .'

'That telephone call *scared* me, Fredric. I know these people and what they do, I *saw* it, in Germany, and now it's here, in this room.'

'Which is my fault, but I don't think I can do anything about it, except walk away from the movie and leave France. Is that what I should do?'

'You'd better not.'

'Then we have to live with it.' He rested his cigarette on the ashtray, took her hands in his and held them tight. 'Can you do that?'

Some of the tension left her, he could see it in her face. She met his eyes, then shook her head in mock despair, a corner of her mouth turned up and she said, 'Go make love to a sexy man and see what happens.'

Perhaps, he thought, hoped, she wanted him more than peace of mind. 'Speaking of which . . . ,' he said, with the playfully evil smile of a movie villain, a villain more than ready to skip dinner.

'That's for later.'

'Then can we go get something good to eat? My dear Renate? My love?'

She liked that, lowered her head and bumped him gently in the chest. 'Help me on with my coat,' she said.

19 December. The mâche-betterave was superb, what followed on the rue Varlin was even better. Having got *the first time* out of the way on the previous night, they had truly indulged themselves. Stahl reached the Claridge just after dawn, where the night deskman wished him a tender good morning – the hotel clerks of Paris were pleased when a guest enjoyed the delights of their city. Before Stahl left for work he telephoned Mme Brun and, after listening to a silent phone for a few

minutes, was told Wilkinson would see him at 7.15 that evening, and the arrangements for their meeting.

A few minutes early, Stahl got out of a taxi at a river dock on the Quai de Grenelle. A middle-aged couple, apparently waiting for his arrival, greeted him like an old friend. 'Hi there Fredric, what a night for a cruise, hey?' said the man in American English. This dock served the tourist boat that went up and down the Seine, and a hand-lettered sign on the shuttered ticket booth said AMERICAN CHAMBER OF COMMERCE CHRISTMAS CRUISE. Stahl chatted with the two Americans – Bob was a vice president at the National City Bank – until the launch arrived, strings of coloured lights shimmering in the icy mist, a band on the foredeck playing 'God Rest Ye Merry Gentlemen'.

J. J. Wilkinson, in a camel-hair overcoat, was waiting for him in the lounge, a shopping bag from the Au Printemps department store by his side. Holding, Stahl guessed, Christmas presents. 'I've ordered you a scotch,' Wilkinson said as they shook hands. 'I hope it's something you like.'

'It'll do me good,' Stahl said. 'A long day on the set.'

'Am I going to be taking notes?'

'I'm afraid so.'

'They never quit, do they.'

'Well, not yet they haven't.'

As always, the blunt and beefy Wilkinson was a port in a storm, and a good listener. When Stahl was done describing the phone call at Renate's apartment, Wilkinson said, 'Well, another piece of the puzzle anyhow.'

'What's that?'

'They know about Orlova, and they suspect you might have had some secret involvement with her.'

'The man on the phone certainly sounded confident.'

Wilkinson shrugged. 'What else? I suspect they were watching the courier, and went chasing after him when he headed for Morocco. And I believe they, the people following him, couldn't let him do whatever they feared so they killed him. They were on that train, Fredric, and maybe – don't take this badly – didn't know who you were.'

Stahl grinned. 'I thought everybody knew who I was.'

'Luckily they didn't. But once they found the money, they started to investigate all the people the courier had contact with. At this point, Orlova's name came up. Now nobody, anywhere in the world, gets close to a national leader without serious attention from the security services, and that goes double for Hitler. Who is this person? What do they want? Who are their friends? Everything you can think of and some things you'd never imagine. I would guess they have a record, a daily, *hourly* record, of her life in Berlin. They knew that you spent the night with Orlova at the Adlon, so they took a close look at you, then decided to give you a poke to see what you did next. Now, that's the optimistic version of . . .'

A waiter arrived with two scotch-and-sodas. '*Salut,*' Wilkinson said in French. To Stahl, the bite of the whisky felt comforting on a cold, raw evening.

'The optimistic version, as I said. The other possibility is that they've caught Orlova spying and arrested her. Which means she's been interrogated, and given them your name. However, if they really felt sure you were spying on Germany I doubt they'd fool around with telephone calls. So, there's a chance that Orlova got away and they're looking for her. One thing I do know is that she's not in Berlin. She's vanished.'

'Is she in Moscow?'

'For her sake, I hope not.'

'She *is* a survivor,' Stahl said.

'She'd better be. And I suspect she'll be doing her surviving in Mexico, or Brazil. Even so, the Gestapo has a long arm.'

'Was that where the phone call came from? The Gestapo?'

'I would think so. The crowd from the Ribbentropburo, Emhof and his friends, wouldn't be involved at this level.'

'Oh,' Stahl said, meaning he understood. But something had jumped inside him when Wilkinson said 'Gestapo'. 'Is there anything I can do about it?'

Wilkinson thought it over. 'You can go to the police, maybe the Deuxième Bureau – I can help with that, but protecting you would involve a lot of time and money and many people. Still, they might do it. The danger comes if they say they'll do it but don't do much, the danger comes when, because you're a movie star, they say things to make you feel better.' Suddenly, Wilkinson turned grim and uncomfortable. 'It's been known to happen,' he said.

It *has* happened, Stahl thought. Why on earth had he assumed he was the only one involved in Wilkinson's operations? Now he knew he wasn't and that, for some of the others, things had gone badly.

The launch pulled into another dock to pick up more passengers. The band on the foredeck began to play 'O Come All Ye Faithful', Wilkinson swirled what remained in his glass, then drank it off and said, 'Care for another?'

Stahl said he would.

Wilkinson turned halfway round and signalled to the waiter. 'Actually, you don't have too much time left here, only a few weeks, right? You'll just have to be cautious – where you are, who you're with. You know your way around the city and you aren't going anywhere else.'

'I'm going to Hungary.'

Wilkinson looked at him, clearly alarmed. 'Fredric, that's not a good place for you, the Gestapo can do anything it wants there.'

'Still, I have to go,' Stahl said. 'I am curious about one thing, why did you have the American couple on the dock?'

'It seemed odd to have you go to an event like this by yourself. And I didn't want you standing alone in a deserted place.'

The drinks arrived, Stahl took more than a sip, so did Wilkinson.

20 December. True to the words of the voice on the telephone, the colleagues in Paris got in touch with him. A second phone call, this time in the morning, as Stahl, barely awake, was having his morning coffee. 'Good morning, Herr Stahl, how are you feeling today?'

Stahl started to hang up the phone when the voice called out, 'Oh no, you mustn't do *that,* Herr Stahl.'

Holding the receiver, Stahl looked around him.

'Over here, Herr Stahl, across the street.'

Directly opposite the Claridge was an unremarkable, but no doubt expensive, apartment building and, at a window that looked into his room, Stahl saw a hand waving at him. The voice on the phone said, 'Yoo-hoo. Here I am.' Then the hand disappeared.

'Yes, I see you, and so what?' Stahl said.

'If I had a decent weapon I could just about put a little hole in your coffee cup.'

As Stahl slammed the receiver down he heard a laugh. Not a portentous or threatening laugh, but the honest, merry laughter of someone who finds something truly funny. And that, Stahl realized, was worse.

Out at Joinville that morning, Stahl asked Avila when they were going to Hungary. 'A few days from now,' Avila said. 'Paramount has rented the castle, and we can stay in the rooms there, most of us anyhow. There's a hotel in the town for everyone else. Wait till you see it, Fredric, the location is perfect.' So much for Stahl's faint hope that the trip might be cancelled. He worked with particular concentration that day, making a point to himself: he wasn't going to allow voices on a telephone or someone waving from a window to distract him from doing his best. He did think about it, between takes, but finally realized this led nowhere and turned his mind to other things.

By four o'clock Stahl was back at the hotel, where a square parcel in brown paper awaited him at the desk. Holding it in his hands – it hardly weighed anything – his defensive instincts surged: *another one of their tricks?* But the return address on the package said, *B. Mehlman, The William Morris Agency* and Stahl relaxed – his agent had sent him a Christmas present. In the room, he tore off the brown wrapping, which revealed fancy gift paper, silver stars on a blue background, tied with a red ribbon. Given the size of the box, Stahl suspected sweaters. Not like Buzzy to do this, he'd never done it before, perhaps it heralded good news about his career. The card would tell the story – where was it? No doubt in the box. And so it was. A small sealed envelope lay on crumpled white paper, in the middle of what he realized – after a few seconds of blank incomprehension – was a garrotte. Sickened by the look of the thing, he held it up and examined it: some kind of very strong cord, like a bowstring, that had a knot in the middle and two wooden handles. With some difficulty, his hands not their usual selves, he tore open the envelope and read the card, which said, in German, 'Merry Christmas'.

He went out a few minutes later and eventually came upon an alley where, by the open back door of a restaurant, he found a garbage can and threw the box on top of a mound of potato peelings. The card he kept.

21 December. Renate had to work late so Stahl, in for the evening, had a brandy and started a new Van Dine murder mystery. He'd thought about going to a movie – the Marx Brothers' *Room Service* was playing nearby – but preferred to stay home and rest. He wasn't precisely afraid, he just didn't want to be out in the street. Some combination of Philo Vance and brandy had him dozing by 10.20, when the telephone rang. He went over to the desk and watched it for a ring or two, then thought *what the hell* and picked it up. And was relieved when a voice on the other end said, 'Hello, Fredric, it's Kiki,' but then, a moment later, not so relieved. This was not a late-evening call from a former lover – there was real urgency in her voice as she said, 'Fredric, there's something I must tell you, it has nothing to do with, with you and me, it's something . . . very different. And not for the telephone. Can you meet me at a café? It's not far from your hotel, a little place on the rue de la Trémoille. Please say yes.' Whatever motive lay behind the call he did not know, but it wasn't seduction. 'All right,' he said. 'Are you at this café?'

'I can be there in twenty minutes.'

Stahl paced the room for a time, then threw a trench coat on and left the hotel.

The rue de la Trémoille was lined with imperious apartment

houses built, lavishly, in the nineteenth century – here there were rich people. But it was after ten at night and the street was dark and silent, a condition that the inhabitants, inside their fortresses, no doubt found restful and much to their taste. Not so Stahl. Wilkinson's cautionary words, about being aware of where you were, echoed in his memory. Not a soul to be seen, not a light visible in the draped windows. When a car's headlights turned a corner and came up behind him, he stepped into a doorway. Slowly, as though the driver were searching for something, the heavy car rumbled past, its taillights glowed red for a moment, then it went on its way.

Minutes later, Stahl found the café, an old-fashioned oasis in the desert of a fashionable neighborhood. Inside it was all amber walls and a haze of Gauloises smoke, and crowded with the usual cast of characters: old women with their dogs, men in workers' caps at the bar, lovers without a place to go. From a far corner, Kiki waved to him and Stahl wound his way past the close-set tables, and they kissed hello. Kiki, despite the cloud of expensive perfume, seemed to be playing a chaste version of herself; the seductress make-up was gone, leaving her fresh-faced and younger, and she wore a sweater of very soft wool in a colour that reminded Stahl of mocha cream. Inside the shawl collar of the sweater, a silk scarf decorated with gold anchors replaced her pearl necklace. 'Thank you for coming,' she said, meaning it. 'You sounded like you were half-asleep.'

'I was,' Stahl said.

'I should've called earlier,' Kiki said, 'but I couldn't make up my mind, and I was afraid you'd just hang up on me.'

'That's not like you, Kiki.'

'No, I suppose it isn't, but you'll see why. Are you going to order something?'

'I don't really want coffee, it will keep me awake. Anyhow, I'm getting more curious by the moment, so . . .'

Kiki took a breath, then said, 'I'm here as a messenger, Fredric. And the message comes from the Baroness von Reschke. She knew you wouldn't agree to see her, and she regrets that, though she does understand. But I must tell you this: when she told me what she wanted me to say to you she was, how to put it, intense, *serious,* and not her usual self – you know what she's like.'

'I do know,' Stahl said. 'All charm and smiles, the baroness.'

'Not when I saw her. She wanted to make sure, absolutely sure, that you received what she called "a final warning". According to her, certain people, her words, no explanation, certain people require your cooperation, and it would be unwise not to help them. What she said was, "please make him understand that he won't be warned again." Does that make any sense to you?'

'It does.'

'Who are these people, to threaten *you*?'

'Being in the movies, Kiki, doesn't shield you from what goes on in the real world. And the people she's talking about are very much from the real world, where politics is a game with no rules, and they're determined to make me help them.'

'Do you know who they are?'

'Well, they're friends of the baroness, and sure of her to the point that they've used her, and thus you, to send their message.'

She stared at him. 'What if you don't do what they want? Are you in danger?'

'Not really. You shouldn't worry about it, and I'll only be in Paris for a few more weeks.'

'I care for you, Fredric, being with you meant a lot to me. I don't want you to be – hurt.'

'Likely that won't happen, though it's hard to predict.'

'What shall I tell her? She said, "I must have an answer," and she meant it. Not like her at all, not the baroness I know. Suddenly, right there in her parlour, she was a different woman. Cold, and almost, well, *cruel*.'

'The answer is that you gave me the message. I heard what she wanted me to hear.'

'Nothing else?'

'No, nothing else.'

'Fredric' – she reached across the table and took his hand in hers – 'is there anything I can do to help you?'

He shook his head. 'Leave it alone, Kiki. Forget this happened. There is no point in your being involved, in fact there's every reason you shouldn't be.'

She let go of his hand and sat back. 'Very well,' she said. 'But the offer is still there, if you change your mind.'

Amid the low burble and clatter of the night-time café, Stahl was silent for a time, then leaned forward and said, 'Kiki, maybe I shouldn't ask, but I will anyhow. Are you more a part of this than you're telling me?'

Slowly, she shook her head. 'I'm only Kiki de Saint-Ange, Fredric, that's all I know how to be. And when you go back to America I'll just be a girl you knew in Paris.'

Stahl and Renate spent Christmas Eve together – had a champagne supper served in his suite, then stayed for the night. Renate Steiner was a supremely sophisticated woman, but a supremely sophisticated woman who had lived in penury for a long time and Stahl was secretly delighted to watch as the luxurious surroundings went to her head. A glass of champagne in hand, she took a bubble bath in the glorious bathroom, then, pink and excited, lounged around the suite in Stahl's pyjamas as the radio played Christmas carols – 'O the rising of the sun, the running of the deer'. Finally, drunk and happy, they went to bed, made love, and woke in the morning to the icy fog of a northern European winter.

Late that morning they took a taxi to Renate's apartment, where she was giving a buffet lunch for her émigré friends. Perhaps twenty people were packed into the tiny apartment, all of them fugitives; artists, leftists, Jews, the sort of people the Nazis loathed, the sort of people the Nazis murdered. A ragtag lot, all of them poor to one degree or another. The lunch was abundant – Stahl saw to that – and practically all of it was eaten. And drunk. A few tears were shed, and La Belle France was toasted as their saviour, though one of the guests turned to Stahl and whispered, 'For the time being, anyhow.' Stahl had visited his bank the day before and, as a line of guests left en masse – 'I don't want these opened at the party,' he'd told Renate – each was given an envelope containing a thousand dollars in one-hundred-dollar bills. He was plenty rich enough to make such gestures, and so he did.

Trouble came the following day, from an unexpected direction, and it also affected a group of émigrés, including Stahl and Renate. Avila called a meeting of the cast and crew on the set, where he announced that Paramount had declined to pay for air travel to Budapest. The cast and crew would, the studio executives had declared, have to go by train. A certain hush fell over the set when Avila said this. It took a moment, but soon enough everybody realized what that meant: the eleven émigrés working on *Après la Guerre* could not cross the German border. The Gestapo list of those who had fled Germany illegally was precise and thorough, and the émigrés would certainly be arrested. And to reach Hungary from France you had to go through Germany. 'Deschelles fought hard,' Avila explained, 'but the Paramount executives wouldn't budge. As Jules put it to me, 'I did the best I could, but I am an ant and they are a thumb.'

In the discussion that followed, the émigrés didn't say much, but the rest of the company was passionate on their behalf. 'We are a family,' Justine Piro said. 'Every good production company becomes a family, we can't leave people behind.' At the end of the discussion, it was worked out that the eleven would fly on a small chartered aeroplane; Deschelles would 'borrow' some money from production funds, and those who could afford it – which meant Stahl, paying for himself and Renate, and two others making high salaries – would contribute. Avila would donate, and so would Piro, Pasquin, and Gilles Brecker. At the end of the discussion, a carpenter from Hamburg, formerly a communist streetfighter, stood and thanked everyone there. 'I'll tell you it's a fucking pity,' Pasquin said to Stahl as the meeting broke up, 'that the whole country won't work this way.'

Early on the morning of 28 December, Stahl took a taxi to Le Bourget. As they left the city, the driver said, 'Excuse me, monsieur, is it possible that someone is following you?'

'Why do you ask?'

'Because there's a car that's been behind us at every turn.' Then, with the bellicose flair of the Parisian taxi driver, he said, 'I'll lose them if you want me to, monsieur.' Stahl told him not to bother. An hour later he was in an aeroplane, looking down at the snow-dusted forests of Germany.

28 December. They circled Budapest as the lights of the city came on, then landed at the nearby airfield. The customs officers were amiable enough, smiling and silent as they stamped passports – silent because they knew that nobody spoke Hungarian, and they didn't care to conduct business in German, the second language of Hungary, and what had been the Austro-Hungarian Empire. Next, the eleven émigrés crowded into two rattletrap taxis. Avila had given Stahl a hand-drawn map of the castle's location, near the Danubian port of Komarom, and Stahl handed it to the taxi drivers. After some head scratching and a spirited argument, inspiration struck and the taxis drove off over snow-covered roads. Soon enough the driving grew difficult, the bald tyres spun, the drivers cursed, everybody got out and pushed. Finally, at the edge of a tiny village, the drivers gave up. 'Can't go,' said one of them in rudimentary German. Stahl paid him, the driver said they should stay where they were and that someone would come for them. Then the taxis got turned around and headed back towards Budapest.

As the émigrés stood by their baggage, rubbing their hands and stamping their feet, they wondered what would become of them. A cold hour passed, and just when they'd decided to walk into the village, they heard the jingling of little bells. Then, from the darkness, there appeared two sleighs, each of them drawn by two immense horses. Once again, Stahl produced his map, but these drivers took one glance and knew where they were going. The émigrés seated themselves in the sleighs and were then covered by large blankets, more like rugs, thick wool with canvas backing. A crown and Cross-of-Lorraine design, red on grey, decorated the wool, which smelled like horse sweat and manure. At last, with long plumes steaming from the horses' nostrils, they trotted off towards Komarom.

The moon cast blue-tinted light on the snow and, except for the muffled clop of hooves, the jingling bells, and the occasional gentle 'hup' of the driver, there wasn't a sound to be heard. 'We've gone back in time,' Renate said as she pressed against Stahl, sharing his warmth. The road wound through a forest, where bare branches glittered with ice in the moonlight, then returned to the white fields. Far off in the distance, they heard two wolves, howling back and forth. The grinning driver turned halfway round and, rubbing his tummy, said something in Hungarian which made him laugh. After an hour or so, and just as the frigid air started to hurt the skin on their faces, a dark, massive silhouette appeared in the distance. The driver pointed with his whip and said, 'Castle Polanyi.'

In the moonlight, the castle rose from a hill high above the grey Danube. A jagged ruin, black as soot, destroyed not so much by time as by stones flung from siege machines, by cannon, by fire, by the wars of three hundred years. Here and there, broken towers climbed above the crumbling battlements. The castle's factotum, manager of noble estates, greeted the frozen travellers at the end of a bridge over the empty moat, and led them into a rebuilt part of the castle, then up a stone stairway where rooms awaited them, each with a blazing fire. As the factotum, who introduced himself as Csaba, pronounced *chaba,* showed Stahl his room, he said that the Count Polanyi intended to visit the castle while filming was in progress. 'You should be honoured,' said Csaba. 'He doesn't often come here, except in hunting season. The count is a diplomat at the Hungarian legation in Paris. A great man, you shall see.' Stahl and Renate stayed together, huddled under many blankets, the chill air in the room so cold that Stahl slid out of bed from time to time and added a log to the fire.

As night fell on the following day, the cast and crew arrived from Budapest. 'We only just made it,' Avila told Stahl. 'There were trucks waiting for us at the railway station, but we had to stop and dig them out of the snow every few miles.' In the morning, the last day of December, the last day of 1938, they once again began work on *Après la Guerre.*

In the movie it was autumn, but in Komárom it was winter, so two of the count's stablemen shovelled the snow off the castle's courtyard. The prop man had brought large burlap bags of dead leaves and, with the help of a fan, these blew across the ancient sett stones. Stahl, in his legionnaire's uniform, and Piro, in black kerchief and a man's torn coat, sat on a low wall, where the leaves swirled past their feet – to be gathered at the far end of the courtyard and sent across again, though the rough surface did them no good. Once Avila had the camera properly angled, so that it captured the profile of the black tower above them, the day's shooting began.

'I think,' Ilona says, 'before we go in there, I must tell you the truth about myself.'

'What truth is that?' says Vadic, his hair ruffled handsomely by the leaf fan.

'I am no countess, Colonel Vadic. It was all . . . a lie.'

'Are you Ilona? Are you Hungarian?'

'I am Ilona and, at least on my mother's side, Hungarian. I was afraid you wouldn't take me along, so I made up a story.'

'Oh well, it was nice to have a countess with us. I suppose that if we go in there, they won't greet you with open arms.'

A rueful smile. 'They will stare at me, they will wonder, "who is this ragged woman, pretending to be a countess?"'

'Beautiful woman, I'd say.'

'You flatter me, but I don't believe they'll care. They will have the servants throw us out, or worse.'

They will – a reluctant nod from Colonel Vadic. 'So, no jewels, no loyal lady's maid.'

'No, colonel. Not even dinner. It was only my daydream of a different life.'

'Well, all is not lost. We shall just be wayfaring strangers, going home after the war. They still might feed us.'

'Are you angry with me? I wouldn't blame you.'

'I can't be angry, Ilona, not with you. And beautiful women are allowed a few lies.'

As they sit for a moment in silence, a noisy flock of crows – no part of the script – lands on the tower above the wall. Then Ilona says, 'Why do you keep saying I am beautiful? Just *look* at me.'

'To me you have always been beautiful, from the first moment I saw you.'

She looks up at him and in her eyes, in the subtle alteration of her face, is the slow comprehension of what he's been trying to say. Slowly, he leans towards her, he is going to kiss her but a voice from a window shouts 'Get out of here, you filthy tramps.'

'Cut!' Avila said. 'Let's try another take, that *can't* have been as good as I thought it was.' Then, to the soundman, 'Gerard, let's keep those crows. Have somebody throw a stone up there, maybe we can get them to caw for the next take.'

Count Janos Polanyi arrived late in the afternoon and, by way of Csaba, let Avila, Stahl, and Justine Piro know they were expected for dinner at 8.30. The dining room had a long table of polished walnut and vases of fresh flowers. In December, fresh flowers. Polanyi was well into his sixties, a large, heavy man with thick white hair, who smelled of bay rum, cigar smoke, and wine, and wore a blue suit cut by a London tailor. He had the easy warmth of a wealthy host, and the distance of power and privilege.

The main course was a spit-roasted haunch of venison. In response to the exclamations of delight at the first taste, the count said, 'I would like you to think this came from a great stag, that I brought down with a single shot. But the truth is, I picked it up at my Paris butcher on the way to the airport.' Thus Polanyi. A brief rumble of a laugh followed, joined by the guests at the table.

With the pears and local cheese, and having drunk more than his share of Echézeaux Burgundy, Polanyi became reflective. 'My poor old battered castle,' he said. 'It's the border of northern Hungary now

– the treaty that followed the Great War turned the other side of the river into Czech territory. But for this castle, it was just one more war. It began life as a Roman fortification, was taken by the Hungarian Grand Duke Arpád in 895 – legend has it that the Milky Way was formed from the dust raised by his army's horses. Then it was destroyed in 1241 by the Mongolian Tartars – a costly invasion, half the people of Hungary were murdered. Rebuilt, it was besieged by the Turks in 1683, then recaptured by Charles of Lorraine in 1684. History has *always* been bloody in this part of the world, and is about to be once again. But, what can we do. Now we'll have to sign some sort of treaty with Hitler and his thugs and, once the French and the British have dealt with them, oh how we shall suffer for that.' He paused for a time, then said, 'Well, here comes the brandy, would anyone care to join me for a cigar?'

1 January, 1939. New Year's Day for much of the world, but there were no holidays for film crews on location. But Stahl didn't mind. As long as production went smoothly, the reality of a good location inspired the cast, so Stahl was eager to work. At breakfast, on trestle tables set up in the entry hall, the company raised their cups of coffee or tea and drank to a better year in 1939, peace on earth, good will towards men.

But not just yet.

As Stahl rose to leave, the cameraman came running down the stairway, his face blank with shock. 'Jean!' he shouted. 'The cameras have been stolen!'

The room had gone dead silent. Avila stood up and said, 'What?'

'They were taken from the room we're using for storage. Sometime last night.'

'We'll have to find cameras in Budapest,' Avila said. 'How could this happen?'

'I don't know. I don't know.' He was frantic, close to tears.

'Calm down, Jean-Paul. Was the door locked?'

'No, there's no lock. All I found was . . .' He gave Avila a piece of paper. Avila read it twice, then handed it to Stahl. 'What do you make of this?'

The note was in German, hand-printed in ink, and said, 'If you want your cameras back it will cost you a thousand American dollars.' Then went on to describe an inn, outside the town of Szony. 'If you alert the police,' it went on, 'you will never see your cameras again. Come to this place promptly at 5.15 tonight.' There was no signature.

'Jean,' Stahl said, 'I must speak with you in private.'

They went out into the hallway, where Stahl told Avila what was going on. Not all of it, there wasn't time, but enough. German secret police, he said, were after him because of a suspected connection with a woman who had been spying on the Nazi leadership. 'This could be a coincidence, Jean, just a simple robbery, but I don't believe in coincidence. This theft is my fault, and I will be the one to go to the inn, pay the ransom, and get the cameras back.'

Avila, too well aware of conspiracy and its strategies, wasn't slow to see the implications of the note: Stahl lured to some isolated place and abducted. 'You are the target, Fredric, and so you *can't* be the one to go – I will take care of this. However, we can do nothing without telling Polanyi, it happened in his house, he'll never forgive us if we don't tell him.'

'But he will involve the police, and we'll lose the cameras.'

'Then we'll have to insist. It's our equipment, and we're responsible for retrieving it. That means me and one other person, because you can't go anywhere near that inn.'

'Jean, we have to see Polanyi, right away. Then, later on, you and I can argue. But I warn you, I can't just sit here, I cannot. Will not. Because if something happened to you I couldn't live with it. As for the money, I've got about six hundred dollars with me, and we'll have to find the rest.'

'I have it,' Avila said. 'I brought dollars with me, because they work when nothing else will. Christ, what an evil thing to do.'

They went off in search of Csaba, who led them upstairs to Polanyi's suite of rooms. The count, in a green satin dressing gown with lime silk lapels, was having his breakfast. An egg cup, of near translucent porcelain, held a boiled egg with its top neatly sliced off. Tiny spoon in hand, he said good morning as Csaba showed them into his room. When Avila told him what had happened, and added Stahl's explanation, Polanyi barely responded – raised eyebrows, little more. As a diplomat, he was conditioned to hearing bad news and had long ago learned not to react to it. 'Very brazen of them,' he said, 'to sneak in here at night. What do the Nazis want with a thousand dollars?'

'Perhaps,' Stahl said, 'to make it look like the work of a local thief. Who would get nothing like a thousand dollars from some pawnbroker.'

Polanyi almost smiled. 'A local thief? Clearly they've never met the local thief. Tell me, what exactly did they take?'

'Five Mitchell Standard film cameras, packed in five large suitcases. The tripods travel separately.'

'Well, if they're at Szony, you'll soon have them back.'

'Will you notify the police?'

'In Budapest, I would. There are detectives there who could take care of this in a hurry. But, out here in the countryside, we have the gendarmerie, and they aren't . . . what we need. But, gentlemen, don't despair! I have a couple of friends in the neighbourhood, old cavalry friends from the war. And *they* know how to deal with people who do such things.'

'Count Polanyi,' Stahl said, 'this happened because of me, and I am honour-bound to take part in the recovery.'

Now Polanyi did smile, a bittersweet smile. He put his spoon down by the egg cup and said, 'Honour-bound, are you? It's been some time since I've heard that expression, people don't often use it these days. So then, you wish to come along with us? Is that what you want?'

'"Us" you say. Does that mean you're going?'

'It is my house, sir. And my honour that has been affronted. So of course I will go.'

Stahl had been rebuked and he showed it.

And then, after a moment's thought, Polanyi relented. 'Oh all *right*,' he said. 'I do understand.' With a sigh he put his hands on his knees, rose to his feet, walked across the room to an elaborate antique dresser and opened the top drawer. From which he took a well-worn leather holster that held an automatic pistol with an extra clip bound to the barrel with a rubber band. Handing it to Stahl he said, 'Have you ever used one of these?'

'Only in the movies, with blank cartridges.'

Polanyi nodded and said, 'Naturally. Well, you won't need it, but bring it along.' Then, after a glance at his cooling egg, he looked at his watch and said, 'Now, gentlemen, I must get dressed. It is the first day of the new year, and I will be going to mass.'

Polanyi's friends arrived before three, Csaba came for Stahl and he went downstairs to meet them. They were both in their late forties, Ferenc and Anton, with dark eyes and black moustaches. Tall and lean and weathered, they looked to Stahl as though they'd spent their lives on horseback. Stahl was wearing the holstered automatic on his belt and, after they'd all been introduced, Ferenc said, 'What've you got there?' Stahl drew the pistol and handed it to him grip first. Ferenc had a professional look at it, worked the slide, then said, 'Very good, the Frommer 7.65, our military sidearm for a long time. Do you plan to shoot somebody?'

'I don't plan on it but, if I have to, I will.'

'Well, if it turns out that way, and sometimes it does, just aim for the centre of the body and you may hit something. Of course, with a weapon like this, closer is always better.' Ferenc handed the pistol back to Stahl and said, 'We should be leaving in about ten minutes.'

Stahl returned to his room, where Renate awaited him. Earlier, when he'd told her what he was going to do, she'd simply said, 'I see,' in the flat voice of the practised fatalist but, after he'd buttoned up his warm jacket, she put her arms around him, pulled him close, and held him tight. Then she stepped back and said, 'Now you can go, but for God's sake be careful.'

A low, cloudy sky that afternoon, with winter light and a liquid tang in the air that meant it would snow. Polanyi appeared in the entry hall, dressed for hunting, a shotgun held by the barrels resting on his shoulder. Ferenc and Anton, rifles slung on their backs, holstered pistols on their hips, joined them. 'So, off we go,' Polanyi said.

'How do we get there?' Stahl said. All afternoon he'd been apprehensive about horseback riding. He could do it, he'd done it, but he wasn't good at it.

'By launch,' Polanyi said. 'Szony is just down the river from here, maybe twenty minutes – the current is with us.'

'I thought the note said five-fifteen,' Stahl said.

The courteous Polanyi, trying to hide his amusement, said, 'Indeed it did, but it might be a good idea to have a look at the place in daylight.' He patted Stahl on the shoulder with a heavy hand. *We'll be fine.*

They walked down the hill to a wooden dock, its pilings forced askew by the downstream tide. The launch was small and compact, with flaking grey paint on its hull – one more working boat on a commercial river – but when Polanyi started it up the engine roared with power before he cut back the throttle. Nobody said much – a compulsion to chatter when facing action was considered to be bad form. As Polanyi steered for the centre of the river, Stahl, standing on the deck behind the open wheelhouse, could feel the heavy strength of the current. Polanyi, raising his voice over the chug of the engine, said, 'In one way we're lucky – usually the Danube would be frozen up by now, but not this year.'

Twenty minutes later they passed the port of Szony, on the same side of the river as Komarom, and larger than Stahl had imagined, where two Danube freighters were being serviced at a refuelling dock. Then, once the port had fallen astern, Ferenc, standing watch at the bow, said, 'There it is.' Partly hidden by the tangle of poplar and willow that traced the shoreline, was a one-storey building of wooden slats with a faded sign above its door and its windows boarded up. Looking past the inn, Stahl caught a glimpse of the road that ran along the river on the Hungarian side.

Once the launch, following a slight curve, had passed the inn and it was no longer visible, Polanyi slowed the engine. Turning to Stahl he said, 'I think I know what they were planning. Once they'd got hold of you, all they had to do was throw you in the boot of a car, drive west to Komarom, then take the bridge across to Slovakian territory. Slovakia is Germany's great friend – they hate the Czechs – and from there it's not that far to the Reich, and a cellar on the Prinz-Albrecht-Strasse, Gestapo headquarters.' Stepping partway out of the wheelhouse, he called out, 'Hey Ferenc, is the road passable?'

'It's snow-covered, but I've already seen a small truck go by. Not driving fast, but making way well enough.'

Polanyi cut the engine back and steered the boat towards the shoreline. At the stern, Anton tossed an anchor over the side, and the launch tugged at it but stayed where it was. 'Now we wait,' Polanyi said and shut the engine off. He took a silver flask from his pocket, had a drink, then passed it to Stahl, saying, 'This will keep you warm.' It was fruit brandy in the flask, slivovitz, distilled from plums. Stahl remembered it well – a good way to get plastered when he'd been a teenager in Vienna.

By four-thirty, the twilight was fading fast, soon enough it would be dark. A rowing boat suspended from davits at the stern was lowered into the water by Polanyi and Ferenc. 'We're going to have a look at the inn,' Polanyi said to Stahl. 'If somebody tries to board the launch, shoot him, don't waste time on conversation. Otherwise, your job is to wait here.'

Stahl acknowledged the order and settled on the landward side of the launch, his back against the wall of the wheelhouse. The rowing boat moved off into the marsh at the edge of the river and, once the dip of the oars could no longer be heard, the silence deepened, broken only by gusts of wind that rustled the high reeds. Staring into the darkness, he thought he saw a momentary gleam of light near the inn – perhaps a flashlight – then it was dark once again. As the brandy's warmth wore off, Stahl felt the cold, and wanted to move around but stayed where he was. If the launch was being watched, he wasn't going to make himself an easy target. He couldn't see the dial on his watch, but guessed the time set for the meeting had passed.

Then, in the distance, he heard a voice. Only a syllable or two, maybe a shout, maybe a cry of alarm, he couldn't tell. Staying low, he moved to the railing and opened the holster, drawing the automatic, holding it ready in his hand. From the direction of the inn, two flat snaps, gunshots, followed by a fusillade that went on for a few seconds and shouting from various voices, the words indistinguishable. Something went whistling through the reeds, hit the water, and whined off into the night. Had somebody shot at him? No, a stray round from the gunfight. A moment of dead silence was ended by a single report, louder and deeper than the others, and the sound of a car's ignition and an engine with the gas pedal on the floor in first gear. The car was headed away from him, back towards Komarom. Then, nothing. Where were Polanyi and the others? He started counting, because if nobody appeared he would have to go and see what had happened. Somebody hurt? Somebody dead? All of them dead? He counted to one hundred, then stood up, prepared to go into the marsh and work his way towards the inn.

But, it turned out, he didn't have to. As the rowing boat emerged from the darkness, weaving through the reeds and willows, Polanyi called out, 'It's your friends, Herr Stahl, please hold your fire.' Stahl relaxed and let out a long-held breath. Polanyi and his two friends pulled themselves over the open stern, then the count came towards him and handed him a shoe. Puzzled, he stared at it – a well-made man's shoe, black, and recently shined, the sort of shoe worn in a city, worn in an office. 'Booty from the raid,' Polanyi said. 'And yours if you want it, perhaps a trophy.'

'What happened?' Stahl said.

'Well, they were there all right, three of them, wearing overcoats and hats. They were waiting for you outside the inn, in the trees on the far side of the road. Basically, we surprised each other, which happens in combat, and we fired at them as they fired at us, and nobody hit anybody, despite a lot of bullets flying around. But they weren't there for a gun battle, they were there for an abduction – they were armed with pistols, and when the rifles took pieces out of the tree trunks they yelled in German and ran for their car. On the way, one of them lost a shoe.'

Ferenc, standing next to Polanyi, cleared his throat, a sound of polite disagreement. Then he said, 'The Count Polanyi fired both barrels as they were running away and I believe he may have hit one of them, possibly in the backside – he leapt into the air and squawked – but maybe that's just wishful thinking. We had a look around where the car had been parked and there may have been blood on the weeds. But who knows, it was dark, and torches don't really give you enough light. Still, it might have been blood.'

'Maybe,' Polanyi said. 'In any event, they ran away. So, honour satisfied. However, we did break into the inn and had a look, and I'm sorry but there was no sign of any suitcase or camera, or anything, really. The inn is closed for the winter, chairs stacked, windows boarded up, no sign of use.'

'I want to thank you, Count Polanyi,' Stahl said. 'And to thank Ferenc and Anton as well. For doing this, for . . .'

Polanyi raised a hand. 'You are welcome. As it happens, we don't like seeing Germans with guns on Hungarian soil and we would do it again tomorrow if we had to. In fact we *may* have to, time will tell. And, as for the cameras, I will telephone to Budapest in the morning and see what can be arranged. We make plenty of movies in Hungary, and I know one or two people who might be able to help.'

'I can only say thank you once again.'

'Well, wait until tomorrow for that. By the way, do you want to keep the shoe?'

'I think not,' Stahl said.

'In that case . . . ,' Polanyi said, nodding towards the river.

Stahl flipped the shoe over the railing.

Polanyi went to start the engine while Ferenc and Anton cranked the rowing boat back onto the launch. As they pulled away from the shore, Polanyi turned on a spotlight mounted on the roof of the wheelhouse and the beam swept the black water ahead of them as they made for Komárom.

There were cameras in Budapest – in fact there were two Mitchells, which made life easier for the cameraman and, by the morning of the third, the company was again at work, shooting inside the castle, and then staging the climactic gun battle, using for background the blackened stone walls and two windows that opened on the courtyard. And it did look, once Avila worked out the angles, like 'somewhere in the Balkans'. The first part of the scene, a fight in a bar, had been shot at Joinville, so what they filmed now was the climax: Colonel Vadic's heroism, Pasquin's jolly bravery, and the lieutenant's wounding that leads to his death speech. The actors playing the Balkan thugs were more than frightening, one of them a Russian giant discovered by Avila, who found him working as a nightclub doorman.

From Stahl's perspective it worked perfectly well – mostly running and shooting, no subtle acting required. But he sensed that the cast and crew had been rattled by the theft and were more than ready to go back to Paris. There were, according to Avila, two or three retakes they could do at Joinville, or perhaps not, it would be up to Deschelles. Essentially, for all practical purposes, the filming of *Après la Guerre* was complete. The movie would have its final edit and music would be added in the weeks to come, but Stahl's work on the production was finished.

That night, Stahl and Renate had the discussion that they had been, for some time, avoiding. They pulled two wing chairs up to the huge fireplace and Stahl built a splendid fire. Once it was blazing, he settled in his chair and said, 'We haven't talked about this, but I think the time has come. I don't like it, but, with everything that's happened, I had better get out of France as soon as I can.'

'Yes, I saw it coming,' Renate said. 'Once you got that telephone call at my apartment I started thinking, and I began to realize that, after the movie was done, you'd be better off leaving the country.'

'I did want to stay, there was a time when I thought about staying for a while, or even longer. In a proper world, Paris is where I belong.'

'I know,' Renate said. 'It's no secret, how you feel.'

'And you as well, Renate. No?'

'Oh yes, it was . . . When my husband and I were struggling to get out of Germany, Paris was my dream. Just get there, I thought, and everything will be perfect. But it turned out that this wasn't so, not for my husband, wherever he is tonight, and not really for me either, until I met you. Then it, the city, kept its promises.'

'How would you feel if you came back to California with me? You wouldn't have to stay if you hated it. Because people do, you know, truly hate it.'

'Oh I'm sure I would hate it – I'm a European, in my heart. And I doubt I could work there.'

'You could. I know people who can make it possible.'

'But what about a visa? It takes months now – half the world wants to go to America.'

'That won't be a problem. I think the embassy might move you up the list. And, if for some reason they won't, we'll just have to get married.'

It gladdened Stahl's heart to see her smile in the usual way as she said, irony just barely touching her voice, 'A proposal?'

They looked at each other for a time, then Stahl said, 'I don't want to lose you, Renate. We should be together.'

'Then that is what we shall do,' Renate said. 'Now, no more of this, let's get into bed before we freeze to death.'

8 January. There was to be no end-of-production party at the castle – the cast and crew voted – but Avila said he would arrange something when they were back home. And so they all packed, and Stahl spent a few minutes saying goodbye to Polanyi. The count had no appetite for sentiment, and waved off Stahl's expression of gratitude. 'I'll see you in Paris, my friend,' he said. 'That's where I work, at the legation, and I like the idea of having a movie star at my social evenings.'

'I would enjoy it,' Stahl said. 'But I suspect I'll be heading off to California.'

'Oh I think you'll be back, once the current mess is resolved. So, until then . . .' They shook hands, and Stahl realized that Polanyi had thoroughly enjoyed saving his life and was sorry to see him leave.

'I'll just go to my room,' Stahl said, 'and bring your pistol back.'

'No, no,' Polanyi said. 'You keep that, it's my gift to you.'

The road to Budapest was now open and Stahl and Renate and the other émigrés headed for the airfield, and the chartered plane, in three taxis that came to get them at the castle. Staring out of the window at the winter fields, Stahl wondered about Polanyi. Something about him, Stahl couldn't say exactly what that was, reminded him of J. J. Wilkinson. Maybe Polanyi was a working diplomat, but Stahl thought there might be a little more. He had, Stahl thought, some spy in him. Maybe more than some.

The airport was crowded and busy, but the émigrés were in good spirits, they had worked hard, earned money, were now headed home to the people that cared about them. Stahl, as the leader of the group, stood at the end of the passport control line, Renate at his side. What they had together had grown, in front of the castle fireplace; they had a future now, and that changed them. The passport officers were slower that day, they checked photographs against faces, asked about Hungarian money and art, and took their time making sense of various official papers: some of the émigrés were travelling on French documents, some on the Nansen passports issued to stateless persons by the League of Nations, and some on German passports that would never be renewed but were still valid. The officers also had a list. One did not like seeing a list, one knew what that might mean.

And so it did.

When it came Renate's turn – the rest of the émigrés waiting on the other side of the desks – the officer, a rather intellectual-looking fellow with a trim beard, said, 'Madam Steiner, I must ask you to wait for a minute. I'll see to the gentleman with you first, it won't take long.'

It didn't. Stahl's American document was quickly stamped. Then the officer excused himself and walked a few steps to an office directly opposite the passport control area.

'What could be wrong?' Stahl said. 'Have you used your passport before?'

'Not since I came to Paris. And we crossed into France at night, like everyone else, through a forest. The Nazis weren't going to let us out. One of my friends tried to leave in the official way, to her sorrow.'

The door of the office was open and they could see the control officer, in conversation with a man who wore a suit. Back and forth they went, not animated in the least, simply dealing with some sort of problem. Finally, the officer returned to his desk. He looked at Stahl and said, 'You may proceed, sir, you don't have to wait here.'

'I don't mind,' Stahl said. 'We're travelling together.'

'I'm afraid there's some difficulty in approving Madam Steiner's exit. Apparently, German officials wish to question her regarding her husband, who is being sought by the German police, and they have requested that we detain her until she can be questioned. I regret the inconvenience, but we must honour their request. It's not usually done this way, but it does happen sometimes.'

'Are you sure?' Stahl said. 'Steiner is a common name in Germany.'

'Perhaps they've made an error. But, even if they haven't, this shouldn't be too hard to straighten out, she needs simply to visit the German legation here in Budapest. However, since she'll have to travel later, there's no reason you should miss your flight. Madam Steiner will surely be following on in a day or two.'

'Go ahead,' Renate whispered to him. 'Go. Get *out* of here.'

'I believe we'll travel together,' Stahl said to the officer. 'So I'll have to wait as well.'

The officer met Stahl's eyes, then, with a covert nod of the head towards the other side of the control desk, he let Stahl know that he had best join his friends while he still could. Stahl didn't move. 'Well,' the officer said, 'that's up to you.'

In a taxi, headed for the Hotel Astoria, Renate tried, and failed, not to show her reaction to the denied exit. After a brooding silence, she said, 'I really thought we were safe. I really did. But that kind of thinking is a curse. Funny, but I never learn, a fault in my character perhaps. But it was nice while it lasted, wasn't it. Should I go to the German legation?'

'Don't be like that, Renate. You'd never come out and you know it.'

'Then what?'

'There's surely an American consulate in Budapest, I'll get in touch with them as soon as we're settled in the hotel.'

'But the chartered aeroplane is gone, Fredric. It's gone, it flew away to Paris. And, when I looked at the notice board in the airport, every flight, it seems, requires a transfer in Berlin. Where will I go?' She was, he thought, close to tears, but would get no closer.

He put his arm around her shoulders. 'You're going with me,' he said.

The Astoria was almost full, but a small single room remained and Stahl took it. They didn't unpack, they sat side by side on the edge of the bed and schemed. There was no telephone in the room, so Stahl went down to the desk and placed a call to the American consulate. The woman who answered the phone was, by her accent, American, and Stahl spoke English with her. She knew who he was, and told him he could see a consular officer that afternoon. America would help them, he believed, but, just in case, he booked a call to Buzz Mehlman. 'As soon as the foreign operator gets through,' he told the hotel clerk, 'please call me. I'm in room sixty-five.'

It was three-thirty by the time he reached the American consulate, six-thirty in the morning Pacific Coast Time, so he was safe there because he'd called Buzz at the William Morris office. The consular official was a young fellow called Stanton, and he, a committed movie fan, was eager to help. Yes, he would telephone Mr Wilkinson at the Paris embassy but he doubted there was much he could do, this problem had to be dealt with locally. Stahl explained what had happened in the airport but went no further. It was Renate Steiner who needed help, because the Reich officials were being . . . Stanton filled in the word: 'Difficult?'

'A polite word,' Stahl said. 'At least that.'

'Okay,' Stanton said. 'Basically you and your friend have to get out of Hungary, and the difficulty here is that she's technically a German citizen. Now what I can do is this: I'm going to approve a visa for her to travel to the US, giving us at least some official standing to intervene with the authorities in Budapest – they don't *have* to honour the German request.'

'How long will that take?'

Stanton drummed his fingers on the desk. 'I always hope for days, but I've seen days become weeks. Still, it's a chance. And once the Hungarians release her, you can charter another aeroplane and fly right over Hitler.'

'This is very good of you,' Stahl said. 'I think I'll go back to the Astoria and bring her over here.'

'See you later,' Stanton said. 'And now I can write to my mom in Ohio and tell her I met *Fredric Stahl*.'

On the street outside the consulate was a long line – people applying for American visas. The line disappeared around the corner, Stahl had no idea how far it went after that.

At the hotel, he told Renate to grab her passport and they would go immediately to the consulate. She had set her suitcase on the luggage rack and unpacked a few things. 'Do you think you could lend me a handkerchief?' she said. 'I seem to have left mine back in the room.'

'Of course,' he said, put his suitcase on the bed and opened it up. Renate, standing by his side, said, 'What's that?'

'An automatic pistol that Polanyi gave me.' After a brief search, he found a handkerchief, handed it to her, and said, 'Now can we go?'

By 5.15, Hungarian time, Renate had a visa to travel to America. If she could ever get out of Hungary alive. At 7.40, Stahl's call to the

William Morris Agency was put through and he went down to a telephone cabin in the lobby. The secretary who answered the phone found Buzzy right away. 'Fredric? Can you hear me?'

'Yes, I can.'

'What's going on?'

'It's a long story, but what's happened is that I'm with a woman friend, we were shooting on location in Hungary, and the border officials won't let us out.'

'Won't let *you* out?'

'I go where she goes.'

'Oh. Okay, now I understand. Let me make some calls, I'll see what I can do.' Stahl had heard this line before, and, when he'd heard it, good things had followed. Not always, but often enough.

'Her name is Renate Steiner, Buzz. She's officially a German citizen but she's a political émigré and lives in Paris.'

'Can you spell her name for me?'

Stahl spelled out the name.

'Now, where are you? In Budapest, I know, but I need a telephone number.'

Stahl went to the desk for the number and, miraculously, when he returned, the line was still open. After he'd made sure the hotel and the number were correctly written down, he said, 'Buzzy, do you think you can help?'

'I'll give it one helluva try.'

'That's all I can ask.'

'Everything okay, otherwise?'

'It is.'

'You sound serious about this woman, maybe sometime I'll meet her.'

'God willing,' Stahl said.

'We'll talk soon,' Buzzy said, and hung up.

10 January. Stahl had no idea what Buzz Mehlman had done or who he'd talked to but, by eleven that morning, it produced, at the Astoria

desk, one Jerry Silverberg. Short, pudgy, and nervous, wearing glasses in tortoiseshell frames with lenses so thick they distorted his eyes, Silverberg was wearing what Stahl suspected was a brand-new suit, possibly bought for this meeting. They went to a coffee shop in the hotel lobby, where Silverberg ordered a glass of seltzer. 'I'm the Warner's rep in eastern Europe,' Silverberg said. 'I work with all the distributors in Poland, Hungary, Roumania, and Bulgaria. After I got the big call, I took a train down here from Warsaw, because you are one important guy, Mr Stahl.'

'The big call. From Buzz Mehlman?'

'Who?'

'My agent.'

'Oh no, I got the call from Walter Perry, which, as I'm sure you know, means Jack Warner. So, believe me when I say I'm going to help you.'

'I hope you can.'

'I *better*. Mr Perry talked to me for a while, he told me who he was, which I knew, and he mentioned he was the Warner Bros. man who deals with people in Washington, D.C. Which I didn't know, but I suppose somebody does that and he's the one. He also said that Mr Warner himself was concerned about you, and told me to give you five thousand dollars, which I have with me. So, as I said, you're one important guy.'

'Very encouraging, Jerry, but the German police want to question my woman friend, and the Hungarians won't let us out until she goes to the German legation.'

'Mr Perry seemed to know all about it. And he wants me to help you. "Any way you can," he said to me. So, first of all, if you're thinking the Hungarians, with the Nazis looking over their shoulder, will let you out of here, don't. You'll be here forever. No, this has got to be done another way, what I like to call *informally* – in this part of the world it's the way things get done, you understand?'

'I do.'

'Good. So here's how it will work. You take a train down to a place called Arad, which is now in Roumania but it was Hungary for hundreds of years, and the people there are Hungarian. Including the border police, see? And there's a certain major, Major Mihaly, who runs the Arad border control. To him you give three hundred bucks, no more and no less, and you tell him Mr Sobak sent you. And he'll let you into Roumania. Here, write it down.'

Jerry Silverberg handed him a pad and a pencil, then repeated the information and spelled the names. That done, Stahl said, 'Who is Mr Sobak?'

'I do favours for Mr Sobak, Mr Sobak does favours for me. He owns a movie theatre in Warsaw but he's one of those people with fingers in a lot of pies.'

'Do you actually speak Polish, Jerry? And Hungarian?'

'A little. A little of everything, really, but mostly I speak German – I grew up in Minsk speaking Yiddish, then when I was twelve we moved to Brooklyn. Later on, my brother-in-law was hired as an accountant at Warner Bros. and, after a while, he got me this job. I owned a dry cleaners at the time, nothing but headaches. So now I work for Warner Bros.'

'No headaches there.'

Silverberg laughed. 'Plenty, but they pay better. You want to hear the rest?'

Stahl nodded.

'From Arad there's a train to Constanta, the Roumanian port on the Black Sea, then you take a steamer to Istanbul, and from *there* you get a ship to Lisbon. Where you board the boat for New York, and then you can catch the 20th Century Limited to L.A. You're finished with your movie, aren't you?'

'Yes.'

'Then it's time you went home. I took the liberty of booking all your passages, and your friend Miss Steiner is included. First class all the way! You pick up your tickets from the Thomas Cook office in Constanta. Now this will take a long time, but it's the southern route and it avoids German Europe – you won't be alone on these boats, you'll see.'

'You did all this?'

'Who else? And when you get back to Hollywood, and you see Mr Walter Perry, maybe put in a good word for me. Now, here's the money.'

Stahl took the envelope and said, 'Jerry, can I buy you lunch? A drink?'

'Thanks. Kind of you, but as long as I'm in Budapest I might as well see some people.' He stood, put out a pudgy hand and said, 'Good luck, Mr Stahl, I hope everything goes all right. And, when you get back to L.A., you ought to write an article or give a speech, tell people what goes on here in Europe, because they just don't know.'

In the room, Renate was wide-eyed as Stahl read the itinerary off the pad. 'A long voyage,' she said. 'And everything in Paris, just . . . left there.'

'Three weeks or so, maybe a few days more. Think of it as a honeymoon.'

'Maybe I can get my friends to send me some things; photographs, my scissors.'

'I don't see why not.'

She took a breath and said, 'When do we leave?'

'Now,' Stahl said.

For three hours, the local to Arad chugged its way southeast. When the train rolled around a long curve, Stahl could see the tracks up ahead of them, two dark lines that disappeared into the winter countryside. In the late afternoon, they got off at Arad station, where the signs were in Roumanian. Going to the border control, Stahl asked to see Major Mihaly and an officer went off to find him, at the café where he spent his days. The major appeared when he was good and ready, a man with a waxed moustache who nipped in his waist with a corset and reeked of hair oil. The six fifty-dollar bills slipped magically from sight into his uniform as he said, 'When you see Mr Sobak, tell him the price is going up, and give him my best regards. So many people lately, passing through here, he'll understand.'

'I'll let him know,' Stahl said as the major stamped their passports.

'Enjoy Roumania, if you can,' said the Hungarian major and saluted with two fingers to the brim of his uniform cap.

It took a long eight hours to get to Constanta, and the best they could do was a run-down waterfront hotel called the Princess Maria. Stahl went off to the Cook agency, the boat to Istanbul would leave in three days, on 14 January.

12 January. The professional assassin Herbert was also in Constanta, though at a much better hotel. He was, as usual, accompanied by his colleague Lothar, and that night they visited one of Constanta's better brothels, which catered mostly to the many German visitors in the city that winter. After spending time in the rooms upstairs, Herbert and Lothar sat comfortably in the parlour, ordered schnapps, and relaxed, not having to go to work until the following day.

'Have we been here before?' Lothar asked.

'No, that was last fall. We were in Varna, the *Bulgarian* port, taking care of some Frenchman who ran away with bribe money.'

'Ah, that's right. Is this man Stahl somebody I should know? The name is familiar.'

'A movie actor, a Viennese who lives in America.'

'That's unusual,' Lothar said. 'For us.'

'Somehow he got tangled up with the Ribbentropburo, in Paris. Then the Gestapo got involved, and there was some sort of debacle in Hungary. For which Himmler himself blamed von Ribbentrop, he had to blame *somebody*. So now the Ribbentrop people – you know, Emhof – want to be rid of Herr Stahl before anything else goes wrong. They're afraid of Himmler, this operation is meant to appease him.'

'I guess it doesn't matter.'

'Not to me it doesn't, as long as somebody pays.'

'Who's doing the job?'

'I found us a new Russian, Volodya he calls himself, an émigré in

Bucharest. He'll be here tomorrow, we'll do it then.'

'Care to go back upstairs?' Lothar said.

'I'm thinking about it, one's never quite enough. Maybe that little blonde thing, whatever her name is. What about you?'

'I'm tired, the train was miserable. But I'm happy to wait for you.'

'Then I think I'll indulge,' Herbert said. 'It's cheap enough.'

13 January. As was their usual practice, Herbert and Lothar were to meet their gunman at a local bar in a workers' quarter. Their Russian, however, was late – two o'clock passed, then two-thirty. In time he showed up – through the window they could see him coming, weaving from one side of the pavement to the other, and chuckling to himself. Herbert swore – there wasn't much more he could do. Volodya entered singing, and backed up a step when he saw his employers. Then he made his way to their table, collapsed on a chair, and said a few choice words in Russian, which neither Herbert nor Lothar understood.

Herbert was enraged, though you would have had to know him well to see that. Shaking his head, smiling away, he handed Volodya some money, far less than he was supposed to be paid, but he seemed happy enough as he staggered away from the bar. 'And what do we do now?' Lothar said.

'I'll have to handle it myself,' Herbert said. 'Just like the old days. There isn't time to find somebody else – they sail tomorrow.'

'Want company?'

'No, you wait for me here. I won't be long.' From a briefcase he took an old Luger pistol and tucked it in his waistband. Then he rose, shook his head once more, and said, 'Something always goes wrong, doesn't it,' and left the bar, headed for the Princess Maria Hotel.

Stahl and Renate were lying on the bed, reading their books, waiting for the hours to pass until they sailed, when someone knocked at the door. Stahl got to his feet and said, 'Yes? Who is it?'

'Desk clerk, open up, please.'

Stahl and Renate looked at each other. The desk clerk spoke a form of hotel German, what had been said in the corridor was the language of a Berliner. Stahl called out, 'One moment,' and got down on his knees, peered through the crack beneath the door and saw a pair of very well-made shoes. Standing up, he said, 'What do you want?'

From the other side of the door: 'Open up, sir.'

This was no desk clerk. As Renate watched, Stahl tiptoed to his open suitcase and took the automatic pistol from its holster. Then he stood in front of the door and waited for the man in the corridor to go away.

Now Herbert, who had had an irritating day, smacked the side of his fist on the thin wooden door, which made it bang against the simple lock. 'Open up!' the voice repeated and something surged inside Stahl. The loud report deafened him, a splintery hole appeared in the door. Renate gasped and leapt to her feet, horrified. 'What happened?' she said.

Listening at the door, Stahl heard only silence. He made himself wait for a full minute, then looked out into the corridor, but there was nobody there.

Later that afternoon, Stahl went downstairs to pay the bill – they had decided that it was wiser not to stay at the hotel overnight. The desk clerk said to him, 'Did someone upstairs fire a gun?'

'They did. A while ago. Some madman in a uniform, I think, on the floor above us. I wouldn't go up there, if I were you.'

The clerk's eyes went from Stahl to the staircase and back, then his Adam's apple rose and fell, and he took the money that Stahl offered him.

The Princess Maria Hotel was on a broad avenue that faced the sea, where benches set beneath lime trees invited passersby to spend a moment. On one of the benches sat a man who was going to spend more than a moment, his head at rest against the uppermost wooden slat, one eye open, a hand inside his jacket. As people walked by, they had a brief glance, then looked away. Was a dead man sitting on a bench, in the Roumania of 1939, of no consequence? Perhaps so. In any event, the men and women in the street went about their business. As to the unpleasant sight on the bench, there was nothing they cared to do.

Someone would see to it.

It *was* a long voyage: fourteen days at sea, a few days waiting to embark in the ports of Istanbul and Lisbon, three weeks by the time they reached New York. There were fierce storms in the Mediterranean and heavy seas in the January Atlantic, where they sailed on a Dutch liner much favoured by students and intellectuals – a melancholy group on that leg of the voyage, sad to leave Europe to its fate, or just sad to leave Europe. Stahl and Renate spent the time together, fought and made up, made love, slept in the afternoon, sometimes just stared at the sea, hypnotized by the long swells, and got to know each other very well indeed but were, more than ever, by the time the ship entered New York Harbor, friends and lovers. Just after dawn that day, the ship blew three long blasts on its foghorn. The more seasoned travellers knew what that meant and flocked to the railing on the port side of the ship as the Statue of Liberty appeared from the morning mist. Here Stahl and Renate joined the crowd and held hands, not letting go until Renate required the use of a handkerchief, and Stahl had to touch the corners of his eyes with his fingers. And they weren't the only ones.

France was attacked by Germany on 10 May, 1940, and surrendered on 21 June.

Mission to Paris

Reading Group Notes

About the Author

Alan Furst is the author of twelve highly acclaimed espionage novels, including the TV Book Club choice *Spies of the Balkans*. He has lived for long periods in France, especially in Paris, and has travelled as a journalist in Eastern Europe and Russia. He has written extensively for *Esquire* and the *International Herald Tribune*.

For Discussion

- On the first page of *Mission to Paris*, the author pulls us back to 1938. How has he achieved this?

- The seasons and the weather create very strong moods in *Mission to Paris* – how has the author created these tones?

- 'I don't think anybody actually *likes* it.' What sense of Hollywood do you get from the novel?

- How do your feelings about Frederic Stahl develop through *Mission to Paris*?

- 'The French looked away from evil, it drained the pleasure from life. *Perhaps*, they thought, *it will just go away*.' How does the author feel about the French?

- Did Frederic make the right decisions? What would you have done?

- 'The people in Hollywood cast you as they do for a reason, Monsieur Stahl, they build on what is already there.' True for spies as well, do you think?

- How does the author use pace in *Mission to Paris*, and how does this affect the tone?

- Why do you think the author has chosen a film star for his central character?

- Whilst the author created a feeling of a classic crime novel in *Mission to Paris*, he also has had to write with a modern readership in mind – how has he set about meeting these two objectives?

In Conversation with Alan Furst

Q *Whilst a sense of authenticity is crucial to a novel like* Mission to Paris, *is absolute historical accuracy also needed, or can it hinder the flow of the plot?*

A Actually, it is used as the plot – the situations of the characters follow the flow of the history. So it doesn't hinder the flow of the plot, it enables it.

Q *Why are you drawn to this period in history?*

A For a novelist who writes about politics and espionage and intimate relationships, the 1930s are a period when good and evil were sharply demarcated, a time when Soviet Communism or German Fascism threatened, seriously, to rule the world.

Q *Your novels have a strong film noir quality to them – how do you go about creating that tone?*

A I'm not sure. It happens word by word, sentence by sentence, and clandestine meetings and clandestine love affairs are natural generators of what we call film noir.

Q *Is Frederic Stahl based on a real actor?*

A His looks may be based on Fredric March, also his name, though March was born in Ohio. Also, the kind of actor Stahl is, is reminiscent of March's career.

Q *Did you always know how Frederic was going to behave, or did he develop as* Mission to Paris *grew?*

A I had a general idea of who he was and how he worked, but once you're writing, your character will show new parts of his or her personality and history.

Q *How important is Frederic's nationality?*

A Frederic doesn't really have a conventional nationality. In the book, he's been a traditional expatriate artist, then an émigré to Hollywood and is in the process of becoming an American, as in the novel's final scene.

Q *Are you like Frederic? How would you have behaved differently?*

A Hard to know what would have become of me in the '30s. I would have been strongly anti-Nazi, and that was a dangerous thing to be. Some survived, some didn't.

Q *How did you physically write* Mission to Paris, *and why?*

A I wrote *Mission to Paris* in about nine months, which is what these books usually take. There was a lot of research before that – explicitly in political warfare and in émigré film people in the late 1930s.

Q *Silence or music while you write? If music, who do you listen to?*

A I listen to classical music when I write, sometimes jazz. But there's a fine classical music station where I live, so that's what I listen to.

Q *Which authors do you admire and why?*

A I admire the great '30s writers, which means Eric Ambler, Graham Greene, Rebecca West, George Orwell, Isaac Babel, Curzio Malaparte, T.E. Lawrence, the wonderful Olivia Manning, Joseph Roth – they lived the decade and wrote from the heart.

Q *What's your most treasured possession?*

A I have wonderful photos and maps from the period.

Q *What single thing about you would surprise us the most?*

A Not very much. I'm just the usual novelist from the Upper West Side of Manhattan, where they breed writers.

Q *What's your most vivid memory?*

A I have a very precise and good memory, lots of things, though I never linger on personal memories.

Q *Any clues about your next book – any snippets for us?*

A Sorry, I'm just now figuring out what I'm going to do.

Suggested Further Reading

Tinker Tailor Soldier Spy by John le Carré

After Many a Summer by Aldous Huxley

Our Man in Havana by Graham Greene

Above Suspicion by Helen MacInnes

Berlin Game by Len Deighton

*Read on for an exclusive sample
chapter of Alan Furst's new novel*

MIDNIGHT IN EUROPE

Available from Weidenfeld & Nicolson
in hardback and ebook

On a soft, winter evening in Manhattan, the fifteenth of December, 1937, it started to snow; big flakes spun lazily in the sky, danced in the lights of the office buildings, then melted as they hit the pavement. At Saks Fifth Avenue the window displays were lush and glittering – tinsel, toy trains, sugary frost dusted on the glass – and a crowd had gathered at the main entrance, drawn by a group of carollers dressed for a Dickens Christmas in long scarves, top hats, and bonnets. Here then, for as long as it lasted, was a romantic New York, the New York in a song on the radio.

Cristián Ferrar, a Spanish émigré who lived in Paris, took a moment to enjoy the spectacle, then hurried across the avenue as the traffic light turned red and began to work his way through the crowd. In a buckled briefcase carried under his arm, he had that morning's *New York Times*. The international news was as usual: marches, riots, assassinations, street brawls, arson; political warfare was tearing Europe apart. Real war was coming, this was merely the overture. In Spain, political warfare had flared into civil war, and, the *Times* reported, the army of the Republic had attacked General Franco's fascist forces at the Aragonese town of Teruel. And, you only had to turn the page, there was more: Hitler's Nazi Germany had issued new restrictions on the Jews, while here was a photograph of Benito Mussolini, shown by his personal railcar as he gave the stiff-armed fascist salute, and there a photograph of Marshal Stalin, reviewing a parade of tank columns.

Cristián Ferrar would force himself to read it, would ask himself, *Is there anything to be done? Is it hopeless?* So it seemed. Elsewhere in the newspaper, the democratic opposition to the dictators tried not to show fear, but it was in their every word, the nervous dithering of the losing side. As Franco and his generals attacked the elected Republic, the others joined in, troops and warplanes provided by Germany and Italy, and with every victory they boasted and bragged and strutted: *It's our turn, get out of our way.*

Or else.

He'd had a long, long day. A lawyer with the Coudert Frères law firm in Paris – 'coo-DARE', he would remind his American clients – he'd spent hours at the Coudert Brothers office at 2 Rector Street. There'd been files to read, meetings to attend, and confidential discussions with the partners, as they worked on matters that involved both the Paris and the New York offices, whose wealthy clientele had worldwide business interests and, sometimes, eccentric lives. Coudert had, early in the century, famously untangled the byzantine affairs of the son of Jacques Lebaudy. Lebaudy *père* had earned millions of dollars, becoming known as 'the Sugar King of France', but the son was another story. On receipt of his father's fortune he'd gone thoroughly mad and led a private army to North Africa and there declared himself 'Emperor of the Sahara'. In time, the French Foreign Legion had sent the emperor packing and he'd wound up living on Long Island, where his wife shot and killed him.

But the difficulties of the Lebaudy case were minor compared to what Coudert had faced that day: the legal hell created by the Spanish Civil War, now in its seventeenth month; individuals and corporations cut off from their money, families in hiding because they were trapped on the wrong side – whatever side that was – burnt homes, burnt factories, burnt records, with no means of proving anything to insurance companies, or banks, or government bureaucracies. The Coudert lawyers in Paris and New York did the best they could, but sometimes there was little

4

to be done. 'We regret your misfortune, monsieur, but the oil tanker has apparently vanished.'

Ferrar had left the Coudert office at five-thirty and headed uptown to his hotel, the Gotham, then, as a favour to a friend at the Spanish embassy in Paris, he'd walked over to the Spanish Republic's arms-buying office at 515 Madison Avenue. Here he'd picked up two manila envelopes he would take back to Paris – the days when you could trust the mail were long gone. He went next to Saks, meaning to buy Christmas presents – a hammered-silver bracelet and a cashmere sweater – for a woman friend he was to meet at seven. This love affair had gone on for more than two years as, every three months or so, he flew to Lisbon, where one could take the Pan Am flying boat to New York.

Actually, Ferrar was not precisely a Spaniard. He'd been born in Barcelona and so thought of himself as Catalan, from Catalonia, in ancient times a principality that included the French province of Roussillon. A Castilian from Madrid might well have recognized Ferrar's origin: his skin at the pale edge of dark, a gentle hawkish slope to the nose, and the deep green eyes common to the Catalan, with thick, black hair combed straight back from a high forehead and cut in the European style; noticeably long, and low on the neck. In June he'd turned forty, went horse-riding in the Bois de Boulogne twice a week, and stayed lean and tight with just that exercise. Heading towards the entrance to Saks, he wore a kind of lawyer's battle dress: good, sober suit beneath a tan, delicately soiled raincoat, fedora hat slightly tilted over the left eye, maroon scarf, and brown leather gloves. With the briefcase under his arm, Ferrar looked like what he was, a lawyer, a hardworking paladin ready to defend you against Uncle Henry's raid on your trusts.

As he reached the entry to the department store, Ferrar saw once again a thin little fellow who wore gold-rimmed spectacles, hands in the pockets of a blue overcoat, shoulders slumped as from fatigue or sorrow, who had followed him all day. This time he was leaning against the door of a taxi while the driver read a newspaper by the light of a streetlamp. The man in the blue overcoat had been with Ferrar at every stop, waiting outside at each location but not at all secretive, as though someone wanted Ferrar to know he was being watched.

Now who would that be?

There were many possibilities. For the secret services of Germany, Italy, and the USSR, the civil war in Spain was a spymaster's dream, and attacks were organized against targets everywhere in Europe: politicians of the left, diplomats, intellectuals, journalists, idealists – all much-favoured prey of the clandestine forces, be they fascist or communist. At embassies, social salons, grand hotels and nightclubs, the predators worked day and night. As for the man who followed him, Ferrar suspected he might be a local communist in service to the NKVD, since the USSR – the Republic's crucial, almost its only, ally – famously spied on its enemies, its friends, and everybody else. Or could the man be working for Franco's secret police?

Ferrar was determined not to brood about it, he could think of nothing to do in response, and he was not someone easily intimidated. He dismissed the man's presence with an unvoiced sigh, pulled the massive door open, and entered the store. Barely audible above the din of the shopping crowd, yet another band of carollers was singing 'joyful and tri-umm-phant'. Momentarily adrift in an aromatic maze of perfume and cosmetics counters, Ferrar searched for the jewellery department. The man in the blue overcoat waited outside.

P. J. DELANEY it said on the window. Then, below that, BAR & GRILL.

The very perfection of what the gossip columnists would call 'the local saloon'. It had been there forever, on East Thirty-Seventh Street in Murray Hill, a neighbourhood of boarding houses and small hotels, a low rung on the middle-class ladder where office workers, shop assistants, and people who did

6

God-only-knew-what lived in genteel poverty. But their lives were their own. The neighbourhood had, for no particular reason, a seductive air of privacy about it. You could do what you liked, nobody cared.

Delaney's, as it was known, was down four steps from the pavement, open the door and the atmosphere came rolling out at you; decades of spilled beer and cigarette smoke. Cristián Ferrar sat in a booth by the wall; a stout wooden table – its edges scarred by cigarette burns – was flanked by benches attached to high backs, the tops handsomely scrolled. He had his *New York Times* spread out before him, ashtray to one side, whiskey and soda on the other.

Ferrar tried to read the newspaper, then folded it up and put it back in his briefcase – at least for the moment he would spare himself the smoke and fume of Europe on fire. He was in Delaney's to meet his lover, Eileen Moore, so turned his thoughts to the pleasures they would share. As he thought of her, his eyes wandered up to the window and the pavement outside where, since the bar was below street level, he could see only the lower halves of people walking by. Could he identify Eileen before she entered the bar? In his imagination he could see her strong legs in black cotton stockings, but she might be wearing something else. Outside it was still snowing, a little girl paused, then bent over to peer through the window until her mother towed her away.

Ferrar had a sip of his drink; then, when he put the glass down, there she was. 'Hello, Cristián,' she said, hands in the pockets of her wool coat. He stood, his smile radiant, and they embraced – a light, public embrace which lingered for the extra second that separates friendship from intimacy. Then he helped her off with her coat, finding ways to touch her as he did so, and hung it on a brass hook fixed to the side of the booth. She sat, slid next to the wall, he settled beside her, she rested a hand on his knee, there were droplets of melted snow in her hair.

'It's been too long,' he said.

7

'It has.'

'We'll make up for that,' he said.

Her hand tightened on his knee. Their eyes met, followed by a pair of knowing smiles. Grins, almost.

She had auburn hair, parted in the middle and falling in wings to her shoulders – easy to brush into place, cheap to maintain – and a pale, redhead's complexion with a spray of freckles barely visible across the bridge of her nose: an Irish girl, raised in the Bronx, now, in her early thirties, living a Manhattan life. She wouldn't be called *pretty,* but her face was animated and alive and good to look at. She wore a grey wool sweater that buttoned up the front, little gold earrings, no makeup, French perfume he'd bought her in August, black skirt, and the black cotton stockings with a seam up the back.

'Seeing you made me forget,' she said. 'I meant to say *buenas noches.* Did I get that right?'

'You did,' he said. Then, 'The old greeting – they don't say that these days.'

By this she was startled. 'And why not?'

'It would mean that you were of the upper classes and some-one would arrest you. Now they say *Salut,* or *Salut camarada.* You know, "comrade".'

'I'm not much of a comrade,' she said. 'I marched here, back in November, and we have a *Help Spain* coin jar at work, that's about as far as I go with the politics.' *At work* meant, he knew, at the Public Library, where she shelved books at night. By day she wrote novels – cheap paperbacks with lurid covers.

'Have you eaten?' he asked.

'No, I'm not all that hungry. What's on the blackboard?'

'"Chicken à la king", it said. Which is . . . ?'

'Pieces of chicken in a cream sauce on toast. If the cook is feeling his oats there might be a pea or two in there.'

'And what king ate this?'

Her laugh was loud and harsh. 'You,' she said.

'Let me get you a drink.'

'What've you got there?'

'Whiskey and soda.'

'Rye whiskey, in here. Yes, I'll have that.'

He went to the bar and returned with the drink. Eileen took a pack of Chesterfields from her purse, smacked it twice on the table to firm up the tobacco at the smoker's end, then peeled back the foil. Ferrar drew a Gitane from his packet and lit both their cigarettes. She raised her glass and said, '*Salut,* comrade,' then added, 'and mud in your eye' and drank off a generous sip.

'In my *eye?*' He was being droll, which she really liked. And it sounded good in his accent – vaguely foreign, with a British lilt, because he'd learned his English in Paris, where the teachers were British expatriates.

'Are you still living at the same place?' Ferrar said.

She nodded. 'The good old Iroquois Hotel. A room and a hotplate, bathroom down the hall.'

And a bed, he thought. A fond memory, that narrow bed with a lumpy mattress and iron rails at head and foot. Not much of a bed, but wonderful things happened there. With Eileen Moore he shared two great passions; they loved to laugh, and they loved sex – the more they excited each other, the more excited they became. Attraction was always mysterious, he believed – he didn't really know what drew her to him – but for himself he knew very well indeed. Yes, he had a fierce appetite for her small, curved shape, for her round bottom in motion, but beyond that he was wildly provoked by her redhead's colouring: her white body, the faded pink of her nether parts. He believed, deep down where his desire lived, that redheads had thinner skin, so that a single stroke went a *long* way. In Ferrar's imagination, amid the crowd in the noisy bar, he recalled how, when he first touched her nipples, her chin lifted and her face became taut and concentrated. *Stop it,* he told himself – it was too soon to leave. He finished his drink and went off to get two more.

Waiting at the bar, Ferrar remembered the first time he'd seen her. She'd been working as a clerk in a warehouse near the

Hudson River, there'd been a sudden fire, two of the workers had been injured and were carried out as the building burned to a shell. The owner, a German Jew who'd fled to Paris, had filed a claim with his insurance company, the company stated that the fire was arson and refused to pay, the owner retained Coudert and sued. When Ferrar, in New York for meetings, had interviewed some of the workers, Eileen Moore sat across from him at a desk while a secretary recorded the deposition in shorthand. She did not record, but may have noticed, that attraction between Eileen Moore and Ferrar was instantaneous and powerful. Three months later – the insurance company had settled – he was back in the city; he called her, they met at Delaney's, they went to her room.

Returning to the table, a drink in either hand, he said, 'Are you writing a new book?'

'Yeah, I am. *Fatal Friday* did OK, so my editor wanted another. My working title is *Death of a Dame,* what do you think?'

'Well, I'd read it.'

'Aw, go on,' she said.

'I would read it because you wrote it.'

She snorted. 'No trace of me on the cover, as usual, at Phoenix Press only men write naughty crime books – that's the rule.'

'Do you mind?'

'A little, maybe. My friend Dawn thinks I should.' By Dawn she meant Dawn Powell, the reigning novelist of Murray Hill.

'Would you try one with your name on it?'

She shrugged. 'I don't know. Maybe some day.'

'I think you will, Eileen,' he said, touching her thigh beneath the table.

Suddenly she leaned over and kissed him on the cheek. 'Damn, I'm happy you're here.'

He took his hand from her thigh and ran his fingers up under the silky hair on the back of her head. 'Have what you want of that,' he said, indicating her glass. He left the rest unsaid, she knew what he wanted.

She finished her drink and then, with mischief in her smile, and that quick nod and glance towards the door which meant *let's get out of here,* she sped them on their way.

Outside, the snow was sticking here and there as the night grew colder but was no more than a coating on the pavement. As they climbed the steps in front of the bar she took his arm and then, as he transferred the Saks bag to his other hand, he noticed, a little way up the street and on the side opposite Delaney's, a taxi with its lights off, engine thrumming, two white faces in the front seat.

'What's in the bag, Cristián?'

'Presents for you, but you'll have to . . . earn them.'

'Oh no,' she said. *Not that.*

Madrid, 17 December, 1937. Castillo wasn't the bravest man in the world but he was probably somewhere on the list. No movie hero, Castillo — he was a pudgy fellow, fiftyish, who might have been taken for a bookkeeper at a small factory. On the night of the seventeenth he found himself in the besieged city of Madrid, where he shouldn't have been. Madrid was a bastion of the Republic, but the city was run by the Communist party; cold, hard, suspicious people uninterested in explanations or excuses, and very dangerous. But Castillo was trying to do a good deed and, as far as he knew, had managed it. Now he had to get out of Spain and go home to Paris.

A freezing night in Madrid, bitter cold, and where the water pipes had been ruptured by bombs or artillery shells, rivers of ice ran across the paving stones. Castillo was on his way to the Hotel Florida, haunt of American celebrities, writers and journalists from everywhere, and stray dogs like himself. To keep the hotel from being bombed, the top floor had been crowded with fascist hostages so it was, for the moment, safe enough. Eager to be out of the weather, Castillo took a shortcut through an alley that led onto the Calle Victoria. There was a bar tucked into a tenement building in the alley, a poster taped to its cracked window – there weren't many whole panes of glass left in the city – showed a man with a green face, listening intently, his hand cupping his ear. A spy! A young woman next to him held an index finger to her lips. Above her head, the message: 'Sh! Comrades, not a word to brothers or friends or sweethearts.' Spy mania had become a passion in the city.

When Castillo was halfway down the alley, there was a white flash above the Calle Victoria and the concussion blew his hat off. Other bombs followed, and when their explosions lit the sky, a thousand roosters, mistaking the light for dawn, began to crow. Dust filled the air and something, a metal something, clanked on the street as it came down from wherever it had been. A woman screamed, the dogs began to bark. Castillo stood still – should he run? Throw himself to the ground? Realizing he was bareheaded, he looked around for his hat and finally saw it, upside down, a few yards behind him. Suddenly he shivered with fear and frantically searched his shirt and trousers for bloodstains, but found none.

He took a deep breath, steadied himself, and retrieved his hat. Now, how to get back to the hotel. A crowd would gather in the Calle Victoria; people – looking for survivors – digging frantically in the rubble, soldiers, police, ambulances with blue paper concealing their headlights from Franco's spotter planes. And officials, with authority from some bureau no one had ever heard of, whose sole purpose on earth was to demand to see one's papers, which would lack a validating stamp that no one had ever heard of. For Castillo, a frightening prospect. So he began to walk back the way he'd come. This was a mistake, the sort of decision that seems obvious at the time but then turns out to have been wrong, when it's too late. He had almost reached the end of the alley, then a voice in the darkness said, 'You, *camarada*.'

Castillo stopped dead. From the shadows came a child with a rifle. He had a long look at Castillo: heavy overcoat, blue suit, white shirt, a tie, maybe one of those upper-class Franco sympathizers caught in the city by the war.

'Your papers,' said the child. Who, Castillo now saw, wasn't a child at all. He was small and dark, maybe fifteen, with a child's face. His feet were wrapped in rags.

As Castillo reached for his passport and permits, he said, 'Who are you?'

'I am the sentry for this alley.'

Castillo handed over the documents, the sentry held the papers upside down and pretended to read them. 'Are these *your* papers?' he said.

'Yes.'

They weren't.

'Are you a spy?'

'No. Certainly not.'

That was a lie.

The sentry was trying to decide what to do, Castillo could see it in his face. A few, very long seconds went by, then the sentry said, 'I will take you to the officer.'

'Of course,' said Castillo. 'Which way do we go?' He almost pulled it off – the sentry hesitated because Castillo had done the trick very well, his confident voice just faintly suggesting that the officer might not be pleased when he discovered what the sentry had done. Finally the sentry said, 'I'll take you there, it is not far.' He had best be polite, this man in a suit could be somebody important.

The walk took fifteen minutes and ended at the service entrance to the Palace, the largest hotel in Europe, which had been converted to a hospital. Before the war, most of the hospital nurses in the city had been nuns but they had fled to Franco-occupied territory and the wards were now staffed by the prostitutes of Madrid – their hair growing out black because the city's supply of peroxide was needed as antiseptic for the wounded.

The sentry led Castillo down one flight of stairs, then another, to a room that had once been part of a kitchen; zinc tubs lined the walls and the still air smelled of grease and sour wine. When his eyes adjusted to the darkness – the room was lit by two candles at either end of a table, electricity being an occasional thing in the city – Castillo could see the forms of men standing in line. As he took his place at the end of the line his stomach clenched with fear, because the man seated at the table was in civilian clothes and he was wearing glasses. *Officer of what?*